*Who do you turn to when your love life
is going to the dogs?*

From "ATHENA'S CHRISTMAS TAIL"

For what seemed like an eternity Robert was close enough
to take Mercy in his arms. Her green eyes were wide—and
anxious. Was she afraid? That wouldn't do. He started to
back away himself and came up against Hannibal. What was
the blasted dog doing so close, hemming him in?

"Hannibal," he began. And then Athena reared up on her
hind legs and the next thing he knew, Mercy slammed into
his chest. His arms went around her automatically, clasping
her to him. She fit perfectly against him. For the merest
second, he let himself enjoy it.

Then she lifted her shocked face to his. "Robert, I—"

Her mouth was so close, so tempting. He stared at it,
mesmerized, leaning toward it as it came toward his. And
then she raised up on her tiptoes and kissed him.

It was a chaste kiss, the kiss of an innocent, and short. But
it left him shaken in a way Emerine's kisses, or those of the
many women he'd had before her, had never done.

Santa Paws

VICTORIA ALEXANDER,
NINA COOMBS,
ANNIE KIMBERLIN,
MIRIAM RAFTERY

LOVE SPELL BOOKS ◆ NEW YORK CITY

LOVE SPELL®

November 1997

Published by

Dorchester Publishing Co., Inc.
276 Fifth Avenue
New York, NY 10001

ISBN 0-505-52235-7

SHAKESPEAR
AND THE
THREE KINGS
Victoria Alexander

*This story is for Tory and Alex
who loan me their names,
and on Christmas and every day of the year,
show me what love is really all about.*

Chapter One

October 23, 1893

My Dearest Oliver,

If indeed you are reading this it means my idiot doctors were correct and I shall not be here when you return from your travels. They insist I am about to breathe my last breath upon this earth and will not see another Christmas. Pity. I do so love Christmas. Of course, I have no intention of proving them right. Still, it is wise to be prepared.

First, I do not wish you to be unduly upset by my passing. I have lived an excellent life full of all the affection and adventure any woman could ask for in this day and age. If I am to leave this world behind I am eager to get on with it and be reunited with my beloved Charles. It has been nearly twenty-two years since he had the temerity to die without me. I shall have a few firm words for him on that score before we spend eternity together. All in all, I am quite looking forward to it.

In spite of himself, Sir Oliver Thornton Stanhope could not suppress a slight smile. He could well imagine Great Aunt Eleanor berating Uncle Charles for having the audacity to die without her permission. Oliver knew Charles only from the portrait that hung next to Aunt Ellie's in the front hall of Thornton Manor but he'd always thought there was a twinkle in the old man's eye. Ridiculous notion, of course.

I have never particularly believed in regrets. Yet I find I do have a few and they concern you, my dear boy.

As you well know, it has always been a source of irritation to me that your parents did not provide the proper affection that was your due as their son. I would not have wished their untimely deaths yet it does seem to me perhaps fate had a hand in it as it brought you into my keeping. If you recall, you were not at all pleasant at age eleven. And since Charles had only recently passed on it was a trying time for us both.

An image of soap shavings tossed discreetly into a kettle of tea and the resulting foamy chaos flashed through his mind. His smile widened to a grin.

How did we manage to muddle through those days? Quite well, I think, in looking back upon it. You have been as a son to me, Oliver. I have

8

loved you without reservation for these long years and, while you have always been reticent to display your emotions, I have no doubt you returned my affection. Still, I fear the legacy of your parents' lack of regard lingers within you.

His smile faded.

I did so wish before I left this earth to see you with a wife and children of your own. I had hoped you would find the same kind of love Charles and I shared. I am well aware that you sampled it once with disastrous results. Still, life goes on and I did try my best.

A seemingly endless parade of eligible young women marched through his mind. Every time he had visited Aunt Ellie in recent years she'd had a houseguest or a house full of guests—most of them young, charming and eminently suitable to be the wife of Sir Oliver Thornton Stanhope.

It is the greatest failure of my life that I was not able to help you find a lasting love. There is little I can do about it now. However, in addition to the manor and my fortune, which you really do not need—but one can never be too wealthy or too intelligent in this world—I leave in your keeping the last loves of my life.

Oliver glanced over the top of the lilac-scented stationery to meet three pairs of black, beady, unflinching eyes. He grit his teeth and dropped his gaze back to the flowery writing on the page before him.

My little darlings have brought great joy to me. I consider them my children just as I consider you my son.

Oliver rolled his eyes at the ceiling and sighed.

I can see you now in my mind's eye, gazing heavenward and heaving a great sigh.

She always knew exactly what he was thinking. Even now, from the grave.

I well know your opinion of my three tiny kings yet I also know you will provide them with a good home. It may not be easy. I have spoiled them shamelessly. In order to ease your adjustment to them, and theirs to you, I have procured the services of an American . . .

His eyes narrowed.

. . . a recent acquaintance, who is skilled in the training of dogs. D. K. Lawrence should arrive at the manor by December eighteenth and has agreed to stay for as long as is necessary.

Bloody hell. This was already the seventeenth. There was no time to head the damnable man off.

Shakespeare and the Three Kings

The last thing Oliver wanted was some blasted American dog lover in his home for an undetermined period of time.

I am well aware of your feelings about Americans. Still, it is the season of goodwill toward all and I do expect you to honor that spirit as well as my wishes.

As if she had left him a choice.

If you will permit them, my little ones will provide you with a great deal of affection. It is my hope, if you open your heart to them it will help you learn to open your heart to others.

Never forget, my dearest Oliver, how very much I have loved you and how very much I pray you will find love in the future. It is my final Christmas gift to you. The gift of love. The greatest gift of all.

Yours always,
Aunt Ellie

An unaccustomed ache stung the back of his throat. Damn, he would miss her. Why had he never told her how much she meant to him? Although, if he had read the tone of her letter correctly, she knew of his feelings. He should have been here with her. If he'd returned but two weeks earlier . . .

Regret surged through him and he shook his head. He couldn't help that business for the crown had taken him out of England for the last six months. Even though he'd moved to London a de-

11

cade ago, he did manage to make the three hour train trip to Thornton an average of every other fortnight and he'd never missed a holiday. Yet at this moment, it did not seem enough for the woman who had taken him in and given him a life and a future.

He dropped the letter on his desk. He'd learned of her death when he returned to England last week and came immediately to Thornton Manor. He'd met with her solicitor and discovered she had arranged all the loose ends of her life in a tidy manner. This letter tied up the rest. Dear Aunt Ellie. His life would not be the same without her.

He raised his gaze and all sentiment vanished in the face of three pairs of intently staring eyes. Yorkshire Terriers. Rats with fur was more like it. They were far too tiny to do much of anything but yap and get underfoot. How could she have done this to him? He detested the minuscule beasts and had a strong suspicion they were not fond of him either. Perhaps this Lawrence person would be willing to take them off his hands.

He glared at the toylike animals and they glared right back. No, of course he couldn't get rid of them. It was Aunt Ellie's last request of him and he could never deny her anything.

"Blast it." He got to his feet and strode to the door of Aunt Ellie's library, or rather, his library now, and flung it open. "Miles!"

Aunt Ellie's butler appeared from nowhere as was his custom.

"Yes, Sir Oliver?"

"It seems we are to have a visitor my aunt invited

before her death. Please make the appropriate arrangements."

Miles didn't so much as raise a brow. He'd been Aunt Ellie's family retainer for as long as Oliver could remember and news of an unexpected houseguest, even one invited posthumously, did not daunt him in the least. "As you wish. When will Lady Eleanor's guest arrive?"

"Tomorrow." Oliver shook his head. "I am not pleased at all about this, Miles, but it was my aunt's doing so we shall have to acquiesce to her wishes. Besides, it is too late to head the bloody man off."

"I shall see to it that suitable accommodations are found."

"Thank you, Miles."

The butler nodded and vanished into the shadowy hall. Miles, and most of the other servants at Thornton, were as much a part of his family as Aunt Ellie. In his youth he recalled having long conversations with Miles on the deeply philosophical matters that plague a young man's mind. As an adult, Miles treated him with the deference his position demanded but Oliver always suspected, or perhaps hoped, should he need to have a discussion of a more personal nature, Miles would serve as his confidant. Not that he needed anyone to talk to. Oliver prided himself on keeping such matters private. He had learned, in an exceedingly painful manner, to keep his thoughts, and more, his emotions, to himself. That may well be the very reason why none of the young women Aunt Ellie had herded in his direction had appealed to him. He had allowed himself to fall under the charms of a woman once. And once was quite enough.

Oliver started toward the stairs. Tiny footsteps sounded behind him. He glanced over his shoulder. The Yorkies lined up at his heels. "Where do you think you're going?"

They stared as if to say he was their master now and he was stuck with them. They appeared no happier about it than he was.

"What are your names anyway?" Oliver frowned. "Ah yes. How could I have forgotten? Aunt Ellie's three kings: Melchoir—"

The ears of the middle dog perked upward.

"—Balthazar—"

The creature last in line took a step forward.

"—and Gaspar." The animal closest to him wagged its stubby tail. "Ridiculous names for such tiny beasts."

They gazed at him with a steady stare. A bit unnerving, that. Why, they seemed quite intelligent. Almost human. Nonsense. They were the living playthings of an elderly woman and nothing more. Still, now they were his.

He heaved a sigh of surrender. "Very well, come along but stay out of my way."

Oliver headed up the steps, the scrambling of twelve tiny paws on the polished wood of the stairs echoing after him. They were so small, did they need help negotiating the climb? He resisted the urge to turn. No, if indeed they were all to coexist together they'd best learn to be independent. There would be no coddling from him.

Perhaps there was something beneficial to the arrival of the American after all. If nothing else, he could teach the miserable excuses for canines to be dogs and not pampered children.

At least the Yorkies and the American would provide a needed distraction. He'd spent the last twenty-two Christmases in the wonder of the holiday atmosphere his aunt created at the manor—the only place in the world where he knew without question he was welcomed and loved. It was going to be lonely without her. He was used to being alone, of course, but he was also used to Aunt Ellie's unconditional affection. Christmas was her favorite time of year and this Christmas would be difficult at best.

An impatient yap sounded behind him. Oliver groaned to himself and continued up the steps.

On the other hand, there was something to be said for solitude.

Chapter Two

"If you require nothing else then, miss, I shall take my leave."

"Thank you, Miles." Diana Lawrence stood in the middle of the elegantly appointed bedroom suite. Her hand rested lightly on the head of the Great Dane she'd recently acquired, hoping to draw her own strength from that of the gentle beast. "I'm sure I'll be fine here. It's a lovely room."

"Lady Eleanor would be pleased by your compliment. She prided herself on her home."

"Could you tell me, where is—"

"Sir Oliver has gone for a walk, miss. He is expected back within the hour."

"Oh, I see." Disappointment battled with relief within her.

"I shall have your things sent up at once." Miles nodded and stepped toward the door, then turned back. "Might I say, miss, it is good to see you here again and I wish you every success on your endeavor."

"My endeavor?" Diana's eyes widened. "You know?"

A slight smile pulled at the corners of the older man's mouth. "Indeed, I do. If I may speak frankly?"

"Please."

"I have served in Lady Eleanor's employ for more than thirty years and I am proud to say she considered me her friend as well as her servant. I am well aware of the real reason for your presence. Should you need any assistance whatsoever, please consider me at your service."

"Thank you, Miles." Diana smiled with relief. "It's good to know I have at least one friend in the castle."

Miles raised a brow. "I beg your pardon, miss, it is not a castle, merely a manor house."

"Sorry. We don't have either in America."

"Pity." Miles nodded and left the room, shutting the door behind him.

"Apparently it's just the two of us for the moment, Shakespeare."

The Great Dane looked up at her, wagged his tail and padded toward the huge, four-poster bed. With an awkward leap, he jumped into the center of the coverlet and settled down, his large paws dangling over the side of the bed. "Well, at least you're making yourself at home."

Diana laughed and stepped to a full-length mirror. She pulled the pins from her fashionable hat and tossed it on a chair. Her dark hair gleamed in the weak winter sunlight filtering in through the tall windows.

What would he see when he looked at her? She had not changed much in the last decade. Oh, her face was leaner, her figure more mature. She was once a pretty girl and was now an attractive woman. Men seemed to think so at any rate. She'd discovered that fact, quite to her surprise, after her father died and, for the first time in years, she'd attended civic events and social gatherings. The vast wealth he'd left her and her own liquidation of his assets, as well as his respected name, gained her entrance to circles she never knew existed. At first, she'd been something of a curiosity; attractive, unmarried, respectable women of her age were rare. But money and her father's position had triumphed. Diana had quite enjoyed the attention she'd received.

She pulled off her jacket and it joined the hat, her gaze returning to the mirror. The real differences in Diana were not reflected here. She quite liked the woman she'd become as much as she detested the girl she'd been. There was a strength of purpose, and therefore pride, in her nature now and a sense of self-confidence she never would have imagined in her younger years. It was her father's last, and if truth were told, only real, gift to her.

Her father. Ketterson. A hard glint shown in her eye. If she had only known. But ten years ago she was a scared, shy eighteen-year-old too afraid of her father's wrath to fight for the man she loved. The man she still loved.

That girl, Diana Ketterson, no longer existed. It was a scant nine months since she'd learned the horrible, yet liberating, truth. After that, she took her mother's maiden name and set in motion the actions that would lead her to England and to him. And thanks to Lady Eleanor's scheme, she would have a second chance.

"Come along, Shakespeare." The dog slid leisurely off the bed and in one step was by her side. "Let's go greet the kings and their master."

She lifted her chin, straightened her spine and firmly pushed away the heavy, uneasy weight that settled in her stomach.

She was Diana Lawrence now, and more than ready to fight for love.

Diana paced the wide width of the parlor, her arms folded tightly across her chest in the manner of someone cold or terrified. Lord, she was nervous. What would he say when he saw her? What would he think? He could, in all likelihood, throw her out, although Lady Eleanor had foreseen that possibility and had taken precautions against it. If only the dear woman was still alive to give Diana courage.

Shakespeare matched her step for step for a good five minutes before plopping down in the middle of the room. Now only his dun-colored head followed her progress. The animal looked for all the world as if he were watching a tennis match. In spite of her agitation she could well see the humor in his stance.

A door slammed in the hall and she heard a muttered oath and the distinct sounds of tiny nails clicking on the floor. Her breath caught. Shakespeare's ears perked up. He leapt to his feet and sprinted through the open parlor doors.

Yapping, barking and a man's irate yell filled the air. A crash sounded and a yelp. Noise reverberated through the house. Diana winced. Wasn't there a lovely antique vase on a table in the hall?

A moment later, the Yorkies raced into the room, Shakespeare right behind, all four animals in a state of canine chaos. The dogs circled the parlor at a breakneck pace, the smaller animals ducking under sofas, the big dog leaping over tables in a breathtaking blur of fur and frenzy. A chair fell to its side. A fern tottered on a stand. A lamp shattered on the floor.

"Shakespeare," she said in the commanding voice his previous owner had instructed. "Down, boy! Sit!" The Great Dane froze, then obediently smacked his haunches on the carpet. The Yorkies stopped as one and stared.

"Where in the name of all that's holy did this great hulking beast come from? Brandy, Miles! Now." Oliver strode into the room, his angry gaze on the Great Dane. "Who brought this creature into my home? It's not bad enough—"

"He's mine." Her voice quavered and his gaze jerked to hers.

"And who—" His eyes widened. Astonishment and recognition flashed across his face.

She drew a deep breath and thrust out her hand. "I'm D. K. Lawrence."

Diana?

"You're D. K. Lawrence?"

She nodded. Stunned disbelief flooded him and rooted him to the floor. She dropped her hand. "My aunt hired you? *You?*"

She squared her shoulders. "Yes, she did."

He stared for a long moment, groping to find words through his shock. Miles stepped into the room bearing a tray laden with a decanter and two glasses. The servant placed it on a table near the fireplace and left without saying a word.

Oliver turned on his heel and strode to the waiting brandy. He poured a snifter of the amber liquid and his hand shook. "Were you aware that my aunt died last month?"

"Yes." Her voice was soft. "I'm very sorry." She paused. Was she as affected at this moment as he? Or did she simply not care? His fingers tightened on the crystal. "When we me—corresponded, she was well aware of that possibility. That's exactly why she wished me to come at this time."

He pulled a deep swallow of the pungent liquor and savored the burn down his throat. He turned to face her.

Gad, she was far lovelier than he remembered. He would not have thought it possible but the years had molded her in the way a sculptor carves a rough-hewn piece of marble into an exquisite work of art. She'd been a pretty girl. She was a magnificent woman. And he wanted nothing to do with her.

"My aunt was wrong." His words were cold and hard. "I have no need of your services. I will have my solicitor see to your fee and—"

"I've already been paid." A surprising note of stubbornness rang in her voice.

"Very well, then. Miles will make arrangements for you to return to London or wherever you wish." He nodded his dismissal.

"I'm afraid you misunderstand." A determined gleam shone in her deep brown eyes. "I've been retained to render a service. I've received compensation for my work in advance. I have a job to do here and I will not leave until that job is completed."

He clenched his jaw. "The need no longer exists. Therefore—"

"I beg to differ with you. From what I just saw, the situation here is far worse than your aunt led me to believe. She suspected you would not be able to handle the terriers." She raised a delicate brow. "Or am I mistaken? Was the upheaval in the hall to your liking, then?"

"The upheaval in the hall was the direct result of that horse you brought into my home!"

"I see. I assume therefore your walk with the dogs went well? They were well behaved and responsive to your commands?"

The memory of the last hour with his small herd of dogs flashed through his head. Each of the creatures had insisted on going in his own direction and not one had paid the least bit of attention to Oliver's vain attempt to instill order from canine anarchy.

He tossed off the rest of the brandy and slammed the glass down on the table. "Very well. Stay. Just do something about those bloody beasts. They are driving me stark, raving mad." He stalked toward the door. He had to get away from her. Now. Before the wall he'd constructed so carefully around his emotions, around his heart, shattered. She'd destroyed him once before. He would not permit it again.

"Wait. Pardon me."

"What?" He halted and threw her a scathing glare. She should have cringed. Others had. Instead, she raised her chin and met his gaze.

"What, precisely, did you wish me to do with the dogs?"

"I don't give a bloody fig what you do with them. Roast them for supper for all I care!"

A low chorus of growls sounded.

"I mean, what do you wish me to accomplish?" She tilted her head and his heart thudded at the long-remembered gesture. Lord, had he forgotten nothing about her?

"I just wish them to behave as well-mannered dogs and not overindulged brats."

Oliver nodded sharply, strode through the doorway and stalked the short distance down the hall to the library. He threw open the double doors and slammed them shut behind him. A decanter similar to that in the parlor sat on the desk. Thank God for Miles. He poured a glass and downed the contents in one swallow.

"Diana," he whispered, and closed his eyes against a wave of pain he'd thought long since vanquished to some irretrievable part of his past.

He hadn't forgotten, of course, he'd simply chosen not to think about it. But every moment of the days the young Englishman had spent with the pretty American swept through his mind as vivid as yesterday. They'd met at some social function or other and met again at museums and galleries and parks until they'd made meeting a priority and, for him, the only priority. He loved her with all the passion of his youth and wanted her as his wife. And he thought she loved him as well. Believed it with his whole heart, right up until the time when he came to ask her father for her hand.

He poured another glass and sank into the chair before the fireplace. Jonathan Ketterson was a wealthy American in London on business. The vehemence of Ketterson's reaction to Oliver's suit still rang in the younger man's mind. . . .

* * *

". . . I would never allow my daughter to marry an Englishman." Ketterson's voice swelled with bitter anger. *"I would see her in her grave before I would permit such a match."*

"But sir," Oliver said, struggling to keep his tone calm, *"we love each other."*

"Love? Rubbish. A foolish emotion at best." Ketterson's eyes narrowed. *"If you have dishonored her—"*

"Not at all, sir! I wish her to be my wife."

"Not as long as there is breath in my body. I know better than most the deceitful nature of Englishmen. I have taken precautions to prevent any further contact between you and my daughter. I have sent her home. She and her mother sailed this morning." A spiteful gleam shown in Ketterson's eye. *"Besides, she is to marry a man of my choosing. The arrangements have already been made."*

Oliver shook his head. *"Forgive me, sir, but I cannot, I will not, believe that."*

"Believe what you wish. She, no doubt, was playing you for a fool. Regardless, the fact is that you will not see her again. I will make certain of that, do you understand? Never . . ."

Oliver hadn't believed. He wrote letter after letter to Diana. Every day for weeks, every week for months, with no reply. Until finally he realized the inevitable truth: she had indeed deceived him. He'd been an idle diversion, a distraction to keep her amused during her stay in London. Nothing more.

He raked his hand through his hair. Ketterson and his daughter had changed his life forever. His heart hardened. He threw all the passion he'd felt for her into furthering his governmental career. He never permitted another man to speak to him as Ketterson had. He never allowed himself to be taken in by the wiles of a woman. And he never expected to see her again.

Now, by some dastardly fluke of fate, or the hand of his beloved aunt, she was here. In his own home. Why?

Diana Lawrence. Lawrence must be her husband's name. Where did he fit into all this? Perhaps she was a widow? Perhaps—no! He drew a deep swallow of the brandy. Whatever her true purpose for being here, he would not fall victim to her charms again. The feelings he'd had for her had died with his youth.

She'd been hired to do something about those bloody dogs and he'd tolerate her presence for that and that alone. He would resist the impulse to pull her into his arms and taste of the lips he had tasted so briefly so long ago. He would turn his back on the deep velvet of her eyes. He would deafen his ears to the dulcet sound of her voice.

And he would ignore the ache that centered near his heart and crush the hope that sprang unwillingly from his soul.

Chapter Three

Diana stared at the doorway. Unbidden tears clouded her vision and she angrily sniffed them away. She had cried once for him and would not cry for, or because of, any man ever again. Her tears were a surprise; she thought she was stronger than that. Oliver's reaction, on the other hand, was no surprise at all.

Lady Eleanor had warned her that he would not welcome her with open arms. Still, somewhere deep inside, she had hoped for some acknowledgement of what they'd meant to each other. Aside from a momentary flash in his eyes, Oliver hadn't even indicated he remembered her. Even so, he was letting her stay. Diana pulled a deep breath. It was so little but it was a beginning.

A soft head nudged her hand. She glanced down to meet Shakespeare's mournful gaze.

"Did you understand all that, boy?" Diana sank to the floor, and Shakespeare settled next her. She scanned the room. The Yorkies sat beneath a sofa, black eyes trained on her. She patted the carpet beside her. "Come."

Shakespeare and the Three Kings

Obediently, all three trotted to line up before her. She couldn't help but smile. "You're all quite adorable, you know."

The terriers seemed to smile in a smug manner.

"Ah, I see, you know what darlings you are. Let's see if I can remember who is whom." Diana studied the dogs, each subtly different from the next. "You are Gaspar."

The smallest dog wagged his tail.

"And you are Balthazar."

The ears of the dog next in line perked upward. This animal had more of a silver color in his coat than the other two.

"And that means you must be Melchoir."

The last and roundest animal tilted his head.

Diana smiled. "I do hope that's right. Lady Eleanor said I should be able to tell you apart after a few days. Of course, what I'm going to do with you will be a bit more difficult to determine." She lowered her voice confidentially. "I've never even owned a dog, you know. Why, I only acquired Shakespeare last month and he was already trained. The man who owned him gave me some advice and a pamphlet on the training of canines but"—she shrugged—"I suppose we'll simply have to work together on this. Everything would be so much easier if Lady Eleanor were here."

Diana shook her head in regret. She'd loved Lady Eleanor from the moment she'd walked into Thornton Manor in October in hopes of finding Oliver, and had wondered since then how differently life might have been for them all if she'd met his aunt when she'd first met him. The elderly women had put Diana at ease at once and listened to her story without censure or criticism. Diana had related only the bare facts but the shrewd look in the other woman's eye told her Lady Eleanor could well guess the portions of Diana's story left unsaid. The woman she'd become was embarrassed, even ashamed, of the weak, frightened girl she'd been.

Absently, she scratched behind Balthazar's ears. Even now, the horror of the day she'd told her father of her feelings for Oliver haunted her. Jonathan Ketterson had flown into a rage unlike anything she'd ever seen. He'd called her a fool and worse. He'd said Oliver was merely toying with her affections and was in fact already betrothed. He'd screamed and raved and torn her dress from her back, beating her at the base of her spine with his cane until she swooned from the pain. Anna, her mother, tried to interfere but he backhanded her with enough force to fling her halfway across the room.

From that moment on, nothing in her life was the same. Jonathan had never been especially affectionate toward her and his attitude grew ever worse. Her sweet, quiet mother seemed to lose whatever meager spirit she had possessed and died within six months of their return home. Diana had often wished she could follow her.

Jonathan kept her isolated from the rest of the world after that. She was more servant than daughter and she lived in terror of his displeasure; one misunderstood word and he'd take his cane to her. While he ventured into society, all invitations for her were refused. When at last he died, three years ago, she grieved not for his death but for the life he had denied her.

Shakespeare and the Three Kings

It clearly wasn't his intention, but his treatment fostered the growth of a strength and an instinct to survive that would have shocked him, and as well, prepared her to manage with an unfeminine ruthlessness his finances and his business. She never had the courage to defy him in life, but, upon his death, vowed no man would cause her pain again. She had wealth now and therefore power. She handled his affairs with a shrewd, firm manner that surprised herself and everyone she dealt with. And she reentered society. It wasn't until she began seeing dressmakers that she discovered the latticework of scars crossing the small of her back. Jonathan Ketterson's legacy.

With his death she thought his ability to hurt her had died as well, but she was wrong. In the past year, she'd discovered a cache of letters among some overlooked papers. All but one were from Oliver to her. He had not been engaged. And he had loved her.

The letter that remained had been written before her birth by her mother to her father. It was a tale of confession and a plea for forgiveness. While on a trip to visit distant relatives, Anna Ketterson had apparently fallen in love with another man, an Englishman, and had conceived a child: Diana.

At once, everything in her life became clear. Her father had never cared for her because he was not her father at all. He obviously viewed her love for Oliver, another Englishman, as betrayal, just like her mother's. It was a relief to discover the vile man who had nearly destroyed her was not connected to her in any way.

She liquidated all of his holdings with a bitter

pleasure. He loved his businesses and his mansion and his possessions, and she sold them all, just payment for the scars on her body and her soul, and sailed for England, determined to find Oliver. To see if there was even the slightest chance that they could recapture the love they'd shared so long ago.

Melchoir rolled on his back and waved his paws in the air. She smiled and rubbed his fat tummy. This ridiculous deception of posing as a dog trainer had been all Lady Eleanor's idea. . . .

"It's the perfect ruse, my dear. As much as I hate to admit it—" Lady Eleanor clucked her tongue in dismay, "—I fear Oliver's heart is too, shall we say, hardened, by the pain of your past for him to accept your story at once. No, it would be far better if we could manage to put the two of you in close proximity and allow nature to take its course. And this is really exceedingly clever."

"I don't know." Diana shook her head. "It sounds rather deceitful."

"Well, of course it's deceitful, my dear. That is entirely the point." Lady Eleanor leaned forward as if to impart well-kept secrets shared only by women about men. "Women have been deceiving men since the world began, usually for their own good. It all works out quite nicely in the end.

"You see, Diana, men rarely, if ever, know what's good for them. It is up to us to guide them in the right direction. Train them, as it were. In that, they are not unlike my little darlings. . . .

Diana had her doubts but she was certainly willing to try. Oliver was the only man she'd ever had and, probably, ever would love. If there was even a remote chance of recapturing what they'd once shared, it was worth any effort. She simply had to be patient. She had waited for him for ten years, a few more weeks shouldn't matter.

Now, she had to put on something of a show of training these little creatures. But training them to do what?

Diana surveyed the dogs lined up before her like children before a schoolteacher. The kings sat to her left, Shakespeare to her right.

"Very well, then." Diana pulled her brows together. "The gentleman I purchased Shakespeare from had already given him a considerable education. Pay attention now. Shakespeare." The Great Dane cast her a steady gaze. "Sit up."

Shakespeare stared for a moment as if trying to decide whether or not to obey, then rolled his weight back on his tail, hoisted his front legs and pawed the air.

"Good boy." Diana grinned at the huge beast. "What a wonderful dog you are. Now, were you watching?" She turned toward the terriers. They eyed Shakespeare with identical expressions of doggy disdain. "It's your turn. Sit."

The little dogs shifted their attention from the Great Dane to Diana.

"Sit. Up."

Gaspar yawned. Balthazar scratched behind his ear. Melchoir sniffed. Shakespeare dropped his front feet to the floor.

"Very well." Diana studied the animals. "Perhaps we can start with something a bit easier. Shakespeare, roll over."

31

Obediently the big dog tumbled to the carpet, rolled and stood.

"Perfect." Diana beamed. "Let's try that. Melchoir, Balthazar, Gaspar, roll over."

Gaspar stretched. Balthazar scratched his other ear. Melchoir lay on the carpet and rested his head on his paws.

Diana narrowed her eyes. "This is not precisely the spirit of cooperation I had hoped for."

Shakespeare cast the small dogs a questioning look, as if he had definite concerns about their intelligence, then padded to the doorway, let out a low "woof" and returned.

"A walk?"

Shakespeare sat down in front of her and thumped his tail on the floor.

"I think a walk will do us both—" the Yorkies stared intently, their manner abruptly interested. She laughed. "Very well, then—all of us—a world of good. I suspect your recent outing with your new master was more a trial than a romp. Besides, if I am to do anything at all with you three, we should get to know one another." Diana headed toward the hall. "We'd best hurry, there's a hint of rain in the air. I'll get my cloak and then we'll go."

It was perhaps for the best that the terriers were resistant to her commands. It meant that teaching them to do anything at all would take time. And time in Oliver's home, in Oliver's life, was exactly what she needed.

The Yorkies sat three abreast, the lines of their bodies alert and at attention. The small dog, the chubby dog and the silver dog all cocked their heads to one side as if listening to something, or someone, with rapt attention. The Great Dane swiveled his large head from side to side and growled. Then, his ears perked and he too appeared to hear something beyond the range of mortal man.

One by one, each terrior sat upright, tiny paws flailing in the air. One by one, each small dog dropped back down and rolled over, scrambling to its feet and wagging its stubby tail.

Miles stepped back deeper into the shadows of the hall to watch the animals unobserved. He'd had his doubts as to this plan of Lady Eleanor's. Miss Lawrence hadn't the least experience with dog training or with dogs at all for that matter. In point of fact, Lady Eleanor's kings were already quite well behaved and remarkably intelligent. Of course, Sir Oliver had no knowledge of that. No, indeed, the Yorkies seemed to delight in annoying him whenever he visited. Obviously, they had no intention of displaying their knowledge or skills to Sir Oliver or to Miss Lawrence. Why, that would doom Lady Eleanor's scheme before it had a chance to succeed.

The dear woman only wanted the best for her nephew, as did Miles and the rest of the staff. The entire household was aware of the Lady's wish to bring happiness to the man she'd raised as her own child. And no one, from the cook to the stableboys, ever doubted the matriarch's belief that, if given enough time, Miss Lawrence would be the instrument of his happiness.

All four dogs stared with rapt attention in the general direction of the fireplace. Miles smiled to himself. He should have known Lady Eleanor would not be content to leave her plot in the hands of mere living creatures, be they human or canine. Lady Eleanor was never one to allow a task she'd started to remain undone.

Even in death.

Chapter Four

Oliver dropped his fork with a clatter and glared at the plate before him. Whatever was wrong with Cook? His aunt's cook had always created the most delightful meals. But his beef had no flavor, his potatoes no taste. Even his wine lacked sparkle. He shoved the tray aside with disgust. What he needed was brandy. He rose to his feet and strode across his bedchamber to the waiting decanter conveniently placed on a table by the chair facing the fireplace. The silver flask had appeared the very day that woman had arrived. Miles always knew what he needed.

He poured a glass and downed it in a single swallow. He was drinking far too much these days. Had been ever since he set eyes on D. K. Lawrence. But liquor made no difference. Nothing seemed to dull the ache that he'd thought he'd rid himself of years ago.

In the three days since Diana had invaded his home he'd managed to avoid her except in passing. It was easy during the day, when his legitimate concerns about the state of Aunt Ellie's properties kept him away from the manor in spite of the dreary winter rains that did nothing to dispel his foul mood. Evenings were more difficult. Oliver was forced to retire to his own chambers, taking his evening meals there. Alone. With only his brandy and his thoughts and his anger.

He refilled his glass. In these last few days of self-imposed exile, his mind had wandered back through his life. He couldn't avoid recalling the magic of the days they'd been together. Magic she destroyed without so much as a backward glance. The remembered pain of her betrayal triggered hard memories of another loss. Until now, he had put the misery he'd known as a small boy well in the past. He rarely thought about his parents. They were probably decent enough in their own way, he supposed. Oh, he'd had excellent governesses and suitable care as a child but there had never been even the slightest inkling of affection from his own parents. They were far too busy in their world of society and travel to remember they had offspring. He'd always wondered what exactly was wrong with him. What had he done to fail them so? When they died, on a trip abroad, his foolish dreams of being a cherished son died with them. Aunt Ellie was the only one in his life who'd ever truly loved him. And the only one he'd ever cared for. Until Diana.

Why was she here?

The question rang over and over and over again in his mind. She'd been the only love of his life and she'd crushed his heart with devastating ease. She'd never responded to his letters and apparently married that Lawrence person. What did she want from him now?

He pulled a long swallow of the liquor. She had him hiding in his bedchamber like a chastised child. What was he afraid of?

Nothing. He clenched his jaw. Oliver Thornton Stanhope was no coward. And enough was enough. He was the epitome of success, respected in society and in government, and he would not be cowed by any man. Or any woman.

This was his home, blast it all, and he would not allow her the run of it simply because he was too caught up in emotions that should have died long ago. First thing in the morning, he would go on with his well-ordered life. He would no longer go out of his way to avoid her. He would not take another bloody meal in his room. He would ignore the past and treat her as exactly what she was: an employee.

Nothing more.

"The beef is quite good. In fact, everything from the soup to the wine is excellent tonight, Miles." Diana smiled at the ever-present butler. "Please give my compliments to Cook."

"Thank you, miss. Cook will appreciate it. Although she will question why you did not partake of it."

Diana looked down at her plate. Miles was right. Her meal was barely touched. She shook her head. "I don't seem to have much of an appetite tonight."

Miles sniffed. "Your appetite has been sadly lacking ever since your arrival."

She glanced around the huge dining room with

its high-beamed ceiling and leaded glass windows. A massive sideboard filled most of one wall. A crystal chandelier sparkled overhead. Candles burned in silver candelabra on the table that could easily seat twenty. Tonight, and last night and the night before, it seated only one.

Diana sighed. "I just hadn't expected to be dining alone every evening. It's rather odd, actually. I am very used to eating by myself."

"Sir Oliver is in his chambers, miss."

"I suspected as much." She leaned back in her chair and folded her hands in her lap. "My presence is rather a waste of time if I can't get him out of his room."

"Your presence is at the request of Lady Eleanor."

"It would all be so much easier if she were here."

"Lady Eleanor would say there is little value in anything achieved too easily."

"I have waited ten long years," she said sharply. "I would scarcely call any of this easy."

Miles raised a brow.

"Forgive me, Miles. I do apologize. I did not mean to snap. I simply . . ." She spread her hands out in front of her. "I don't know what to do.

"Perhaps, miss"—Miles removed her plate and headed toward the kitchen—"you first need to get Sir Oliver's attention." He pushed open the swinging door and disappeared into the kitchen.

"Get his attention?" Diana drew her brows together thoughtfully. She pushed her chair back from the table and crossed her arms over her chest. Excellent idea. What a shame Miles hadn't been a bit more specific on exactly what getting Oliver's attention would entail.

Shakespeare and the Three Kings

A short bark sounded from the floor. All three Yorkies and Shakespeare sat expectantly, alert for any possible table scraps.

"And what do you think, gentlemen?"

The dogs stared at her intently as if they were about to respond.

Diana smiled her encouragement. "Now then, don't be shy. I am entertaining any and all suggestions, recommendations or ideas no matter how far-fetched they might be.

"So, what do you think? How on earth does one attract the attention of a man who refuses to leave his room?"

The night was long and restless and this morning Diana was no closer to determining how to attract Oliver's attention than she had been when she'd slipped into bed. Her thoughts churned endlessly in her mind as she walked down the upstairs hall, the Great Dane by her side. There had to be a way to reach Oliver. Why, they had scarcely even spoken since her arrival. She certainly was not ready to give up. Not yet anyway.

A roar resounded from behind a closed door. Diana pulled up short. Shakespeare growled softly. The door on the left side of the hall flew open with such force it banged against the wall.

"Miles!" Oliver strode out of the room, knotting the tie of his dressing gown. "Miles! Where in the bloody hell are you?"

Diana widened her eyes. Oliver was a quivering tower of rage. "Is there something I can do to help?"

Oliver's gaze jerked to hers and surprise flittered across his face. "You? What are you doing here?"

"I was simply on my way to breakfast." She squared her shoulders and glared. "There is no need to use that tone with me."

"I—" He shook his head and ran his hand through his already tousled hair. "You're right, of course. I do apologize. Although"—his jaw clenched—"this is to some extent your fault."

"What is my fault?"

"This." He grabbed her hand and pulled her into his room.

"What are you doing?"

"Look." He released her and gestured at the massive four-poster bed that dominated the spacious room. "Well?"

"Well what?" She shrugged helplessly. He narrowed his eyes, grabbed her hand and pulled her closer to the bed. Panic fluttered in her stomach. "What on earth are you—"

"There." He stopped at the edge of the mattress. "Now do you see?"

The Yorkies lolled in the middle of the bed, half covered with blankets, looking for all the world as if they had found a home. And looking, as well, as if they had no intention of leaving.

Diana bit back a smile. "Indeed I do. It appears you have made a few friends."

"Hah! You call these friends? That's the last thing I would call them." His voice lowered in a menacing manner. "One of the little buggers actually bit me."

"Come now. I find that difficult to believe." She waved at the bed. "If you paid the tiniest bit of notice to them you'd find they're all very sweet and quite well behaved."

"Apparently, one is not as well behaved as the rest."

"I'm certain you're mistaken."

"I assure you, madam, I am quite capable of knowing when I have been tasted!" Indignation rang in his voice. "And if you doubt my word, I have the teethmarks to prove it."

Diana struggled against laughter threatening to burst free. "Really? And might I ask precisely where these teethmarks are?"

He glared at the animals on the bed and they glared right back. "My toe."

She choked out the words. "The big toe?"

"No." He narrowed his eyes in an unmistakable threat. The kings didn't so much as flinch, but Diana could have sworn Melchoir's black eyes also narrowed. Did Oliver realize his challenge may well have been met and possibly matched? "The smallest toe. Right foot."

"I see." Her eyes watered with the effort of stifling her laughter. He did not think this was even the slightest bit amusing and would, no doubt, not take her reaction at all well.

He slanted her an accusing glance. "You think this is funny, don't you?"

"Not at all." She shook her head vehemently. "I'm certain dog bites can be extremely painful."

"Indeed." He appeared a bit mollified.

"Especially when a dog is as ferocious as these."

"Well, I daresay I wouldn't—"

"Oh, but I think you should." She leaned forward and scooped up Gaspar. The tiny animal just barely filled her hands. "My goodness, these beasts are positively dangerous—"

"Mrs. Lawrence!" Oliver fairly growled the words.

"—a hazard to society—"

"I am not suggesting—"

"—and should no doubt be kept caged."

Oliver's brows pulled together in irritation, but deep within his dark blue eyes, she could see the faintest glimmer of amusement. "I do not appreciate being made sport of."

"Why, Sir Oliver," she forced a note of innocence into her voice. "I would never dare make fun of a wounded man. Would you, Gaspar?" She held the dog up before her and gazed into his eyes. "I didn't think so. But perhaps an apology is in order." She thrust the dog close to Oliver's face. "I do believe he is extremely sorry."

"I am not at all certain he is the culprit." The corners of Oliver's mouth quirked upward ever so slightly.

"Even so, he no doubt was encouraging of the deed and therefore must be the one to ask your pardon." She nodded firmly.

Oliver stared at the dog, his manner skeptical. "He does not seem the least bit repentant."

"Are you sure?" She turned Gaspar toward her, perused him for a moment, then held him back before Oliver. "I think you're mistaken. I think he's quite contrite."

Gaspar leaned toward Oliver, flashed his tiny pink tongue and flicked it across the man's nose. Oliver jerked backward. "Ugh! Contrite? I call it disgusting. Extremely disgusting."

"Not at all. He likes you." Diana winked at the dog and set him back on the bed.

"No doubt." His voice was dry but Diana suspected even Oliver could see the humor in the situation. Excellent. Shared laughter was the beginning of friendship. And friendship was surely the first step to recapturing love.

"I shall, however, remove them from your rooms for now. Come, gentlemen." Diana snapped her fingers and the Yorkies bounced to the edge of the bed, leapt lightly, one by one, to the floor and trotted out the door. Diana grinned with relief. She preferred Oliver not know how little his dogs really listened to her. Shakespeare glanced from the kings to Diana and back to the small pack, then he too padded out the door. She turned to Oliver. "There we are. Now, then . . ."

Had he stepped closer while she was preoccupied with the dogs? It seemed only a bare inch or two separated them now. She gazed up into the deep blue of his eyes and her breath caught. He was exactly as she remembered. His hair was a dark, rich blond, nearly gold. His jaw was strong, his nose straight, his lips full. His features seemed to have sharpened through the years, maturity bringing a greater definition to the planes of his face. Anyone else in the world would term him attractive, perhaps handsome, but not overly so. Diana thought him magnificent.

The cozy warmth and sleepy scent of a man just roused from his bed surrounded her. She wanted to lift her hand to his face and caress his rough, unshaven cheek. To run her fingers through his ruffled hair and smooth the silken strands into place. To throw herself into his arms and beg him to love her again as he once had.

He stood perhaps six inches taller than she and his gaze searched hers with an intensity that pierced her very soul. She couldn't breathe, couldn't think, couldn't do anything beyond lose herself in the depths of his smoldering eyes.

"Why are you here?" Was it anger that echoed in his voice? Or pain? Or hope?

"Why?" *Because I love you. Because I've always loved you. Because we should have already had a life together.*

"I . . ." She wanted to tell him everything. How Ketterson's bitter nature and vile lies had separated them and kept them apart. How she'd learned the truth. But Lady Eleanor had warned her against confessing all. She'd said Oliver had erected too many barriers against his own emotions, and against Diana, to accept her story at once. No, his aunt knew him far better than Diana did and she would follow the older woman's counsel, no matter how difficult it might prove to be.

"The dogs." She waved at the door. "I'm here because of the dogs, of course."

"Of course." His voice was quiet, cool and considering. He stared for a moment longer and then nodded toward the hall. "You had best see to your charges then. I should expect improvement in their behavior soon. And try to keep them out of . . . my bed."

"I shall," she said, swallowing past the lump in her throat, "do my best."

Diana wrenched her gaze from his and hurried out of the room. She imagined she could feel the heat of his stare boring into her back—appraising

44

her presence, evaluating her answers and, perhaps, reaching a decision.

Was the resentment and the misery of a lifetime ago too much too overcome? Lady Eleanor hadn't thought so. Diana wasn't as convinced. But this morning, perhaps, there was a difference in Oliver. Slight but encouraging. His tone was no longer as hard as it had been, the look in his eye not as cold as when she first arrived. Why, the man had nearly smiled at her.

Her lips curved upward at the thought. There was definite progress here. The kings had started it all. They had indeed attracted his attention.

Now, it was her turn.

Chapter Five

She had changed.

Oliver stared at the financial statements before him on the library desk without seeing even one of the figures laid out on the ledger pages with pristine precision.

Diana had definitely changed. He knew it the moment he had stormed out of his bedroom. The shy, reticent girl he'd once known would have shrunk away in fright at the sight of any man in such a raging temper. Especially a man in his nightclothes.

He smiled to himself. No, this Diana had chastised him for the sharpness of his voice. This Diana had accompanied him into the sanctity of his bedchamber without protest. This Diana had almost made him laugh.

His smile faded. Who was she and what was she doing here? As much as he hated to admit it, he'd probably known somewhere in the back of his mind from the second he saw her again that he would not be able to resist her company for long. Oh, certainly, he had made a good show of avoiding her, but his solitude had only served to concentrate his every waking thought on what they had once shared. More and more since her arrival he'd relived the days they'd spent together: glorious days of innocent love and blossoming passion and fervent vows of forever.

The joy had been far overshadowed by the pain at the end, the happiness they'd shared forgotten. But to his surprise, once he allowed himself to remember, those happy memories were remarkably vivid. The more he considered them, the more he wondered if perhaps he hadn't been wrong to accept Ketterson's tirade. If it hadn't been a mistake to believe Diana had simply used him for her own amusement. She hadn't had the flirtatious disposition of a girl of that nature and he'd had no doubts of her love. Not then. It was only later that Ketterson's charges seemed completely valid.

"But, damn it all, I wrote to her." Oliver's voice echoed in the empty library. He ran his hand through his hair in frustration. Bloody hell, the woman had him talking to himself now.

What if she never received my letters?

The thought hit him with an unexpected jolt and his spine stiffened in his chair. Why had he never thought of that before? Had he been so blinded by her apparent betrayal that his senses had abandoned him entirely? Was he so foolish?

Or was he simply so young? He'd only been twenty-two. Barely old enough to know his own mind. Not nearly the self-possessed, experienced man he was now. Today, he would never accept the statements of a man as clearly irrational as Ketterson had been. Today he would—what? Insist on hearing the truth from her own lips? Fight for her hand? Follow her to America?

He groaned and leaned back in his chair, his gaze straying to the coffered library ceiling. Was it even remotely possible that their separation had been a ghastly mistake? Or worse, the vile work of her father?

Still, she had married that Lawrence fellow. But when? Had she actually been betrothed when she left Oliver? Or did her marriage come much later? He had no idea.

"But I intend to find out," he said under his breath. Diana wasn't the only one who had changed with the years. Oliver, too, had a strength of character he hadn't known before. He rose to his feet. He wanted answers and, more, he wanted to know this virtual stranger who'd once altered his life forever and now, suddenly, appeared to be influencing it yet again.

A sharp rap sounded and the door swung open.

"Sir Oliver?" Diana stood in the doorway.

"Mrs. Lawrence." He nodded coolly but his heart thudded in his chest. "Do come in."

"Thank you." She swept into the room with a gleam in her eye and a definite purpose in her step.

"Is there something you need?" How inane. How inadequate. How insipid. He had a hundred questions to ask her. A thousand burning inquiries. That was not on his list.

"Your assistance."

"Really?" He raised a brow. *And I need the truth. Why did you leave me? Why are you back?* "In what way?"

"Well . . ." She stepped closer to the desk. The rains had finally stopped and pale morning sunlight shone through the library windows, highlighting streaks of gold in her dark hair. "It's about your aunt's dogs. Or rather, I should say, your dogs."

"Go on." Her gaze met his with a steady, unblinking stare. Were there flecks of gold in her eyes as well? How could he have forgotten?

"In order to properly train animals, one must get to know them." She clasped her hands together primly before her, the simple movement drawing attention to her fashionable gown and the intriguing way the eminently proper attire molded to the lush curves of her body.

"Get to know them . . ." he murmured, his gaze wandering over her, greedy to memorize every aspect of her face and form or, perhaps, to remember.

"Sir Oliver?"

"Yes?" His gaze jumped to hers.

She tilted her head slightly and a frown creased her brow. "I know you are not at all fond of the dogs but I honestly feel if you, or rather, if I, am to make any sort of progress at all it would be—"

"Of course." Oliver stepped out from behind the desk.

"Of course?"

"You are the expert in these matters, are you not, Mrs. Lawrence?"

Her eyes widened and a look of confusion flashed across her face.

"Mrs. Lawrence?"

"The expert." Her words were measured as if she were trying them on for size. Was she avoiding his gaze as well?

"Indeed. You are the one with the knowledge of dog training." He studied her intently, willing an answer he wasn't sure he was ready to hear. "Precisely the reason why you're here, is it not?"

"Well, yes, but—"

"But what?"

She shrugged in a far too casual manner. "I didn't expect you to agree so quickly, that's all. I had the rather distinct impression that you are not altogether fond of the animals."

"Nor are they fond of me. But my aunt's death has left me little choice in the matter. Like it or not, I'm stuck with the annoying little buggers."

A smiled curved her lips and amusement lit her eyes. "Not buggers. Kings."

He snorted. "They have certainly been treated like royalty."

"Lady Eleanor loved them."

"Indeed she did. And I suppose I shall get used to them eventually. But aside from the clashes of our respective characters, Yorkshire terriers are not exactly the breed I would choose."

"Oh?"

"No indeed. Dogs are, for the most part, decent hardworking animals who should be employed for useful pursuits. Why, they should hunt or herd or guard. They should live as such creatures were meant to live: out-of-doors or in a stable or a barn. They should not be found indoors. They should not be permitted to settle themselves in the lap of some unsuspecting person. And they should never"—he pulled his brows together in a stern manner—"be allowed anywhere in the vicinity of my bed."

"I see."

"And furthermore, they are not a man's breed."

"Yorkies are extremely popular these days."

"With women such as my aunt, perhaps, but a man needs a different type of dog. Something more substantial. Something large and sturdy." He nodded firmly. "Something like that Great Dane of yours."

"Shakespeare?"

"An excellent name, as well. Noble and renowned. According to Miles, he appears to be quite well trained. A tribute to your methods, no doubt."

"No doubt," she said faintly.

"Have you had him long?"

"Long?"

He eyed her curiously. Why was she hesitating? "Yes. I would think to have achieved such a degree of obedience you would have to raise a dog from a pup."

"Well, yes, of course, that is the ideal way to go about it." She pulled a deep breath. "And in fact, I have learned everything I know from my . . . um, work with Shakespeare."

Her voice was even and cool, yet Oliver suspected there was something amiss. What could it be? He added yet another question to his growing list.

"Very well, then. How do you suggest we proceed?"

The faintest touch of relief flushed her face. "I thought perhaps a long walk might be the best place to start."

"Capitol idea." He smiled. "I shall get my coat and meet you and your charges, on the front drive."

"In, shall we say, five minutes?"

"Excellent." He nodded and she turned to leave

Abruptly she swiveled back to him. She stared at him with a considering gaze if she were looking for an answer to a query not yet voiced. "This is the first time I've seen you smile since my arrival."

His voice was soft. "This is the first time I've wished to smile."

"I wondered if you knew how."

"Of course I know how. In point of fact, I am considered to have a highly developed sense of humor." Indignation edged his tone. "I enjoy a good jest as well as the next man. I not only smile, I have been known to grin, chuckle and engage in a hearty laugh on occasion."

"I didn't mean to insult you." She bit back a smile. "I was simply starting to believe you had forgotten such things."

"I have forgotten . . . nothing." At once the lighthearted nature of the moment shattered and tension hung in the air.

She caught her breath and seemed about to say something. Would she now bring up their past? Was this the moment he ached for? The moment he dreaded? She shook her head slightly as if to clear it.

"Five minutes, then." Diana turned and strode out the door.

He exhaled a breath he didn't know he'd held. Was it too soon to bring up what had once been between them? Was she as apprehensive about confronting their past as he was? Could she possibly know how devastated he had been?

Of course! The answer struck him like a slap across the face. Aunt Ellie! This was all her doing. Why hadn't he realized it before now? Obviously, his aunt must have contacted Diana, or perhaps it was the other way around, and devised a plan to bring the only woman he'd ever loved back into his life. It was just the type of endeavor Aunt Ellie would undertake and not the type of thing even death would dissuade her from.

If Ellie had had a hand in this that went beyond the ridiculous notion of helping him adjust to her pets, she must have liked Diana a great deal. She would never allow the woman who'd destroyed her nephew's heart to come anywhere near him, or for that matter, her kings, unless she firmly believed it was best for Oliver.

A sinking sensation settled in his stomach. Were his newfound suspicions about the events of a decade ago true after all? He'd wager Ellie thought so. In all his years with her, he'd never known her to make a serious error in the judgement of the integrity of any man or any woman.

Still, he would have to be cautious until he was certain. It was best if he took this possibility with a healthy dose of skepticism. For so long he had believed in Diana's treachery, had lived with its bitter taste in his mouth. It would be wise to proceed slowly. He wasn't ready to pull her into his arms and declare the past behind them, although, with each passing moment in her presence, that was exactly what he wanted.

No, this self-reliant woman who refused to flinch from his steady, assessing gaze was a far cry from the quiet innocent he'd once loved. And for that, if for no other reason, he had to tread with care and keep the hope and desire that grew within him under control. At least for now.

It would not be easy. Especially with the realization that, regardless of how much time had passed, no woman in her right mind would return to confront the man she'd so cruelly deserted unless she had never truly deserted him at all.

Chapter Six

"Now, gentlemen, I should very much appreciate it if you were on your best behavior." The Yorkies looked up at her with an air of indifference in an obvious debate over the pros and cons of honoring her request. "It would be a great help if I was able to show him at least a tiny improvement in your attitude. Shakespeare, I am counting on you to lead the way." The Great Dane cocked his head, alert and ready. He really was a wonderful dog, not that she knew a great deal about dogs, but this huge beast had already worked his way into her affections. If nothing else came of this venture, she at least had a loyal friend for life.

Oliver strode across the broad, winter-browned expanse of the lawn toward the end of the long drive where Diana and her charges waited. Her heart caught. He was so handsome, his step so firm, his bearing so self-assured. He was at once just as she'd remembered yet so very different. The passage of time had taken a reserved young man and molded him into a fine figure of fortitude and strength.

How on earth could she resist the temptation to throw herself into his arms and tell him everything she'd learned since Ketterson's death? No. She took a deep breath. It was far too soon.

"Patience, my dear." Lady Eleanor's instructions rang in her ears. *"Remember, men are very much like dogs when it comes to how they view the world around them and their relationship to it and other creatures."*

If there was any chance that he could love her again, he had to accept her first.

Oliver stepped up beside her with a cordial nod. "Where do you suggest we begin?"

"Begin?" She wished she knew.

"Yes." He stared in a quizzical manner. "You said I needed to better know the animals. I admit I have no knowledge about the training of dogs, but this idea strikes me as a bit unusual."

"It's American," she said quickly. "And quite the latest method for canine instruction."

"It does seem rather unique."

"It's very progressive. I suggest we simply walk with them for a while and see how that goes."

He raised a brow. "I attempted to walk with them on the day you arrived and it did not go at all well. The creatures insisted on darting off the road and disappearing into the bushes. I was quite afraid I would lose them entirely. I found myself chasing after them like a lunatic."

She stifled a smile at the image. "Did you call them in a firm, yet pleasant tone?"

"I was exceedingly firm," he said wryly.

"And pleasant?"

Oliver grimaced.

Shakespeare and the Three Kings

"Very well, then. I see we shall have to start from the beginning." Diana started off down the lane, all too aware of Oliver at her side. If she closed her eyes, she could imagine another walk in another time and a single kiss in a moment stolen with the man she loved.

The dogs trotted before them in a haphazard display of obedience. Not at all impressive but far better than nothing at all. What was it that the pamphlet instructed? Oh yes. "Consistency is the key to training a dog. They will come to understand what it is you require of them if you are consistent in your commands."

"And pleasant," he muttered.

"Obviously, we shall have to work on that. It appears you and the kings have started off on the wrong foot, or rather"—she cast him a teasing smile—"I should say the wrong paw."

"They do not like me." Oliver's eyes narrowed. "They have never liked me."

"And do you like them?"

"I do not precisely dislike them. I simply find them annoying, noisy, snapping little blighters."

"Dogs are extremely intelligent animals. I daresay they know full well your opinion of them." She shook her head. "Perhaps you need to be trained as much as they do."

"Hah. My behavior is not in question here. They are the problem." He nodded at the dogs, who seemed to pay no notice to them at all. "I say, shouldn't we be issuing commands of some sort?"

"No, no, not today," she said with a conviction she didn't feel. "As I said, you need to get to know one another. You and the Yorkies have to accept each other's company. You must first learn mutual trust and even respect before any kind of serious training can begin." Good Lord! What kind of rubbish was she spouting? Although, even to her own ears, it did seem to sound rather knowledgeable.

"Respect?"

"Certainly. Why, you would not listen for a moment to anyone you did not respect. Dogs are no different. It shall certainly take a great deal of work but it will be worth the effort in the end." Another phrase from the pamphlet leapt to mind. "A well trained dog is a delightful companion."

He snorted with disdain. "I rather doubt delightful can be achieved in this case. We may have to settle for a simple armed truce."

She laughed. "It's far too early to give up. Patience is nearly as important in training as consistency."

In your training as well as theirs.

"I suppose." He shrugged. The dogs ambled before them in a surprisingly well-behaved manner. Diana heaved a silent sigh of relief. At least they were not distracting her from her chat with Oliver. And that, after all, was the true purpose of this outing.

"I have to confess, I am rather surprised by your expertise." Oliver slanted her an admiring glance.

"Oh?" Her stomach clenched but she kept her tone even. "Why is that?"

"You must admit it is rather unusual for a woman to have any sort of profession, let alone be engaged in the education of dogs."

"Do you think women are unfit for such professions?"

"No, not really, I suppose." He chuckled. "Frankly, I had never given it any consideration one way or another."

"I have heard of numerous women who have pursued various methods of earning a living."

"Perhaps not numerous but indeed, I have heard of a few as well. For the most part they were widows who had taken over the business activities of their deceased husbands." He paused as if choosing his words with care. "Did you learn your skills with animals from your husband?"

"My husband?" She stopped short and stared.

"Lawrence." He studied her carefully.

"Lawrence," she echoed.

"I am sorry. I simply assumed, since you are so obviously independent, that you were a widow."

"A widow." Of course. He'd called her *Mrs. Lawrence*. He must think she'd married. She knew from his letters that Ketterson had told him she was to be wed. She'd been far too preoccupied with other considerations to note his use of the married title until now. "Yes, well, I am indeed . . . independent." She turned and continued down the lane.

"It must be very difficult." His voice was quiet. "For a woman alone, that is. Even one with a profession."

"It is always difficult to be alone." She glanced at him. "Don't you think?"

"Very difficult, indeed."

He stared down at the graveled lane, his brows furrowed as if he were deep in thought. What was he thinking? Was this finally the moment to reveal the truth? They seemed to have developed a quiet companionship today or, possibly, an unspoken agreement as to the bounds of discussion. Could this be the time to bring up the past? She squared her shoulders.

He drew a deep breath. "Mrs. Lawrence—"

"Yes?"

"I was wondering . . ." He shook his head. "Never mind. It's of no consequence."

She nodded, her courage evaporating in the wind. His feelings were too raw, too fragile. He simply was not trained enough to her company to pursue anything further. It would take time. She could wait.

They walked on in silence. Diana kept her gaze directed on the ground before them, too full of her own concerns to pay attention to anything beyond the turmoil churning within her.

"I do realize you are the expert in matters pertaining to dogs."

She looked up at him. Amusement danced in his blue eyes. "Yes?"

A smile tugged the corners of his lips. "Yet I am curious, don't you think we should at least keep an eye on the animals? I suspect I can't possibly get to know the beasts if they are nowhere in sight."

"What?" Diana scanned the road ahead. The dogs had vanished. "Where on earth have they gone?"

"This is precisely what they did to me when I attempted an outing." He shrugged. "However, I assumed with your expertise . . ."

She widened her eyes and stared at him. Why, the man was teasing her. Her heart soared. It was a very good sign.

"So, what do you suggest now?" The smile grew

to a grin. Did he suspect she hadn't the vaguest idea how to handle dogs?

"Now?"

"I suppose we shall have to find them."

"That's exactly what I was about to say," she said, a bit more sharply than she intended. She lifted her chin and hurried down the road. He chuckled behind her. Honestly, he was behaving as if she didn't know what she was doing. She didn't, of course, but he needn't be so smug about it.

As if cued by an unseen hand, a chorus of frantic yelps broke out a few yards beyond them from a small grove of trees. Diana sent a prayer of thanks toward the heavens. Losing the dogs would not do at all.

"I believe they're in this direction."

"That would be my guess. After you, Mrs. Lawrence." She could hear the laugh in his voice. "You're the expert. As far as I'm concerned, those animals can go straight to—"

"Sir Oliver! Your aunt expects you to take care of them," she said over her shoulder, "and even anyone who knows nothing at all about dogs can certainly tell they're in some kind of predicament." She stepped briskly off the road and into the lightly wooded area.

"I rescind my earlier statement," he called after her. "I do dislike them! I detest them! If the truth were told—"

Diana plunged through the brush and pulled up short. The ground banked down gently. It was not a difficult incline under usual conditions, but today it was slickened with mud. A small pond lay a few yards beyond. Puddles of rainwater dotted the area.

Shakespeare struggled at the bottom of the slope to pull himself out of some sort of hole. But the poor beast couldn't get a grasp on the muddy ground and every effort left him covered more and more with muck. He gazed up at her with a mournful expression. The Yorkies sat to one side of the big dog, their long hair plastered to their tiny bodies, looking quite pleased with themselves. They had, after all, summoned help and their task here was done.

"Did you find—" Oliver stepped up beside her and winced. "That's a bloody mess."

"He's stuck down there."

"So it appears," Oliver said mildly.

"In some kind of hole."

"A foxhole I suspect." Oliver bent forward slightly and peered at the display. "Yes, indeed, looks like a foxhole from here."

"Aren't you going to do something?" She waved at the Great Dane. "Rescue him?"

"You're the dog expert." He crossed his arms over his chest and bit back a grin. "You do something."

She glared in annoyance. "Very well, I will." She picked up her skirts, set her jaw and stepped forward firmly.

"I say, don't be—"

Her feet slipped out from under her, her balance fled and she toppled backward, plopping down on her rear end and siding the full length of the incline like a child on a sled.

"Mrs. Lawrence!"

She turned just in time to see Oliver scramble down the hill to her side. He pulled her to her feet, concern evident on his face. "Are you all right? I am sorry. I never meant for you to actually try to negotiate this slope by yourself. But you started off before I could stop you and I—"

"Oh, honestly, Oliver," exasperation colored her words, "I'm covered in mud. We've been together much of the day. I should think we can dispense with formalities. Can't you call me Diana?"

He stared down at her. His midnight gaze bored into hers and her heart pounded in her ears. Time seemed to stop. The world faded away and all that mattered was the question in his eyes. "Diana."

He spoke her name like a caress, and it shivered through her blood. She never thought she'd hear him say it again.

"Why . . ." He grabbed her shoulders and pulled her closer, his gaze searching hers, hungry and hopeful. Then abruptly, the look in his eye vanished, as a flame extinguished by a puff of breath, and he dropped his hands.

"Oliver, I—" Disappointment rushed through her. And relief. And fear. She wasn't ready. Not yet. Diana turned toward Shakespeare and waved helplessly at him. "He is much too big for me to handle alone."

"I'll do it." Oliver stepped toward the dog, grasped his midsection and pulled him out of the hole. Shakespeare cast him a grateful glance, reached his huge head forward and slapped his tongue across Oliver's face. Oliver jerked back but not fast enough. Shakespeare shook his solid body in an impressive display of energy. Droplets of water and chunks of mud flew. In a split second, Oliver was drenched and covered.

"Damnation!" Oliver sputtered and glared at his ruined clothing.

Shakespeare scrambled up the hill and gazed down at him, wagging his tail in a manner that distinctly said this was a grand game. Diana stifled a laugh of her own.

"Blasted creatures."

"It's precisely what you deserve."

"Oh," he raised a brow. "In what way?"

"I told you once," she said in a lofty manner, "dogs can sense when somebody dislikes them."

Oliver glanced up at Shakespeare. He wagged his tail. "He seems to like me well enough."

"You rescued him. Shakespeare is very willing to like everyone. Now the kings, on the other hand"—she nodded at the Yorkies who watched their every move—"are perhaps a shade more discriminating." She bent over and snapped her fingers. "Come here, gentlemen."

The dogs scurried to her side. She scooped up Balthazar and Melchoir and thrust them at Oliver. "Here. You shall have to carry them up. I doubt they can make it by themselves. I'll carry Gaspar."

He accepted the squirming, wet and rather pungent animals with a grimace of distaste. "And who will carry you?"

Her gaze locked with his and once again it seemed the question hanging between them had nothing to do with the words. She wrenched her gaze away, bent and picked up Gaspar. "You said it yourself, Oliver: I am an independent woman. I'm certain I shall manage."

· She turned, examined the slope and started toward a spot that seemed slightly less steep than the rest. Intent on her climb up the hill she wasn't at all certain but she could have sworn she heard Oliver comment softly.

"Ah, but my dear, will I?"

Oliver swirled the brandy in his glass and stared at the flames licking at the logs in the fireplace. He'd planned on dining downstairs tonight but both Miles and Mrs. Collins, the housekeeper, had insisted he and Diana go straight to bed after bathing and a light supper.

Oliver and Diana had not exchanged more than a few words on the brisk walk back to the manor. Oliver was not entirely certain what he wished to say. Diana shivered at his side, cold and miserable. He could do little but offer her a coat that was not substantially better than what she had. The temperature had dropped and a stiff breeze carried the scent of snow. He'd wanted to wrap his arms around her but . . .

Miles had greeted them at the door with no more comment than an upraised brow. Apparently, he'd seen the kings in this state before. Within seconds, the Yorkies were handed over to kitchen maids, Shakespeare was on his way to the stables and servants were drawing baths. Miles always knew what he needed.

But did Oliver?

He pulled a thoughtful sip and considered the day's events. Yes, Diana had changed with the years and to an equal, if not greater, extent, so had he. Gone was the foolhardy youth who wore his heart on his sleeve and fell in love with a shy, dark-eyed American. Vanished was the very proper, well-behaved young lady who had just enough of a hint of passion in those eyes to tantalize the equally respectable young man. But he could no longer deny that whatever had pulled them together once before lingered now.

He still wanted to know exactly why she was back in his life. Could she possibly want him again after all these years? The answer, one way or another, would make what he had to do so much easier. At least he would know. He'd almost done it today, grabbed her and jerked her into his arms and demanded the truth. Had she left him of her own accord? Did she break his heart for her own amusement? Or were they both victims of another's deceit? But his courage failed. The words simply wouldn't come.

Oliver emptied his glass in one long swallow and set it carefully on the table at his side. He was not a man easily frightened. He considered himself possessed of a certain moral fiber and a satisfactory physical presence. He did not doubt his own capabilities. Oliver Thornton Stanhope was not one to run from a fight.

But today when he'd said her name and stared into the endless depths of her eyes, fear such as he'd never imagined, intense and primitive and heart-stopping, rushed through him. Fear triggered at the moment he realized the past no longer mattered. The moment he knew with clarity that stunned his senses and his soul that once again he loved her.

And very likely, always had.

Chapter Seven

"Where is she, Miles?" Oliver strode into the breakfast room, determination adding a spring to his step. The night had been long and restless, his sleep fitful, but this morning's decision had renewed his spirit.

He didn't give a bloody fig about the events of a decade ago. That was over and done with. All he cared about was today. She was in his home and in his life and that's where he would fight to keep her. He was not the same man who'd lost her once, for whatever reason. He would not lose her again.

He had no idea what her feelings were, but more and more he believed she would not be here at all if she didn't harbor some affection for him. Nothing else made sense. It was the only logical explanation. Odd, what love did to a man's mind. He'd been too distracted by her arrival to recognize the absurdity of this dog training nonsense.

"Get on with it, man, where is she?"

"Who, sir?" Miles stood holding a small silver tray bearing a white vellum envelope in one hand. Oliver's coat hung over his other arm.

"You know who." Impatience pulled his brows together. "Mrs. Lawrence, that's who."

"Miss Lawrence is not down yet."

"Very well." Oliver pulled out a chair. "I shall wait."

"I'm afraid not, sir." Miles offered the tray. "This arrived for you a short while ago. I believe you've been called back to London."

"Blast it all." Oliver ripped open the envelope and scanned the tersely worded message. "Some sort of question over the clauses in a rather obscure treaty of little importance. Ridiculous to call me back for this. I daresay—" Resignation washed through him. "Damnation. Well, there's nothing to be done for it, I suppose. At least it shouldn't take long." Oliver pulled out his watch. "I believe there's a train to London within the hour. If I make it—"

"I assumed you would want to leave at once, sir." Miles assisted Oliver into his coat. "A carriage is waiting to take you to the station."

"You always did know what I needed, Miles."

"Indeed, I do, Sir Oliver," Miles said under his breath.

Oliver started toward the door, then turned back. "When you see Mrs. Lawrence . . ."

"Yes, Sir?"

"Tell her—" *Tell her—what?* "Never mind. Just tell her I'll be home this evening. And I should like to see her. Tell her it's important. No. Tell her it's urgent. No. Don't tell her anything. I'll tell her myself." Oliver hurried out the door to the waiting carriage, his mind turning to the barely remembered business awaiting him in London.

It wasn't until the train was approaching the city

that the strange nature of the summons to return dawned on him. Miles had rushed him out of the manor too quickly to give it much thought. He pulled the letter from his breast pocket and studied it.

The signature was scrawled and unreadable. He'd simply assumed, given the emergency nature of the missive, it was from his superiors. There was no letterhead, no official insignia, nothing of that sort. It was a simple, yet expensive, sheet of fine writing paper. The type anyone of means might have access to.

Odder still, the more he regarded the dispatch, the more the handwriting seemed familiar. In fact, it bore a startling but very distinct resemblance to Aunt Ellie's.

"Where is he, Miles?" Diana stepped into the breakfast room, Shakespeare at her side, the three kings scampering about her feet.

"Sir Oliver was called to London, miss."

"Oh." Her spirits dropped. "I see."

Miles pulled out a chair and absently she sat down. Through the long hours of a sleepless night she'd finally decided the time had come to confront him about the past. She would not beg his forgiveness: she'd done nothing to forgive save a weak character that had blindly accepted Ketterson's words. But she would tell him the truth of what had happened. And she would confess her love and admit her feelings for him had never dimmed.

Miles set her breakfast plate before her with a loud sigh.

And if Oliver rejected her? So be it. Unconsciously, she lifted her chin in defiance. It would be painful but she would survive. She would always survive. She had matured enough to recognize and accept with pride her own strength.

Miles poured her coffee and again released a heartfelt sigh.

"Miles?" She gazed up at the hovering butler. "Forgive me for intruding, but is something the matter?"

He sighed again. "I hate to trouble you, miss."

"Don't be silly. Please. I'd like to help."

"Well . . ." He hesitated as if debating the propriety of his admission. "I'm sure you're aware this is the first Christmas at Thornton without Lady Eleanor."

In the midst of dealing with Oliver and the dogs, she'd nearly forgotten all about Christmas. "I am sorry. You must miss her."

"Lady Eleanor loved Christmastime."

"Of course."

"She made certain the manor was decked in finery from one end to the other." A reminiscent light shone in Miles' eyes. "It was a sight to behold."

"I can well imagine."

"Sir Oliver loved the way the manor looked at Christmas.

"Really?"

"Indeed. He used to say that coming back here for the holidays was the best part of his year."

"Did he?"

Miles sighed once more. "The staff and I have been saying it's something of a shame not to celebrate the season this year. For Sir Oliver that is."

Diana tapped her finger thoughtfully on the table.

"Lady Eleanor would have wanted it." Miles pressed his point home. "For Sir Oliver."

"Consistency is the key to training a dog," she murmured.

"Miss?" Miles raised a brow.

"Nothing, Miles, nothing at all," she said slowly. "When is Sir Oliver expected to return?"

"The train trip is approximately three hours and ten minutes each way. That, given the time it shall take him to resolve whatever matter it is he finds there, and considering as well the limited number of trains available . . . He should be back quite late I should say."

"Do you think . . . would it be possible . . . I mean, could we—"

"Decorate the manor? Fetch Lady Eleanor's decorations from the attic? Bring in boughs of fir? Select and cut a tree?"

"Dear me." It was her turn to sigh. "I hadn't realized there was so very much to accomplish. Christmas was never much of an occasion in my home and not marked at all after my mother's death. It does seem impossible."

"My dear, Miss Lawrence." Miles drew himself up in an imperious manner. "Lady Eleanor's staff at Thornton, including gardeners and stable hands, consists of thirty-seven of the best-trained servants in England. She considered us not as mere employees but as members of her family. Each and every one of us feels her loss. And each and every one of us views Sir Oliver with a great deal of affection." A determined gleam shone in his eye. "Nothing is impossible. Not for this staff. Not in this household and especially not at Christmas."

Diana shook her head. "Miles, you are amazing."

"Yes, miss, I am." The corners of his lips curled but his staid expression didn't so much as flicker. "Shall I give the orders, then?"

"Please do." Diana rose to her feet. "Can I be of any assistance?"

"You already have, miss." Miles nodded and hurried out of the room.

Diana glanced down at the dogs sitting expectantly beside the table. "It appears, gentlemen, once again, we are going to get Oliver's attention."

Within the hour, the manor exploded with activity and exhilaration. Everywhere, servants scurried, arms laden with evergreen branches and boxes of the fragile ornaments collected by Lady Eleanor. Laughter rang through the hall and echoed in every chamber of the huge house. Now and again a rousing, if off-key, version of "God Rest Ye Merry Gentlemen" or "Deck the Halls" would break out, the joy more in the singing than the sound.

The Yorkies bounded from one group of chattering workers to the next as if overseeing the proceedings. Shakespeare, too, seemed caught up in the excitement, his wagging tail smacking more than one unsuspecting backside.

Chambermaids festooned the grand stairway with garlands. Stable boys and coachmen found the perfect tree and erected it in the main parlor. The cook and her helpers gathered huge bows out of ribbons and laces and odd bits of silk and then retired to the kitchen.

The smell of cinnamon and clove, nutmeg and spice and all things delightful soon mingled with the clean scent of fresh pine and fir. Diana helped with a decoration here, a bit of direction there, but it was all somewhat overwhelming. She'd never seen the like before. Even as a child, in a house nearly as grand as the manor with almost as many servants, Christmas had been a quiet affair. A holiday observed with due reverence but little more.

But this—this was a celebration. A celebration shared by friends who were as much family as any blood relations. And she was welcomed among them and made to feel a part of the gathering, of the family. She'd never been a part of anything even remotely like this before.

And she'd never had so much fun.

The door to Miss Lawrence's room swung open. Miles frowned with annoyance. The American was downstairs assisting with the effort to bring Christmas to the manor. Her rooms were made up earlier today. No one should be here now. He started toward her door with every intention of chastising whatever servant had intruded in her private chambers, then stopped.

Gaspar trotted into the hall followed by Balthazar and Melchoir, the chubby creature carrying something in his mouth. From where he was standing it appeared to be a document, perhaps a booklet of some sort or a small sheaf of papers. The door closed behind them and the dogs continued down the hall.

Miles smiled and shook his head. He knew without looking that there was no one in Miss Lawrence's room. At least no one he would be able to see.

What was Lady Eleanor up to now?

*   *   *

By late evening, the miracle had been wrought. Every inch of the manor from overmantles to door frames, sideboards to chandeliers, was adorned with greenery and gilded nuts and bright red holly berries. Even the portraits of Lady Eleanor and her husband in the hall were decked with pinecones and silk ribbons. The tree was trimmed to mythical perfection with bows and sweets and glass ornaments imported from Germany, and glistened in the lamplight like magic or a wish come true.

Everywhere Diana looked it was Christmas.

And there was love.

Oliver still hadn't returned and she preferred not to destroy the enjoyment of the day with the inevitable emotional upheaval she suspected lay ahead. Their discussion could wait until the morning. Tomorrow, after all, was Christmas Eve, and what better time to lay aside the past and look toward the future than a day so laden with hope.

Diana climbed the stairs, now appointed with the joy of the season. How very ironic. She'd come to Thornton Manor to recover the lost love of a single man and had discovered instead the affection of a family and a home.

No matter what happened with Oliver, her stay here would linger in her memory forever.

And so would the love.

"Bloody hell." Oliver stamped his feet and brushed the snow off his shoulders. The steady snowfall had started during his trip home and who knew how long it would last. His foul mood did not allow for appreciation of the scenic beauty of the night.

"Sir Oliver." Miles appeared to take his coat and hat. "Was your trip to town successful?"

"Successful?" Oliver snorted. "Hardly. There was nothing to it. I have been on some sort of devious wild goose hunt." He narrowed his eyes. "Who did you say brought that message this morning anyway?"

"I didn't say, sir. I believe it was received by one of the parlor maids." Miles' expression remained noncommittal. "I can ask her in the morning if you wish, sir."

"Never mind," Oliver snapped. "I suppose it's of no significance at this point. Where is Mrs. Lawrence?"

"She's retired for the evening, sir."

"I see." Disappointment surged through him. Still, perhaps it was for the best. He was in no mood to confront her tonight. No, tonight he might well allow his irritation with his completely wasted day to influence what he wished to say to her. "I suppose I shall retire then as well."

He turned and started toward the stair, then stopped. His eyes widened. His gaze skimmed over the evergreens in the hall, the ribbons on the banister. He turned on his heel and strode into the parlor. The room was transformed, touched by the hand of Christmas magic. Just as it had always appeared when Aunt Ellie was alive. Just as he'd always loved it.

"Miles." There was an odd catch in his voice he couldn't quite hide. "What is all this?"

"Christmas, sir."

"Yes, I recognize Christmas when I see it." Oliver's voice was quiet. "How did—"

"Miss Lawrence, sir."

"Diana did all this?"

"Actually, Sir Oliver, the staff did most of it. But it was Miss Lawrence's suggestion."

"Was it?"

"Yes, sir." Miles paused as if waiting for another question. "If there is nothing else, sir?"

"No, nothing." Oliver couldn't seem to pull his gaze away from the spectacle before him. "Go to bed, Miles. I shall speak to Mrs. Lawrence in the morning."

"Yes, sir." The butler turned to leave.

"And Miles?" The butler halted. "Thank you."

"The thanks go to Miss Lawrence, sir."

"Of course," he murmured.

He hadn't expected all this. But more, he hadn't expected the overwhelming feeling of warmth that swept through him. It was as if he were a boy again spending his first Christmas in a new house with a new family. Family. He'd never truly had that with his own parents. It was only when he'd come to live with Aunt Ellie and the remarkable people who were called servants but were so much more, that he'd ever had a sense of belonging.

Diana had had a hand in this. His heart swelled. Surely that was a good sign. He'd talk to her tomorrow, first thing in the morning. Tomorrow was Christmas Eve and there was no better time to lay to rest the specter of the past and plan the rest of their lives together.

He was convinced of her feelings. What she'd

done here was confirmation. But even if he was wrong, in this house, with these people, even with those blasted dogs, he could face it.

He was home and here was love.

Chapter Eight

What in the name of all that was holy made him believe he'd get any sleep tonight? Oliver paced the length of his chamber, tightening the belt of his dressing gown. He hadn't had a decent night's sleep since she'd arrived and this evening was no different.

He couldn't get her out of his mind. What he wanted to say and, more specifically, how, kept going around and around in his head like a dog chasing its tail. It was nerves, of course, plain and simple. He drew his brows together in annoyance. What was wrong with him? He was confident and successful and nothing had ever effected him like this.

Except Diana.

Brandy, that's what he needed. He strode across the room toward the silver decanter. A slight scraping sounded at the door.

"What on earth?"

Oliver stopped and listened. The noise sounded again. It was more of a scratch than a scrape. He stepped to the door and yanked it open. The three Yorkies sat lined up before him.

"Well?" He glared at the dogs. "What do you want?"

Almost as one, the three kings stood and padded into his room, heading toward the bed.

"Wait just a moment." Oliver skirted the animals and blocked their approach. "Where do you think you're going?"

Gaspar cast him a rather smug look as if to say he was going anywhere he damn well pleased, and dove under the bed.

"Oh, no you don't." Oliver dropped to his hands and knees and peered under the bed. Where was the creature? "Come out from there, you little bugger. I have no intention of allowing you, any of you, in my chambers. Not under my bed. Not on it. Do you understand?"

A soft yap sounded above him.

"What?" Oliver scrambled to his feet. The Yorkies sat amidst his bedclothes, looking very much as if they were settling in for the night. "Very well. You've outsmarted me for the moment but I will not permit you to stay. Not on my bed." He released an exasperated sigh. "I suppose you can sleep on the floor if you insist, but only for tonight."

The kings did not appear to take him seriously. What was that in Melchoir's mouth? He reached for it. Someone growled and he snatched his hand back.

"Very well," he snapped. "Don't give it to me."

The dogs cocked their heads and stared intensely in the general direction of the window, almost as if they were listening to something or someone. Then

Melchoir tripped lightly over the rumpled blankets to lay his burden at the edge of the bed. It appeared to be a pamphlet of some sort.

Oliver picked it up and studied it. For a long moment his mind refused to accept the evidence before his eyes. His blood roared in his ears. His breath caught in his chest. A grin broke across his face.

"Do you have any idea what this means?" Oliver wanted to laugh for the sheer joy of it. "I was right, gentlemen. She's not here for you. Not at all. You're an excuse. Nothing more. She's here for me. She's come back to me. And this time," he said, waving the pamphlet at them, "I'll never let her go."

The dogs stared warily.

He laughed. "I am sorry. I should have said we'll never let her go. Whether I like it or not, we're in this together. Thanks to Aunt Ellie."

He couldn't wait until morning. He had to see her now. This very minute. He started toward the door, turned and cast the dogs an admonishing look. "This doesn't mean I have completely reversed my opinion of you three. I still think you're pampered and spoiled and barely deserved to be included in the honorable world of canines.

"However"—he shook his head—"you are exceedingly clever and you have earned a modicum of respect from me. And, I suspect, my thanks as well." He nodded and strode out the door and down the hall to face his past.

And his future.

She simply couldn't sleep. Diana rolled over and punched the pillow. Although why she'd thought she could in the first place was ridiculous. Far too many emotions cluttered her mind to allow her to rest. She threw the covers off, slid out of bed and lit the gas lamp.

Diana had put it off far too long. Lady's Eleanor's advice notwithstanding, enough was enough. She pulled on her robe and started for the door. She'd wait for him downstairs and the moment he returned she'd confront him. She squared her shoulders. It was past time for the truth between them.

She brushed her hair away from her face with one hand and yanked the door open with the other.

Oliver stood in the hall, his hand upraised as if to knock.

"You're home." At once everything she'd planned to say, all the phrases she'd rehearsed flew out of her mind.

He nodded. "Within the hour." He hesitated as if uncertain how to proceed. "I wish to speak with you."

"Very well."

He stepped into the room. She closed the door behind him and leaned against it.

He swiveled toward her, his eyes dark and searching, his words blunt. "Why did you leave me?"

This was it then. "I didn't. My father, Ketterson, sent me home. He said—." She crossed her arms over her chest and stepped away, her gaze focused on the floral carpet beneath her feet. Why was it so hard to admit what a fool she'd once been? She drew a deep breath. "He said I was nothing more than an amusing flirtation for you. He said you were to be married."

"Why didn't you answer my letters?" His tone was even.

"I never got them. Ketterson died a few years ago and I only found your letters recently. That's when I learned he had told the same lies to you."

"Why didn't you write to me then?" Was it anger in his voice? Or pain?

She lifted her chin and stared into his eyes. "I did better than write. I came."

"Why didn't you tell me all this when you arrived?"

"You were scarcely in the mood to listen," she said sharply.

"By God, the last time I'd seen you you'd broken—" he waved the rest of the unspoken sentence away.

"If I recall, you ordered me to leave."

"Of course I ordered you to leave. Seeing you was something of a shock. I was expecting someone who was here to deal with the blasted dogs." He glared. "I never expected it to be you."

"Yes, well—"

He grabbed her shoulders, his gaze trapped hers. "Why are you here, Diana? Tell me. Why are you back in my life? What do you want?"

"What do I want?" Electricity arced between them. She searched the depths of his smoldering eyes for a sign, a clue of what he wanted her to say. She swallowed hard. Her voice was shaky but her tone was fervent. "I want what we should have had ten years ago. I want the happiness and joy that was stolen from us. I want . . . you."

"Are you certain?" The question echoed in his gaze. "I am not the same man I was a decade ago."

"And I am not the same girl."

"No." He brushed an errant strand of hair away from her face. "But you are a rather remarkable woman and I'm exceedingly grateful to have found you again." He smiled. "Even though it's rather obvious that you are no trainer of dogs."

"It is?"

"I found your pamphlet."

"Oh dear."

"I was beginning to wonder, you know. Was there a purpose to that farce?"

"Lady Eleanor thought it was best if you were to . . . well, adjust to my company before I told you the truth."

"Adjust to your company?" His eyes narrowed. "Get to know you, perhaps?"

"Perhaps," she said weakly.

"Just as I am to get to know her beasts?"

"Something like that."

"You've been training me?" Disbelief colored his face.

"Only in the vaguest—"

"You've been training me just as you have those damn dogs?"

"You needn't sound so outraged," she snapped. "In point of fact the dogs have been far easier to work with than you. After all, *they* have a rather keen degree of intelligence."

"Was that my aunt's idea as well?"

"Oliver, she simply wanted—"

"Trained! Like a bloody dog! Betrayed by my own flesh and blood—"

"I scarcely think betrayed—"

"Trained!" In two long strides he reached the door, jerked it open and slammed it behind him.

His roar echoed through the hall. "Trained!"

Diana stared at the door shuddering from the force of his exit. At once it flew open and smacked against the wall, the noise reverberating deep inside her.

"I never forgot you." His eyes flashed. He snapped the door closed behind him and stepped toward her.

"I never forgot you either." Defiance rang in her voice and she resisted the impulse to step back.

"You were always there, at the edge of my mind." He took another step. "In my dreams."

Her heart thudded. "You filled my dreams as well."

He stepped closer, so near she could see the rise and fall of his chest with every breath. Feel the warmth of his body pulse against her own. Breathe the masculine scents of brandy and heat and all things Oliver. "I never stopped loving you."

"And I," she stared up at him, "I never stopped loving you."

He pulled her into his arms. "Do you realize I've never really kissed you?"

"You did once."

"Ah, but that was the kiss of a young man barely out in the world and an innocent girl."

"I remember," she said softly. "It was my first kiss." *My only kiss*.

"It scarcely counts." He brushed his lips across hers and her knees weakened.

She could barely breathe at the nearness of his body. "Doesn't it?"

"No indeed. That and this"—his lips whispered across her mouth in a touch so gentle it was

84

scarcely a touch at all—"is the kiss of a youth for a girl."

"And," her voice quavered, "will it be so different now?"

"Indeed it will, my love." His words murmured against her lips. "Indeed it will."

His mouth met hers, his lips firm and warm, and a trembling started from somewhere deep inside her. She wrapped her arms around his neck and pressed close to him. His kiss grew harder, his lips demanding and insistent. Without warning everything she'd held inside her through the long years of missing him and wanting him and loving him and meeting him only in her dreams burst free, and she clutched at him as if he were a life raft and she a drowning soul.

She ran her hands boldly down his chest and under his dressing gown, pushing at the silk of his garments with an undeniable urge to know him and feel his naked flesh beneath her fingers. Impatience spiraled through her. Surely he felt the same? His mouth, his hands, were everywhere at once, exploring and claiming her for his own. He rained kisses down the length of her throat and she moaned and lost herself in the sheer thrill of his touch. Oliver pushed her robe off her shoulders and fumbled at the ribbons on her nightdress, until he swore under his breath and tore them away, the fabric itself ripping free. Dazed with a need she'd never imagined, Diana scarcely noted how, but at once their nightclothes were a heap of rags at their feet and their bodies naked and wanting.

He was solid and strong and his flesh scorched hers with a heat that mirrored the blaze consuming her body and her soul. The hard length of him pressed against her. Anticipation shivered through her and mingled with fear, abrupt and unforeseen. Dear Lord, he expected a widow! A woman familiar with the ways of love. A woman who'd known the passion of a man before. Not a virgin. She should tell him. Now, while there was still time. He was her first love. Her only love.

He cupped her breasts in his hands and the exquisite sensations rushing through her overwhelmed any rational thoughts of what was still unsaid between them. Here and now she was in his arms and nothing else mattered.

He swept her off her feet, carried her to the bed and lay down beside her. "I should warn you." His voice was a growl deep in his throat. "I am not at all well trained."

She gathered him close against her, reveling in his heat and the promise of what was to come. "That's quite all right," she breathed. "I have a pamphlet."

She was hot and tight and he wondered how long it had been since her husband died and he vowed to make her forget Lawrence. He slid into her with a care born of love, and she cried out once but clutched him tighter and within moments matched her thrusts to his own. She was all he'd dreamed, all he'd imagined, all he'd ever wanted. He cursed the lost years and swore this would be the start of a new lifetime with the one woman he'd always loved.

She brought him to heights he'd never known and he did all in his power to bring her there as well until she jerked beneath him and called out his name with a joy that gripped his heart. His release matched hers and his spirit soared with ecstasy and the certain knowledge that it was love that had brought him here.

They made love again and again through the long night and traded promises of forever and pledges of tomorrow until at last exhaustion claimed them both.

He wrapped his arms around her and she nestled her back against his chest. Peace and contentment filled him and he marveled that after so long without her his world was so right with her. He buried his face in the sweet smell of her hair and smiled to himself at her murmured words heard in the last hazy moments before sleep.

"A well-trained dog makes a delightful companion."

Chapter Nine

The first feeble rays of dawn drifted in through the window. Oliver propped himself up on one elbow and gazed at Diana. She lay on her side, turned away from him, sleeping peacefully.

Lord, had he ever been so happy? He hadn't even remembered how much she'd meant to him, suspected how much she still meant to him, until she came back into his life. Thank God for Aunt Ellie. He chuckled softly. If she only knew how well her scheme had worked.

He pushed away Diana's dark hair and kissed the nape of her neck. "Good morning, my love."

She sighed sleepily. "Ummmm . . ."

He kissed the top of her shoulder.

"That's nice," she murmured.

He smiled, the unmistakable urge to make love to her again rising within him. "You are so beautiful."

"I love you, Oliver."

"And I love you." He trailed his fingers down her spine and marveled at the silken feel of her skin. A faint crosshatch of faded, white scars marked the small of her back as if . . . He stared for a long moment. A heavy weight settled in his stomach.

"Diana." His voice was soft. "Did Lawrence do this to you? Did your husband do this to you?"

Her muscles tensed beneath his touch. His breath caught. The minutes stretched by.

Diana drew a ragged breath. "I've never been married. Lawrence was my mother's name."

Of course. He should have realized she'd never been with a man before. "Then who—" At once the answer was clear. The violence of Ketterson's response to Oliver's suit slammed into him and he knew Diana's father would have taken his anger out on her. "Your father?"

"Ketterson." She rolled over, her dark gaze met his, direct and calm. "But he wasn't my father at all. I didn't learn the truth until after his death. My real father was an Englishman my mother fell in love with." She laughed softly, a resigned, mirthless sound. "Odd, the tricks life plays on us. He hated you simply because you're a countryman to the man my mother loved."

Dear God! This was his fault! All of it! He'd been so consumed by his own pain all those years ago he failed to consider what her fate might be. Of course, he had believed she was marrying someone of her father's choosing and had never dreamed the man was lying, but that was no excuse. He should have followed her to America. He should have forced her father's acceptance or, failing that, taken her far away. He should have fought for her. His jaw clenched.

He rose from the bed and shrugged into his dressing gown.

"Oliver?" She sat up and clutched the coverlet to her naked breasts.

"Yes?" His voice was hard.

Concern flickered in her deep brown eyes and her voice was soft. "It was a very long time ago. It scarcely matters now."

"I find it matters a great deal."

"Oliver." She smiled and reached out her hand. "Come back to bed."

"I think not." He steeled himself against the hurt and confusion that flickered across her lovely features. He turned and stalked toward the door. "We will talk later. I should return to my own rooms now, before the servants notice my absence."

"I—I don't understand." Pain sounded in her voice but he couldn't face her. "Oliver?" He pulled the door open and closed it sharply behind him, her words echoing after him.

He strode down the hall, his mind numb with the understanding of what she had endured for him. He should have been her rescuer, her salvation, her hope. Instead he had failed her. Forsaken her to face her fate alone. And she had suffered horribly for his abandonment. The only woman he'd ever cared for had paid for loving him. How much more had she endured through the years? What scars had she that didn't show on her flesh but on her soul?

She said it didn't matter and perhaps she had come to terms with his negligence years ago. But the revelation of his failure to protect her struck him with an almost physical force and sickened him to a point where he couldn't bear to be in her presence one minute more. How could she possibly have forgiven him? How could he forgive himself? She'd paid an awful price for loving him once.

How high would the price be for loving him now?

"Oliver." She stared at the door. Shock gripped her. His eyes had been as dark and blue as a winter night and just as cold.

Dear Lord, he hated her!

Oh, not for the scars themselves. She knew him well enough to know he was not so shallow as to allow a physical imperfection to turn him away. But for what they said, more than words could ever say, about who she was. Who she had been. How could she have ever expected a man as strong as he to accept someone as weak as she once was?

Shame and self-loathing coursed through her. She disgusted him and she could scarcely blame him. She disgusted herself. She should have stood up to Ketterson. She should have fought for Oliver. For love. Instead she'd cowered beneath the wrath of the man she'd called father for years until she was freed only by his death.

It made no difference that strength had grown out of those horrible days. No difference that she was not the same insipid coward she once was. The girl Oliver had loved in his youth was not someone he could love as a man. And her scars were a vivid reminder of all she had been.

Tears scalded her eyes and she brushed them angrily away. This was the end, then. So be it. She jerked her chin up. She knew all along coming here was a gamble. She'd always known it could fail. She simply hadn't realized how very much it would hurt.

Pain mixed with resolve. She didn't want to see him again. She couldn't. It would be far too easy to throw herself into his arms and beg for his forgiveness and his love. She had to leave Thornton. Today. At once. She had no home to return to. Perhaps she'd travel Europe. Wander the continent alone. And someday the grief of losing the only man she'd ever loved, not once but twice in a single lifetime, would surely fade. Diana had survived before and would survive this as well.

Of course, she had Shakespeare now and his affection was unconditional. And she had last night and memories that would linger in her heart always.

And what more could a survivor expect?

"I would not wish to presume, my lady, but if you are planning to do something, now would perhaps be an excellent time," Miles said under his breath. He stared at the portrait of Lady Eleanor in the front hall. "All is not working quite as we had anticipated this morning."

Miles had no idea what could have gone wrong. He, together with the rest of the staff, was well aware Sir Oliver had spent the night in Miss Lawrence's room. In fact, once that was ascertained, he and Cook and Mrs. Collins had shared a celebratory brandy in the kitchen. But something had obviously happened. Sir Oliver was heard slamming things about in his rooms and Miss Lawrence was packing to leave. This would not do. Not at all. Why, it was Christmas Eve and it was

Lady Eleanor's desire to leave Sir Oliver one last gift.

The three kings trotted into the hall followed by the Great Dane. Miles stepped closer to the wall and watched the massive front door swing open as if by an invisible hand. The dogs ambled out into the winter morning and the door closed gently shut behind them.

Miles drew his brows together thoughtfully, then allowed a slight smile to play across his lips.

"My apologies, my lady, I shouldn't have doubted you for a moment."

"Miles!" Oliver walked slowly down the front stairway. In the hours since dawn he'd tried to come to grips with the emotions that raged through him. He had resolved nothing. His body and his soul felt as if he'd been trampled by a team of horses.

The butler appeared in the front hall. "Sir?"

"What are those doing here?" Oliver pointed at the valises stacked by the front door. "Who's are they?"

"They belong to Miss Lawrence, sir. She is leaving this morning."

"Leaving? What do you mean leaving?" Panic flickered through him.

Miles raised a brow.

"Never mind." Oliver raked a hand through his hair. How could he let her leave? How could he expect her to stay? She obviously didn't blame him for the past, but he blamed himself. How could he live with that? In a spilt second he knew: he'd have to learn to do just that. He couldn't live without her. Not again. Not now. Not ever. "Where is she?"

"It appears the dogs are missing, sir."

"All of them?"

"All of them." Miles nodded. "Miss Lawrence couldn't leave without her animal so she has gone to find them."

"Blasted beasts. Miles, fetch my—" Miles held out Oliver's coat. "—coat. Thank you." He threw on the greatcoat. "How long ago did she leave?"

"Just a few minutes ago, sir. I suspect you can—"

Oliver was out the door before the words were out of Miles' mouth. He didn't know what he would say to her, how to reconcile the past. He only knew he couldn't let her go.

He spotted her up ahead on the lane. Her head was bowed; she was obviously following the paw prints of the dogs in the newfallen snow.

"Diana!" He called to her and she stopped but didn't turn around. He sprinted toward her. "Diana, I—"

"The dogs are missing, Oliver," she said quietly, refusing to meet his gaze. "It is far too cold for the Yorkies to be out of doors for any length of time. We need to find them as quickly as possible."

"Of course." He fell into step beside her. Good God, what could he say?

They walked silently for a few long moments.

"I want you to know"—she lifted her chin in that defiant little way she had and his heart tripped—"I quite understand."

"You understand what?"

She pulled a deep breath. "I realize why this will not work between us. Why you detest me so. I cannot say I—"

"Detest you?" He pulled up short, grabbed her

arm and swung her to face him. Sorrow and regret filled her brown eyes. "Why on earth would you think I detest you?"

"It's very obvious to me, Oliver." She shrugged and tore her gaze from his. "A man such as yourself couldn't possibly care for some one who was as . . . helpless as I was." A note of disgust underlaid her words.

"Diana, that's absurd." He gripped her shoulders. "You were a girl. Scarcely more than a child. No one in their right mind would expect you to challenge your father. I certainly wouldn't have." He cupped her chin and forced her gaze to his. "You were young and sweet and lovely and what happened to you was out of your hands There was nothing you could do."

"Then why do you hate me so?" Her voice was barely a whisper.

"I don't hate you." He drew his brows together in surprise. "I've never hated you."

"Then what—"

"Tell me this, Diana. The scars on your back," he swallowed hard, "they were just the beginning of Ketterson's ill treatment, weren't they?"

"It doesn't matter."

His hands tightened on her shoulders. "It does matter! Tell me. Was there more?"

"Yes," she snapped and wrenched out of his grasp. "Through the years, there was more. The wrong look on my face, the wrong word, even the wrong dish at dinner—yes! There was much more. But it's over and done with and best forgotten!"

"How can you forget?" He shook his head and

dropped his hands. "How can you forgive me for that?"

"Forgive you?" Her eyes widened with confusion. "You had nothing to do with it."

"Didn't I?" He clenched his fists and turned away. His gaze wandered over the snow-covered scenery but he saw none of it. "I should have protected you, Diana. I should never have let you go. You have lived through hell on earth and it's my fault."

"Your fault?" Anger rang in her voice "How dare you think that? It had nothing to do with you."

He swiveled toward her. "It had everything to do with me. It started with me. I should have known Ketterson was lying."

"How could you possibly know that?"

"I should have trusted you. Trusted in the love we shared. I should have saved you."

"No, Oliver." Her eyes flashed. "I should have saved myself."

"You? You were a mere girl. What could you do?" Bitterness colored his voice. "I was the one who should have acted. I didn't. I failed you. And you paid for my failure."

"No, it wasn't—"

"Bloody hell, Diana!" The words exploded from him with all the regret and despair and guilt that had overwhelmed him from the moment he realized the truth. "I should have fought for you! Moved mountains for you! By God, I should have rescued you!"

The words froze between them in the still winter morning. He held his breath. Silence stretched endlessly.

"Then rescue me now, Oliver." Her voice was

even and intense. Tears misted her eyes. "Rescue my heart. My soul."

"Diana." Her name caught in his throat.

"You said you failed me once before. Don't fail me now. Don't fail . . ." A tear slipped down her cheek. "Us."

"Diana." His voice broke and he stepped toward her and at once she was in his arms. "Dear Lord, Diana, I swear to you I will make it up to you. I will spend the rest of my life doing all in my power to make you happy."

She wept against him, her body shaking with the force of her emotions.

A wave of helplessness swept through him. "Diana—"

"I'm crying, Oliver." She raised her tear-stained face to meet his gaze. "I vowed I'd never cry again. And I haven't. Not until now."

"I'm so sorry, my love." He pulled her tighter against him. "I promise I'll never make you sad again."

"No." She sobbed. "I'm not sad. Not at all. I'm happy. I'm really very happy."

His heart soared and he grinned in spite of himself. "Then I suspect we are in for a great deal of tears. I plan on making you very, very happy."

She sniffed and smiled up at him. "You already have, Oliver, you already have."

He bent his lips to hers in a kiss long and loving and full of promises, and marveled at the miracle that had brought her back to him. And sent, as well, silent thanks to Aunt Ellie for ensuring, before she left this life, he found the happiness she'd always wished for him.

Without warning, Diana pulled back. "Oliver, we still have to find the dogs."

Oliver glanced over her shoulder. "The beasts are fine. Look."

There, on the end of the drive, lined up like an audience, sat the Great Dane and the Yorkshire terriers. Each and every one of them appeared to sport a smug smile.

"Oliver," Diana said thoughtfully, "do you think . . ."

Ridiculous notion, of course. Still . . .

Oliver wrapped his arm around her and started toward the manor. "I think they have earned a place in our lives."

"Of course. A well-trained dog—"

"Is a delightful companion." He raised a brow. "And what of a well-trained man?"

She tilted her head and considered him. "I suspect he too would be a delightful companion."

He laughed and she joined him and arm in arm they headed up the drive toward the manor and their future. Life would indeed be delightful with Diana by his side. He had no doubt that every day, every year that lay before them would be full of love and laughter. And every Christmas would be filled with joy and wonder and one day, he hoped, children, and always, always miracles.

And yes, God help them all, even dogs.

Starting this very moment, this very Christmas, with these very beasts: Shakespeare and the three kings.

Chapter Ten

Miles gazed up at the portraits in the front hall. He could well be mistaken but it seemed the smile on Lady Eleanor's lips was a touch more satisfied. And in the twinkle in the eye of her husband, a shade more pronounced.

And why not? It was Christmas Day. The joy of the season filled the manor. And love lingered in the air.

Miles wasn't quite certain precisely what had transpired but it didn't matter. Sir Oliver and Miss Lawrence were together and would be together for the rest of their days. In spite of the holiday, they had already summoned the minister to determine how soon they could be wed.

He suspected he would not see the dogs listening to commands issued by an unseen master again. There would be no more doors opening of their own accord. Lady Eleanor's last task on earth was completed and Miles hoped she was once again with her beloved Charles.

She had made certain her dear Oliver had finally

found a love to fill his days and his nights and his future. It was her final Christmas gift to him. The gift of love.

The greatest gift of all.

ATHENA'S CHRISTMAS TAIL

NINA COOMBS

For Warren
with love

Chapter One

Athena bounded down from the carriage and looked around. An awful lot of tall houses here, all squeezed together. Humans had strange ways, living in cities, all on top of each other. But Grosvenor Square was a good place to live. Mercy had said so. And Mercy never lied.

Athena sniffed the early October breeze. In some kitchen nearby, sausages were sizzling. And in the other direction a goose was browning. It smelled so good that she had to lick her chops. She sniffed again. No rabbits were lurking within smelling distance, but then, it was hard to see where rabbits could live around here.

She wasn't sure she was going to like this place Mercy called London. The country was better. Though she had to admit that there had been some intriguing scents when the carriage passed through that noisy part of town—Trafalgar Square, Mercy called it. But the Viscount had made Athena get her paws off the seat, so she hadn't had a chance to see out the window.

"Athena," Mercy called, from the carriage. "Stay."

Athena sighed and sank to her haunches. She wasn't stupid enough to run off in a strange place. Mercy ought to know that. But then the poor thing had been having a hard time of it lately. That new husband of hers was a real disappointment. The odor of sadness hung around her so much that anyone—well, any dog—could smell it.

The new husband stepped down from the carriage, and with a frown looked down at his leg. Robert, Viscount Brockton, was a fine looking man, in spite of the slight limp that he'd brought home from his fight with Napoleon. When she'd first seen him, Athena had been pleased. Mercy deserved a good man. She might be a little plain looking, at least that's what her father often said, but Mercy was beautiful inside, where it counted.

And I ought to know, Athena thought.

She could remember very little from the time when she'd been whelped, but she *could* remember the cold and the hunger and the awful loneliness. She could remember being a whimpering ball of misery, and the sound of a soft voice saying, "You poor little thing," and the warmth of Mercy's arms enfolding her. From that moment on, Mercy was the most wonderful person in the world. And nobody better ever say differently.

The viscount extended a gloved hand to Mercy to help her down. She put her gloved hand in his. Framed in the carriage doorway, she paused a moment in her new traveling gown of gray bombazine. A fashionable bonnet covered her dark hair. Her face was composed—it wasn't plain, it was a beautiful face—but she was nervous. That was the viscount's fault. The man was so cold and standoffish.

Why, in the carriage, he hadn't even put his arm around Mercy. There they were, newly married, and they rode all the way to London without him ever even touching her. No wonder the poor thing was upset.

People were often strange. They did some queer things. But this was really weird. Because Mercy *wanted* him to touch her. That was easy enough to see, even if you couldn't smell it, which Athena certainly could.

Mercy's smells were always easy to read. She was a good person, a wonderful person.

The viscount—now, he was harder to understand. He smelled as though he liked Mercy, but he treated her as if she were someone he hardly knew.

"Come, Athena," Mercy said, and took the viscount's arm to go up the sidewalk to the door of the town house. Athena followed, of course. She never disobeyed Mercy. That would have been the height of ingratitude, to ignore the wishes of the person who had saved her life.

The front door opened and the butler said, "Good afternoon, milord, milady." As round as an apple, except for a nose which was long and thin, he looked down at Athena. The nose twitched slightly, as though he smelled something bad. But it wasn't her. Mercy had made sure she was clean and sweet smelling before they set out for London.

"Good afternoon, Stoddard," the viscount said.

"Is this creature supposed to be here, milord?" the butler asked, his tone disbelieving.

Athena refrained from snarling, but she did allow her lips to slide back from her teeth the littlest bit.

That man needed to be put in his place. A good nip in his fat calf, maybe—but no, Mercy wouldn't like that. She always said you had to be a friend to have a friend.

"The dog belongs to her ladyship," the viscount said, in a voice that brooked no disobedience. "She will have the run of the house."

"The run . . ." At a look from the viscount the butler squeaked to a halt. "Yes, milord."

The viscount would have made a good pack leader. He knew how to put people in their place.

Mercy took off her new bonnet and pelisse and gave them to the butler. Athena waited, sitting quietly. She wasn't going to let Mercy out of her sight in this strange place. If that husband of hers didn't treat her right, he was going to answer to her dog. And as for that butterball of a butler . . .

Mercy let Robert lead her up the wide staircase. It hardly seemed possible that she was really here, really in London. But this was her home now, and she was the wife of a viscount.

She took a quick glance at Robert. He'd limped quite a bit coming up the walk. "Milord," she began.

"My name is Robert," he reminded her. "You will call me by my name."

"Yes—Robert." She swallowed. "I'm sorry. Sometimes I forget."

He nodded. "You'll learn."

"I just wondered if your leg is hurting and—"

"My leg is fine," he said curtly. "We will not discuss it."

"I just thought—Your wound isn't long healed and—"

106

"We will not discuss it," he repeated, his voice icy.

"Yes, Robert," she answered with a sigh.

He led her into a bedchamber, lavishly decorated in rose satin and gilt. "This is your room," he said.

She couldn't help herself—she glanced toward the other door, the one that must connect to his chamber as was the custom of married people in the ton. The door was closed. Like his heart.

"I'll leave you to freshen up," he said in that distant voice he used when he spoke to her. "Perhaps you'd like to rest a bit before dinner."

"Yes," she said. What else *could* she say? She could hardly ask, *Robert, what have I done? Why do you treat me so coldly?*

He nodded, and went out, closing the door behind him.

She sank down on the rose-colored cushions of the chaise and swallowed hard. She wasn't going to cry. She just wasn't.

But this wasn't at all like she'd imagined it would be when she consented to this marriage. She'd known Robert didn't love her. She was plain and she knew it. So she couldn't expect him to love her. But he had married her. And so she'd thought . . .

But they'd been married a whole week, a week in which he'd only touched her to help her in and out of the carriage.

What was wrong with him? He hadn't always been this way. When he was a boy . . .

She leaned back against the cushions, remembering that day, the first day she'd met him. She was six, and even then busy caring for her animals. And Robert was about twelve. She remembered the breathlessness that had come over her just at the sight of him. And the fear. He was the son of a viscount, after all. And she was just the daughter of a poor country vicar.

But her fear had soon vanished. He'd been kind to her, visiting the animals she'd been caring for. Telling her stories he'd learned in school, wonderful stories about Greek gods and goddesses. No one knew those stories had lodged in her memory, sweet, wonderful memories that she cherished just as she'd cherished the sound of his voice, his wonderful smile.

So when Papa said she could learn to read, could have the schooling boys usually had, it was to those stories that she'd gone, those stories that brought her closer to Robert. Probably people would say that a child of six *couldn't* fall in love, but she knew better. She *knew*. She'd loved him then. She loved him now.

When Papa said she could marry Robert, marry the man of her dreams though Papa didn't know it, she'd been so happy. And now here she was, the wife of the man she'd loved these long years.

A sob rose in her throat. The wife in name only.

Chapter Two

When Mercy went downstairs for dinner, she had washed her face and hands and changed from her traveling gown to another. It was hard to get used to all the new clothes. Before their marriage Robert had insisted that the modiste make her a whole new wardrobe. At the time, she'd welcomed the idea, because she wanted to look nice for him. But now it didn't seem to matter.

Still, she'd never given up on something she really wanted. She'd persuaded Papa to let her learn Greek, no easy task. And she would *make* Robert treat her with respect. He owed her that much, at least. And perhaps he could grow to love her.

She straightened her shoulders and swept into the dining room, Athena at her heels. Athena went everywhere with her as a matter of course. That had been the one thing that she'd insisted on when they'd told her about Robert's offer. If she married Robert, Athena went wherever she did.

The dining room was empty. "Where is he?" she murmured to Athena. Since the day she'd stumbled across the bedraggled, soaking-wet ball of fur in the bushes outside Papa's study, she'd talked to Athena. She'd spent so much of her childhood alone, it was good to have a friend to talk to. Athena didn't talk back, of course. But it seemed that she understood. Her warm brown eyes gave back love, the kind of love Mercy imagined Mama might have given if she hadn't died in birthing her, the kind of attention Papa was too busy with the parishioners to give. So now Athena was her best friend.

She turned. "I guess we'll have to go find—"

"Good evening, Mercy," Robert said from the doorway. "That gown looks nice on you."

"Thank you," she said. "It was kind of you to buy it for me."

He shrugged his broad shoulders. "It was nothing."

Nothing to him perhaps, but to her those gowns were a lot. She looked at the table, for the first time noticing that there were three places set. "We are having a guest for dinner?" she asked.

A strange expression crossed his face. "Yes. My friend Cranston. He wants to meet you."

Surprise made her voice squeak. "Meet—me?"

Robert nodded. "Cranston's my best friend. We served together in Spain. I tried to dissuade him, thinking you'd be tired tonight, but—"

"It's quite all right," she said. "I understand." She didn't understand at all. But they might as well have a guest. Perhaps *he* would talk to her. And if he didn't, she could at least listen to them talk. She wouldn't have to try to make conversation with Robert, try to get past the cold wall he'd erected between them.

"Do you—"

"Harold, the Marquis of Cranston," Stoddard intoned from the doorway.

Mercy turned. The Marquis was a short man, probably a head shorter than Robert, but a little taller than she was. And he was fair while Robert was dark. But the biggest difference between them was in their smiles. The Marquis's smile was broad, not the faint upward twitch of the lips that was the only smile Robert seemed to have anymore.

The Marquis crossed the room. "Milady," he said, his blue eyes twinkling at her. "Please call me Cranston." He grinned. "Harold is not a name I favor."

"Yes, Cranston."

He bent over her hand. "You're looking ravishing tonight."

"And you are a great flatterer," she replied. She didn't know what it was, but something about him put her immediately at ease.

He grinned. "I see you have taken my measure." He looked down to where Athena sat beside her. "And who is this beautiful shaggy creature at your feet?"

Mercy smiled. "This is Athena."

The Marquis raised a slender eyebrow. "Athena?"

Robert nodded. "Mercy has an affection for Greek mythology. She names all her animals after ancient characters."

"All?" the Marquis inquired.

She laughed. "Yes. I'm afraid that I also have an affection for lost and hurt animals. And for nursing them back to health."

The Marquis nodded. "You have a tender heart. No harm in that." He glanced at Athena again.

"Though I have to admit seeing Athena here did give me pause. Stoddard has been adamantly against animals in the house for lo these many years."

Mercy looked at Robert.

He shrugged. "I am the lord here. What Stoddard wants doesn't matter. And I gave you my word."

Cranston looked to her, curiosity all over his face. "His word about what?"

"Come sit down," Robert said. "And I will tell you all."

He helped Mercy into her chair and settled himself beside her.

"Do tell me," Cranston said. "I'm all ears."

"When I asked Mercy to be my wife," Robert said, "she had only one request to make. Can you guess what it was?"

"A new wardrobe?" Cranston asked, grinning. "A bigger carriage? A diamond necklace?"

"No," Robert said. "Her only request was that she be allowed to bring Athena with her." He smiled at her, an almost real smile. "Can you wonder that I was pleased to grant her such a request?"

"Not at all," Cranston said, nodding. "Not at all. But I have one more question, if I may."

Robert shrugged again, but it was obvious to her that he was feeling better. His features were more relaxed and some of the sadness had left his eyes. "Ask away," he said.

Cranston turned to Mercy. "I am curious as to why you decided to name her Athena."

Mercy chuckled. "If you remember the story of Athena's birth—"

Cranston looked a little sheepish. "I'm afraid I

didn't pay much attention to my Greek."

"Athena was born from Zeus's head. No mother bore her. I found my Athena in the bushes—no mother."

Cranston nodded. "Thank you for enlightening me."

Stoddard served the meal then, and Mercy turned her attention to eating. The food was good, though perhaps more highly spiced and sauced than the simple fare she was used to at the vicarage. She found that her appetite, which had been failing the last couple days, had returned. Having Cranston there made her feel better. It had even made Robert seem more friendly. Still, she couldn't help wishing she knew what was wrong between them, why he treated her so coldly.

"I saw her today," Cranston said, through a mouthful of pigeon pie.

Something in the tone of his voice made her glance at Robert. His mouth had grown so grim. "I don't care to—" he said.

"She was at Lady Davenport's having tea," Cranston went on. "She asked about you."

"I don't care to—"

"Well, you'll have to," Cranston said cheerfully. "You can't go about in the ton without running into her, you know."

"I don't mean to go about in the ton," Robert said crisply, giving his old friend a hard look.

Both Cranston's eyebrows shot up. "Surely you can't mean that!"

"I can and I do," Robert said. "I have no desire to be part of that foolishness again."

"But you have a wife. She'll want to take her rightful place in society."

Robert shrugged again. "She may do so if she wishes. I don't intend to."

"Really, Robert." Cranston was plainly upset, his pleasant features pulled into a frown. "That's no way to treat your wife. Besides, Emerine is not—"

Robert glowered at his friend. "You will not repeat that name in my presence."

Cranston shook his head. "I never thought to see you behave in such a ragged fashion."

"I don't recall asking you for your opinion," Robert said in a voice laden with sarcasm. He shoved back his chair. "I'm going to my room. Mercy can see you out."

And without so much as a good night to her, he limped out.

Mercy looked down at the fork that trembled in her hand. She put it carefully beside her plate, her appetite gone. Was this the reason for Robert's coldness? This woman named Emerine?

"I'm so sorry," Cranston said, his merry face twisted in a frown. "I had no idea. I didn't mean—"

"It's all right," she said. "But please, if you can do so without divulging a confidence, tell me about this—Emerine."

He stared at her. "You mean he didn't tell you? Nothing?"

"I'm afraid not," she said, composing her features as best she could.

Cranston shook his head. "Well, it's common knowledge. And I suppose if I don't tell you, someone else will. He can't keep you cooped up in here forever."

She was not so sure about that, but she needed to know about this woman. So she waited, her gaze on his face.

"Well, they were engaged to be married," Cranston said. "Got promised at the Christmas Ball before we went off to fight old Nappy. She promised to wait, of course. But when we got back, Robert with his wounded leg and me with a hole in my shoulder, Emerine decided she didn't want a a husband with a gimpy leg and—"

Shock brought Mercy to her feet. "She said that!"

Cranston nodded. "Right to his face, so I heard. Said she didn't want a man with a gimpy leg and broke the engagement right then and there. A little later she married the wealthy Earl of Rorston."

Mercy sank back down into her chair. "This earl, did he go to fight Napoleon too?"

Cranston laughed. "Hardly. The Earl's fifty if he's a day. It's his blunt that's attractive to Emerine. His blunt and his title."

Mercy tried to absorb this. Finally she asked, "What does she look like, this Emerine?"

Cranston gave her a speculative glance.

"Please?"

"Well, she was the belle of the ball her season. She's tall, willowy, with dazzling blue eyes and a figure to make a man think—" He broke off abruptly. "Sorry. She's not any nicer looking than you."

"Please, Cranston," the words broke from her in

a half-sob. "There's no need to lie to me. I know what I am. And now I know what's wrong with my husband. For that I thank you. I thank you very much."

Chapter Three

Late the next morning Stoddard stopped Robert in the foyer. "Milord?" Stoddard's round face was approaching a shade of purple and his nose twitched violently, a sure sign that he had reached the limits of his endurance.

"Yes, Stoddard?"

"Milord, we have never had a dog—" He made the word sound like something completely and utterly vile. "In this establishment."

With some effort, Robert overcame a desire to laugh. The desire surprised him—he'd laughed little since he'd returned to England. But there was something about Stoddard's expression that invited mirth.

"The *animal*," Stoddard went on. "The animal tripped me on purpose this morning, so that I fell and dropped the plate of breakfast sausages."

Robert bit his lip to hold back the laughter that bubbled in his throat. Stoddard, on his round rump on the floor, surrounded by scattered sausages, would certainly be a hilarious sight.

"Did she eat them?" Robert inquired, when he could control his voice.

Stoddard's mouth fell open. "Eat?" he repeated.

"Eat," Robert said. "If the dog tripped you on purpose, it must have been to get to the sausages. Did she grab them and run off?"

"No, milord." Stoddard looked crestfallen.

"What *did* she do?" Robert inquired, impelled by a strange curiosity.

"She—she—came over to me and—and—she licked my face." Stoddard's composure crumpled at having to report this ultimate indignity.

"Licked . . ." The laughter forced its way out of Robert's throat, but he managed to turn it into a cough before Stoddard could grow affronted.

"So you must see, milord," Stoddard continued. "Why I really cannot stay in an establishment with such a creature."

Robert swallowed a sigh, his good humor gone as quickly as it had come. He was used to a well-run establishment and if Stoddard left, comfort would leave with him, until another butler could be installed and get things running smoothly again.

But there was his promise to Mercy. He could still see her earnest expression the day he'd asked for her hand. She'd told him then that she was agreeable to marriage with him, but only on condition that wherever she went Athena went too. And he *had* given his word. Now it was up to him to keep it. He had taken Mercy from the life she knew and the father she loved to bring her to London where she would know no one and lead a life of seclusion. He could not, in good conscience, take her only friend from her.

Stoddard was gazing at him with the expectation of a servant who knew his worth, but in this case it wasn't going to work. Robert could get a new butler. He couldn't repair a breach in his honor. "The dog belongs to her ladyship," he explained. "The dog will stay here."

Stoddard's face reflected shock. "But, milord—"

"I'm sorry, Stoddard, if you feel you cannot deal with the animal. Of course I will give you good references." Some hesitancy in Stoddard's expression made him go on. "However, I would appreciate it if you'd stay out the month. Perhaps," he added, as though the thought had just occurred to him, "perhaps, after you get to know—"

"I doubt that, milord," Stoddard said with wounded dignity. "But I will stay out the month. Of course."

"Thank you," Robert said. "Did her ladyship say how soon she would—"

"I am ready now, Robert," Mercy called from the landing above.

He looked up. She was wearing a day gown of sea-foam green, and over it a hunter green pelisse. She came down the stairs toward him, swinging her matching bonnet by the strings like a little girl. "It's kind of you to take me to the Minerva Lending Library. I have always wanted to go there."

"I am going out anyway," Robert said. That was true enough, and she needn't know that he was feeling guilty about his boorish behavior last night. But Cranston should have known better. Discussing Emerine in front of Mercy—it just wasn't done. "You need to get some fresh air."

She reached the bottom of the stairs and set her

bonnet on top of her dark curls. Funny, he'd never noticed how her hair shone. Plain—her father had called her. She didn't look plain today. She looked different than the ladies of the ton, of course. But that was probably because there was a freshness about her, an innocence. That was one of the reasons he hadn't insisted on his nuptial rights on their wedding night. Give her a little time to get used to the idea.

But now—now he didn't want her to see his leg, the twisted scarred leg that had cost him Emerine. He couldn't bear to see that look of pity come into Mercy's eyes. Pity that might turn to distaste.

Mercy turned to him. "Is my bonnet on straight?"

"Yes," he said, looking away from her green eyes. Why should he find her eyes disturbing? They were just eyes like any others, except that they were the exact color of her gown. Had the modiste chosen the fabric for that reason?

Mercy tied the ribbons under her chin and moved toward the door, the dog at her heels as always. He had no objection to being seen with the dog. She was well-behaved, though not the most dignified looking of animals. But he did doubt that she'd be welcome at the Minerva. Maybe he should suggest— But a look at Stoddard's apoplectic face stayed his tongue. Maybe Stoddard would be lucky and the dog would run off while they were inside the Minerva.

But some time later when they returned to the carriage, loaded down with Mercy's selections and skirting puddles left from the autumn shower that had passed while they were inside, the dog was sitting patiently on the squabs, watching out the window. She got off the seat when they opened the door.

Mercy smiled. "Good dog, Athena."

Robert put the books inside and offered Mercy his hand. She took it, like she might have taken anyone's. A twinge of disappointment went through him. Now why should he feel that way? After all, she wasn't Emerine. Emerine who could make a seduction out of a simple thing like climbing into a carriage.

He climbed in too, and settled beside Mercy. "Home, John," he called, and let his eyes close, remembering. Emerine, with the flashing eyes and golden curls, and the figure that spilled out of her gown. He could remember every inch of that figure, every magnificent inch. He hadn't loved her, so it wasn't his heart that had suffered at her betrayal. But he *had* wanted her. And he had his pride. He wasn't going to be the focus of the ladies' pitying glances.

He made a face of disgust. He should have known that with Emer—

"Robert?" Mercy's gloved hand settled on his sleeve. "Robert? Robert, are you in pain?"

He opened his eyes. She was staring at him, concern in her eyes, on her face.

"Pain? No, no."

"I thought maybe your leg—" She caught herself and stopped, her gloved hand going to her lips. She looked at him for another moment, and then, when he didn't say anything in reply, she bent to pet the dog. "Good dog, Athena."

The dog quivered and stiffened, then reared up

on her hind legs to peer out the window. "Mercy," he began. "I really don't think—"

But she had already reached for the dog. "Athena, you know better. You mustn't—Oh no!"

The terror on her face sent his stomach plummeting to his boots. "What—"

"Stop!" she screamed. "John Coachman, stop the carriage this instant!"

And the carriage stopped. So fast that Robert had to throw out a hand to prevent himself from being dashed to the floor. "What on earth?"

She grabbed his arm, almost ripping the sleeve out of his new coat. "That man!" she cried. "He's beating his dog!"

Robert looked. The dog was an ungainly spotted hound, long legged, bones showing through a dirty white coat. And the man was definitely beating it. The dog looked as if it would have run, but the brute had one end of a rope around its neck and was beating it with the other.

Mercy tugged at his arm. "Robert!"

"I see," he said, but having said that, he was at a loss as to what she expected of him. Obviously the dog belonged to the man. He could beat it if he wanted to.

Mercy gave him an exasperated look and reached for the door handle.

"What are you doing?" he asked.

"I'm going to stop that man," she said, her eyes flashing. "Someone has to."

"Stop—" Words failed him. He pushed her back on the squabs, rather roughly, he was afraid.

"Robert," she said indignantly. "I cannot sit here and allow—"

"I'll go," he said in exasperation. And before she could protest any more he pushed past her and dropped to the pavement, his game leg protesting at such rough treatment. He ignored it and the mud that squished beneath his boots, and advanced on the brute, who stood in the middle of the mucky street belaboring the dog.

"Ah, sir?" Robert began.

The bully looked up, his eyes gin-bleared and his mouth twisted in a snarl. "You talking at me?"

It was obvious that no appeal to humanity would move this poor excuse for a man. But then he had an idea. "I was wondering if perhaps you'd be interested in selling that—dog."

"This 'ere dog?" the bully asked, spitting from between rotten teeth.

Robert nodded. "That dog."

The bully cocked his head. "Whatcha give me fer 'im?"

"How much do you want?"

The bully considered, sucking what was left of his teeth. "Five pound," he said finally.

"Five—"

"Aye." The bully raised the rope again.

Robert could almost hear Mercy scrambling out of the carriage behind him, landing in the mud. "Very well," he said, surrendering to the inevitable. "Give me the rope."

The bully stood fast. "Gi' me the fiver first."

Robert passed over the money with one hand and received the rope with the other. The cur came to his side willingly. Little wonder in that.

Robert moved off toward the carriage. He had no desire to have his carriage infested with fleas, but

123

the door flew open and Mercy leaned out. "Lift him in," she said. And before he knew what he was doing he had hefted the filthy muddy beast in his arms. Oh, well. He set the dog down on the floor of the carriage and stepped over him. Both coat and trousers were probably ruined. But his tailor would be pleased to see him again.

Emerine, now, would have refused to let him into the carriage with his clothes in such disorder, but Mercy didn't even notice. He had hardly hit the seat before she called up, "Home! And hurry!"

And hurry John Coachman did, setting off with a jolt that nearly threw Mercy down on the floor with the cur and sent another twinge of pain through Robert's game leg. The cursed thing. Wasn't it enough that it had ruined his life? Was it going to pain him forever?

But Mercy didn't question him about his expression this time. All her attention was on the dog. "Don't you worry," she told the sorry animal. "You're safe now. We'll take care of you."

As the cur and Athena exchanged sniffs, Robert wondered how Athena had known to look out the window at precisely that moment. Or did Mercy just pull strays to her?

She raised tear-filled eyes to his. "Thank you, Robert. Thank you." Her bottom lip quivered. "I know it was better to buy the dog. And a gentleman can't go around brawling in the street. But—" A watery chuckle escaped her. "I should so have liked to see you give that a bully a good smack in the chops. *He* should feel what it's like to be beaten."

She looked down at the dog again. "The poor thing. He's so thin. We'll have to feed him up and—"

Robert cleared his throat. "Might I suggest a bath first? And since I don't care to have the house infested with fleas, John Coachman can have a stableboy—"

"No," Mercy said. She didn't raise her voice or change her expression. But that *no* was granite-hard. "I will bathe him. And I will care for him. He has been mistreated." Her voice quivered. "And he must be given love."

Love—for a dog. But he knew that tone of firmness. He'd encountered it when they were children. She would give on many things, but not when she used that tone. So it looked like he'd met his match. Still, he tried again. "Stoddard gave notice this morning."

"That's too bad," she said, fondling the dog's filthy ears. Her gloves would have to be discarded too.

"Mercy!" Exasperation tinged his words. "If Stoddard leaves, the house will be all at sixes and sevens!"

"I can manage it," she said, examining one of the cur's ragged ears. "I managed Papa's."

"No," he said, copying her earlier tone.

She looked up at him again, her eyes questioning.

"You will not take over Stoddard's duties. If he leaves, we'll find someone else." He paused, but she didn't argue. "But perhaps you might persuade him to stay."

"Me?" Astonishment widened her eyes, those green eyes that he found so disturbing.

"Yes. If you could keep Athena from tripping him up—"

Her eyes got even wider. "Athena tripped him?"

125

"So he says. And while he was carrying the breakfast sausages."

"I can hardly believe—"

"But that was not the final indignity."

"It wasn't?"

For some reason he wanted to laugh, though losing a butler was no laughing matter. "No. Stoddard informed me that when she had him down she licked his face."

Mercy stared at him. "She licked—" And *she* began to laugh.

He managed not to join her, but only because the carriage had stopped in front of their townhouse. John Coachman opened the door. A peculiar expression on his ruddy face, he let down the step and stood aside. Robert stepped over the dogs and down.

She took the hand he offered and let him help her down. "I think he can walk," she said, and waited while Athena and then the cur jumped down. She started up the walk, the thick rope looking incongruous in her dainty hand. Robert followed her. Undoubtedly this would be the last straw for poor Stoddard and his much-abused dignity.

The door opened and Mercy sailed in, followed by the dogs. "I'll want the biggest tin tub we have," she said, ignoring the fact that Stoddard's mouth had fallen open—and stayed that way—and that his nose was twitching violently. "Have it brought to the kitchen and filled with warm water. Oh, and this is Hannibal." She indicated the dog with an airy wave of her hand. "He'll be living here now."

Stoddard made an inarticulate sound. "Tell the footmen to hurry," Mercy added. Was that a twinkle in her eyes? "His lordship doesn't want the place infested with fleas."

And while Stoddard struggled to find words adequate to voice his indignation, Robert followed Mercy to the kitchen. He meant to find out why she'd named that scroungy cur Hannibal.

Chapter Four

White's was crowded that November afternoon. Robert gazed around, seeking Cranston's blond head. There he was, holding a table for them. Robert crossed the room to him. About time Cranston got back from the country. A whole month without anyone to talk to—well, anyone but Hannibal—was giving him bats in his belfry.

"You're looking—different," Cranston said, curiosity in his voice. "Sit down. Tell me how married life agrees with you."

Robert sank into a chair. Trust Cranston to put his finger right on the sore spot.

"And how is Mercy?" Cranston asked. "She made a deep impression on me, that girl. How's she doing?"

"She's well," Robert said, signaling to the waiter for a drink.

"And Athena?"

Cranston's eyes gleamed with mischief. Robert felt a sinking in the region of his heart. Did the whole ton know what went on in his house? He shifted uncomfortably in his chair. No one *could* know that the connecting door from his room to Mercy's remained unopened, that night after night he sat staring at it, wondering, wishing—

"Well," Cranston prodded, "are you going to tell me or are you going to sit there like a gape-fish?"

Robert managed a smile. "Athena is well—and we have a new addition to the household."

Cranston grinned. "You're increasing already? I say that's—"

"No, no. We have another dog."

Cranston chuckled. "I trust that Stoddard has departed in a dudgeon."

Robert shook his head. "No. Actually, he was going to. His month was out last week, but Mercy persuaded him not to leave us during the holiday season. She appealed to his pride—and his honor. And he consented to stay on till the New Year."

Cranston raised an eyebrow. "Will wonders never cease?"

"That isn't all," Robert said.

"Tell me more." Cranston took some wine. "I was sorry to desert you as I did, but my estate business wouldn't wait."

"I understand. But let me tell you how we acquired the animal. Athena heard him being beaten." He saw Cranston's raised eyebrows, but continued. "Athena alerted Mercy, who looked out the window and spied this surly brute beating a mangy cur."

Cranston leaned across the table, all attention. "Go on."

"Mercy yelled to John to stop the coach and was about to jump out and accost the bully herself."

"You didn't let her—"

129

"Of course not. I jumped out into the mud myself and ended up giving the brute five pounds for the animal—fleas and all."

Cranston was grinning from ear to ear. He was really enjoying this. "And then?"

Robert grinned too, at the memory. "Then Mercy thanked me, but wished I'd given the bully a smack in the chops. We went home and she sent Stoddard to get the tub filled and she bathed Hannibal right there in the kitchen."

"Hannibal?" Cranston asked, laughter in his voice.

"I wanted to know that too," Robert said. "So I asked her. And she said she looked at him and his name was Hannibal."

"Amazing."

"When he was cleaned up, he wasn't a bad looking animal. And he, well, he sort of attached himself to me. I suppose because I rescued him from that brute. So there we are. Wherever Mercy goes, Athena goes. Wherever I go, he goes. And he even sleeps—" He broke off. He couldn't tell Cranston, not even Cranston, about that closed door.

"And yesterday, Stoddard—can you imagine— Stoddard came to me and said that Hannibal is some new breed of dog. From Dalmatia, he said, an island near Venice."

"White with black spots?" Cranston said. "Tall and rangy?"

"Yes." Robert winced. "And with a tail that'll raise welts on your legs, if you get too close while he's wagging it."

"So you're one big happy family. And if Mercy

isn't increasing now, she will be soon. You'll have a house full of—"

Cranston stopped and stared at him, comprehension creeping across his face. "Good God, man! Don't tell me you're having trouble in the bedroom! You! I can't believe that you—"

At least Cranston hadn't forgotten Robert had once been quite the man about town. Those days seemed so long ago. Another lifetime. He was another man now—and he hadn't been with a woman since before he'd been wounded. "No, I haven't had any trouble."

"Then what is it? What's wrong? Mercy may be young and innocent, but surely she wouldn't deny you—"

"She hasn't had the opportunity." How had he ended up talking about this?

"She hasn't what?" Cranston stared at him stupidly. "Have you lost your senses?"

"Sometimes I wonder."

"Good grief, man. What has happened to you? Tell me."

And Robert found he wanted to talk about it, *had* to talk about it. "Well, you know our marriage was rather—"

"Hasty?" Cranston said, with that grin of his.

"Yes. I suppose you could call it that. Anyway, after I could walk again, and Emerine . . . did what she did, I retired to the country."

"A wise move," Cranston agreed, nodding.

"So I thought. Well, while I was recuperating Mercy's father came to call and we were discussing the ton and its ways. He said he was glad Mercy didn't aspire to such heights, that she was content

131

with her life. He *was* sorry, he said, that she wouldn't have a husband and a family, but he wouldn't marry her to just any lout. And so I offered to marry her myself."

"You what!" Heads turned and Cranston lowered his voice and leaned further across the table.

It did sound rather lame, put so baldly like that. But at the time it had made perfect sense. "She needed a husband. I wanted a wife."

"But, but . . ." For once Cranston was at a loss for words. "I could see you marrying Emerine like that—without feeling. But a girl like Mercy? How could you?"

"I knew the girl. I liked her. I thought we'd deal well together."

"Then what's wrong?"

"Nothing. We do deal well together."

"Then why—"

"I don't know. At first, I didn't go to her because—because of that innocence of hers. I wanted to give her time to get used to the idea."

"Considerate," Cranston agreed. "But that was a month ago, man. Anyone could get used to the idea in that length of time."

Robert shrugged. It had been a mistake, taking Cranston into his confidence. Cranston might think the hole in his shoulder made him more dashing, a hero to the ladies. And maybe it did. But that was a simple scar, not a limb twisted and torn, ridged with lumps of proud flesh. Not the kind of wound that made a man an object of pity, of disgust. If he lived to be a hundred, he'd never forget the loathing on Emerine's fine features when she told him she didn't intend to marry a man who was disfigured, a man with a gimpy leg.

Cranston leaned still closer. "Robert, tell me. Why don't you just approach her?"

"I don't know." He straightened. "Enough about me. How are things in the country? Did you get that problem cleared up?"

Mercy dropped the needlework into her lap. She was tired of stitching. She'd done just as Robert asked—she'd talked Stoddard into staying till after the holidays. But she almost wished he'd gone. There was so little to do here, not like at home where the whole management of things had fallen to her.

She heaved a sigh, and Athena and Hannibal came to put their heads in her lap. She chuckled weakly. "You always know when I need comfort, don't you?" She smoothed their silken fur. The youngest footmen had become quite proficient in giving them baths. And the herbs she'd brought from the country kept the fleas away. She smiled sadly. At least she could please Robert that way. But nothing she did seemed to lighten his spirits.

At first, she wondered if he'd brought home some kind of a fever from the war. But now she thought it must be a sickness of the mind. Or the heart.

"He's pining for that woman," she told the dogs. "She's so beautiful. And he loved her so much." She swallowed. "That's why he's so cold and distant to me. I'm not beautiful. Even Papa says I'm plain. Just a plain country girl." The tears came then, and she let them fall. Who was there to see? Or to care?

Nina Coombs

Robert spent most of his time away at his club, or in his library.

"But I don't understand why he *married* me," she sobbed. "I'm his *wife*. Why doesn't he *treat* me like a wife? Why doesn't he at least give me some children to love?"

Hannibal moved his head just a little, so his nose touched Athena's. Athena was sad. He could smell it. He was sad too. A woman like Mercy, a woman so full of love, shouldn't be unhappy. What was wrong with Master that he left his wife to cry alone like this? Didn't he know that people who gave so much love to others needed to have some love given back?

It was hard to understand. He liked Master. Well, who wouldn't like being saved from old Duffy? But there was more to it than that. Master was a good person. He never kicked or yelled. He always gave plenty of pats. The food bowls were always full.

That first night, after he'd been bathed and fed and petted, Athena had told him to follow Master. She said Master *needed* him.

That seemed strange. What did Master need *him* for? Master had everything. But now that he'd been here for a month, sleeping in Master's room, he knew what Athena meant. Master was a troubled man. Every night he tossed and turned, till the covers in the great bed were a tangled mess.

At first he'd thought Master was in pain. That first night he'd followed Master up the stairs and into his room, because Athena had told him to. He'd rather have gone with her, into Mercy's room, but she had this idea that he could help Master. And when she put it that way—well, if it wasn't for Master, he would be nothing but a bag of bones, slinking through the mews, searching for something to put in his gnawing belly.

But he didn't know *how* to help. Master's leg looked bad, twisted and ridged with scars. Master cursed every time he took off his britches and saw it. But that was anger in his voice, not pain. Hannibal sighed. It was too much for him to understand. But Athena said humans were puzzling and needed lots of love. And since he'd come here to live—and learned about love from Mercy and Athena—he wouldn't argue with that. He just gave Master all the love he could. Athena said that would do it—sooner or later.

Chapter Five

Two days later Mercy turned from the cheval glass and dismissed her maid Nancy. The new gown of pale blue satin shot with silver thread was very pretty, but it didn't make her feel better. She wore the gowns because Robert had provided them for her, but she let Nancy choose which one. Robert wouldn't notice anyway.

She straightened her shoulders. No feeling sorry for herself tonight. Not when Cranston was coming to dinner. *He* would talk to her. It wasn't that she lacked people to talk to. Ladies came to call, or left their cards if she was out. But the things they talked about—or rather, the people—meant nothing to her. For people who purported to be friends, they had very little good to say of each other. And they asked so many questions—personal questions— about Robert and her, that they made her uneasy. To think that people actually *wanted* to be part of society. She much preferred the company of the dogs. At least Robert had let her have them. But she missed caring for the hurt and lost as she had at home.

She gave herself one last look in the glass and started downstairs, Athena at her heels. Hannibal was in with Robert, as always when Robert was home. Mercy moved along briskly. She was eager to see Cranston. He was always—At the top of the stairs, Athena whimpered deep in her throat—a sound of distress. Mercy stopped. "What is it, girl?"

Athena bounded down the stairs, right toward Stoddard's back. "Athena, no!" Athena skidded to a halt. What was wrong with her? She'd been really good about Stoddard. No more spilled breakfast sausages. No more incidents of any kind.

Mercy lifted her skirts and hurried down, just as Stoddard turned toward her. "Stoddard, I'm so—Stoddard?"

The butler gave her a sheepish smile. "I—ah—I heard this strange noise. And I looked—and—" The bedraggled kitten in his arms mewed pitifully. "I—ah—thought perhaps you—"

"Of course." She reached for the kitten, but Stoddard drew back. "Your gown, milady."

The gown didn't matter. "But if it's hurt . . ."

"I—ah—looked it over. It just seems to be hungry. With your permission, milady, I'll give her to the footmen to bathe and—"

Mercy swallowed a smile. "I believe that would be appropriate, Stoddard."

Stoddard didn't turn away. "I thought perhaps . . . We might . . . A kitten in the house might be a good idea. But milady, dogs and cats . . ."

Mercy allowed her second smile to surface. "The dogs won't hurt her. I promise."

Stoddard smiled then and turned toward the kitchen. "Yes, milady. Very good, milady."

Mercy continued toward the sitting room. Imagine, Stoddard of all people, rescuing a kitten. *And* suggesting that it be kept in the house.

"Hello," Cranston said from a chair near the fire. "You're looking very pleased with yourself."

"It's Stoddard," she explained. "He's found a lost kitten. And he wants us to keep it."

Cranston's blond brows shot skyward. "Stoddard!"

"Yes," she said. "Stoddard. Why, I believe—"

"Cranston," Robert said from the doorway. "Good to see you."

"Robert." Cranston grinned as Robert came in, Hannibal at his side, and settled in a chair. "I hear that you're opening a menagerie here."

Robert shrugged. "Two dogs hardly constitute a menagerie."

"Two dogs *and* a kitten," Cranston amended, giving him the details.

Mercy watched as the men talked, watched as the tightness in Robert's face eased and he actually laughed. Why couldn't *she* make Robert laugh like that? Why couldn't she even make him smile? She did everything he asked, everything she could think of, to make his life pleasant. But nothing worked. His face was still set in those hard lines that made it look like stone. Sometimes it softened, sometimes when Hannibal put his head on his knee and Robert stroked him. Robert never refused the dog, she'd noticed. And sometimes in her lonely bed during the long nights she wished *she* could be a dog. Hannibal, after all, got to sleep in the same room as Robert, got to feel Robert's touch. While she—

"Have you thought about decorating for Christmas yet?" Cranston asked.

"Not yet," Mercy said, looking to Robert. "I wasn't sure—"

"Whatever you want to do," Robert said, his face growing tight again.

"Of course you'll decorate," Cranston said. "It's not Christmas without the Yule log and holly everywhere."

Mercy nodded. "We always had the biggest log we could drag in. And lots of holly."

"Which kind?" Cranston asked. "Rough or smooth?"

"Both," Mercy said.

Cranston nodded. "At home in Derbyshire we say that the kind of holly determines the master."

Robert's face was a study in disbelief. "Cranston, whatever are you babbling about?"

"Not babbling," Cranston said. "It's simple enough. Prickly holly is referred to as *he* and smooth holly as *she*."

Robert shook his head, but she could see his exasperation was feigned. "And what has that to do with being master?" he asked.

"The saying goes that whichever holly is used to decorate determines whether husband or wife will be master during the next year."

"I'll order the prickly and—" Mercy began.

"No!" the word was so explosive that both she and Cranston turned in surprise.

Robert gave a little chuckle. It sounded artificial, but it *was* a chuckle. "We'll have prickly *and* smooth." His hand went to Hannibal's head again. The dog was obviously a big comfort to him.

"Very well, Robert," she said, wondering what Cranston suddenly looked so pleased about.

"Stoddard will send out for the Yule log," Robert said. "And the holly. And anything else you require."

Cranston cleared his throat. "I'd be honored if you'd let me provide the holly." He glanced at Robert with mischief in his eyes. "I promise to provide both kinds in equal quantity."

"If you like," Robert said, "but only if you promise to join us on Christmas Day."

Mercy held her breath. Would Cranston say yes? It would be much pleasanter if he were there to help Robert relax. Cranston hesitated and she was about to add her plea to Robert's. Then Cranston said, "I will. If it's all right with Mercy."

"Of course it is," she hurried to say. "We'll enjoy your company."

From her place by Mercy's chair, Athena considered the strange behavior of humans. Mercy wanted to make Master happy. That was no secret. Master's friend, that nice man with the bighearted laugh, he wanted Mercy to be happy. Master, too. Those two were easy to understand.

But Master? He seemed fearful of Mercy. That was a puzzle. Athena and Hannibal had discussed it many times. But neither of them could figure out why anyone would be afraid of Mercy. Mercy had a big loving heart. She was good to everyone whether they were good to her or not.

Athena got up and went to put her head in Mercy's lap. Mercy was unhappy in this house. In spite of her cheerful smile and her kind words, she spent her nights in tears. Athena sighed. There wasn't a thing a dog could do about it. The only person who could make Mercy happy again was Master. And he didn't seem to have the least idea how to begin. Even if he wanted to.

Chapter Six

The days passed, each very much like the other for Mercy and the dogs. The kitten, which she'd insisted Stoddard name, had been christened Aphrodite. In keeping, Stoddard had said, smiling shyly, with the family she was now a part of.

Ditey, as they took to calling her, turned out to be a cute ball of black-and-white fluff. She followed Stoddard wherever he went, evidently having decided that if she let him out of her sight she'd be abandoned again. And Stoddard did not object—indeed, he seemed to enjoy it. The young footmen, Griggs and Benson, had taken to bringing home injured animals and birds, and John Coachman had made a special place in the stable where Mercy cared for them.

And through it all Robert continued to be polite—and distant. Sometimes she found herself wishing that he would fly into a rage and scream at her, as she often felt like screaming at him. At least then she'd know he was feeling *something* about her.

Still, the days passed. And one day Cranston arrived with the greens he had promised. Stoddard came to the sitting room door to tell her. "The Marquis is here with the greens, milady." A chuckle escaped him. "It appears that his whole carriage is full of them. I sent Griggs and Benson out to help."

Mercy dropped her needlepoint and hurried to the front door. "Cranston! Hello!"

He turned from the carriage where, in spite of a light snow, he was supervising the unloading, and waved at her.

A heavy shawl settled around her shoulders. "Milady," Stoddard said. "It's too cold for you out here. You'll catch a chill."

"Thank you, Stoddard." She gave him a smile and pulled the shawl closer around her. "Cranston. Do come in out of the snow."

"Coming." He bustled up the path toward her.

"Did you bring us the whole forest?" she asked, laughing.

"Not quite." He grinned sheepishly. "But I was having such fun. Could I . . . Do you suppose . . ."

In the weeks he'd been a visitor here, she'd never known him to be at a loss for words. "What is it? What are you trying to say?"

"Could I help with the decorating?"

"Oh yes!" She'd been dreading doing it alone. "I should like that very much." She took his arm and pulled him into the house. "I mentioned the subject of decorating to several ladies last week when they came to call. But they turned their noses up and said that was for servants to do."

"Did you enjoy the ladies' company?" Cranston asked, stepping around the kitten to hand Stoddard his hat and greatcoat.

"Well—"

"Come, come," Cranston said, his eyes twinkling. "You can be frank with me. What do you really think of the ladies?"

She shrugged. "Well, they seem to talk only about each other. And they ask so many questions."

"Questions?" Cranston raised an eyebrow. "Questions about what?"

"Personal questions," she said, dropping her shawl on a chair. "About Robert. And me."

Cranston shook his head. "You don't have to answer them, you know."

"Oh, I don't. But I wish they'd stop."

"You don't have to be at home for such *ladies*."

"I know that," she said. "But the dogs can't talk to me and—" Oh dear, she didn't want to complain about Robert to his friend. "Look, they're bringing the holly in. Where shall we begin?"

Robert came down the front stairs and stopped. That sounded like Cranston in the sitting room. It would be good to see his friend. Cranston was one of the few good things left in his life. He was good for Mercy too. Robert knew she received lady callers, but he never joined her. Cowardly, perhaps, to let her face them alone, especially since he knew they would try to wrest as much information as possible from her.

But in her innocence she was strong. And these days he felt anything but strong. If someone made remarks about Emerine, as they almost certainly would, he might not be able to control his reaction. And besides, he didn't care to spend his time parrying cattish innuendoes from the gossips who would descend if word got about that he was receiving callers.

He paused in the door to the sitting room, taking in the scene. Mercy was passing a length of greens to Cranston, laughing up into his face, laughing, Robert thought, as she never laughed with him. A twinge of pain shot through him. Why did she never laugh like that when the two of them were alone?

He stood there for a few minutes, watching in envious silence, unobserved. Then Mercy turned and saw him. The smile faded from her face. Cranston saw it and turned too. "Robert! Come in, man. We need your help."

It was plain to him that they *didn't* need his help, that they were doing quite well without him. But just as he was about to say so and retreat back to his library, Hannibal slammed into the back of his legs, and, taken off balance, he stumbled forward into the room. The next thing he knew Cranston had slapped some holly in his hand. "Prickly," he said, his eyes twinkling. And Mercy put another strand in his other hand. "Smooth," she said with a little laugh. "He brought half of each, just as he said he would."

"Cranston is a man of his word," Robert said, surrendering to the inevitable. "You can count on him." And then he was swept up in the hustle and bustle of decorating. For the first time in weeks, he forgot about his blasted leg.

Forgot until Cranston turned with that wicked gleam in his eyes and asked, "Where shall we hang this?"

Mercy's cheeks turned pink. "Really, Cranston, we have no need of mistletoe."

Yes, we do, Robert thought. And he knew Cranston was thinking it too.

"It isn't Christmas without the mistletoe ball," Cranston said. "Now let me see." He surveyed the room, then grabbed a chair and dragged it to the doorway. "There," he said as he stepped down. "That will do famously."

"It looks fine," Mercy said, her cheeks still pink. And she turned away to busy herself with something else.

"You mean you're not going to let me try it out?" Cranston said.

"Really, Cranston." Mercy gave him a smile that revealed her nervousness, at least to Robert. "Behave yourself. We still have a lot to do."

"Very well," Cranston said with a deep sigh, and returned to the holly.

By the time they finished, it was late. "You'll stay to eat with us, of course," Mercy said, laying a hand on Cranston's arm.

"Yes, of course," Robert added. Looking at that small hand, he felt another twinge. Had she formed a *tendre* for Cranston? Were his best friend and his wife . . . No, that was craziness. Mercy was an innocent. She just enjoyed company. After all, she spent a lot of time alone. And whose fault was that? he asked himself. His. But he didn't know what to do about it.

Every time he meant to approach her, he lost his nerve. Just the thought of her looking at his disfigured leg clenched his stomach into a hundred knots, turned his mouth into a desert and his hands into a swamp. He felt like the biggest coward, but he seemed unable to do what once had been second nature to him. He, who had once been a great ladies' man, couldn't approach a simple country girl.

He had some idea why, of course. He remembered so clearly the day he'd reached home, still in pain but not caring because at last he'd be with Emerine. And then Emerine, instead of going into his arms, had opened her beautiful mouth, her face distorted with loathing, and told him she was breaking off their engagement. She couldn't abide marriage to a man who was disfigured.

Oh, he didn't think Mercy would regard him with loathing. She was too compassionate for that. But to see pity in her green eyes, even fear—*that* he wouldn't be able to stand. And so the door between their rooms remained closed.

"I'll just go freshen up a bit," Mercy said, putting a hand to her tumbled curls. "And then we'll have dinner." And off she went, Athena at her heels.

Later, at the dinner table, Mercy smiled to herself. It was good to have Cranston here. He made life seem almost normal. And the holly and other greens gave the place a festive air. She felt better already, more in the holiday spirit.

But during dessert, Cranston turned to her. "So, where are you getting your new gown made?"

"I'm sure I don't need any new gowns," she said. "Robert saw to it that I have more than enough."

"But surely Robert is going to get you a gown for the Christmas Ball." Cranston said this nonchalantly, without even looking up from his plate, but she wasn't deceived. He knew exactly what he was asking.

The trouble was, she didn't know how to answer.

She hadn't even thought about going to the Christmas Ball. Her hand that was bringing a forkful of cobbler to her mouth stopped halfway there, trembling in midair, while she turned to look at Robert. And then she wished she hadn't. All the hard lines had come back into his face and his mouth had settled into the grimness it usually wore.

Robert didn't want to take her anywhere. She'd been in London for almost three months. And aside from that first trip to the Minerva Lending Library, they hadn't gone out of the house together. No theaters, no museums, no shopping. Whatever she'd done, she'd done alone. Except for Cranston, Robert didn't come down to receive callers. He certainly wasn't about to take her to the biggest ball of the year.

"I am not going to the Christmas Ball," Robert said finally.

Cranston looked up. "Do you think that's fair to your wife? Keeping her from the season's biggest ball?"

He had kept her from the others, Mercy wanted to say, but something in Cranston's face silenced her. That, and the lump that had come into her throat.

Robert didn't look at her. He focused an icy stare on Cranston and said, "Mercy may go if she likes. Perhaps you'd like to take her." She'd never heard him speak in a colder voice. It made her want to shiver.

"No," she cried. "I don't wish to go without you." She wasn't going to any ball without her husband. She'd been shamed enough already. Everyone must know about Emerine, know that Robert had loved

148

Emerine. And that he didn't love his wife.

"Really, Robert," Cranston began, ignoring Robert's glare. "You should take Mercy out in company. She hasn't been to Covent Garden. She hasn't—"

Robert put down his napkin and pushed back his chair. "Cranston, we've been friends for a long time. I hope we'll be friends all our lives. But I must tell you that I don't appreciate your interference with my marriage. And if you persist in this line of discussion, I shall have to ask you to leave my home." He skewered Cranston with his eyes. "Is that understood?"

Cranston nodded, his face serene. "Oh, I understand. I don't like it, but I understand." And he went on eating.

Mercy let out the breath she hadn't known she was holding. Robert had so few friends. He shouldn't fight with this one. But how did Cranston bear up under Robert's awful icy stare? It didn't seem to bother him in the least.

Silence settled on the room—and grew till she could scarcely bear it. "Ah, Cranston," she said finally. "Tell me. What else do people in the city do to celebrate the holidays?"

Cranston began to tell her about sleigh rides and charades, and other things city people did. She forced herself to concentrate on that, not to look at Robert, though she did notice with relief that he had settled back in his chair.

Under the table, Athena touched noses with Hannibal. He'd done a good job getting Master into the sitting room earlier. When she'd seen them there in the doorway, she'd smelled Master's hesitation, known he was getting ready to turn away. And smart Hannibal had stopped him, even pushed him into the room. But there was only so much two dogs could do. The people had to do a little of it themselves.

Mercy loved Master. That was easy to see—and smell. But Master—Athena still had trouble deciphering his smells. He was such a contradictory man. He acted cold and distant, but she could smell wanting on him at the same time, especially when they hung up that mistletoe thing.

Smells were important. Smells told her things—like how Mercy felt, or that Hannibal was looking for her. Or where a rabbit was crouching. Of course, she hadn't smelled a rabbit since they'd left the country. But she didn't want to go back to the country now. Rabbits couldn't compare to being with Hannibal.

And before long there would be the puppies. Hers and Hannibal's. Mercy had been so wrapped up in her own problems that she hadn't noticed yet. But she would soon. Athena could almost feel them growing inside her, bigger day by day. Soon they'd be running around the house, playing with Ditey—a cute little thing for a cat. Yes, wonderful days were coming.

Athena put her head down on her paws. They'd just have to be patient with Master. Be patient and love him.

Chapter Seven

Hannibal sat beside Master's chair while the humans were at breakfast. Meals were one of the few times during the day that he got to be with Athena. Then, and when Master went out. But Master didn't go out much, except in the evening. He spent most of his days in his library.

That mistletoe thing had been up for two days now and nothing had happened. Somehow Athena had found out that it had to do with one of those strange human customs—kissing, it was called. He couldn't see the sense of it himself. He'd rather sniff noses—or other things.

But Athena said kissing was important to Mercy. And Athena had come up with a plan. Well, actually two, since he hadn't liked the first plan. He wasn't too sure about the second either. But if it hadn't been for Athena, Mercy would never have seen Duffy beating him that day and Master wouldn't have come to his rescue. So he owed them all.

It wasn't that he didn't want Mercy and Master to be together. He did. For one thing, it would mean that he could sleep in the same room with Athena.

Still, that first plan—He didn't want to make Master mad at him. And besides, tripping Master might hurt his leg. So Athena had come up with a second plan. He just had to stand there, in Master's way, and Athena would do the tripping. *She'd* get Mercy to fall into his arms, and right under the mistletoe ball. Surely that would do the trick.

Hannibal wasn't so sure. Master was a stubborn man. Smart, too. It was hard to imagine him being tricked into anything. But Athena was wise. And Athena said Master already loved Mercy—he just didn't know it. That was the hardest thing of all to imagine—loving without knowing it. After all, love was so special, so important.

Mercy and Master got up from the table. Athena looked at Hannibal, and he got up too. Time to do it, her eyes said.

Heaving a sigh, Robert followed Mercy out of the dining room. The mistletoe still hung where Cranston had put it. But though they passed under it many times a day, nothing happened. What was *wrong* with him? He couldn't even kiss his own wife!

He was so tired of the stilted conversation between them. He wanted to see her smile, to laugh—not to see that look on her face that meant she was considering her words before she let them out of her mouth.

She'd changed so. The little girl he'd once known, with the green eyes that widened at his stories of Greek gods and goddesses, had laughed wholeheartedly. She'd giggled as she chased a playful puppy under a bush. And she'd told him anything and everything that came into her head. Or so it seemed.

But now he had no idea what Mercy was thinking. Her face was closed to him. He was living with a stranger. And it was his own fault. *He* had made her that way. He had thought to make life better for her. But he wasn't sure that he had.

"Have you enjoyed your books from the Minerva?" he asked, seeking a neutral topic of conversation. Something to keep her there for a moment longer.

She turned, surprise on her face. "Yes. Very much. I go there nearly every week. It's marvelous to have so many choices."

He nodded, his heart leaping into his throat. She was standing right under the mistletoe. He took a step toward her. *Do it*, he told himself. *Just do it.* He took another step. He was almost to her. Something flickered in her eyes. He couldn't tell what. She started to back away, but Athena was behind her and she couldn't get past. *Now*, he told himself. And froze there—just a step away from her.

For what seemed like an eternity he was close enough to take her in his arms. Her green eyes were wide—and anxious. Was she afraid? That wouldn't do. He started to back away himself and came up against Hannibal. What was the blasted dog doing so close, hemming him in?

"Hannibal," he began. And then Athena reared up on her hind legs and the next thing he knew, Mercy slammed into his chest. His arms went around her automatically, clasping her to him. She fit perfectly

153

against him. For the merest second, he let himself enjoy it.

Then she lifted her shocked face to his. "Robert, I—"

Her mouth was so close, so tempting. He stared at it, mesmerized, leaning toward it as it came toward his. And then she raised up on her tiptoes and kissed him.

It was a chaste kiss, the kiss of an innocent, and short. But it left him shaken in a way Emerine's kisses, or those of the many women he'd had before her, had never done.

Mercy pulled out of his arms, pink flooding her cheeks. "I—I have to go out to the stable," she said. "Griggs found a hurt bird. I've got to check its wing."

"Of course," he said. Why didn't she invite him along? Probably because he'd been behaving like a boor, because he couldn't relax with her. He'd like to go out to the stables with her. He liked to see that look of compassion and love on her face. She'd had it even as a child. She had such a loving heart. His Mercy. If only there could be love in it for him.

Mercy turned and stumbled toward the foyer. She wouldn't think about that kiss. The hurt bird was waiting, and the other animals in her little hospital. A shawl should be enough since she was just going to the stables. She glanced down at Athena, pattering along at her side as usual. It was strange, though, Athena knocking her into Robert's arms like that. She'd definitely felt Athena's paws on her back as she fell forward.

Athena's blocking the doorway was odd, too.

Though she followed everywhere, she was never in the way. Now twice in a very little time she'd behaved strangely. Mercy reached down to touch Athena's nose. It was cold and wet. Well, she wasn't sick.

In the foyer, Mercy accepted her shawl from Stoddard with a thank you and smiled when she saw Ditey's head poking out of his pocket. Stoddard saw her look. "She insists on going everywhere with me," he said. "And her legs are just too short."

"It's quite all right, Stoddard. You don't need to explain it to me."

"Yes, milady," Stoddard said with a satisfied smile. "I know."

Funny, she thought, as she made her way toward the back of the house, how that kitten had changed Stoddard. He smiled a lot now. And his nose never quivered in indignation as it had that first day when he'd spied Athena. Well, at least some good had come of her being here.

She opened the back door and sighed, warmth flooding her cheeks again. It was no use trying not to think about it. She had kissed Robert! She could hardly believe it. How could she have done such a forward thing? Kissing him! But they'd been under the mistletoe and she'd been thrown there, right against his waistcoat. Right—she had to admit it to herself—where she really wanted to be. Had wanted to be for a long, long time. But to kiss him like that! Of course, he had kissed her back. At least, she *thought* he'd kissed her back. She'd never kissed anyone before, so it was difficult to know for sure.

Afterwards she'd wanted to burrow into his arms, to stay there forever. But she knew that doing that wouldn't mean anything, just as his kissing her back didn't mean anything. Robert still pined for Emerine, and if he were kind enough to his plain little wife from the country not to push her away, it was only because he was a good man.

She reached the stable and pushed open the door. She couldn't be thinking about Robert now. Her animals needed her whole attention.

Athena settled on her haunches to watch Mercy at work. Her hands were so sure and gentle. All the animals seemed to know that she wouldn't hurt them, that she just wanted to help them. Well, since Mercy was the most wonderful person in the world, that wasn't so unusual. The unusual thing was that Master couldn't see what she was. Hannibal knew, and Ditey, and Master's friend, and even grumpy old Stoddard, who wasn't grumpy anymore.

Well, she and Hannibal had certainly done their part. They'd gotten Master and Mercy into each other's arms at last. They'd even gotten them to kiss. How much more would it take to make Master realize that he loved Mercy?

Athena scratched her ear. She didn't like being separated from Hannibal so much. But it was obvious Master needed to learn about love. She raised her head. Maybe . . .

Chapter Eight

The next afternoon Hannibal trotted into the sitting room and flopped down in front of the fireplace with Athena. Master had gone out, so now he could be with Athena and Mercy.

Master was all right, Hannibal thought. Master gave lots of pats—absentminded pats, but pats nevertheless. And he didn't shout or kick. Or beat his dogs like Duffy did.

But still, being with Athena was better. And when Mercy talked to them, that was best of all. Mercy didn't just give pats, she talked. And she talked right to them, looking directly into their eyes. It was easy to tell that she loved them. She would love the puppies too. But she didn't know about them yet.

Mercy looked up from her needlepoint and smiled at him. "Hello, Hannibal." She sighed, one of those big sighs she gave so often. Probably she was thinking about Master, and the strange way he behaved. "I guess Robert has gone out again. Otherwise you'd still be with him."

She glanced over at Athena, who was dozing with

157

her head on her paws. A worried expression crossed Mercy's face. "Are you all right, Athena? You're doing an awful lot of sleeping lately." She dropped her needlepoint in the basket and patted the skirt over her knees. "Come here, girl. Let me feel your nose."

Athena got up and went to put her head in Mercy's lap. Mercy felt her nose. "Well, that's cold enough. And wet. Let me look at the rest of you."

She ran a hand over Athena's back. Hannibal sat up, his ears perking. Mercy wasn't stupid. Soon now she'd realize about the pups.

Mercy examined each of Athena's legs. "Well, nothing wrong there." She reached under her, ran a hand along her stomach and stopped.

Mercy looked up, a big smile on her face. "Of course! What's wrong with me? Puppies! You're going to have puppies!"

Hannibal got up and went to her too. "Hannibal, you old devil," she said, grinning as she ruffled his ears. "What've you been up to?"

He grinned back. Mercy always knew the right thing to say. Mercy was just as wonderful as Athena said. Wonderful and good and kind. What was wrong with Master? Why didn't he love such a fine woman?

Mercy rubbed the dogs' heads, paying attention to the special places she knew they liked to be scratched. Thank goodness she had them. She didn't know what she'd have done if she didn't. "I'm sure Robert doesn't mean to be cruel to me," she told them, gazing into their warm, comforting eyes. "It's just that it's lonely here in London. I have no friends. Those ladies who come to call—no one could make friends with them. They don't *want* friends. They're only looking for gossip to take on to the next house. They just want to trick me into saying something. Something about our marriage, or Emerine, no doubt. Well, I won't give them that satisfaction."

Athena nosed at her hand, and Mercy smiled. "Yes, I know. You want me to keep scratching. But I'm used to saying what I think. Or I was when I was at home. I don't like having to consider every word before I speak it. And it's the same way when I'm with Robert. I'm not to speak of his wound, or of Emerine, or of the Christmas Ball. I'm afraid to say anything for fear it will be the *wrong* thing."

She smiled and gave them a final pat. "Go lie down again. I know you like it by the fire." The dogs settled on the hearth rug together and she picked up her needlepoint again.

All of a sudden, tears welled up in her eyes. Yesterday afternoon she had kissed Robert. Right there under the mistletoe. And for a moment, there in his arms, she had imagined what life might be like if he really loved her. But that had lasted only a moment. He'd kissed her back, but that was because he was a good man and didn't want to hurt her feelings.

"But if he's such a good man," she said aloud. "Why does he treat me like this? Why doesn't he at least give me a child to love? Why?" she cried in her pain.

But there was no answer. She looked down at the needlepoint clutched in her hands. Two tears glistened on its woolen surface. She brushed them off. There was no sense in being a waterworks. Papa had always taught her to make the most of what she had. And after all, she had her animals. And Cranston—he had become a good friend. She didn't have to think before she spoke to *him*. Unless Robert was there.

If only Cranston would not bring up the Christmas Ball again. Not that she wouldn't like to go to it. To dance the waltz. The ladies said the waltz was scandalous, but they said it with those little giggles that showed how much they enjoyed it.

She leaned back in the chair and closed her eyes. To whirl around the floor in Robert's arms—oh, that would be the most wonderful thing. And in some marvelous gown. Her new gowns made her presentable at least.

Nancy often insisted she was beautiful. But of course, Nancy was her maid. Mercy knew she wasn't beautiful, but even she could see that in her new gowns she wasn't so plain after all. In a fancy gown, with her hair swept up, and jewels around her throat and—

Her eyes flew open. What on earth was she thinking? Hadn't Papa taught her that it was foolish to yearn after what she couldn't have? She'd never done it before. She wouldn't do it now. Besides, going to the ball wasn't really what she wanted. She wanted Robert to love her. She wanted—God help her—she wanted to be his wife. Really his wife.

That night at the dinner table, Mercy took a sip of water and looked to Robert. As usual they had spoken only of the weather and other trivial things. He asked about the animals and her hospital. And she'd told him. Now she wanted to tell him about

Athena—and the puppies. But it seemed, somehow, personal.

"Robert?"

He looked up from his pigeon pie. "Yes?"

With him looking at her like that, she grew nervous and blurted out, "We're going to have puppies!"

He raised an eyebrow. "We are?"

"That is," she stammered, "Athena is."

He shrugged. "What did you expect? After all, Hannibal—"

"I guess I just didn't think about it. I've been busy with the animals—and decorating for Christmas. I'm happy about it, of course."

A rare smile crossed his face. "I wouldn't have thought otherwise."

She nodded and sipped her tea. "It'll be nice to have babies around the house."

"The kitten isn't enough?" Robert asked.

"Well, Ditey is fun. But she's really Stoddard's."

She looked down at her food. "Or he's hers."

"Yes, I suppose that's true. Incidentally—" He paused to take a swallow of tea. "You've certainly made a great change in Stoddard."

Mercy looked up from her plate. "I?"

Robert nodded. "You."

"But what have I done?"

"Well, the man used to be a stern-faced martinet, that nose of his quivering with indignation at the mere mention of an animal in his establishment. And now he goes around smiling all the time—and carries a kitten in his coat pocket. I certainly call that change. And I lay that change at your door."

Why must he look at her like that? So sternly.

Like she'd done something really horrible. "I suppose he *is* different. I am sorry for disrupting your well-run establishment, but I did warn you, and—"

"There's no need to apologize," Robert said. "I find the change beneficial."

He what? Her mouth fell open. "You do?"

"Yes, of course." He glanced down at Hannibal, who was in his usual place by his side. "I never realized that having an animal could be such a comfort to a man." He straightened and gave her an odd look. "To Stoddard, of course. I'm speaking of him, of course."

"Of course," she agreed, pretending that she couldn't see the truth in his eyes.

He pushed back his chair. "I'm going out. Have a pleasant evening."

And he was gone. She stared down at her half-finished tart, her appetite gone. He'd changed the subject and she'd never gotten to say anything about *her* wanting a baby. He did that every time she brought up something he didn't want to discuss. Either he changed the subject, or he told her flatly that he didn't wish to discuss it. She pushed back her own chair and went to the sitting room, the dogs behind her.

Later that evening, Mercy climbed the stairs to her bedchamber. Robert was still out. With Cranston, probably.

She let Nancy help her out of her gown and into her nightdress. Then, sending Nancy to her own bed, Mercy sat down before her dressing table to brush her hair. One hundred strokes every night. It was nice hair, if she did say so herself, thick and glossy. Her best feature. She liked to brush it herself, as she had for so many years at home. She had used that quiet time to think about the day and what had happened during it.

One hundred. There, she was finished. She put down the brush. The candlelight gleamed off its silver back. Robert had provided that brush for her—and all the other beautiful things in this room. She sighed. She would trade everything in this room—well, not the dogs, but everything else—to have Robert's love.

She blew out the candle and got up. "Come on, Hannibal. Out you go."

Hannibal gave her a reproachful look. He got to his feet, but he went to the door to Robert's room instead of the one to the hall. "No, Hannibal. Out in the hall."

But Hannibal didn't move.

Oh well, Robert was still out. Instead of dragging the dog out into the hall, she'd just open the door a little, and let him into Robert's room.

She put a hesitant hand on the knob. She could open the connecting door without looking in. She'd never seen Robert's room. Not that she hadn't been tempted to peek in some day when he was out. But she hadn't. This was the first time she'd even touched the door.

Slowly she turned the knob, opening it just wide enough for Hannibal to get through. Just one—no! She looked away. She wasn't going to peek. She turned back, and there went Athena, right after Hannibal, into Robert's room.

Oh dear! What was wrong with the dogs? They'd

never disobeyed before. And Athena—she never left her side if she could help it.

Mercy sighed. Now what should she do? She couldn't leave the door ajar. Robert wouldn't like that. Well, since he wasn't home yet, maybe she could just go in and get Athena. And when she got her back in her room—

She pushed open the door. Where *was* that dog?

She crossed the room, step by step, looking around, behind a chair, under a table. No Athena. The click of an opening door brought Mercy erect, her heart in her throat. The blood left her face and she put out a hand to steady herself. Robert! He stood there, in his dressing room doorway, half unclothed, his dressing gown hanging from his hand.

He must have been as astonished as she. For an eternity he stood there, frozen. She stood too, unable to move. And she saw his wounded leg—ridges of proud flesh and the scars where it had been ripped open. No wonder he was cross sometimes.

She looked up to his face. His eyes burned at her, dark, glowing. The blood rushed back to her cheeks. This was awful! She was standing in Robert's bedchamber in her nightdress! Her hand went to her mouth. What he must be thinking!

"I—" she stammered. "Hannibal wanted to come in—And I didn't think—And Athena—"

"Get out!" Robert said, struggling into his dressing gown. "Go, now!" he cried, limping toward her.

She turned and ran to the safety of her room, Athena at her side. The door slammed shut behind her, rattling the paintings on the wall. Why had he been so angry?

* * *

In the room Mercy had just fled, Robert cursed. He cursed his leg, Napoleon Bonaparte, King George III, the French army, the English army, Emerine, the ton and its gossips, and most of all himself. But cursing didn't help. Mercy had seen his leg. And she'd been appalled at the sight of it. Her hand had gone to her mouth in that gesture of horror. She'd backed away, then run from him.

He threw himself down in a chair by the hearth and stared at the fire in dejection. What was he to do now? There was no hope of a real marriage, not when the sight of him sent her into revulsion.

What had she been doing in here anyway? What had she mumbled? Something about Hannibal wanting to come in. And Athena. Those two *had* been acting strangely, but for Mercy to blame them for her invasion of his privacy—that wasn't like her. Still, maybe he'd misunderstood.

"God," he moaned. "What am I going to do?"

A cold, wet nose shoved its way under his hand. He looked down, into Hannibal's warm brown eyes. "Hannibal," he said. "You're one lucky dog. You're hale and hearty. Athena doesn't run from you."

He stroked the dog's long ears. "You know, I'd give anything to be whole again. I know I'm her husband. I could insist on my nuptial rights. She'd give them to me too."

He sighed. "But I can't do that. I won't appeal to her duty. Or her pity. I love her too much for that."

What a pretty kettle of fish he'd gotten himself into now! What had he been thinking that day he'd offered for her?

He leaned back in his chair and tried to remember. He'd been hurting that day, not his leg as much

165

as his pride, though at the time he'd thought it was his heart that was giving him so much trouble. And when they'd gotten to the subject of marriage and Mercy's father had bemoaned his daughter's lack of a husband, Robert had remembered that little girl who'd been so cheerful and good to be around. How she'd hung on his every word that summer he told her stories of Greek gods and goddesses. How tenderly she'd touched her animals, love in her face.

He hadn't seen her since she'd grown to adulthood, but her father had assured him she was much the same. And suddenly she had seemed like the answer to everything. He would marry Mercy. She would have a husband. He would have a wife. The ton could go to hell—and Emerine with it.

He must have been half out of his head with misery to think that he could take an innocent young girl and saddle her with a cripple. And he'd never, ever, thought that he'd come to love her. But he had. He had, and he didn't know what to do about it.

Chapter Nine

The next morning after breakfast, Mercy made her way to her sitting room, the dogs at her heels. She went in, closed the door, and stood there, breathing heavily. She had never been this angry in her life. In fact, she seldom got angry. But this morning she wanted to break something—anything—most of all Robert's head!

She had come down to breakfast with trepidation. After all, last night she had cried herself to sleep—finally. And this morning her eyes had been so red and puffy that no amount of cool water would make them look normal. Still, she had refused to cower in her room. She had made a mistake going into Robert's room, a simple mistake. Surely he had been able to see that once he'd calmed down.

This morning he would say he was sorry, she'd thought. She would say she was sorry. And it would be over.

Robert had been already at the table when she reached it. He'd looked up and nodded. "Good morning."

Her knees had threatened to give way. He sounded just as he had yesterday morning—and the morning before that. As though nothing had happened between them.

"Good morning," she'd replied, keeping her voice level.

She'd managed to get through breakfast, even to reply to whatever he said. But the food had seemed lodged in her throat and would not go down. And finally it was over and he had gone out.

Now she stomped across the sitting room. "Damn, damn, damn!" she muttered, throwing herself into a chair. "I didn't know it would be like this. I knew it would be hard, but not like this!"

The dogs came to put their heads in her lap. She fondled their ears. "He just makes me so mad! Yelling at me like that just because I came into his rooms in my nightdress. My goodness! I'm his wife!" She heaved a great sigh. "I wish I knew what to do. Some way to make him behave sensibly instead of moping after that foolish woman." Anybody who preferred an old earl to Robert had to be foolish.

"You always make me feel better," she told the dogs, smiling down at them. "But I still need to *do* something. You know, Athena, how hard it is for me to do nothing. Besides, doing nothing doesn't seem to have improved the situation the least bit. So—" She scratched behind their ears. "We're agreed then. I must *do* something. Now the question is, what do I do?"

Athena lifted her head and gazed into Mercy's eyes. "Oh, Athena, I wish you could speak. I'm sorely in need of your wisdom."

Athena wriggled out from under her scratching fingers and moved to the center of the rug. "What are you—" Mercy began. "Athena! I didn't know you could dance!"

On her hind legs, Athena pirouetted around the rug once. Then she dropped to her haunches and sat there, her tongue hanging out, staring at Mercy as though she expected something from her.

"I didn't know you could dance," Mercy repeated. "But why are you dancing now? It must be hard with the puppies and all."

Still, Athena sat there—waiting. Mercy picked up her needlepoint. She was sick of it, but she had to do something with her hands. Athena's pirouetting like that made her think of the Christmas Ball—the forbidden Christmas Ball. She looked at Athena again. At the ball there would be dancing.

Her fingers hesitated, but her mind raced. Athena was really wise, but—no. There was no way she could bring up the ball to Robert. Unless . . . She put down her sewing and went to the desk to pen a note. For this she was going to need Cranston's help.

Dinner was nearly over before Mercy screwed her courage to the sticking point and said to Cranston, "I have changed my mind. I find I should like to go to the Christmas Ball after all."

From the corner of her eye, she saw Robert opening his mouth.

"Of course, Robert does not wish to go," she hurried on before he could speak.

Robert closed his mouth.

"It's his choice, of course. Though if *I* were in his shoes, I should certainly go."

"And why is that?" Cranston asked, the very picture of innocence.

"Why, if *I* were in Robert's shoes," she said, "I would go to the Ball and act madly in love with my new wife. That would certainly put Emerine's nose out of joint."

Cranston chuckled. "I had not supposed you to have such a vengeful turn of mind," he said.

Mercy shrugged. "She deserves it. What she did was un—un—unladylike," she stammered.

"An interesting idea," Robert said.

And her heart nearly leapt right out of her mouth.

"But I doubt it would work," Robert went on.

Cranston looked to her, but her mouth had gone suddenly dry and she was unable to speak. "And why is that?" he inquired.

"It takes two people to pull off a deception like that."

"And you don't think Mercy could bring it off?" Cranston looked at her again, his eyes urging her on.

She pulled in a deep breath. "Oh, I'm sure I could convince such a shallow woman. What does she know of love, anyway? But, of course, this is all conjecture. Robert doesn't wish to go. So I shall go with you."

"I shall be honored," Cranston said, bowing his head.

She clapped her hands, pretending happiness, though her heart was breaking. The plan hadn't worked. But she'd have to go to the ball anyway. She looked to Robert. "I hope I may have a new gown. Cranston will want me to look my best."

Robert put down his cup. His heart was pounding so hard he thought the others must be able to hear it. He didn't care about putting Emerine's nose out of joint. Actually, she had never really meant anything to him. Though he hadn't known it at the time, he knew it now. She meant nothing to him at all.

But the chance to have Mercy look at him with love—even if it was pretend love—was worth more than he could say. And if their stratagem got the ton to talking again, at least it would be good talk.

Mercy had fallen silent and was looking down at her plate. No wonder. He hadn't answered her question about the gown. "I believe green silk will do nicely. We'll go to the modiste tomorrow."

Mercy's head snapped up—and her eyes grew wide. "*You* will?"

"Of course," he said. "If we're going to pull this off, we have to do it right."

"You mean—" Mercy began.

"I mean I like your plan. It appeals to the—" He grinned. "Suffice it to say that I like it."

"I do too," Cranston said. "If the gown is going to be green, maybe my sainted mother would loan—"

"Mercy will wear my mother's emeralds," Robert said, pushing down his jealousy. Cranston was just trying to help.

Robert turned to Mercy, who was still staring at him as though she couldn't believe her ears. Well, no wonder, considering how he'd behaved last night. "You can do it, can't you?" he asked. "You *can* pretend to be madly in love with me?"

"Yes," she said, pink tinting her cheeks. "I can pretend."

"Then it's all decided," Robert said, before she could change her mind. "We'll go to the modiste as soon as she opens tomorrow."

"Yes, Robert." Her voice had regained some strength. She was doing this to help him, out of her compassionate heart. He knew that. But it wasn't fair to her—to take her to a ball and not dance with her. He *could* dance. His leg seldom pained him now. And she would enjoy dancing.

"Mercy, do you waltz?" he asked.

She stared at him in amazement. "I? A vicar's daughter? No, Robert. But I shan't need—"

"Yes, you shall need," he said. "We must waltz."

"But I can't!"

"Then you must learn. We'll start tonight."

"But your leg! Oh!" Her hands flew to her mouth. "I'm—"

"My leg is fine." He managed a smile. "Besides, Cranston is here. He will help."

Later that night Athena followed Mercy up the stairs to bed. What fun and laughter she'd heard that night. She smiled to herself. This was the way a home was supposed to be, full of fun and laughter. Mercy had laughed and laughed. Master's friend Cranston, who was so jolly, laughed till tears came into his eyes. And Master had laughed too, dancing around the room with Mercy in his arms while Cranston beat time with his foot and counted. They had all laughed—and now Mercy was happy—for a little while, at least.

Master did love Mercy. Athena was sure of it.

Maybe this would make him realize it. And Mercy *wasn't* plain. Any fool could see that, Athena told herself as she crossed Mercy's room to the pallet Stoddard had fixed for her. She lay down carefully. The puppies were growing fast. She could feel them tumbling around inside her. And they were getting heavy. A good thing she didn't have to dance anymore.

She put her head on her paws and closed her eyes. Yes, the Christmas Ball should do the job.

Chapter Ten

The days passed quickly. Robert took Mercy to the modiste and supervised the ordering of her gown, the most beautiful dark green silk she'd ever seen. And while they were there, they practiced pretending to be madly in love. Robert was so good at it, lavishing her with smiles and warm glances. And she did her best to reciprocate. Of course, *she* didn't have to pretend.

And Cranston came to the house every day, counting out the steps while she and Robert waltzed around the sitting room. They danced, and laughed at their mistakes. He said the mistakes were *theirs*, not his. He was like another person, this Robert. He laughed and joked, and seemed to enjoy everything.

While they practiced, she tried to concentrate on the steps, not to think about being in Robert's arms. But it was very difficult. She wanted just to dance forever, on and on in his arms. And at night, in her sleep, she dreamed of that very thing.

The night of the ball finally arrived. Mercy let

Nancy help her with her gown, and do her hair, and rave over her good looks. She let Robert put his mother's emeralds around her neck. And through it all she wondered if this too was a dream.

But they reached the ballroom and she didn't wake up. She stopped in the doorway. "Oh!" she breathed. She'd never seen such a magnificent sight as this. The whole room was wreathed with holly—the windows and doors, and even the chandeliers. Candles gleamed everywhere, casting a glow over the assembled guests. So many people! Lords and ladies arrayed in their very best, ladies dripping with jewels, gentlemen looking their handsomest.

"Well," Robert whispered from her right. "Ready to play your part?"

"Ready," she said, turning her best smile in his direction. "Will this do?"

On her other side, Cranston chuckled. "I should say it does, admirably."

Robert pulled Mercy's arm tighter against his side. He could hardly believe this was happening. He had never seen Mercy smile like that before. She was getting really good at this acting thing. Of course, he and Cranston had coached her in this as well as in dancing, coached her how to hold his arm, how to languish against him, how to look up at him with soulful eyes. Sometimes he could almost forget that it *was* an act. Sometimes—for as long as a minute—he could convince himself that he had a chance with her. And then he remembered that look of horror on her face—and he knew better. But if tonight was all he was going to have, he was going to enjoy it, every last second of it. He had that much—at least.

He led her up to the receiving line. "Lady Jersey, may I present my wife, Mercy?"

He held his breath while the Jersey inspected Mercy. Mercy, the innocent, not knowing she was facing the ton's fiercest arbiter of fashion, smiled her usual friendly smile, and said, "I'm very pleased to meet you, Lady Jersey. It was kind of you to ask us."

And finally the woman smiled and nodded. "A wise choice, Robert. I approve."

Mercy gave him another adoring look that almost buckled his knees. But he gave her back one just as good and told the Jersey, "Yes. I know. She's the very best."

"Enjoy the ball," the Jersey said, and turned to the next guest.

"Robert," Mercy said, as they advanced into the room thronged with guests. "Where is the duchess? Emerine?"

"Forget about her," Robert said. "And remember to smile."

"I can't forget about her." Mercy's cheeks turned pink. "I—ah—want to do a particularly good job when she's watching. After all, this charade is for her benefit."

"Do a good job all the time," he whispered. He meant to savor every precious moment of this time. He'd probably never get a chance to have Mercy look at him like this again. There would be no more dancing sessions, either. God, how he'd enjoyed those dancing sessions. He hadn't laughed like that, genuinely laughed, in many years. If only there were some way he could—

"Where is she?" Mercy asked again, turning those

green eyes of hers on him. "Please, I want to meet her and—"

"Well, it looks like you're going to get your wish," Cranston said dryly. "She's on her way over here. The tall blonde in the blazing red gown, just coming around the portly gentleman to the left there."

Robert looked down. Mercy's arm was trembling in his. Her face had paled. "Buck up," he whispered. "Don't let me down now."

He was beginning to regret the whole thing. Mercy was such an innocent. She was no match for someone of Emerine's sophistication. But it was too late now to turn tail and run. They'd have to brazen it out.

Emerine wove her way through the crowd, her hips moving in the rhythm he remembered so well. Only now he found it cheap. The scarlet gown, too.

She stopped in front of them, her eyes gleaming balefully.

But before she could speak, Mercy turned to him. "Robert, my love," she said, and his heart jumped at the endearment, however false it might be. "Do you know this lady?"

"Oh, he knows me," Emerine said, shrugging the white shoulders that emerged from her gown. "He knows me very well."

Marriage had clearly not softened her tongue. Nor, evidently, had it changed her desire to display her body to all and sundry. The gown *was* spectacular. He had to admit that. Its décolletage was calculated to show off her breasts, almost all of them. And the rest of the gown clung to her body, revealing every sumptuous curve. And yet, as voluptuous as she looked, he felt nothing but distaste.

He swallowed a curse. Mercy was no match for Emerine. Still, he was fairly caught, so he made the proper introductions. "This is Emerine, the Duchess of Rorston," he said. "My wife, Mercy."

Emerine looked Mercy up and down. "Your wife," she said flatly, as she might have said, "Your horse."

"Yes," Mercy said, smiling sweetly. "I'm Robert's wife. Robert's very happy wife." And she flashed him another of those blinding smiles.

He bent and nuzzled her neck. When he straightened, he asked Emerine, "Where's your husband tonight? I hope he's not ailing again."

"Not at all," Emerine said, smiling seductively. "He's over there talking to the dowagers. The old biddies seldom get to talk to a man, so they enjoy his company." She leaned toward Robert provocatively, her red lips parted. He heard Mercy's intake of breath at the wealth of bosom so blatantly revealed.

He ignored it, turning to Mercy instead. "Come, my dear," he told her. "The music is waiting for us. I can hardly wait to waltz with you."

He led her to the dance floor. "I'm so nervous," she whispered. "What if I step on your foot?"

He chuckled, relieved that she didn't want to discuss Emerine. He wasn't sure he could face that. "Don't worry about it. You can step on them all night, for all I care. Seeing Emerine's face—" He beamed down at Mercy. "You were quite right, my dear. We did put her nose out of joint. We did it royally. And now we shall celebrate." And he swung her out onto the dance floor.

* * *

It was almost dawn when the three of them climbed into the carriage for the ride home. "Oh my," Mercy cried, leaning back on the squabs. "I have never had so much fun in my life. Dancing is so—so invigorating."

"You will be exhausted in the morning," Cranston observed with a grin. "Take my word for it."

"Oh, I don't think so," she said, and yawned.

Robert laughed. She loved the sound of his laughter, so deep and hearty. Before this week she'd never heard it. Not since he was young. She could remember his boyish laughter, though. She'd loved it too.

She closed her eyes. She wanted to remember this night, every wonderful moment of it.

"Mercy was the belle of the ball," Cranston said.

The heat rose to her cheeks. "Oh, I was no such thing. Just because a few men asked me to dance."

"A few!" he declared. "Every man in the place asked you."

She opened her eyes. "Oh, Cranston, you exaggerate."

"I don't," he said. "But in spite of your turning them all down, including yours truly, your husband's best friend, I think you made quite a hit."

She didn't want to talk about those men. When they'd asked her to dance, she'd simply said that she was newly wed and wanted only to dance with her husband. She hadn't minded them asking, though. Few men had asked her to dance when she was the plain daughter of a country vicar. So she'd enjoyed the attention tonight. But most of all, she'd enjoyed the loving looks Robert kept directing at her.

She turned to him. "I thought it went well. Don't

you? I mean, we did convince them, don't you think?" Goodness, why was she running on so? He would think her a regular babbler.

He reached over to pat her gloved hand. The first time he had ever offered her a touch in comfort, she thought.

"You were perfect, my dear. You should have gone upon the stage."

She laughed nervously. "I don't believe Papa would have approved of that."

"I suppose not," Robert agreed, laughter in his voice.

If only he could stay like this. Life would be so wonderful if he really loved her. But this was all make believe. No matter that it *felt* real. Tomorrow everything would be back to normal—painfully lonely normal.

The carriage came to a halt and Cranston turned to them. "I thank you for letting me share in your escapade."

"You're most welcome," Robert said. "We couldn't have done it without your help."

"Don't forget Christmas," Mercy cried. If he didn't come—

"I won't," he assured her. "I'll be there bright and early. And spend the day."

"Good," she said.

Cranston climbed out. "Good night," he called, as the carriage drove away.

Mercy leaned back. If only they could take Cranston home with them.

They rode in silence for some minutes. Well, what else had she expected? The ball was over. No more dancing. No more laughing together. She tried to see the expression on Robert's face, but the carriage lamps were too dim. A sigh welled up out of her and she couldn't quite stop it.

"Tired?" Robert asked.

"Yes," she said. "I didn't realize till now *how* tired." She felt limp as an old rag. But it wasn't from the dancing. It was because they were alone, and going home to the same old loneliness.

And then they *were* home. Robert climbed out and offered her his hand. She took it—and her fingers trembled. Strange, she'd been touching him all evening and she hadn't trembled. Well, only when Emerine had confronted them, and then only for a moment.

Robert escorted her into the house, waited while she gave her wraps to Stoddard and made her hellos to the dogs, and then went up the stairs with her. At her door, they stopped. She looked up into his dear face—and wished for the mistletoe. But it was downstairs, and there was no one here to pretend for.

"Thank you," Robert said. "For your plan. And for your brilliant execution of it."

"It was nothing."

"Yes, it was," he insisted. "And I thank you for it."

"You're welcome," she said, holding her breath, hoping, praying . . .

For a long moment they stood there. And then Robert said, "Good night," and turned away.

"Good night," she whispered over the lump in her throat, and after his door had closed behind him, "my love."

Chapter Eleven

On Christmas Eve, Mercy and Robert retired early, making their usual formal good nights. She would not cry, she told herself firmly. It was pointless. Besides, she should be grateful for all the good things in her life.

After Nancy helped her into her nightdress and was sent off to bed, Mercy sat down before her dressing table and took the pins from her hair. She picked up the silver-backed brush and began to brush. One. Two. Tomorrow Cranston would be coming.

Thank goodness. The week between the ball and Christmas Eve had passed so slowly. More than once she'd wished they'd never attended the ball at all. After all their laughing and dancing, after her feeling wonderfully special, the next day had been awful. Just as she'd feared, things had gone right back to the polite formality they had lived in before. And it was even harder than it had been. The laughter was gone from Robert's eyes and his mouth had reverted to its former grim line. And her happiness had fled.

It wasn't that she'd expected things to be different, though she *had* hoped. It was just that laughing and dancing with him had given her a glimpse of what might have been. And was once again beyond her reach.

But she'd made the preparations for Christmas, checking with Cook to discover Robert's favorites, and ordering a huge plum pudding. And she looked forward to Cranston's being there. Maybe Robert would laugh again—for a little while.

Thirty. Thirty-one.

A strange sound came from across the room. She turned to look. Athena was on her pallet and the noises were coming from her. Mercy got up and went over. It looked like the puppies were on their way. Mercy sank to her knees. "It'll be all right, girl. I'm here."

Some time later, Mercy raised a worried face to the clock in the corner. Six puppies squirmed beside Athena, but she was still struggling. No more puppies had arrived for some time, but Athena was still in labor.

Mercy looked at the connecting door. Robert wouldn't like being disturbed, but Athena was in trouble. Real trouble. She couldn't just let her suffer like that. She might even—Mercy patted her head. "I'm going to get Robert, girl. Don't worry. I'll be right back."

She pushed herself to her feet and straightened her dressing gown. There was no time for worrying about Robert's reaction. Athena needed help now.

Mercy raised a hand and rapped briskly on the connecting door. Once. Twice. Pray to God he wasn't sound asleep.

She raised her hand again. And the door opened. Robert stood there in his dressing gown, amazement on his face at the sight of her.

"It's Athena," she stammered. "The puppies are coming. But something's wrong. I don't know what to do and—"

"Let me see," he said, hurrying past her, Hannibal at his heels.

She followed them to Athena. After Hannibal sniffed Athena's nose, he went to a corner out of the way and sank down to wait. Then Robert knelt, patted Athena's head, and felt her heavy belly. Finally, he looked up, his face serious. "It's turned the wrong way."

She sank to her knees. "Can you—"

"I've delivered foals," he said, getting to his feet. He untied the belt of his dressing gown and stepped out of it, then rolled up the sleeves of his nightshirt, exposing strong well-muscled arms. "I'll have to turn it inside her."

"Will it—hurt her?" she asked, terror sounding in her voice.

Robert gazed into her eyes. "It may. But it has to be done. If we don't—"

"I understand," she said. "I'll hold her head."

"Then let's get to work." And he got back on his knees. In doing so, he exposed his scarred leg. She averted her eyes. It wasn't kind to stare at the injury that had ruined his life.

She watched his hands instead. They were so gentle, so tender as he worked with Athena. "Easy, girl," she whispered. "Robert will help you. Easy now."

Robert gave Mercy a glance. He'd seen her look

at his leg and then quickly away. But he couldn't worry about that now. The dog was in bad shape and Mercy's pale face told him she knew it. She loved this dog. He had to save her. The pup too, if he could.

Breathing a silent prayer, he went to work.

It was near midnight when he finally got the last pup delivered and took care of the afterbirth. He sat back on his heels and breathed a sigh of relief. Then he looked up into Mercy's worried face. "She should be all right now."

He got to his feet. "I'll just go wash up and—"

"Use my basin," she said, her voice hesitant. "I—I wish you could stay a little longer. Just in case—"

"Of course." He crossed the room to her basin and pitcher. When he finished washing and turned, she was holding his dressing gown open for him. She couldn't stand the sight of his leg now that the dog was all right. He slipped into it and pulled the belt tight.

"Thank you," she said. "Thank you so much. I was awfully worried."

"I think they'll be all right now," he said. "All of them. You should get to bed too."

"I suppose so. But I won't be able to sleep. Could you look at the puppies now that she's got them cleaned up? Just once more?" She put a hand on his sleeve.

"Of course," he said. She was being kind to him because he'd saved her beloved dog. Well, beggars couldn't be choosers. He'd take what kindnesses he could get from her.

He stood beside her, gazing down at the puppies.

Athena finished cleaning the last one and looked up at him with grateful eyes. He leaned down to ruffle her ears. "You did a good job, girl," he said. Hannibal came to his side and nosed his hand. He chuckled and ruffled his ears too. "You did a good job too," he said.

"Oh dear," Mercy breathed. "The littlest one has a twisted leg."

Anger swept over Robert, huge irrational waves of anger. All that work and worry—and for a cripple whose life wouldn't be worth anything. Bile rose to choke him and he blurted out, "I'll have him destroyed." He started to reach out. The sooner the better.

Mercy grabbed his arm with the strength of ten, outrage on her pale face. "You'll do no such thing! How can you even suggest it?"

"He's crippled," he said patiently. "He's better off dead."

She glared at him. "That's the most ridiculous thing I've ever heard."

"I know what it is to have a twisted leg," he said. "It's miserable. My leg ruined my life."

"That's plain stupid!" she cried, her eyes blazing with righteous anger. "With love that puppy will be just as happy as the others. And as for you—what's wrong with you isn't your leg. It's your *head*. The stupid way you think. Just because that Emerine doesn't love you, you act like your life is over." Her bosom heaving, tears rolling down her cheeks, she glared at him. "There are other women who could love you. Who *do* love you!"

Her eyes widened and she covered her face with

her hands and turned away, her shoulders heaving with sobs.

His heart almost beat its way out of his chest. She couldn't mean . . . He limped after her, took her by the shoulders and turned her to him. "Mercy? Look at me."

She raised her tear-stained face. "Did you mean that?" he asked. "Did you mean that *you* love me?"

She nodded, her face a study in misery.

"But I thought—the way you looked at my leg—I thought it disgusted you."

"Oh no!' " she cried. "You were wounded fighting for your country. That only makes me—love you more." She shuddered, her bottom lip trembling. "I'm sorry. I shouldn't have—"

"Oh yes, you should," he said, and he pulled her into his arms.

"But—" Her voice was muffled against his chest.

"I love you," he said. "I've loved you almost since the day I married you."

She looked up at him with disbelieving eyes. "But you never said anything, you were so cold."

"I was afraid," he said, looking into the loving eyes so near his own. "I thought my leg made you pity me."

She reached up and kissed his cheek. "Never, Robert. I couldn't pity you. I've loved you since I was six years old. I'm surprised you couldn't tell."

"I've been blind," he said. "But no more." And he bent and kissed her right and proper.

"Oh, Robert," she said. "I can scarcely believe—"

"Believe," he said, loath to let her out of his arms. "Let's check the pups and Athena once more and then I'll prove it to you." He smiled at the look of delight on her face. "We'll become man and wife in reality—tonight."

"Oh yes!" she cried. "Yes! That will be the loveliest Christmas gift I've ever had."

Hannibal watched them go off into Master's chamber, their arms around each other's waists, leaving the connecting door wide open. At last.

Moving closer to Athena, he curled up beside her. He gave her ear a lick and she raised her head and licked him back. Then he put his head down on his paws and watched her clean their puppies.

She was paying special attention to the little one, the one with the twisted leg. Good little fellow, Hannibal thought. He gave the pup a few comforting licks himself. That pup had already done a great thing, bringing Master and Mercy together like he had. Hannibal snuggled closer to Athena's back. Yes, Athena was right. All the little one needed was love. That was all anyone needed.

AWAY IN A SHELTER

SHELTER

ANNIE KIMBERLIN

*To Leslie, a confirmed cat person
(thanks Ann and Roni for being late).*

*Special thanks to Janet Kupay and to
Cheryl Holloway.*

A portion of the author's royalties supports THE COMPANY OF ANIMALS, a nonprofit agency that distributes grants to animal welfare agencies providing emergency and ongoing care to companion animals throughout the United States.

Chapter One

"Well, hello there. Who are you?"

The answer was a frantic wagging of tail as the little dog pulled and strained against the rope tying her to the door handle of the Greene County Animal Shelter. Camille knew the policy about stray dogs, but technically this was not a stray. *Splitting hairs again, Counselor?* she asked herself.

"No," she whispered out loud to no one. The little dog seemed to be looking into her soul, pleading, begging for its life, as if it knew the fate awaiting it. How could she deny this dog a chance? "I'm not splitting hairs," she continued, her whisper an odd juxtaposition to the whining and whimpering of the little dog. "I'm simply breaking a rule. Blatantly. With knowledge and deliberate forethought. Giving a dog a chance, in the first degree."

Softening her posture to show friendliness, Camille knelt down on the steps, which were dusted with early-morning snow, to pet the dog. "I can pet you better if you hold still," she told the wiggling dog. "Someone just tied you up here and left you?

How rude of them. You are such a nice . . . um . . .
dog." She snuck a quick peek at the dog's underside.
"What a pretty girl you are. I bet you're hungry, a
skinny little short-haired thing like you. And cold
too." Camille could feel the little dog, now pressed
to her leg, trembling.

"We need to get you inside, make you warm and
give you breakfast. Let me untie this rope so you
can come with me."

The rope was frosty, making the knot difficult to
undo. Camille peeled off her driving gloves and
went back to work at it with her cold fingers. After
several tries, she held her fingers up to her mouth
to blow on them, warming them up before another
assault on the knot. Whoever had left this dog here
could tie knots brilliantly. She glanced down the
steps to the walk. Except for her footprints, the
snow was undisturbed. That meant the little dog
had been here for several hours, while it snowed.
At least it wasn't the bitter cold and driving snow
that had been predicted for later in the morning.

The little dog sat at attention, tail still swishing
joyously. Her eyes were trained on Camille's face
and contained an expression very akin to worship,
as if she knew this big person was her savior. Camille smiled into the little dog's eyes, acknowledging
the worship, and confirming, with her face, that
everything would be all right. "As soon as I get this
wretched knot out. Okay, girl. I'm going to give it
one more try and then I'll have to haul out my trusty
Swiss Army knife."

After a few more seconds of futile attempts on
the knot, she pulled out her knife and went to work
on the loop around the door handle. "I should have

done this to begin with. Even this knot is no match for the Swiss Army Knife Lady," told the little dog as she held up the cut end in triumph. "Let's go." She pulled the key out of her purse, then unlocked the plate glass door.

The little dog had no hesitation about following her into the building, down the hall to the volunteer office. Even if Camille hadn't been holding on to the rope she probably would have stuck close as glue, and she was completely at ease. The little dog's toenails clicked on the tile floor. It was a cheerful sound, but it meant her toenails needed trimming.

Hanging up her winter parka and setting her purse on the desk, Camille stooped down to examine the dog more closely. She stood about sixteen inches high at the shoulder, and had the very fine bone structure and leggy look of a sighthound. This might account for the skin-and-bones look, she thought. Sighthounds had been bred for speed and therefore carried not an ounce of fat. Yet the muzzle was too boxy, too square for a sighthound. In fact, she had a scenthound's head, complete with typically pendulous ears—ears that, when nose was to the ground, swept and stirred up the scent, making the track easier to follow. Right now that nose was sniffing out the corners of the small room. Her coat was short and flat, solid rusty gold—like a vizsla, Camille noted, but her eyes were dark and rimmed with black, unlike that breed. And her tail was long, not docked as were the tails of many hunting dogs. All in all, she looked surprisingly elegant and refined.

"Where did you come from?" Camille wondered out loud.

At the sound of her voice, the little dog bounded over to her, throwing herself recklessly at Camille, obviously expecting enthusiasm in return. She got it.

He recognized that voice. He'd know that voice anywhere. *And run from it every time.* Roger Matheson grimaced. This time he was stuck. He'd told Casey, the volunteer coordinator, he'd work over the Christmas holidays. After all, he wasn't going anywhere, not doing anything special. Most important, he was between projects, his last computer game had been shipped off and the design plan for his new project wasn't due for a couple of weeks. So when Casey had asked him to be one half of the kennel team for the week, he'd agreed. He'd not thought to ask who the other half would be. He should have.

"Such a pretty dog, fair of face and full of grace. In fact, Grace is a perfect name for you."

The woman's voice carried to Roger. Precise tones, careful enunciation, a voice that reeked of elocution lessons and snobbery. And the woman was a lawyer, of all things. Wasn't it Shakespeare who'd said, "The first thing we do, let's kill all the lawyers"? A dozen lawyer jokes flashed through his mind. Most of them had to do with sharks, or highways with no skid marks. She was probably volunteering at the animal shelter because it made a good public impression. Or maybe it was supposed to work off her karma. Penance for being a lawyer. Though possibly just *being* a lawyer was penance enough.

Be fair, his conscience chided him. *You've never*

talked to the lady, only seen her at volunteer meetings. Casey said she's very bright and nice.

Well, he answered back. *That doesn't mean a thing. Casey loves everyone, just like a dog who was well socialized as a puppy.*

Maybe when he started the design work on his next game the villain would be a lawyer. A lady lawyer.

She heard footsteps in the hall. *The other volunteer,* she thought. The person with whom she'd be spending at least two hours each morning and evening of the holiday week. The little dog—Grace, she mentally corrected herself—must have heard the footsteps too, for she sprang up on her toes, her whole being alert and waiting, neck stretched out.

It was that big guy, she thought as she gazed at him standing in the doorway. Disappointment welled up inside her. Of all the volunteers, why did it have to be the big guy? The one who always looked at her as if she were a pariah. He probably wasn't even aware that she recognized that look. But she had spent much of her childhood being treated as an outcast by the other kids at school. Even when the teachers had admonished them to be nice it was there, that attitude that she was less than they. It had been covered up, hidden from the adults, but Camille had seen it in the way they held their shoulders, their heads. It had been as clear to her as if they were shouting it. But the teachers had not noticed, because the children used their bodies, not their words.

Grace, however, had no such misgivings. She trained her eyes on the man, stiffening for one second as if she were coming to a decision. Then she launched her skinny self toward him, whimpering and wiggling in delight as if he were a long-lost brother. Grace obviously loved everyone, even the big guys of the world.

He tossed his coat on the desk, then stooped down to pet the dog, accepting her licks and whines. *Pet* was not the right word, though. He touched, caressed, fondled her head, communicating in that special way that only someone who knows dogs can do. He totally focused on Grace, murmuring to her, chuckling when she slurped her tongue around his face.

"Very nice dog. Is she yours?" His voice was deep and round, the sound resonant and calm. He let his words go, without holding on to them in his throat or at the front of his mouth. It was the kind of voice Camille could listen to forever. What a tragedy it belonged to the big guy. There really was no justice in the world.

"Evidently someone abandoned her here in the middle of the night. When I arrived a few minutes ago, I found her tied to the door."

He frowned up at her.

"There were no footprints in the snow when I arrived," she explained. "So whoever it was must have left her before the snow started to fall. Last night the weather forecasters predicted the snow would begin by about four o'clock in the morning."

"Elementary, dear Watson?"

"What?" It was her turn to frown. Did she hear a hint of sarcasm in that round voice of his?

He must have realized he sounded on the edge of rude. He had the manners to slightly avert his face, returning his attention to the dog. "I meant that you're particularly analytical."

Not knowing if he was insulting her or complimenting her, she chose to assume the positive. After all, the two of them would be working together for the coming week. Any irritations between the two of them would be picked up by the cats and dogs at the shelter. The animals wouldn't know *what* the discomfort was, only that it existed, and it might worry them. They deserved better than that. "Thank you. I do tend to pay attention to details."

She settled down cross-legged on the floor. "Come here, Gracie," she coaxed the dog. "Let me finish looking at you."

Grace quickly abandoned the big guy—what a smart puppy—and landed in Camille's lap.

"I'm going to look at your teeth now. This won't hurt." Camille lifted the soft golden folds of her mouth.

"Gracie?" Camille could almost hear the big guy lift an eyebrow.

"Grace," Camille asserted, taking a final peek at lovely puppy teeth before letting go of the soft muzzle and glancing at him. "Her name is Grace. Because she once was lost and now she's found," she explained when the big guy continued to look at her in confusion.

"You named her?"

"Yes. I gave her a name. She deserves a name." Camille rolled the little dog gently over to examine the inside of her thighs for a tattoo. The skin was pale and unmarked. She let the puppy roll over again. "Look, I untied her from the front door, brought her in. I know that according to county policy, all stray dogs and cats are to be turned over to the dog warden. I am going to ignore the policy." Still holding on to the puppy, she stretched her arm to open the desk drawer and feel around for the scanner. Ah, there it was. She drew it out. The scanner was about the size of a telephone receiver. "It's a crummy policy, by the way, and ought to be seriously revised." She pushed the "on" button. Slowly, she circled it over the back of Grace's neck, listening for the beeps, and watching for the number display that would signify an identification microchip. "No chip. I also know that we are not supposed to become emotionally involved with any of the cats and dogs that come through. I am also going to ignore that rule. Of course, it's an unspoken rule, so it's not legally binding." She set the scanner deliberately back in the drawer, then glared at him, just to make sure he got her point, daring him to argue.

He didn't move, yet his very lack of motion was alive, full of vibrancy, the pause of a stalking wolf just before he makes the final leap upon his prey.

"I've just looked at her teeth," Camille continued. Even though she was sitting as arrow-straight as possible, and he was stooped down, balancing on his toes, he seemed to loom over her. "She hasn't any of her adult teeth yet, so she's probably between five and six months old. Her color is good, her eyes are bright. Her ears are not hot, so she probably does not have a fever. She shows no sign of any illness, so I'm going to feed her. When the appropriate time comes, I'll save a stool sample so Dr. March can test for parasites. Grace is exceptionally skinny, possibly because she may be part sighthound, but she could also be skinny from worms, or just plain neglect." Her body language was very defensive, even from a sitting position. And she was well aware of it.

"Whoa!" he held up his hands in surrender. "I sure got your dander up. I didn't mean to. I'm sorry." He put a hand down on the floor to better his balance.

The expression in his eyes looked almost sincere. It was still shuttered, but there was sincerity in the way he held his head, his shoulders.

"I'm sorry also." She lowered her defensive tone, not all the way, but enough for civilities. "I don't believe we've ever been introduced. I'm Camille Campbell." She stuck out her hand, but their gazes found each other first, and held.

His hand was rough, warm and as large as the rest of him. Her hand was dropped as soon as courtesy allowed. "I'm Roger Matheson. Nice to meet you." His voice matched her formal tones.

Still their gazes held. She knew that he was doing the same thing she was, evaluating, sizing up, learning which one of them would be the pack leader. Camille liked being in charge, liked leading, was not good at either following or getting out of the way. She did not want him to think that he could order her around during their work together. She knew how to care for the animals. She needed orders from no one. Especially from the big guy.

Evidently he felt exactly the same way, because he did not break eye contact either. She realized he knew exactly what she was thinking. He also was aware of pack behavior.

With gazes still locked, he nodded slightly, acknowledging her authority—not her authority over him, but the power that comes with being an alpha bitch, in the good sense of the word. She gave a slight nod back, acknowledging his power. Eye contact was broken as they looked away at the same time. Neither of them lost face.

"So what are we going to do with her?"

"Do?" she repeated. "What we're *not* going to do is turn her over to the animal control people. It's not her fault she's been abandoned. I bet the people probably would have stayed to do all the paperwork, but"—her quick mind was in action—"they had to leave town in the middle of the night for a family emergency. They left a letter explaining all of it to us, but the wind blew it away, along with the blanket they left with her. Very warm blanket."

"And the dog dishes full of food and water?"

"Yes. And even a chew toy." She stuck out her chin, and ignored his sarcasm. Just let him try to take Grace away from her. She'd find some way to prevent it. There would be some loophole somewhere, she was good at finding loopholes.

"You're right." His voice, all sarcasm gone, brought her back to the little dog. "She is a skinny little thing. Sighthound you think? Maybe she's just anorexic."

It was a truce. Of sorts.

"She does not appear to be anorexic." In spite of herself Camille found herself smiling at the joke. "I do think sighthound—perhaps whippet, the size and coat are right—but only half. I think she may also be part vizsla. Look at her color, and the way she stands up high on her toes, nice tight toes. Great in a vizsla."

"Look at her ears, they look more scenthound. Or are they vizsla as well? I'm not familiar with some of the hunting dogs."

"What do you think it is?" was a never-ending discussion around the many mixed breeds who passed through the Greene County Animal Shelter. Sometimes the mother's breed was known, but the paternity was a great mystery. Yet it was more than idle chatter on the part of the shelter workers. It was important to make the best possible match between the dogs and their new homes. For instance, there were breeds that were well known to love children, and breeds who were nervous around them. Some breeds would probably get along fine with the family cat, other breeds would probably see it as prey.

Camille found it was easy, talking to him about the dog. Easier than she'd ever have imagined, if she'd ever imagined herself talking to the big guy, which she hadn't. No, she'd not thought of him at all. She reminded herself that she hadn't thought of him after the meeting of the shelter volunteers, a couple of weeks ago when she'd started volunteering. She hadn't thought of the way his eyes hardened almost imperceptibly when his gaze fell on her. Probably someone else wouldn't have noticed it, but she was very conscious of body language. But she hadn't thought about it at all. She really hadn't.

"So she wants to name you Grace, eh?" he asked the little dog.

Grace promptly rolled on her back to provide access to her tummy for scratching. He obliged. From her upside-down position, her lips fell back, giving her a silly grimace.

201

Not to be left out, Camille slid her hands under Grace's head to cradle it while she rubbed her velvety ears, and to unwind the rope that was still attached to her collar. Camille stroked the fur under Grace's chin, fur that was as soft as a whisper. It was a marvel that such softness could exist outside of poetry, or a dream.

"But I think," he continued, his voice gentle and intimate when he spoke to the dog, "that we ought to call you Splinter. Because you're so skinny. Or maybe Annie, for anorexic."

"That's a horrible name," Camille protested, her voice pitched low so she wouldn't startle Grace. "Both of them are horrible names." Still, if he was willing to put a name with Grace it meant he might be willing to forget that she was a stray. The big guy would forget the policy for a little dog. Yet Grace was not just any old dog. Grace was special.

"It's a perfect name, isn't that right, Splinter?"

Grace wriggled in delight as he reached her itchy spot, her hind foot starting its rhythmic pumping against air.

"Her name is Grace," Camille insisted.

"Nah," he countered, his attention still on the little dog, almost as if he were ignoring Camille. "It's Splinter. Isn't it girl?"

Grace was obviously willing to agree to anything, Camille thought sourly. Well, she wouldn't give the big guy the satisfaction of an argument. She had a dog that needed to be fed.

"Well, I am going to take her"—she purposely didn't use Grace's name—"to the kennels to get some breakfast. She needs a good meal."

The big guy gave Grace a final scratch, then

stood. His height as well as his size was imposing. Camille refused to be intimidated.

"Then why don't you do the dog runs as well, and I'll take care of the cat wing."

While it was couched as a suggestion, it felt like an order. Her first instinct was to refuse. However, if she protested, she'd end up doing the cat wing and he'd end up with the dogs—and Grace. If she agreed, she would be tacitly acknowledging his right to be in charge. Well, she wasn't a lawyer for nothing. She knew how to play this game. She stood also, pinning him with her gaze.

"While you're taking care of the cat wing," she said, "be sure to empty the used litter bin into the Dumpster. It was nearing full yesterday."

A slight twitch of his lips told her he recognized what she'd done.

"Sure. See you later, Splinter."

He nodded briefly to her, then was out the door.

"Roger," she called. His name felt unfamiliar to her.

He stuck his head back inside. "Yeah?"

"Thanks."

In the brief flash that their eyes met, she could almost imagine she saw a smile.

"You're welcome."

"Hello, little snugglefritz," he crooned to a little black-and-white kitten as he cuddled her in one hand. He held her against his cheek, feeling the vibrations of her purr as he slid the bowl of food into her cage. "You'd rather play face than eat. Isn't that right, little thing? Well you go right ahead and purr. Yes, I like you too. Such a tiny thing, all alone in the world."

He'd long ago quit wondering why they ended up at the shelter. When he first started volunteering, he wanted to know the story of every cat and dog that came in. Then, the day after the staff brought in a number of dogs who'd been found surviving in utter filth in the basement of a senile old man—the dogs in such unspeakably horrible condition that half of them had to be put to sleep—he practically went crazy with rage. Casey, the volunteer coordinator, found him repeatedly pounding his fist into the brick wall. She took him out for a walk. She listened. Then she gave him some advice he'd learned to live by. Becoming emotionally attached to the cats and dogs that came through was to ask for a punch in the gut. Over and over and over again. It could only mean burnout—or a callous approach to the critters. Neither one was a good thing. The best way to deal with it was to live in the present. They were here, they were safe, they were warm and fed. Take care of them, give them affection, and know that you're helping them find their way to a wonderful home.

Yeah, he was a sucker for kittens—and puppies. For baby anythings. Especially furry baby anythings. If he could afford it, he'd take home all the dogs and cats in the shelter. They could all live with him on his farm. Sure. Somehow he thought that even Karen would raise an eyebrow at that—and Karen of all people had no right to question his rescuing a dog. Even fifty-something dogs. Not to mention all the cats.

"Maybe I'll put a black-and-white kitten into my next game, eh? Would you like to become immortalized in a computer game? Maybe the black-and-white kitten will vanquish the evil nasty lawyer."

The kitten rubbed her cheek against his, her ears springing up and flicking his nose.

"But you know, little one, the lady lawyer isn't as evil and nasty as I thought she'd be. I thought she'd be stuck up. I mean, what kind of person wears designer clothes to clean out dog runs, hmm? You should see the silly little Santa pin on her sweater. Honestly, of all the impractical . . . Still, she seems to know something about dogs." It was a high compliment.

As for Splinter, Splinter was not the right dog for her. She should have a bichon frise, or a miniature poodle, something decorative that she could dye to match her clothes. Splinter was built for speed. If she were part vizsla, or even part sighthound, she probably had hunting instinct. She should be out in the country. She should be out on his farm, where there was an acre of rough field to explore. Sanner would have a great time showing Splinter all his favorite rabbit holes. In fact, Sanner would love a puppy to play with. It would liven him up in his dotage. They would be a matched set. The elderly Labrador and the young pup. He imagined them all on his couch, one on each side of him, in front of a crackling fire in his fireplace. It was a comforting picture.

Suddenly, the thought of Splinter spending her days and nights in the kennel at the shelter was unacceptable. She belonged with him. Instead of making something up to put on the paperwork—some cock-and-bull story about a family leaving a letter, hah!—he'd simply take her home. He realized how in those few moments he'd become quite attached to the skinny little dog.

He set the kitten back in her cage. "There you go, sweetie, eat your breakfast."

He watched the kitten discover her food and throw herself into the joy of eating, purring all the while.

As Roger went about the chores in the cat wing, feeding, cleaning, petting, bestowing hugs and kisses on all the cats—inmates, he called them—his thoughts returned again and again to the little black-and-white kitten. And also the rust-colored puppy. And also the high-and-mighty lady lawyer, who for some reason did not act as high and mighty as she appeared to be.

"Karen is right again," he told the little kitten as he passed her cage. "She always says I tend to make up my mind before I know all the facts. But we won't tell her about this time, will we?"

The kitten reached a paw through the bars of the cage, struggling to reach him. He leaned closer, so she could bat at his nose. "Do you like puppies? Rust-colored puppies with long skinny legs and ears as soft as yours are?"

He wondered if the lady lawyer liked kittens.

"Do you like kitties?" Camille asked Grace.

Grace leaned against Camille and thumped her tail on the floor, twisting her neck back so she could gaze adoringly at her savior.

"I guess that means you do. That's a good thing. Because someday soon I'm going to get a kitty. I know you'll like Phoebe. Everyone likes Phoebe. You're about the same age, same color." Was there anything in the agreement that said she couldn't have another puppy while she had Phoebe? She didn't think so, but she'd have to make sure. Or she'd have to find a way to convince them to make an exception, or find another loophole.

She realized that she'd already decided to take Grace home with her. No, she hadn't actually decided, there was no conscious thought about it. It was just a fact of life. Fish have to swim and birds have to fly, and Grace belonged with her. Simple as that.

"Okay Grace, here's the plan. You've had your breakfast, so I'm going to put you in this run, and you're going to stay there while I feed the rest of the dogs. See, there's a beagle for a next-door neighbor on this side, and a little puppy on this side. Maybe you can swap stories. You'll have fun." She raised the latch, opened the door, and scooted Grace in. Grace was not convinced.

"Guard the kennel, Grace," she said in a breezy, casual tone as she lowered the latch on the door to the run and fastened it with a snap.

Grace pawed at the door and whined piteously.

"None of that now. You'll be just fine." Camille kept her voice very matter-of-fact. "I'll be right here, taking care of all these other dogs. If I coddle you you'll think there really is something to be worried about. And there isn't."

There was a full house this morning, Camille noted. Luckily there was an empty run for Grace to borrow. The fifty-four dogs here were lucky as well. At least they had a warm place where they were fed. Lots of dog food, she thought as she scooped out bowl after bowl of the stuff.

"It's soup!" she called out to the dogs as she started down the first aisle of the kennel. In just a few short minutes the air was vibrating with the cheerful sound of kibble crunching and bowls banging against the bars of the kennels as the very last crumb was searched out and devoured.

Camille whistled a sprightly made-up tune as she began to clean the dog runs. She raised the doors to let the dogs into the outer runs, then lowered the doors to hose down the insides with anti-bacterial cleaner. Next she raised the doors, to bring the dogs into their newly cleaned inside runs. Then she'd close them inside to clean the outside of the runs. In came the houndy little thing, then the two furry mixes, side by side, then the Dobe. She made her way down the runs to the beagle, Grace's next-door neighbor. The beagle came in with her tail wagging, full of cheer. Such a nice little dog would undoubtedly find a family soon.

Camille patted the beagle through the bars, then moved to the next run. She pulled the rope that opened the dog door. "Gracie, girl," she called. "Come inside, my pretty Grace."

No Grace.

"Gracie!" she called again.

Still no Grace.

Her heart beginning to pound, and not bothering about her coat, Camille made her way to the door that led to the outside of the runs. She opened it and pushed. The wretched thing was stuck. She firmly kicked it with the toe of her boot. It opened.

Camille hurried outside to the back of the runs. She held on to a post as she rounded the corner. The newly fallen snow was slippery.

Grace's run was empty.

Grace was gone.

Chapter Two

Heart in her throat, Camille assessed the situation. Fact: The latch wasn't undone, and the clip, which prevented a dog from jumping up and opening the gate with its nose, was still properly attached. Fact: Only someone with opposable thumbs could have opened the latch, let Grace out, then latched the gate again. Fact: The only way into this yard was through the doors at either end of the dog wing, or over the high brick wall and across the grass. Fact: There were no tracks in the pristine snow that frosted the yard. However, there were footprints in the snow outside the run, leading to and from the door at the far end. The footprints were too big to be hers. Fact: Besides herself, there was only one other person at the Shelter today.

Given the facts of the case, there could be only one conclusion. The most likely guilty party is the big guy. No, she reminded herself, his name is Roger. He was actually nice this morning, and he did seem to like Grace a lot. He probably came over to keep her company. In fact, that's probably why she'd heard the dogs doing a canine rendition of the "Hallelujah Chorus" while she was hosing down the inside runs. He probably took Grace over to the cat wing for a short visit. Of course, it was against the rules for dogs to visit the cats, as there was a high probability for upsetting all four-footed parties involved.

So find Roger and she'd find Grace. After chores were finished.

She told herself she felt better after this realization. Right now all the other dogs needed her attention. Grace was probably perfectly safe, even with the big—Roger. But "probably" never won a case, Counselor, she reminded herself. A sudden feeling of unease crept over her. She hurried through the rest of her chores. Without whistling.

They weren't in the cat wing. They weren't in any of the offices, or the training room, or the small auditorium, or the staff lounge. The only place she'd not looked was the men's washroom. She would forego that dubious pleasure, she thought in irritation. In fact, she was more than irritated. She was becoming worried. Where had he taken her dog—without permission? And why? What if something was wrong with Grace?

A look in the cat wing revealed that the cat chores had been completed. The used litter barrel was empty, so he'd even dumped the old litter. "Regular superman," she muttered to a black-and-white kitten in a cage.

The kitten rubbed against the metal bars, then stuck out one paw to gently pat her on the cheek.

"Hello, sweet little thing. I wish I had time to

spend with you right now, but that old big guy"—
she refused to use his name—"stole my skinny little
dog and I don't know where to find her."

The kitten sat down primly in the center of the
cage, wrapped its tail around its feet and regarded
her with that unblinking stare peculiar to cats.

She ran through the back part of the building
again. Still no Grace. Then she pushed through the
heavy double doors into the administrative offices.
Her footsteps echoed in the empty halls.

He wouldn't have left and taken Grace. Not without asking her first. That would be reprehensible.

She reached the front doors with their full windows.

She could see the crushed snow in the parking
lot where his truck had been parked. Past tense.
Had been. There was no truck. There were fresh
tracks.

Evidently the big guy—never again, she vowed,
would she call him by his name—was reprehensible.

"Here we are, Splinter girl. Back at the shelter.
But don't worry, this is just a visit."

He heard her wagging tail hit an old hamburger
wrapper.

He didn't dare take his eyes off the road. Even in
his truck, the falling snow made it slow going.
Deepening snow and pitch black outside—at 5:30,
the sun, what there'd been of it today, had been
down for a good hour. As he pulled into the un-
plowed parking lot, his headlights swept across the
expanse of white. The lady lawyer wasn't here yet.

"I'm going to carry you in, little girl. It looks like

211

the snow is over your head." He tucked the little dog under his arm as he threw some oomph at the truck's door until it opened. He stepped out, and the snow was over his boots.

He should've brought his snowshoes, he thought, as he floundered his way up the sidewalk, then the steps to the front door. At least Splinter didn't struggle in his arms. Good girl. He pulled a glove off with his teeth, then fumbled in his pocket for the key. He had to trample down the snow in front of the door until it could open. Before he left this evening, he'd have to shovel the sidewalk between the parking lot and the shelter. If the forecast held and it continued to snow all evening and into tomorrow there'd be too much snow by morning to shovel easily. Not that it would be an easy task right now. The snow was already almost knee deep. "Good thing I ate my Wheaties for breakfast," he told Splinter. "Makes me big and strong."

Splinter, still in his arms, twisted her neck to look at him with a gaze that held pure adoration and admiration.

Just as he got the shelter door opened, he heard a car engine coming in the long driveway. "I bet that's the lady lawyer," he told Splinter. He turned them around to look. "Yup. There she is." He pointed for Splinter, who followed the track of his arm. "If she's not careful she's gonna get stuck."

Splinter wagged her tail and slurped his chin.

The car continued to creep along the driveway, following the tracks made by his truck. When it reached the deeper snow in the parking lot it almost bottomed out. The car backed up, trying to find his tracks, then started to turn into the curb where the parking lines were a foot and a half under the white stuff. Halfway through the turn, the car came to an abrupt stop.

Roger, standing in the doorway of the shelter, couldn't see the lady lawyer in the car, but he could imagine her frustration. He heard the engine vroom, then the distinct squeal of tires spinning.

"She's stuck."

Roger sighed. "I was raised to be polite," he told the little dog. "Even to lady lawyers." He stuck Splinter inside the door of the shelter. "You wait here. I'll be back soon as I rescue the damsel." He shut the door firmly, ignoring Splinter's whines.

He was coming toward her, the reprehensible big guy. However, it appeared that she needed his help, so she consciously reminded herself to be polite. She'd had lots of practice being polite to people even when they were rude to her and her parents. She didn't want to wait for him in her car—that would be a psychologically submissive position—so she pulled on the door handle and gave it the normal slight shove. The door wouldn't open. She shoved harder, putting some shoulder in it. No deal. She rolled her window halfway down and was promptly hit in the face by a blast of snow.

"I seem to be stuck," she called, wiping her face with a mittened hand.

"That's an understatement," he returned, his voice easily carrying through the hushed gloom. "Don't hurt yourself trying to open your car door, you can't. The snow is too high. You'll have to come out the window."

She rolled the window the rest of the way down

so she could see for herself. The big guy was right. She would have to climb out the window. How ignominious, she thought ruefully. How undignified. She hoped the shelter had a shovel so she could dig out when chores were finished.

Then the big guy was at the side of her car. "Well, come on. Your car will be okay until we dig it out; it can't go anywhere. Snow's pretty deep here, I hope you have boots."

"Of course I have boots. They're in my trunk."

She wriggled herself until she was sitting on the window, her legs still inside the car.

"Give me your keys," he ordered. "I'll get them."

"Dumb place for boots," she heard him mutter as he tromped to the back of her car. Why did she feel defensive? He was no one important. She had no obligation to him. Except right now he was helping her.

"These wussy things are no good for snow," he announced, holding up the offending boots.

"Of course not," she answered pointedly. "They're for cleaning dog runs." She held out her hand to take them.

He rolled his eyes in derision, but passed the boots over.

"I suppose I'll have to carry you."

Not on your life, big guy, she said to herself as she slid the boots on over her shoes and fastened them with a snap. "I can manage," she said out loud. Swinging her feet out the window and at the same time keeping her balance took a bit of concentration. The snow was deeper than she'd thought. *Well,* she determined, *if you can wade through water, you can wade through snow, Camille.* She slid off the window into the snow. It was almost up to her knees.

"I'll follow in your tracks." She refused to make eye contact, instead staring ahead at the sidewalk, judging the distance. She winced as a cold clump of snow made its way down her boot to her foot. She'd never have made it to the South Pole with Scott or Amundsen.

She heard him snort.

For a moment she thought he was going to argue, but he merely headed back up the sidewalk.

What right did she have to be angry at him? he thought in disbelief. "What do you mean you never saw my note?" His voice was louder than he'd intended. Splinter lowered her head.

"Sorry, Splinter," he murmured to her. "I'm not angry at you."

The lady lawyer bent down and held out her hand. "Come here, Grace," she coaxed.

Without hesitation, the little dog struggled to get out of Roger's arms. When he set her down she scrambled over to the lady lawyer.

"Her name is Splinter."

He felt stabbed by her gaze. So this is what a baleful look is, he realized. He'd read the phrase, of course, he'd even used baleful looks in his games. The bad guys gave the good guys baleful looks. That was one way you knew that they were the bad guys. But until this moment, he'd never actually had a baleful look aimed at him. It gave him new insight into the feelings of his bad guys.

He decided to explain, trying not to appear humble. "I left you a note. It said I was taking Splinter home with me, and that this evening we would switch chores. You do the cats and I do the dogs." He'd made the assumption that they would not do the different wings together, as he'd have done with any other volunteer.

She raised an eyebrow at him. "Where did you leave this alleged note?"

Forget trying to explain. He matched her clipped tone. "The note is *not* alleged. I propped it up on the desk in the volunteer office. If you don't believe me, ask Splinter. She was with me when I wrote it."

He watched the lady lawyer press her cheek against Splinter's head. Splinter snuggled farther into her arms. Well, there was no accounting for taste. Still, the lady lawyer did have a shape that would be comfortable to snuggle into. She wasn't skinny. Women who were incredibly skinny were probably uncomfortable to cuddle with, all those unpadded bones would likely bruise a man. He liked to cuddle actively, with lots of touching and rubbing. Tonight was definitely a cuddle alert night. Too bad this lady lawyer was such a shrew. She should have a little shrewish dog, something equally disagreeable, to match. Pretty, but with a nasty temperament.

"Her name is Grace," she said insistently. "And unless dogs are specially trained, such as K-9 dogs, their testimony in court usually does not hold up. Besides, she's not an uninterested party. She's my dog."

Her dog, hah! he thought later, as he scooped out puppy food. The younger dogs, under a year old, were fed twice a day. The youngest puppies were

216

fostered out over the holidays so they could get more care. Over Thanksgiving he'd fostered two puppies that'd been brought in a week earlier. "Can't get rid of 'em," the woman had said, as if puppies were an unwanted nuisance, like fleas. Even though those two puppies had lived with him for four days, and were delightful little guys, he'd not felt that they Belonged—with a capital B—with him.

Splinter was different. As soon as he'd seen her he knew that she was his dog. She knew him also, he'd put money on it. Besides, when he brought her home that morning, Sanner had taken one sniff and had fallen in love. And at this point, whatever Sanner wanted, Sanner would have. He'd see to it.

So now this lady lawyer, who wore those useless elementary school red rubber boots, and Santa pins, and *makeup*, for Pete's sake, to do kennel chores, had the audacity to claim Splinter. Just because this morning she'd gotten here first.

He scooped half a cup more food into the bowl for Splinter. She could use the calories. He tossed the scoop back in the bin of puppy food and dropped the lid with a resounding bang.

That lady lawyer didn't know whom she was up against. He stopped his train of thought to reconsider the grammar here. Didn't know against whom she was up? No. Didn't know up against whom she was? He snorted. Grammar be damned, he was ready for a fight. Splinter was his dog.

His dog, indeed! He had absolutely no rights to Grace. Just the fact that he wanted to give her that ridiculous name should be enough to prove him un-

fit. And his voice, while it was round and smooth—
Camille allowed herself a single moment of regret,
for she truly did like the sound of his voice—it was
also somewhat lazy and casual, just like the rest of
his appearance. Why, he always looked as if he'd
slept in his clothes. His favorite item of clothing
appeared to be that ratty sweatshirt that said,
*"Never trust anyone who doesn't have dog hair on
their clothes."* He obviously trusted himself.

She slid a dish of food into the cage with the cute
black-and-white kitten and watched her turn into a
wild beast stalking its prey.

Mr. Big Guy had a lot to learn.

Splinter could learn so much from Sanner, Roger
thought. All day they'd stuck to each other like bur-
dock prickers to sweat pants. They'd washed each
other's faces, shared treats, played tag and tug. Before the snow had gotten too deep, Sanner had
shown Splinter all around the big field and together
they'd terrorized the local squirrel population.
Then they'd come back in, the snow giving them a
decidedly frosted-flakes look. Their tongues were
lolling out, and they had big silly grins on their
faces. After he dried them off, they'd slurped up all
the water in the bowl, then flopped down at his feet,
panting loudly. Yes, Splinter was a country dog, a
guy's dog.

The lady lawyer would probably get her a rhine-
stone collar and open an account at Phydeaux's Canine Bow-wow-tique.

He made sure the dogs were outside so he could
clean the inside of the runs. One by one, he jerked
down the rope that fastened each dog door. The re-

peated sound of metal crashing down on concrete was very satisfying.

Camille turned on the faucet with greater force than necessary. The water shot into the dishes and bounced off against the sides of the sink. A squirt of dish soap made huge lemon-scented bubbles. She smacked a blob of bubbles between her hands, smashing them. "Take that, you old bubbles," she muttered, thinking of the big guy. She grabbed the scrub brush and began scrubbing the dirty cat food bowls with a vengeance.

After he put the dogs inside and closed the dog doors again, Roger dragged the big hose outside. He really needed to cheer up. What better way could he have to spend Christmas Eve than by taking care of homeless dogs and cats? *Love and joy come to you,* he silently told the dogs as he turned on the water. *And send you a happy New Year. With a wonderful family for each of you.*

Even though he hadn't turned all the floodlights on, there was plenty of light. It bounced from the snow up to the cloud cover, and back down to earth. The rays of light were trapped, unable to escape the soft clutches of the snow. Hmmm. Sounded sort of hokey for a computer game. Still, the physics of it was something to think about.

The calm certainty of the laws of nature filled him, and suddenly he realized he wasn't angry at the lady lawyer any more. Of course she loved Splinter, who wouldn't? She obviously knew a quality dog when she saw one. And if she was able to see quality in a dog it meant that she was probably a true dog person. And if she were a true dog person, then he had to give her the benefit of the doubt. Even if she did wear silly little Santa pins and red rubber boots to clean out dog runs. So he'd have to find a logical way to make her realize that Splinter belonged to him. He'd appeal to her lawyerly sense of reason. Besides, getting into a dogfight about it would only upset the little dog.

Speaking of dogs—he had dog runs to hose down. Better get to it before the runs filled up with snow.

Then it hit him like a snowball middled with a hunk of ice.

The snow was decidedly heavier, and a brisk wind had picked up. *Blizzard,* he thought. The roads to his farm would be nasty, if they were even open. He checked his watch. Karen and Katie wouldn't be home yet. He'd wait a little while and then call to make sure they were all right and to check on the road conditions. At least Sanner wouldn't be home alone.

Finished with the cat chores, Camille trotted down the hall to the dog wing. A quick peek in the door assured her that the big guy was still outside. She slipped in, scanning the runs for Grace. There she was!

Grace saw her at the same instant, and her tail started quivering. She made little snuffle noises, and the beginnings of a whine.

"Shh!" Camille cautioned, fingers to her lips, as she fumbled with the snap on the latch. "It's all right. We're going home." She opened the run and scooped Grace up in her arms. "I'm going to take you home now. Going to dig out my car and take you home where you belong."

She turned to leave and was stopped short by the intense longing in the eyes of the puppy in the next run. The puppy also wanted to go home. "Take me home too," he said with his eyes, with his imploring posture. "Please take me, I want to go home too."

Tears rushed into Camille's eyes. "I can't," she whispered to the puppy. "I can't take you."

But the puppy stood up against the metal mesh of the run. His tail wagged furiously, not the wagging of joy, but the wagging of pleading. He was trying with all his might to convince Camille to take him too.

"I can't," she whispered again, the tears spilling over.

She wiped her eyes with the back of her hand, then gazed down the row of runs. Fifty-four pairs of doggy eyes begged her to take them. Fifty-four tails wagged hopefully. Straining through the chain-link mesh, several paws reached out to her in supplication. She stared at these fifty-four homeless dogs, each one of whom would make a terrific best friend for some lucky person. Fifty-four dogs, none of whom deserved to be here, but who were lucky enough to at least have the chance to be found by someone. The pain of it slugged her like an unwanted subpoena.

These dogs, their longing! She could feel it. She could feel their longing, fifty-four dogs strong. She could hear it in their soft whines, see it in their postures, their eyes. It was stronger than all the shouting in the world. How could she bear it? How could she go home knowing that these dogs had no home, no place to go to, no one to come home to them, no one to curl up next to on a couch. These dogs had concrete runs and dog blankets. A great sob welled up inside her. It was Christmas Eve, dammit, and these dogs had no home under the tree.

Holding on to Grace, as if holding on to life itself, with tears streaming, Camille leaned against the wall, for her legs could not hold her. She closed her eyes to escape from the longing, the home hunger, of the dogs. But there was no escape, not for the dogs, and not for her. She felt Grace twist around in her arms, and felt a little wet doggy nose nudge her cheek, then begin to lick the tears. It was Grace's way of trying to comfort her. One of the other dogs, probably the golden retriever, whined and whimpered, as if trying to comfort her as well.

She made herself open her eyes, to look at each dog. One by one. "I just can't take you home," she whispered to the puppy, with his incredibly winsome eyes. Then the shaggy little mutt, then the Dobe, the furry Shepherd mix.

A cry escaped from Camille's being, a cry for all the homeless dogs and cats in the world. "I'm sorry," she cried, her voice sounding ragged. "I'm truly sorry."

"Sorry for what?"

It was the big guy. Camille didn't even try to summon up the energy necessary for the antagonism between them. Not now. Not in front of these fifty-four dogs. She wordlessly shook her head and wearily closed her eyes against the big guy. She didn't care what he thought of her anymore. That was small potatoes next to what she read in the body language of the canine crew before her.

"Why are you sorry?" he repeated.

With a sigh shaky from unshed tears, she opened her eyes, also opening a gate in the wall between her and the big guy. "Sorry that I can't take them all home."

He reached out with one finger and stroked Grace's head. Grace thumped her tail against Camille's arm.

The big guy, his expression suddenly free of the disdain she'd always read there, looked to her. To her, not at her. As if she were a person of worth, not someone to tolerate. Then he nodded.

"Yeah, I know what you mean."

That round voice was warm and soft, the sound of it as well as the words offering her comfort. Somehow the fact that it was the big guy who had offered her such comfort wrenched her heart as much as the dogs' longing had. She leaned her head back and shook with silent sobs.

Suddenly she felt his arms go around her, felt herself, still holding Grace, enclosed in his arms.

He didn't say anything, just held her, allowing her to cry. He knew what was happening, for it had happened to him as well. She needed to cry, to let it out, to get rid of it. Careful not to crush Splinter in her arms, he held the lady lawyer, one hand tracing a small circle on her back, her sweatshirt soft against his fingers. In fact, she was soft all over and just as comfortable as he'd thought she'd be. Her hair smelled of something elusively fragrant. And the night was still young.

C'mon, Roger, he chided himself. *The lady is going through an emotional wringer and you're thinking lascivious thoughts about her. That's really rude.* But still, those lascivious thoughts, once they'd lodged themselves into his head, wouldn't budge. *You're not trying very hard*, he taunted himself. Still, something would be very hard and very soon unless some changes were made. He decided to make them.

"Let's go back into the office and I'll make you a cup of hot chocolate and we'll talk."

He shifted his body so that he had an arm still around her, but they were side by side as he slowly walked her to the door and down the hall. By the time they reached the office, her sobs had lessened to some pretty hefty sniffles. It was with reluctance that he removed his arm from around her.

He opened a drawer in the desk and pulled out a box of tissues. "Here." He held them out to her. "There're lots more, so don't skimp. You and the hound sit down on the couch. I'll be right back. I'm just going to fill the pot with water."

She lowered her head to rub her cheek against Grace's warm fur. Grace made a contented grunting noise. Oddly enough, Camille reflected, she was content also. The big guy might be nice after all. Of course, she'd thought that this morning, and then he'd kidnapped Grace. Still, in all fairness she had to admit that he had brought her dog back. And now he was being very kind to her. A new flood of tears rushed forth, and she yanked a handful of tissues from the box.

"Here." He was back, two steaming mugs in his hand, a somewhat serious expression on his face. She reached for the proffered mug. The homey scent of hot chocolate drifted about them.

"Careful, sweetie, you'll burn your tongue."

Camille started, then realized he was talking to Grace. For Grace was evidently very interested in hot chocolate.

"No chocolate for you, Gracie, it's toxic for dogs," she added, her voice clogged with her tears.

Grace licked her lips in anticipation.

"She's obviously used to handouts," the big guy commented.

"Yes," Camille agreed. "She has the starving waif routine down pat."

"Let's not disappoint her." The big guy opened a cabinet and produced a dog cookie. "Look here, sweetie," he crooned, holding the cookie out.

Gracie was off Camille's lap in a flash, bounding up and down in front of the big guy. She leapt straight up, almost as high as his chest. The big guy's whole demeanor changed. He was In Charge.

"Sit." His voice was firm, a voice that would accept nothing but complete obedience.

Grace sat, though it was obvious that she was not in favor of the idea.

"Good girl," the big guy praised her. "Okay," he said in the tone of voice dog trainers use when they're releasing a dog from a command. He tossed the cookie up in the air. Grace leaped straight up and caught it.

Camille's eyes opened wide. "What a terrific Frisbee dog," she breathed. "And she already knows how to sit."

The big guy shifted his attention to her, and Camille realized that her nose was probably a dead ringer for Rudoph's, her eyes were undoubtedly swollen, her cheeks stained and stiffened from her tears. She'd never managed to learn how to cry gracefully. But he merely studied her for a split second that lasted an eternity. Then he nodded almost imperceptibly. Camille felt as if he'd praised her also. It made her unaccountably happy.

"You're right." He reached down to stroke Grace's head while she crunched away at her cookie. "She has the makings of a first-rate Frisbee dog. She has the build for it, and the agility."

Talking about simple things, pleasant things, felt nice, she thought. Wait a minute. The big guy was doing it on purpose, she realized in wonder. He was giving her a chance to regain her composure. Dammit. She was going to start crying again. Just because he was being nice to her when she'd been so very upset. What a silly reason to cry.

She reached for yet another tissue. "I'm afraid I'm going to use them all up."

"Well, think about it this way," he suggested, his foot scooting the trash can to the side of the couch. "You have justified their existence, and you have fulfilled their purpose in life. You have given them the opportunity to meet their intended fate. Think how relieved they must be to know that they're not going to end up wrapped around a cut finger or something equally inglorious." He handed Grace another cookie. She closed her eyes in bliss as she crunched.

Camille chuckled through her tears. "Or ending up crumpled and unused in the pocket of someone's winter coat."

"Or lying smashed in the glove compartment of a car that's ended up in the junkyard. Now that would really be awful for a tissue. Not a teary eye in sight."

She gave him a watery smile. "Thank you, Roger."

"You're welcome," he answered softly. He settled down on the couch next to her.

"You probably think I'm silly."

"Not at all." It was said with great seriousness. "It gets all of us sooner or later. It bothers the hell out of us because we care so much about them. If we didn't care it wouldn't bother us. But then we wouldn't be much help to them, would we? But then again, if we didn't care about them, we wouldn't be here in the first place."

"I guess not," she admitted. She was fascinated by the way he could switch gears so quickly. One minute he was joking about the consciousness of tissues, the next minute he was helping her understand what she was feeling. He had a very expressive face, she realized. And he used his hands for emphasis a lot when he talked. It was familiar to her. *I like him*, she realized suddenly. *I really like him.*

"We're truly lucky here, at this shelter, to have a terrific staff and a group of volunteers who care about the cats and dogs as much as we all do." He handed Grace another cookie. "That's the last one, girl, or you'll turn into a blimp." He shifted on the couch so that he was facing her. "Trust me, there are shelters that are really in awful shape. Funding only goes so far."

Grace leapt up on the couch between them. She primly sat down as close to Camille as possible, then leaned against her. Camille put her arm around the little dog, feeling the fragility of Grace's bones.

"But how do you stand it?" she needed to know.

"By concentrating on the ones we can save. By celebrating each one who goes to a happy new home. By making sure their new homes are happy ones, and by educating people, teaching people responsible pet ownership. Yes, we have to euthanize an unconscionable number of them. I know it's almost too painful to think about, and I also get angry at people for not neutering their pets, for adding to the problem. But if I concentrate on my anger I'll go crazy, and that wouldn't help them at all."

He reached out to stroke Grace's head and his arm brushed hers. How long had it been since anyone had touched her, even accidentally? Following all the emotional upset she'd been feeling, the simple human contact felt very nice. *I wish it could go on forever*, she thought.

"We can't save every dog in the world," he said gently, "but we can try to save the fifty-four in the dog runs, and," he added, fondling one of Grace's floppy ears, "this little girl here."

She raised her gaze to meet his. Did he feel it too? That surge of something electric and binding between them?

"There once was a man," he told her, his eyes deep as space, holding her gaze. "An old man who was walking by the ocean one morning after a storm. Hundreds of oysters had washed up in the storm, way above the normal tide line. They would die there, with no way to get back into the water. The old man bent over and picked up several oysters. He carried them down to the water and put them in. Then he went back up for another handful, and put them in. Then another and another. A smart young man came walking down the road and saw the old man. 'Old man, what are you doing?' he asked. 'I'm putting these oysters back in the water so they don't die,' the old man answered. 'Old man, there are so many it would take you three days, and most of them would die in the meantime. You can't possibly save them all. Why waste your time?' The old man gathered another handful of oysters and carried them to the water. 'You're right,' he said. 'I can't save them all. But I can save some of them.' He picked up one more oyster. 'And for this oyster, and the others that I can save, it is not a waste of time.' "

She was silent for a moment, caught up in the spell of his story. Yet she felt his eyes continuing to speak. Silent communication was something she knew well, reading the smallest gesture or expression. Now she knew he was sharing with her his courage, comfort, constancy. And something else, something not as easily defined. Something deep and mystical. Something powerful, passionate and right. It drew her in, enveloped her, made her very aware of the fact that he was a man and she was a woman. She could wander in it forever, lose herself in the things she read in his eyes.

Grace sneezed.

Camille wrenched her gaze away from Roger's, and her mind snapped back to reality. What was she thinking? This was ridiculous. She couldn't become involved with a man, even someone as nice as Roger seemed to be. The last time she'd gotten involved and taken a man home to meet her parents

. . . Well, she was not ever going to do that to her parents again.

To give herself mental space, she took a sip of the hot chocolate. So far, so good. Now she had to say something. Something inane and impersonal. "Nice hot chocolate. Thank you."

"You're welcome."

Was it her imagination, or was there a slight hurt in his voice? She steeled herself against it. Yes, they'd apparently shared a nice moment, but that was all there would be. Better for him to get used to it. For her as well. Still, she couldn't just leave things there, as if nothing had happened.

"Not only for the hot chocolate," she explained, still refusing to look at him, "but for the lovely story, and for helping me deal with . . ." She waved her arm vaguely. "For whatever it was."

"I know."

She risked a small peek at him. He was still watching her, though his expression was now guarded.

"From now on, I'll concentrate on the ones we do help." Another quick peek.

He nodded.

"And make sure they have the best homes possible."

Another peek, another nod.

"And give this one here"—she rubbed her head against Gracie's—"the best home of all."

"Nope."

Chapter Three

Startled, she jerked her head around to see him, lazily leaning back on the couch.

"Splinter is my dog," he stated calmly.

"*Gracie* is *my* dog," she corrected.

"Why?" he challenged, suddenly resembling a hunting dog on point, the epitome of alertness. "Because you saw her first? That's no reason. Unless you're validating squatters' rights."

"Squatters' rights have nothing to do with this," she sputtered. "Grace is mine because . . . well, because she just is, that's why."

"That's no reason," he scoffed.

"I suppose you have a better one?" she thrust out her chin and hugged Grace to her more tightly. Grace wiggled against the restraint. Camille didn't let go.

"She belongs on my farm," he argued. "Out in the country where she can run and play and be a dog. Not shut up in some ritzy lawyerish condo where she's not allowed up on the furniture."

"Are you accusing me of not allowing dogs on my

furniture? I hope you can back up such a scurrilous accusation."

"I'm just saying that at my farm, she'd be a dog, not a pampered little thing."

"Oh, so you're saying that I'd dress her in a frilly doll dress and wheel her around in a baby buggy? Buy her doggy lingerie, and paint her toenails? Is that what you think?"

She watched with satisfaction as the big guy squirmed. Let him squirm. She was just beginning. "At your farm she'd probably sleep on your dirty clothes, the ones you dropped on the floor, and would put back on the next morning."

"Are you calling me a slob?"

"Well, look at you. The only thing I've ever seen you wear is that slovenly sweatshirt. 'Never trust anyone who doesn't have dog hair on their clothes.' That's ridiculous."

He proudly drew himself up to his considerable height. "My sister gave me this sweatshirt. Besides, you're the only person in the world who wears makeup to clean out dog runs. Talk about prissy."

Slamming the mug down on the table next to the couch, she surged to her feet. How dare he try to intimidate her. She wasn't about to roll over and play dead. "I'm not prissy!" She stabbed her glare right into his heart. "I'm a professional, and I'm well groomed."

"I suppose," he scoffed, "you have a standing appointment at the Puppy Poos R Us Dog Salon!"

For a moment they both held their stances, both bristling with anger. Then the absurdity of the situation hit her. A solitary chuckle escaped. Then another, or was that one his? No matter. In an instant

Away in a Shelter

they were both holding their sides, laughing.

Camille, weak in the knees, sank back down on the couch still caught up in hilarity. This time, when Grace wiggled out of her arms, she didn't have the strength to stop her.

"Puppy Poos R Us!" she crowed. "That's priceless!"

"If you could have seen your face," he managed, "when you announced that you were well groomed!"

They were off again.

"Splinter, no!" he suddenly commanded.

Camille turned to see where he was looking. Grace had discovered the half-full mug of hot chocolate on the end table. She grabbed the little dog.

"Dogs can't have chocolate," she scolded. "Not good for their tummies."

He groaned audibly. "Talk about pampering. Next thing you'll be training her with baby talk."

"Sure. Why not? Dogs are very intelligent. They can learn commands in German, Latin, Persian, or baby talk. They don't care. Gracie," she said in a high-pitched squeaky voice. "Sitsy witsy like a goodums puppy wuppy."

Grace tilted her head, confusion written in the wrinkles above her eyes.

"Don't you think that's a bit overblown?" Roger asked dryly.

Camille reverted to her usual tone of voice. "Of course. Grace, sit."

Grace sat.

"Good girl," they both said at the same time.

Grace wagged her tail.

* * *

When her guard was down, he thought, watching her laugh, she was almost pretty. When the ice princess melted her face expressed what she was feeling, and it was a very expressive face. She'd make a lousy poker player. She had a tendency to move her hands a lot when she talked. But still, all this admiration would not solve the problem. The problem was simple. They both wanted Splinter.

Suddenly he realized she'd stopped laughing. He glanced her way and found her gaze trained on him. This time however, it was not a baleful glare at all, but something more akin to curiosity.

"You look as if you want to ask me something," he commented.

"I was thinking about Grace. We both want to keep her. I was wondering how we could arrange it. I suppose we could draw up a custody agreement. You know, like for kids, only for Gracie. I'd be the residential parent, but you could have her every other weekend, and once overnight during the week." She frowned in thought. "I know things like this have been created in divorce decrees, but I'm not sure if it's ever been done with a stray dog." Her voice trailed off uncertainly. "What? Why are you looking at me like that?"

"Like what?"

"As if you want to chop my head off, but don't want to be impolite about it."

"Maybe it's because you're assuming that you should be the residential parent. In fact, you're assuming I'd be willing to go along with a harebrained scheme like this in the first place!"

"Well if you have any other suggestions, now is the time to present them," she snapped. "I'm trying to think of Grace and what would be in her best interest. Obviously it would be best if she were in one home, and visited your farm periodically."

"How do I even know," he challenged, "that you'd give her a decent home? When people come in to adopt we don't let them take a dog just because they think the dog is the right dog for them. So let me put *you* through the process, Ms. Campbell."

She didn't even seem fazed. "Okay. Ask your questions, Mr. Matheson. But remember, I'll ask you the same things. After all, how do I know that you'd give Grace a good home?"

"Agreed."

For an instant, Roger wondered if they should shake on it. The prospect of shaking Camille's hand was not anathema to him. In fact, he remembered how she'd felt in his arms and thought it might be nice to touch her again. But then the moment was gone.

"Have you ever had a dog before?" he asked. "And if so, what happened to it?"

"I grew up with dogs." Her voice was deliberate, even, perfectly modulated and devoid of its earlier passion. Evidently the cool, calm and collected lady lawyer was back. It made him want to clench his teeth in disgust.

"My parents always had at least one dog since before I was born," she continued. "They were part of our family and went everywhere with us. Do you want their names? Most of them lived to very respectable ages when they died."

"What kind were they?"

"We had corgis mostly, and we had some mixed breeds. As a matter of fact, we had one dog, Michelle, who could have been Grace's twin. She was terrific." For an instant her face grew animated again, as if she'd forgotten she was a lady lawyer. For that instant he could almost feel her bond to that dog of long ago, and he wondered if the memory of that dog had anything to do with her desire to keep Splinter. Then the lady lawyer was back again, all business. "Now. Tell me about your experience with dogs."

Was this what it felt like to be on a witness stand? he wondered. "I also grew up with dogs," he answered. "We lived in a town so small that it was big news whenever a shopping cart from the grocery store rolled into the lot and hit a parked car. I don't remember a single day in my life when I didn't have at least one dog. When I went to college I lived in an apartment instead of the dorms so I could have my dog with me."

"What happened to him?" she asked quietly.

"I still have him. San Tropez Matheson, Sanner for short." He grinned at her look of confusion. "San Tropez. After the Pink Floyd song. I discovered Pink Floyd in high school. My parents were less than enthusiastic about their music." A memory whisked across his mind. "I remember Mom always had to tell me to turn the music down. At least she called it music; Dad just called it rhythmic noise." He chuckled. "I haven't thought of this in a long time. Tell me, when you were in high school did your parents constantly have to tell you to turn the music down?"

"No."

Her voice was curt, almost sharp, as if she'd slammed a door in his face.

"We didn't play much music when I was young, my brother and I. Music was not . . ." She shrugged expressively, even though her face was neutral. "Music was not an important part of our lives."

How could that be? he wondered. "I can't imagine living without music," he told her. "Music and dogs and computers. All the rest is just details."

"I guess it depends on your point of view." He thought he detected a hint of defensiveness in her tone.

"I guess so," he admitted. *Still,* he wondered, *how could anyone be a teenager without music?* How could he have survived high school without Pink Floyd?

"So tell me," she interrupted his thoughts. "Tell me about your dog. San what?"

"San Tropez. He's a yellow Lab. He's fourteen now, and all gray in his face. He spends most of his time sleeping, and dreaming of the good old days."

"How would he react to a new puppy invading his turf?"

"I'm glad you asked that." He grinned at her. "They spent the better part of this morning together, and all afternoon. He adores Splinter." He looked around for the dog. "Yo, Splinter, c'm'ere girl!" Here she came, to leap into his arms, to wash his face. "Good girl," he murmured. He settled her on his lap, where she leaned into him as closely as she could press her little canine body. Then he returned his attention to the lady lawyer. The lady lawyer did not look very pleased to see Splinter on his lap. Well, that was just too bad. "Splinter adores Sanner too. She thinks he is just the best thing since chew hooves. You have here a case of an adolescent crush. She did not leave his side for an instant." He gently rubbed Splinter's head and was rewarded by a contented puppy noise. "It was good for Sanner to be the object of such hero worship. Made him feel young again."

The lady lawyer was pacing. "Would you be able to provide a recommendation from your vet?"

"Dr. March?" He nodded. "Sure. She's been my vet since she got out of school and opened her practice in town." He frowned. "What about you?"

"She's my vet too."

"Do you have a dog right now? I didn't think to ask."

"I have Phoebe. She's an eight-month-old Pembroke. I'm her foster mom." She stood immovable, yet subtle, not overt, about it "I'm a puppy raiser for Hearing Ear Dogs." It was said as a matter of fact, not as a boast.

He grimaced. "I guess that's a pretty good recommendation. They are known to be choosy about their puppy raisers."

She took a step closer and planted herself in front of him, hands on her hips, no longer subtle. "You don't have to look so sorrowful about it," she accused. "Did you want to find me an unfit parent so you could have Grace all to yourself? Think again, buster. I'm a terrific dog mom."

"You don't look like it."

"Why? Because I'm not covered in dog hair?"

He groaned. Not that again. Still, she had a point. "Okay," he conceded. "Looks can be deceiving."

"They usually are. We assume we know so much about people when we really know nothing about them at all."

Wasn't that what Karen was always telling him? He hated it when Karen was right. Glumly, he looked down at Splinter. "So what are we going to do?"

"I will take her home."

He jerked his head up fast. "Just who—"

"Wait a minute," she interrupted. "You got to spend the day with her—without my consent, I might point out. So it's only fair that I get her for the night."

Much as it irritated him to do so, he had to admit she was right. Still, he didn't want her to think he was relinquishing his claim to Splinter. "Then I'll have her tomorrow."

"Are we going to pass her back and forth like a . . ." Suddenly all aggression was gone from the lady lawyer. She sat down on the couch next to him and reached out to fondle Splinter's ears, her eyes earnest, her face alive again. "She deserves better than a ping-pong life," she exclaimed passionately. "Who knows what kind of a home she came from, how many homes she's had before now. Who knows why she was dumped here, in the middle of the night, in the snow."

Snow. He'd forgotten the snow. Gazing into her eyes, he realized how easy it'd been to forget.

"It's still snowing."

"What?" Her forehead wrinkled in a frown, just like Splinter's.

"It's still snowing," he repeated patiently. "It's been snowing the whole time we've been here. We'll have to dig out before we can even leave."

"But we haven't decided—"

"You take Splinter—the dog," he amended when

she opened her mouth—to protest, he assumed. "You take her tonight, then tomorrow we'll figure out what's best for her. But right now—" He raised a hand to forestall her. "Right now the important thing is digging out."

Digging out, she thought a half hour later, was much easier said than done. The shelter had only one snow shovel, and as a tool it was fairly worthless.

"It's like trying to move a mountain using a teaspoon," he said, as if reading her thoughts. He tossed one more shovelful of snow to the side, then planted it in the snow and leaned on the handle. "The longer we're out here shoveling, the more the snow fills up the places I've just cleared."

"Isn't there a Greek myth about something like this?" She rubbed her mittened hands against her cold cheeks.

He cocked his head and studied her for a few seconds before he answered. "I don't think the ancient Greeks had a lot of up-close and personal experience with snow."

"Not snow," she insisted. "But I seem to remember a Greek myth about something being undone as quickly as it's done, only I can't quite dredge it out of my mind. Sort of like Sisyphus and the rock on the hill, but not quite."

"If there isn't one, there should be. Let's see. Those kinds of sentences were usually imposed upon some poor wretched mortal because he'd done something to offend the gods." He frowned. "Of course, the gods seemed to be easily annoyed."

She chuckled. He was actually enjoyable and good company when he put his mind to it. "I suppose you'll say next that we've done something to annoy the gods."

"Sure," he agreed readily. "Once"—held out his arms as if welcoming an imagined audience, and his voice took on the sonorous and droning properties of a prologue in a Greek drama—"there were two mortals who had the sacred task of caring for the kennels of the gods. They took their responsibilities very seriously. However, one night while a blizzard raged—" He gave her an outrageous wink before continuing. "One night these two mortals displeased the gods by arguing over which one of them should be allowed to care for the favorite dog of the gods. Each mortal wanted to claim the honor. The gods were so angered by the bickering of the mortals they decreed that the two should not be allowed to leave the kennel until the parking lot"— he swept his arm across the lot, showing the audience the magnitude of the task—"was cleared of snow. The two industriously set to work, determined to prove their worth to the gods. Yet no sooner had a spot of lot been cleared, then it was filled with newly fallen snow once more."

"And so," Camille said, also adopting the dramatic voice of the prologue, "the two mortals were doomed to spend all eternity in a snow-covered parking lot while a blizzard raged. Of course," she continued, taking on a moralistic tone, as if instructing the imaginary audience, "if the male mortal had seen fit to allow the female mortal to take a turn shoveling the snow, our story would have had a different ending. For the female mortal was well versed in the art of snow shoveling." She quickly peeked at Roger to see how he would react.

· "But the male mortal," Roger went on, a wicked gleam in his eye, "was a typical protective male type who didn't like the idea of a woman working while he stood by and watched."

Camille met his wicked gleam with her own, then turned back to the imaginary audience. "And so," she pronounced triumphantly, "once more history is determined by the idiocy of the male."

"As opposed," Roger added, deadpan, "to the Odyossey of the Homer."

"That's Odyssey, you idiot," Camille chuckled.

"Call me an idiot, will you?" Roger roared in mock ferocity.

Camille was instantly showered by armfuls of snow. With a shout of laughter, she fought back, armful for armful. Not taking the time to form the white stuff into snowballs, they heaved it at each other, laughing so hard they could barely stand.

Camille dodged to the left to avoid another handful. Suddenly her feet flew out from underneath her. She found herself smack on her seat in the snow. Roaring with laughter, she fell back. It felt good not to have to stand anymore. No matter that it was cold outside, she thought, for inside her heart she was warm.

"What?" she managed to get out. "You're not going to bury me?"

"Nope. Never bury a woman when she's down. It's one of those laws of physics or something. Drilled into me as a child."

"Naw, Matheson, you've gotten it wrong," she chuckled. "You're getting physics confused with common courtesy. Laws of physics are about bodies in motion."

"Yeah, well, right now your body has no motion at all," he teased. "Hence, I can't bury you. What I *can* and will do," he said, and held out a hand, "is help you up. It's the right thing to do."

Her own hand disappeared into his big one. A flash of mischief shot through her. As hard as she could, she yanked on his hand, and at the same time rolled to the side. He ended up chortling beside her in the snow.

Finally their laughter came to an end. Camille closed her eyes. "Hmmm," she murmured. "I can't remember when I've laughed so much."

"Then it's been too long," his voice drifted lazily over to her. "You've been hanging around the wrong people. Probably all those lawyer types don't have much sense of humor."

"If that is a dig, I'll let it pass." Her voice, she realized, was just as lazy.

"Like a ship in the night," he quipped.

"Like a freight train."

"Like time itself."

"Yeah," she told him drowsily. "Just like that."

"Hey, you're not falling asleep on me, are you?"

"I'm thinking about it," she answered, snuggling further into the hood of her jacket.

"No way, Jose," he announced in a determined voice.

She felt him struggling beside her. She opened her eyes as she felt him unceremoniously pull on her arm until she was sitting. "Absolutely no falling asleep in the snow."

"What? Another law of your wacky physics?"

"Yup. Matheson's fifth law."

"Oh, you have laws named for you. I'm impressed."

"If you don't obey this law you'll be in deep trouble." He continued to pull her arm. "C'mon, time to get up and get inside where it's warm."

"Bully," she muttered without rancor. But with his help she struggled to her feet.

She surveyed the parking lot, still buried in snow. "Well, it seems we weren't terribly effective, doesn't it?"

"What?" he asked in mock surprise. "You're not going to take this opportunity to blame me for not allowing you to take a turn at the shovel?"

She grinned. "No. If I'd had a more effective argument you'd have had to allow me a turn. So I will share the responsibility for this one."

He grinned back at her, and she was filled with an unexpected feeling of camaraderie. As they trudged up the walk to the building, she could see Grace through the glass door, standing up on her hind legs, waiting anxiously for them. The faithful hound waiting and watching for her family to return.

"So," she said, trying to make her voice sound casual. "If we can't dig our cars out, what happens next? I don't suppose the shelter is high on the priority list for city snow plows."

He snorted. "High on the priority list? How about not on the list at all? They know we're closed for the holidays. Careful here."

She didn't pull away when he took hold of her elbow to steady her. It was the action of a friend, and she took it for just that. Her feet were proverbial blocks of ice. The red rubber boots were good for cleaning dog runs, but not much else.

"Snow's so deep and drifted," he continued, "that it's hard to tell the steps even exist."

Just a few more feet to the door, and warmth, she thought, wishing she'd had the foresight to stick a dry pair of socks in her purse. But how would she get home tonight? She wouldn't, she realized. And neither would Roger.

Chapter Four

Roger pulled the heavy glass door shut behind them. He kicked his boots against the rough mat to get the snow off. No sense in bringing the snow inside. Besides, it gave him something to do so he wouldn't have to look into Camille's eyes. A few minutes earlier, when he'd stomped down the drifted snow outside the doors so he could pull them open, he'd glanced at her, and he'd seen questions in her eyes. Questions he didn't want to answer now. Questions he didn't want to even ask himself now.

"Did you have supper before you got here tonight?" she asked.

That wasn't the question he thought she'd ask. "No. And I'm hungry enough to steal a big bag of kibble for supper."

"Now *that's* low," she chuckled.

He watched her stand on first one foot, then the other, to pull off those ridiculous red rubber things that clashed with her normal upper-class retrochic. At least they weren't decorated with little bunnies.

246

"Imagine," she said with a slight grunt as one of the boots came off, "stealing food from dogs in a shelter. You can't get much lower than that."

"Low, but probably filling. After all, the dogs devour it with great enthusiasm, so it must be good."

"I don't know about that. Dogs like some things that are pretty gross. And no, Gracie, you may not chew on my boots."

Roger watched in fascination, forgetting the lady was a lawyer as she stooped down to engage in a nose-to-nose with Splinter. Why, he hadn't noticed before, but her hair was the exact color of Splinter's coat, a deep, glowing gold. An image settled in the front of his mind. The two of them, with Splinter and Sanner, cuddled up on the plush rug in front of a crackling fire in his fireplace, while he threaded his fingers through the silky strands of Camille's rusty-gold hair. He could almost feel the smooth river of it in his hands. Whoops! Time to pay attention to the conversation, before he reached out to discover that her hair was truly as thick as he imagined it would be. He cleared his throat.

"We could always try the cat food," he pointed out.

"Somehow I don't relish the thought of eating cat food."

"Do you mustard it, then?"

"Cute." Her voice dripped with sarcasm. "Very cute."

"Thank you," he said. He used one booted toe to pull at the heel of his other boot. She was okay, he realized. Once he got past her uppity-sounding voice, she was actually a lot of fun. She was bright, she was not averse to being silly, and she was very

quick to pick up on his particular flavor of humor—
something not many women could do. Not only did
she pick up on it, but she joined him in it. He liked
her. He actually liked her.

Suddenly, he realized she'd said something.

"Could you please repeat that? My ears seem to
have frozen." He cocked his head and thumped it
with his hand.

"I said, I don't imagine the pizza places will be
delivering tonight."

"Oh, I dunno," he said as he shucked off his heavy
winter parka and spread it on the floor under the
warm air register. "Don't want to drip all the melted
snow into the office," he explained. He set his boots
next to his parka, then helped her off with her coat.
No, he told himself, he wasn't being polite just so
he could have an excuse to touch her. "We could
always try to find a place that makes deliveries by
dog sled."

She set her red boots—though it made him
cringe to dignify the things by calling them boots—
next to his substantial winter footgear. The two
pairs, side by side, were the perfect visual
dictionary definition of incongruous.

"If we had a dog sled we could get carry-out
pizza."

"Gee," Roger pretended to ponder. "I've never
seen a sled in the shed, but we do have enough dogs
to make up a team."

"Sorry, but on second thought, no." She turned
her attention to untying her shoes.

The knots, along with her shoes, had become
completely soaked. She wasn't going to get those
knots untied. He bent down to help her. "Sit," he

commanded, and she sat. "Let me pull your shoes off. The knots will be easier to untie when they're dry."

"I've just not had good luck with knots today," she said with a sigh.

He tugged a couple of times before the first shoe released her foot to reveal a miserably wet sock. "You'll have to get some decent boots if you're going to have interactive experiences with snow," he scolded. "Right now you need some dry socks. I don't suppose you have any with you?"

She scowled. Yet he understood the scowl was not directed at him, but at the situation. "No."

He rocked back on his heels and considered her. "I suppose the male mortal will once more have to rescue the distressed damsel mortal by loaning her a pair of dry socks."

"I suppose the male mortal was a Boy Scout?"

"Yup," he answered cheerfully. "I'm always prepared. Dry socks in my backpack, which is in the office. Now," he asked conversationally as he started pulling on the second shoe, "why don't you want to take a dog sled to pick up the pizza?" This one came off more easily and he set them next to the boots. The three pairs, all in a row, had an odd resemblance to Papa Bear, Mama Bear, and Little Tiny Baby Bear.

"Dog sleds are terrific," she said, still sitting on the floor, looking up at him with her teasing eyes. "But in this case, they would not be practical. By the time we had a team of dogs assembled and trained," she continued in her precise voice, "we'd have been dead of starvation for a couple of months. By then the snow would be gone and the sled would be useless. Not to mention the pizza would be cold."

Suddenly bursting with the need to hold something alive and warm, Roger scooped Splinter up in his arms. With a soft doggy noise, she snuggled into him. He rubbed the top of her head with his cheek. Even if she was not the one his arms most definitely desired to hold, the little dog would do. "There's a big freezer in the back storage room that's usually decently stocked. Let's go put some dry socks on you and then see what we can find."

"Okay," she agreed.

Side by side, the little dog in his arms, he and the lady lawyer padded down the hallway.

"You seem right at home here," she commented. "Have you been a volunteer very long?"

He pulled his upper body out of the freezer chest, a triumphant grin on his open face, frozen pizzas in his hands. "Eureka!" he crowed, carefully setting down the lid. "Let there be pizza! And let there be pepperoni on it. And it was so. And the man and the woman, they rejoiced with gladness and thanksgiving."

"You are stark raving mad," she said, trying to stifle a chuckle. No sense in encouraging his silliness.

"Mad?" He adopted an attitude of righteous indignation, looking down his nose at her. "My dear woman, I am not the least bit angered. Lack of anchovies is no reason for choler."

"Gracie," she confidentially cautioned the dog who was now in her arms, "I must warn you about this person. If he were a movie, he'd be rated ES. Extremely Silly."

Grace took the opportunity to lick Camille's chin.

"I may be silly, but I have found us pizza."

"Are we allowed to eat it?"

He motioned to her to follow him down the hall. "Well, we're not going to just look at it!"

She pulled at his sleeve to make him stop and look at her. "I'm serious," she insisted. "All kidding aside now. That pizza belongs to someone. We don't have the right to go rummaging around in a freezer that does not belong to us and eat whatever we find in it."

"You afraid of a lawsuit?"

"No!" she protested. "Nothing to do with a lawsuit, don't be absurd. It isn't ours. We have no right to take what is not ours."

Instantly he dropped all pretense, all clowning. "Trust me. It is ours to eat or to look at if that's what we prefer. Frankly, I recommend the former. Pizza as art just doesn't do it."

She stopped up short. "How can it be ours?"

"The contents of that freezer belong to the staff of the Greene County Animal Shelter. Once a month it is restocked with goodies."

He continued through the clinic rooms. She followed, Grace in arms.

"Who pays for it?" She'd never heard of this. Of course, she'd only been a volunteer since October, so she really didn't know much about the administration of the shelter.

Roger shoved the kitchen door open with his shoulder and held it for her. "Conroy Abernathy. He owns the big chain of grocery stores in town. He is also a great fan of cats, and for a millionaire is a very nice human being. This is one of the ways he helps us help the animals."

She was curious. "What is another way?"

"He donates half of the dog and cat food every month. The other half comes from some of the big corporations in town. Didn't you ever read the list of shelter benefactors?"

List of shelter benefactors? She shook her head. "No. I've never even seen it."

He cocked his head at her. "It's in the front of your volunteer notebook. I'm surprised you didn't read it cover to cover—you seem the type. Anyway, you should take a look at that list sometime. We have some terrific folks helping us." He set the frozen pizza down on the counter and rubbed his hands together briskly. "Now, let's nuke this pizza and pig out!"

He watched with great interest as she licked her fingers, just like a little child. She sat cross-legged on the couch; his size extra extra large socks flapping around her ankles added to the image. The lady lawyer was nowhere in evidence. "Do you always enjoy your food this much?" he asked. As if by accident, he moved his leg a fraction closer to her knee, just enough so there was the slightest contact between the two of them.

She leaned back and closed her eyes, a dreamy smile on her face. "I think we ought to canonize the person who invented pizza."

"You mean Edgar Allen Pizza? No, Splinter, stay down. And quit drooling."

"Yes," she said dreamily. "St. Pizza. Patron saint of all hungry shelter workers."

"But you didn't eat all your pepperoni," he pointed out. "You can't have your pudding if you don't eat your meat."

He liked the way her eyes popped open. "Pudding? Mr. Abernathy gave us pudding?"

He couldn't help grinning at her. "Just a line from Pink Floyd," he explained. "But there is some sort of ice cream stuff in the freezer."

"I like ice cream," she said hopefully.

Her eyes were full of anticipation, and once again he was struck by how very expressive her face could be. Well, for that look on her face he'd swim through the snow to bring her back gallons of ice cream. Whoa! Where did that come from? Evidently, his feelings for the lady were undergoing a major and serious transition. He didn't know if he liked it. He had to get out of here, find his equilibrium.

"You stay put, I'll go see what I can find in the ice cream department."

He found some breathing space, and four ice cream sandwiches. He hoped she liked ice cream sandwiches. He did.

But he didn't return right away. Instead, he took a few minutes to stand by the window staring out at the snow while he thought. He could be in serious trouble here, with her. He liked her. He liked her a lot, but this was going way too fast for him. He was used to relationships that happened at the speed of a snail, over a matter of months, not boom and you're there. But he'd never been "there" before. None of the women he'd ever been interested in had Camille's . . . Her what? He had no way to describe what it was about her that attracted him.

He only knew that something did, like the prover-bial bees to honey. Maybe because it had happened so quickly he hadn't had time to integrate all of it into his mind. He hadn't spent hours wondering and thinking about this attraction, thinking about her. Was it a phantom? A figment of his imagina-tion? No. It was real, all right. As real as the ice cream sandwiches in his hand that would be drip-ping in a minute.

Take the ice cream to the woman, he told himself, but leave yourself out of it. If you're too anxious to make it happen, it probably won't. If this is real it's worth slowing down.

Yet when he reached the office door and heard her voice, he knew he didn't want to slow down. She was talking on the phone, her back to the door. Splinter was curled up in a corner of the couch, head on her paws, sound asleep. Aware he was eavesdropping, he jerked on his mental leash and gave himself a stay command.

"I don't know," Camille was saying, "the snow in the parking lot is too deep to drive through. Go ahead."

Through the long silence that followed, Roger considered what he'd just heard. There was some-thing strange about the way she was speaking. Her voice was flat, almost devoid of emotion. The words were carefully clear and slow with a pause after every couple of words and ending with "go ahead." What was that all about? Nobody talked like that on the phone.

Curiosity swept through him like a forest fire. Karen had once told him he was the most curious person she'd ever known. It was a polite way of telling him he was nosy.

Forget about Karen right now, he told himself. There was something important here, just on the edges of his mind. Bits and pieces of a puzzle danced just out of reach, waiting for him to fit them together. He couldn't see the whole picture yet, but he knew it was close.

"Maybe, but don't worry," Camille spoke again in that flat voice. "I'm fine. Remember Phoebe hasn't been alert trained yet, so don't depend on her to wake you up. I will see you later. Go ahead." Another long pause. "I love you too. Go ahead." Another pause, then her voice returned to normal as she continued, "Thank you so much. You're probably pretty busy tonight on Christmas Eve. Lots of calls." Short pause. "Merry Christmas to all of you, and thanks again. Bye."

He watched her hang up the phone and turn, only to stop short when she caught sight of him in the doorway. Her face flushed, and he had the sudden impression she felt hand-in-the-cookie-jar about something.

"I just wanted to call my folks to let them know where I am, and to ask them to take Phoebe over to their place."

He wondered about the tinge of defensiveness he thought he heard. *Slowly,* he reminded himself, *don't be a fool and rush in*.

"I hope you like ice cream sandwiches."

"Love them."

Ordinarily, having heard that hint of wariness in her voice, he'd have gently nudged, and nudged again until he found out why she was uneasy. But not this time. Much as he wanted to, he'd move slowly, and slowly meant to not pry.

"Then your folks live in town," he said, trying to make idle conversation while he ripped the wrapper off his ice cream.

Evidently her parents weren't a subject she could be idle about, he realized, as she took an inordinate amount of interest in the way the Cream-ore company wrapped its ice cream sandwiches.

"We share a double," she said in a voice that invited no response.

"That's nice," he added easily, just to see what would happen. *Stop nudging,* he scolded himself. *It would even be obvious to a turtle that she doesn't want to talk about her parents.* But why? Was this the picture to his puzzle?

"Yes. It means I don't have to worry about Phoebe. I thought about bringing her this evening, but I didn't know if my car would get stuck in the snow or something. Usually she comes everywhere with me, to my office, to the police station, even to court. She's a great hit in court, even with the judges. One judge in particular thinks she's the cutest puppy he's ever seen. She just assumes that everyone will love her."

And Camille was very adept at changing the subject, he thought. Well, he'd let her. After all, if his gut was telling him the truth, he had no reason to hurry. They had forever to be together. He'd find out eventually. He decided to relax, and let that forever begin.

How could she have been so careless? she chided herself. Her brother would probably say it was because she subconsciously wanted to find a way to tell Roger about their folks. Yeah, well, her brother hadn't been the interpreter between their parents and the world. Her brother was painfully shy and usually stayed at home while she, the outgoing one, the friendly one, the one with the better spoken English, accompanied their parents to do business in town. So she was the one who saw the looks, heard the comments when the people thought she wouldn't hear; her hearing was just fine. Sometimes her parents also saw the looks, and interpreted them correctly. It was no wonder they stayed in their own community.

"We're not going to get out of here tonight, are we." She deliberately made it a statement rather than a question.

"You're right about that one," he agreed, starting on his second ice cream sandwich.

Grace raised her head and sniffed toward the big guy.

"It's ice cream," he told her. "You wouldn't like it."

Camille grinned at him. "I bet she would."

"But if we tell her she'd like it, she'd convince us to let her try some. Then she'd be a pest."

Warning flag. "Do you mean you don't allow your dog to have people food?"

"Of course I do. He gets everything I do, except chocolate. He's a pest."

"If he can be a pest, why can't Grace? We're talking about a double standard here. Or is it just a gender thing?"

"I bet you went to law school just so you could

get paid to argue," he said calmly right before he popped the last bite into his mouth.

She couldn't resist a chuckle. "That's what my brother says."

"Perceptive man."

"Yes. Very."

"But back to your original observation, no, we won't get out of here tonight. I hope you weren't planning on midnight services anywhere." He raised his eyebrows at her.

"No, I wasn't."

"I hope you weren't planning on getting up early and running downstairs on Christmas morning, because that isn't going to happen either." He crumpled the ice cream wrapper up into a little ball, then threw it across the room into the wastebasket. "Swish." He added sound effects.

"Good throw."

"Even if we got home tonight, chances are we wouldn't be able to get back tomorrow morning, and the critters would not be happy."

"So what? Are you suggesting a slumber party?"

"Yeah. I hope you don't hurt your thin skin sleeping in a sleeping bag on the floor."

"As long as there are no peas around I should be fine," she returned with equal humor. "I only hope you don't snore." Then she noticed the look in his eyes and for a second all humor was gone. His eyes told her he was aware of her as a woman, a woman he'd be alone with tonight. All night. Warmth flushed through her, tingling, sparking fireworks of awareness. Roger was no longer just a big guy, he was a man.

"Then," she said, trying to keep the breathlessness out of her voice, "it's a good thing I got ahold of my folks so they can take care of Phoebe." *Oh no!* She inwardly cringed. She'd brought up her parents. She never did that. Her folks were always kept strictly separate from the rest of her life. Time to change the subject.

"Did you say something about sleeping bags?" Her feelings were a jumble of tangled knots and she felt all thumbs. Needing to put some distance between them, she moved to the desk. There, amid the confusion of papers and pamphlets, the overflowing in boxes and out boxes, she caught sight of a small figurine. She picked it up. It was a china puppy, with a chip out of one ear. She rubbed the chipped spot tenderly, then curled her hand around the figurine, as if it were alive and she were giving it healing.

"I always carry blizzard gear in my truck. Two sleeping bags," he ticked off on his fingers. "Extra blankets, socks, and a sweatshirt, chocolate bars for energy, matches, flashlight and a flare."

"The Boy Scout thing again?"

"Yeah." He appeared to be perfectly at ease on the old couch, one hand on Grace's head, moving gently, just enough so the little dog would know he was there. How could he be so calm about this? She certainly wasn't used to spending the night with strange men. Not that she'd be . . . well, she wouldn't be *with* him with him, but they'd be in the same building together, without anyone else around.

"Have you ever spent the night at the shelter before?"

"Not in a blizzard, but every year, one of the

fourth-grade teachers in town brings her class for an overnight. I help with that. She does a whole unit on pets before they get here, so this is the practical after the theoretical. They learn about pet responsibility, about different kinds of pets. They spend time socializing the animals, and doing some simple chores."

"Sounds like fun." She shoved some papers aside so she could perch on the desk, next to the window.

"I hope it's more than fun. I hope they grow up to spay their pets."

Camille was curious. "Do you like kids?"

"Yeah."

He had a soft expression on his face, as if he were thinking of something nice. She wondered what it was.

"Do you have any of your own?"

"No. I do have a niece, though. Katie. She's beautiful and seventeen and thinks she's all knowing, all wise, and all powerful."

"That sounds about right for seventeen."

He shook his head. "She's a terrific kid, but I still don't envy my sister raising her alone. I'd hate to be a single parent today."

Camille nodded from her spot by the window, and there was a comfortable silence between them, broken only by Grace's soft snores.

She rubbed a patch of condensation from the window and cupped her hands around her eyes to better see the world outside. "The snow looks so peaceful and pure," she murmured. "So innocent."

"Don't forget, along with snowmen and sledding, it can also bring car accidents, school closings and can wreck other kinds of havoc."

Without turning around, Camille shrugged. "I know."

"Still coming down?"

She nodded, half mesmerized.

"I'm going to go out to the truck and bring in my blizzard gear before it gets any worse."

She turned from the window in time to see him gently touch Grace on the nose.

"Do you need help?"

"No. I can do it. And don't get all heated up about gender stuff. This has nothing to do with it."

"I wasn't going to get heated up. I just made an honest offer of assistance. It was declined. No big deal." But she did have something else to ask him, and she needed his good will. "After that, do you think we could bring out a few of the dogs for some socialization?"

The grin he sent her was wide and infectious. "Great idea. They'll love it." He glanced down at the sleeping dog. "So will Splinter."

"I wish you wouldn't call her that."

"It's her name."

"Her name is Grace."

But he merely winked, as if he knew something she didn't. "We'll see," he told her as he sauntered out of the office. She heard him move down the hallway toward the front door whistling a cheerful tune.

Music. He said it was important to his life. There had to be a radio here somewhere. Oh, there it was, behind that stack of notebooks. She reached for the notebooks to set them aside, and something caught her eye. It was her name, scrawled at the top of a paper that was propped against the radio. She picked the paper up. *Splinter's with me.* She read. *I'll bring her back this evening. I'll do dogs, you do cats. Roger.* So he hadn't been lying when he told her he'd left a note. She smiled to herself. Maybe he wasn't quite as reprehensible as she thought. He hadn't put the note in an obvious spot, but it was there. Still smiling, she turned on the radio to find a station playing Christmas music.

She found mostly static and had just snapped if off when the phone rang.

"Greene County Animal Shelter," she answered.

"Is Roger there?" It was a woman's voice.

"Not right now, he'll be back in a few minutes, though. Can I have him return the call?"

"Sure." The voice was chipper and sounded friendly, open. Camille instinctively felt she'd like the person behind that voice. "Tell him to call Karen at home, will you?"

"Karen at home?" she repeated rummaging around for a pencil and paper.

"Yes. This is Karen Matheson."

Chapter Five

It was amazing what you could find when you were looking for something else, Roger thought as he slung his long-lost ball cap on his head. Dragging his blizzard bag behind him out of the back of his truck, he jumped down into the snow. The white stuff was almost as high as his wheels.

The last time the snow was this deep was when he was a child. It had been a major event. School had been closed for three days. The kids today were probably disappointed. What was the use of the heaviest snowfall in recent memory if they were already out of school for the holidays? Still, it would be terrific for forts and snowball fights. He thought of his recent snow fight with Camille. The lady had good aim, he thought with respect. He scooped up a handful of snow and packed it round and firm. Taking aim, he let it fly toward one of the tall lights that shone on the parking lot.

Smack! Right on target!

Wishing he had snowshoes, Roger pulled the hood of his coat up over his ball cap, hefted his blizzard bag onto his shoulder and started on the long trek back to the inside. Inside where it was warm and dry, and he had a night to spend with Splinter, and the lady lawyer.

Speaking of spending the night, he had to call Karen and let her know what was up. She and Katie should be home by now.

Camille was just inside the front door. For an instant he thought she was welcoming him back, but then he caught the look on her face. Nothing welcoming about that expression. She thrust a leash at him. Splinter, on the other end of the leash, bounded straight up in the air. At least the dog was glad to see him.

"Grace needs to go out. I figured you wouldn't mind since you're all decked out for the weather."

"Okay," he answered, taking the leash. He slung the blizzard bag inside. "C'mon, girl, let's go potty."

He bent down to pick the dog up, and when he'd straightened, he got a nice view of Camille's back as she moved down the hall towards the office.

"What's eating her?" he asked Splinter.

Splinter thumped her tail against his parka.

"You don't know either?"

Another bout of thudding.

He set the little dog down close to the door, the only place where the snow was not deeper than she was tall. She nosed around in the snow, making snuffling sounds, sneezing snow and then shaking her head. Finally, after finding the right spot, she squatted.

"Good girl," he praised her lavishly when she finished.

She jumped up to try to reach his face and he

bent down so she could give him doggy kisses.

"You are an absolute sweetheart."

Splinter stood up and leaned into him. He took off a glove and rubbed the soft head.

"Let's go see what is upsetting the lady lawyer."

Splinter was ready.

Professional, she thought. *Be professional and courteous, even friendly, in a remote sort of way. Evidently the man is an accomplished flirt.* The sudden realization hit her. Did she want Gracie raised by such a man? No she did not. That meant there was only one solution. Gracie would live with her.

She heard feet stomping. The big guy was back. Her insides fluttered and fussed into more knots. *Don't be absurd,* she told herself. *You've worked with several attractive men before. You can handle this. But,* she reminded herself, *none of those other men made you laugh like the big guy does, and none of them looked at you with that—Stop! That's enough. There is evidently another Matheson in the picture.*

There was a scrabble of doggy feet as Gracie raced into the office and launched herself joyfully at Camille.

Camille hugged her close. "You got all snowy. Let's dry you off so you don't get cold. You don't have much of anything to keep you warm in this weather."

Still holding on to Grace, Camille went through the office's back door—the one that led to the work areas of the shelter. In a cupboard in the treatment room she found a stack of towels.

"There you go," she told the little dog as she

wrapped the towel around the shivering body. "Now you'll get nice and toasty warm."

"Here you are."

It was the big guy, of course, in his stocking feet—which was probably how he'd been able to sneak up on her. *Now remember,* she told herself, *professional.*

"She was wet. I wanted to get a towel for her."

"Good idea. We don't want her to be cold."

She risked a glance at him. He stood in the doorway, watching her. Wariness was written all over him. *Friendly in a remote sort of way,* she reminded herself.

She smiled at him, an impersonal smile, as if she hadn't spent the last hour thinking the things she'd been thinking. "Oh, while you were outside Karen called. She asked that you call her at home." *There,* she thought, *let's see what he does now.*

His eyes lit up. "Good. I wasn't sure when she'd be home, I'm glad she made it. I'll call her right away so she doesn't worry."

Just that quickly, and he was gone.

Camille frowned. He certainly didn't act guilty. Maybe he was the kind of guy to whom flirting meant nothing. A professional Lothario, so to speak.

"Come on, Gracie," she whispered. "Let's go hear what we can hear."

Inside the towel, Grace grunted softly, then snuggled farther into Camille's arms.

But when they got back to the office, the big guy had the receiver to his ear and was frowning. "No answer." He hung up the phone, and stood for a moment staring at it. "Maybe she's outside with the dogs. I'll try again in a few minutes."

"You look worried,"

He raised his eyebrows. "Not worried, just concerned. We're incredibly close—can sometimes read each others minds—so I'd know if anything was seriously wrong."

Camille, old thing, she told herself, *it looks like it's just you and the girls. So what else is new?* Actually, it was okay, she told herself. This way she didn't have to do any explaining about her family. Yet even that was cold comfort.

Friendly yet reserved. "You said she might be outside with the dogs. Tell me about them." Dogs were always a safe subject.

"She rescues Newfoundlands. Right now she has seven of them."

"*Seven* Newfoundlands," gasped Camille.

"Three of them are hers, and four are foster dogs. She'll find homes for them eventually. And if not, she'll keep 'em. She's a sucker for those guys." He tossed her one of his infectious grins.

She quickly stuck another brick in the wall she was building between them and returned a smile that she did not allow her eyes to share. "She must like dog hair," she said without thinking, then cringed inwardly. How unspeakably catty of her. "I'm sorry," she quickly added. "That was truly uncalled for."

The big guy, far from taking offense, threw his head back and laughed. "You're right," he told her. "She says she's going to spin it into yarn someday and knit something. I told you, she gave me this sweatshirt," he held out the ratty thing he always wore. "She has one that says 'The cook is not responsible for the dog hair in the food.'"

Camille chuckled politely at the saying, which was funny, but her mind was ticking away. He told her his sister had given him that sweatshirt. Something was rotten in Denmark. She decided to do a little espionage. "What does Sanner think of the Newfoundlands?"

"He grew up with 'em. Karen and I each got our own dog on our seventeenth birthday. I got Sanner, and Karen got her first Newf."

"You're the same age?"

"She's four minutes older than I am, so she always tries to do this big-sister routine. Right now she's taking care of Sanner. I dropped him off at her place on the way over here."

His sister. Karen was his sister. The wall came tumbling down, and Camille dropped her face to hide her smile against Gracie's fur.

"Why don't you try calling her again?" she suggested.

After his phone call, Roger felt better, knowing Sanner and Karen and Katie were all right. "She says most of the country roads are closed by now, and Sanner is asleep on her living room couch," he told Camille as he hung up the phone and started for the door.

"I imagine at his age he does a lot of sleeping," Camille suggested, following him.

He waited for her to precede him through the door, and then scooped up Splinter to carry her out to the dog wing. "That's about all he does these days. Today was an exception. Splinter wore him out." He ran his hand along the little dog's rib cage. "You need some good food, little girl. Make you big and strong."

The lady lawyer sniffed. "You want to turn her into a body builder?"

He chuck led at the thought. "Canine body builders. That's great. Lots of possibilities for caricature there." Instantly a parade of overly muscular dogs in scanty panties pranced and posed across his imagination.

"Yoo hoo! Anyone home?"

He turned away from the dog show in his mind to find her standing in front of him slowly waving her hand, blatant curiosity written all over her face.

"Excuse me?"

"You got this dumb smile on your face. You stopped moving. I wondered what had happened."

"Oh. I was thinking about canine body builders."

She frowned at him, considering. "What do you do?"

"What do you mean?"

"Your work. You know, what do you do all day to earn money to buy dog food?"

"I play." He started down the hall again.

"Play?" The skepticism was clear.

"Yeah. I play." He felt like teasing her a little, no harm intended; it was a way of flirting. He fondled Splinter's ears. She was the most touchable dog he'd ever known.

"What do you play?"

"I play on my computer."

"Someone pays you to play on your computer?"

"Yeah." He took a quick peek to see if she was starting to show any signs of frustration. She was.

He took pity on her as he held open another swinging door for her.

"I create computer adventure games."

Her eyes widened and she came to a full stop in the doorway. "What computer games?"

"Games kids play on their PC's. I make up the plots and the characters, write the dialogue, the action. I work with a team of animators, programmers and a bunch of other people."

Understanding came over her face like the sun rising in the east.

"That's why you like to make things up." She snapped her fingers. "That's why you're so good at improvisation. That's why you like playing with words so much," she added, more to herself than to him.

"I create worlds. Worlds where kids have to use their minds and their reasoning ability to survive a situation, or a series of situations."

"It's important to you that they use their minds?"

"Am I under oath?" he teased.

"Absolutely," she grinned.

"Then yes. It's important to me." He matched his tone of voice to his words. Kids were a mission for him. "I want kids to learn to think. If they can develop these skills—mental skills, not just shoot 'em up—playing a game, then when real life throws them a doozie, maybe they can use those skills to change their lives."

She reached out to touch his arm, yet it was from her gaze that he felt truly touched, touched deep down. For one long instant they communicated on a different level, purer than words; for words were merely a translation, an interpretation, of thought. Then she spoke.

"It must make you happy to know that you help kids grow."

"Yes. It does."

She smiled, it was a secret smile, as if she were hiding something precious from him. As if she were smiling not at him, but at something deep within herself. Then she aimed her smile at him, and it was a blazing smile. "Let's go socialize some dogs and help them grow too."

They were, she thought, becoming friends. How unexpected it was. *Merry Christmas to Camille, from the Greene County Animal Shelter. Your gift of one friend.* This was a gift she'd treasure.

"Who first?" her friend asked.

"Why don't we start at one end and take two or three at a time."

"Might as well," he drawled, a glint in his eye. "There's nothing much good on TV."

They took the first three dogs—two mixed breeds and a terrier—to the family-style room. This was where prospective dog owners had a chance to play with the dogs.

Camille and Roger played ball with the dogs, and sock, and generally horsed around with them. Camille was fascinated by the way Roger interacted with the dogs. He seemed to be able to communicate with them on their level. He seemed to speak dog.

So it went, group after group of dogs. Until they were at the end.

The last dog was the puppy who'd begged her to take him home. His joy at being with people was boundless. He thought Grace was the Queen of Everything. Grace did not disillusion him.

"What do you think this little guy is? Care to hazard a guess?" he asked, settling down on the area rug next to the two dogs.

Camille joined him on the floor and considered the puppy who was on his back, flailing his paws at Grace. Grace had one foot on Roger's stomach and was pretending to ignore him. "Hound of some sort?"

"Nope. Half dalmatian. The people who brought him in have his mother, she's a dal. They had no idea who the father was."

"They couldn't find homes for the resulting puppies so they brought them here," Camille stated. "For us to deal with."

"Be careful," Roger cautioned. "That is a road that leads to anger, and in the end will only burn you out. This little guy"—he gently removed the puppy from under Grace's foot and held him up—"is lucky to be here." The lucky puppy licked Roger's nose and Roger nuzzled the puppy's muzzle. "These same people had a litter of pure-bred dals last year. They thought they could make a bundle of money breeding dogs. So they got two dalmatians, probably from a pet store, and had a litter of puppies. Half of the puppies were deaf."

Camille whipped her head up, all senses on alert. "What did they do with the puppies?"

Roger, still nose-to-nose with the puppy, raised his eyes to meet hers. "They gave us the deaf ones. We very carefully adopted them out," he answered slowly, a question in his eyes.

"All of them?"

He set the puppy down. Tail wagging mightily, the little guy threw himself at Grace and began chewing on her ear. She rolled him.

"Why is that so important to you?"

His voice was quiet, even. Camille knew the question was not an idle one. She'd interrogated too many witnesses herself to not recognize what he was doing. He wanted answers.

"All puppies deserve a chance."

"Even deaf ones?"

"Yes," she said fiercely as righteous anger engulfed her, flooded her. She made herself tamp it down, not allow it free rein. This was something she'd had lots of experience doing. "Most people think a deaf puppy should be put to sleep. Why?" she demanded. "Is a puppy less of a puppy, less capable of devotion, less able to love because it's deaf? Is it less able to catch a Frisbee? Less able to chew up a shoe?"

Her questions were rhetorical and she knew it. She shifted her gaze to the dogs. Always to the dogs, for they were safe—the big guy's eyes were not. The big guy's eyes saw too much.

She sat still, watching the dogs, waiting. Waiting for what? She did not know. Some sort of reaction from him, she supposed. For several minutes there was silence between them. Silence in which she did not look at him, would not make eye contact. She wrapped her silence around her like a cloak.

"Which one of your parents is deaf?"

He spoke so softly and gently she wasn't sure if he'd actually spoken the words, or if she'd just imagined it.

She sighed mentally, a sigh coming not from resignation, but from resolution. It was out in the open, no longer suspended over them like the sword of Damocles. Somehow he'd guessed. Now she would know what possibilities there were for anything real between them.

"How did you know?"

"I finally put the puzzle pieces together."

She yearned to look at him, to see his face, yet at the same time she didn't dare. She was afraid of what she might see, what she had seen before in the eyes of men. She didn't want to feel that hurt again, not this time, not with this man. But if she didn't look at him she'd never know.

The puppy squealed and Camille gave herself a moment of reprieve as she watched Gracie chomp on his foot. He squealed again and Grace immediately let go. The puppy bounded up to tear across the room, Grace in joyous pursuit.

"Which one?" he asked again.

"Both of them."

She raised her gaze to meet his and found within his eyes no censure, no condemnation, only understanding and compassion.

"Tell me."

"What would you like to know?"

"Everything."

She cocked her head as she gazed at him. She understood that he was asking her not so he could gain advantage over her, but so he could share in her life. This had never happened before. Not that there'd been many men in her life. In fact, there hadn't been any.

"Both of my parents are deaf. My brother and I are not."

274

"How did you talk to them on the phone?"

"I call the relay service, they call my folks. I talk to my folks. The relay service uses a TTY to transcribe my words and send them to my folks. My folks read my words, use their TTY to answer. The relay service reads their answer to me."

"You said you grew up with dogs. Were they Hearing Ear Dogs?"

She nodded, "My brother trains them. So I had an in when I wanted to be a puppy raiser." She smiled a bit wryly.

"Is that why you usually speak so carefully?"

"Sign language was my first language, spoken language came much later. My speech was not clear when I started school." She took a deep breath. Even now, the memories had the power to hurt, not her, but the child she used to be. "The other kids made fun of me and the way I spoke. After I spent several years in speech therapy I made up my mind that never again would anyone have reason to make fun of the way I spoke."

"And the way you dressed?"

How did he know that? she thought in surprise. "My parents grew up in an era when deaf children were not given much of an education. Their job choices were limited. But they worked hard to give us what they could."

Camille listened to the silence that followed, watching expressions wash over his face, watching his posture slightly shift. She knew he was thinking, readjusting. After a moment he spoke.

"I'm sorry I picked on you for wearing make-up to clean out dog runs."

She shrugged slightly. "Ironic, isn't it? I try to

dress well so no one will have an excuse to look down their nose at me. And then you come along and criticize me for trying to look nice."

"I always was an iconoclast."

She caught a sudden realization, as a dog would catch a tossed ball. "You try to make jokes to cover up what you're really feeling."

"Is this an accusation?" Melodramatically, he drew himself up and placed one hand on his heart, as one horribly wronged.

She smiled at him, for now she understood not just what he was doing but why. "No accusation," she said mildly, "merely an observation."

He dropped his persona. "I guess we all have ways of coping with what's happening inside. You try to overcompensate, or to distance yourself, and I create alternate worlds."

She nodded.

"Why did you want to be a lawyer?"

"So the people in the deaf community would be able to have fair representation." She picked absently at the braiding on the rug, which had started to pill from too-frequent washings. "Not be taken advantage of, not be misrepresented merely because they could not communicate with their counsel."

"Personal crusade?"

"Yes."

Perfectly at ease, he stretched out on his side, propped up on an elbow and regarded her. "I'm all for crusades myself. I think it makes life worthwhile, if we can quest after a noble cause or two."

"As opposed to tilting at windmills?"

"Who's to say what is a windmill and what is not? Isn't it a matter of perspective?"

"We're waxing philosophical here." She grinned at him, then stretched out beside him on the floor. The two dogs nosed over to them to snuffle at their faces and hands. "The two of you guys are becoming great buddies, aren't you?" She gathered Grace to her, and let the puppy have a test chew on her fingers.

Grace curled up in the crook of Camille's arm, her chin on her chest. The brown doggy eyes were drooping. The puppy, however, was still full of energy, still wanted to play.

"Watch out," Roger cautioned. "This one is trying to incite her to riot."

"Grace is too tired to be revolting."

"You look too tired to be revolting as well."

She yawned. "What time is it?"

"Afraid you'll turn into a pumpkin?" He shoved back his shirt sleeve to find his watch. "Eleven o'clock. You have one hour left at the ball."

"Speaking of which, this little guy would probably love to retrieve."

She watched Roger stretch to his feet. On his way to the toy bin he snagged a pillow off an easy chair and tossed it to her. "Thanks," she murmured sleepily. "You're very thoughtful."

"You're very tired."

She nodded and closed her eyes. In a moment she heard the bounce of a tennis ball, and the scrabble of a puppy bounding after it.

He played ball with the puppy until the little guy finally seemed to have worn off his energy. Camille did not move. Neither did Splinter.

The little guy started circling. "C'mere, little one." Roger clapped his hands softly and the little guy came tumbling over. Roger whisked him up. "You look like you need to go outside. Yo, Splinter, I hate to wake you up, but you need to come outside also."

Splinter raised her head and looked at him.

"Yes, you," he coaxed her.

She clambered to her feet and trotted over. "Good girl," he praised her, and gave her a pat on the head. Then he led them out to the backyard of the shelter, set them down and let them find their respective spots. The snow was still falling, but lightly. It looked as if it would stop soon.

Whew! It had been a very interesting Christmas Eve. The most interesting Christmas Eve he could ever remember. He knew that this one would not be forgotten, not by either of them. Something had happened this night, something big, something important.

"Take two very different mortals," he murmured out loud to the snow. "Put them together in a situation they both feel passionately about, and watch what happens." He nudged a snowdrift with his socked foot; his boots were still in the hallway by the front door. "They become friends. Maybe more than friends. The male mortal seems to be falling in love with the female mortal."

The two puppies were finished, so he picked them up, one under each arm. Regretfully he put the little guy back in his run. He was becoming attached to that puppy. He watched the puppy make one tired circle, then curl up. "One tired puppy goes to sleep," he said softly.

He took Splinter back to Camille and set her

down. The little thing was so tired she almost fell down. Camille did not stir.

Next he dragged the blizzard bag into the room. He unrolled the two foam pads and laid them out side by side. He unrolled the sleeping bags, fluffed them up to make them as comfortable as possible, then put them on the foam pads. He went back to the volunteer office to track down another pillow, and a candle. He lit the candle, set it in a dish next to the sleeping bags, and turned off the bright overhead light.

He gently touched her shoulder. "Wake up, Camille." He'd never said her name out loud before. "Camille, you need to wake up."

Her eyes opened slowly, leisurely. He got a sudden flash of what it would be like to wake up with her in his bed. He liked it.

"Is something wrong?" she asked in a sleep tinged voice.

"No," he whispered. "Nothing's wrong. But the floor isn't very comfortable to sleep on, even without peas. So I fixed a sleeping bag for you."

She struggled to sit up, wiping sleep from her eyes. "That's nice of you," she said through a yawn. "You woke me up so I could go back to sleep. How very considerate." She gave him a sleepy grin. "Thank you."

He grinned back. "You're welcome." Yes indeed. The male mortal was falling in love with the female mortal.

She staggered to her feet. "I'll be right back."

He sat on his own sleeping bag, pulled Splinter up next to him, and waited for her. Soon she returned, her face looking freshly scrubbed, and smelling faintly of the strong soap used at the shelter.

"What time is it?"

He glanced at his watch, then returned his gaze to the woman before him. "It's Christmas."

"Merry Christmas."

"Merry Christmas, Camille. Merry Christmas, Splinter." The little creature was not stirring.

She settled down cross-legged on her sleeping bag, facing him.

"Roger?"

"Hmm?"

"Why did you dislike me?"

His eyes opened wide in surprise. "I didn't dislike you," he protested.

"Yes you did. I could tell."

"How could you tell?"

"Sign language is my first language. It's a language of gestures, of body language. The way people hold their heads, their shoulders, says as much as their words do, if not more. Most hearing people rely on their words. They don't even see the unspoken language, so they only get part of what is being said."

"Are you telling me that my body language told you I didn't like you?"

"Yes. Body language does not lie."

He thought for a moment, a peaceful moment. "I guess I didn't trust you."

"Why?"

"Because you were a lawyer. Because I didn't think you could truly care about the dogs and cats here. Because I thought you had some other purpose for volunteering."

"You have a low opinion of lawyers."

"I guess so."

"Based on personal experience, or just herd mentality?"

"Personal experience." He felt he owed her an explanation. "When I was first designing games, and didn't understand all the legalities of royalties and such, I was ripped off by a lawyer. Ripped off big time."

"Well, let me tell you a secret. Lawyers don't have a patent on dishonesty. There are good lawyers, and there are shysters. Just like the population at large. But we never hear about the good lawyers, they're busy doing their work. We only hear about the shysters. And the jokes."

"I guess you're a good lawyer."

"I try to be."

"You're a lawyer for the right reasons. You're a crusader."

"That's right."

"So when are you going to start teaching me sign language?"

He enjoyed the way her face registered surprise. But it was more than her face, he realized. Surprise was in her shoulders, her arms. She was right! No wonder she felt so at ease with dogs, they communicated by body language as well.

"If I'm going to be part of your life—and I *am* going to be part of your life, just as you're going to be part of mine—I'll need to know sign language so I can talk to your parents. You know, tell them my intentions are strictly honorable, things like that."

"Are your intentions strictly honorable?"

"Yes."

"Oh." She seemed almost disappointed.

"Would you like my intentions to be dishonorable?"

"Of course not." But she said it a little too quickly, and her face flushed in the candlelight.

He slowly reached out to her, for her. With a sigh, she moved into his arms. Now this was nice, he told himself. She was very comfortable to hold, soft in all the right places. He smoothed her hair, a river of burnished gold in the candleglow. He held her not as a protector, but as an equal. She held him in return, not passively, but actively. Their arms, hands, heads caressed, touched, nuzzled.

"Roger," she murmured.

"Hmm?"

"Do you like kittens?"

"Love kittens. Do you like kittens?"

"Yes. In fact, I've been thinking of getting a kitten."

"A specific kitten, or a kitten in general?"

"Specific kitten. One who likes to cuddle as much as you do."

"I bet this kitten is black and white and has a purr that's the envy of General Motors."

"That's right," she said contentedly against his chest.

"Sounds good to me. I think you'll be a terrific kitten mom." He streamed her hair through his fingers, loving the feel of its silkiness. "I've been thinking also. About that little guy puppy."

She tilted her head back and even by candlelight he could see the colors in her eyes. "You think he needs a farm?"

"I do."

"I think so too." And she snuggled even farther into his welcoming arms. "As long as you don't name him something like Rambo," she murmured.

"I suppose you'd name him Percival?"

"I might."

They were both quiet for a moment. "You know," he said, "I'm beginning to get used to the idea of calling her Grace."

"I'm sort of used to you calling her Splinter."

"So she has two names?"

"Why not? Sounds reasonable to me. She certainly answers to both names."

He thought about this for a moment. Yeah, it would work.

"So when are you going to teach me?" he asked, his voice husky and soft.

"What would you like to learn first?"

"How about the sign for dog."

She lightly patted her thigh. "Dog."

Splinter raised her head, looked around, then went back to sleep.

"That's it?" He repeated the motion.

"Yup. You learn quickly."

"Now what is the sign for cat?"

She used one hand to run along imaginary whiskers.

"Now, how do I sign 'I want to kiss you'?"

She answered him, not with her hands, not with her words, but with her whole being. Roger knew he was going to be very good at sign language.

MR. WRIGHT'S CHRISTMAS ANGEL

MIRIAM RAFTERY

To Patrice Cassedy

Prologue

Dr. Joy Winters whirled around, sloshing hot
spiced cider onto the cuff of her white coat. She
stared at her six-year-old daughter, who was
perched on Santa's lap in the hospital cafeteria.
"That's right," Holly repeated, giving Santa an angelic smile. "I want a daddy for Christmas."

Joy set down the Styrofoam cup she'd been holding and pressed her fingertips against her aching
temple. How could she possibly explain to her
adopted child that Santa's packful of goodies didn't
include fathers?

Not that Joy hadn't tried to find a suitable man
to fill the void in Holly's life—and her own. But between work and motherhood, she scarcely had time
to date. Most of the men she'd gone out with viewed
children as irritants to be tolerated or avoided—like
dust mites and pollen. The few who genuinely liked
kids didn't want a serious relationship with a

woman devoted to her career as an emergency room physician. Working long, unpredictable hours was hardly an ideal way to attract a family man with old-fashioned values, Joy concluded glumly.

A lump rose in her throat while she watched Holly accept a candy cane from Santa. The little girl's dark curls bounced and her eyes gleamed brightly as she hopped off Santa's lap to join a group of other children playing games beside the Christmas tree. Joy swallowed hard, dreading the thought of seeing her daughter disappointed.

Heaven knows, I've got plenty to worry about without this, she thought, recalling her disastrous meeting with the hospital administrator earlier. If only Holly had asked for something else. Anything else.

Anxious to escape the cafeteria's stifling warmth, Joy slipped out the door into the hallway. The smell of antiseptics assaulted her senses as she fought to control her emotions.

"Looks like you could use a healthy dose of holiday spirit," a full, mellow voice behind her observed.

She turned around, startled to find Santa Claus staring at her intently, as if he knew exactly what was on her mind. "I'm sorry if my little girl caught you off guard," Joy offered. "I can't imagine where she came up with the idea to ask for a father for Christmas."

The man in the Santa suit raised his white eyebrows, which looked surprisingly real. "Children speak from their hearts, something most grownups have forgotten how to do. I take it you don't think she's likely to get her wish?"

Mr. Wright's Christmas Angel

"I gave up finding Mr. Right long ago," Joy sighed. "But apparently, Holly is still hoping for miracles."

"Miracles can happen," he said softly.

She paused, noting the kindly crinkles around the stranger's eyes. "Holly's adopted," she said, wondering why she felt compelled to explain anything to a man in a fuzzy red suit. "Her father was a gang member. He and her sixteen-year-old mother got caught in crossfire. They died the night Holly was born, six years ago this December."

"Tragic, to start life as an orphan."

"I treated Holly's mother in the E.R., just before an obstetrician delivered the baby. She pleaded with me to look after her baby, to make sure Holly would have a better life."

He nodded in approval. "You have a kind heart, Dr. Winters. The hospital is fortunate to have such a caring physician."

Joy blinked. "How did you know my name? I'm not wearing my badge, not that it matters anymore. Unfortunately, caring about patients doesn't count for much around here either," she added, unable to keep the bitterness from her tone.

He laid a comforting hand on her shoulder. "Something more than a child's Christmas wish is troubling you, isn't it?"

She turned away. "It's nothing."

"Seems like more than that to me, and I'm a fairly good judge of character," he said, stepping in front of her. "I'm also a good listener."

She sighed, giving in to the need to confide in someone—even if he was a perfect stranger. "I lost my job today," she admitted. "Fired with no notice," *and hardly enough severence pay to cover the bills through New Year's,* she added silently. "All because I cared about my patients more than obeying dictates from insurance companies or hospital administrators. Seems I ordered too many 'unnecessary' diagnostic tests, not to mention refusing to jeopardize my patients' health by discharging them prematurely."

"Sounds like those administrators could use some charitable sentiments for Christmas. Or perhaps lumps of coal in their stockings." He pulled a list of some sort from his pocket and jotted down a note. Amused at his efforts to cheer her up, Joy managed a smile.

"What will you do now?" he asked, putting the list away.

She shrugged. "Send out resumes, I guess." Joy dreaded the prospect of taking a job in another inner city hospital, quite possibly with even longer hours. If only she could afford to set up a private practice in some nice small town! But she'd only just finished paying off the student loans that had enabled her to put herself through medical school, and hadn't yet managed to save enough to make her dream come true. "Sometimes I think I'd have been happier back in the old days," she mused, "before health insurance companies were ever invented."

"Interesting thought," Santa observed, furrowing his brow. "Though it might be tougher than you'd think, adapting to old-fashioned times."

"I'd settle for an old-fashioned Christmas," Joy mused. "Like the ones my family celebrated when I was a little girl, before my parents passed on. I'd give anything to let Holly experience an old-fashioned family Christmas . . . but of course, that's impossible."

"Those are mighty tall orders," Santa mumbled, stroking his beard thoughtfully. "Though nothing is impossible, as long as you have faith."

He reached in his pocket and handed Joy an envelope. "What you need is a change of scenery," he informed her.

Baffled, Joy opened the envelope. Inside were two plane tickets to Alaska—reserved for Kriss Kringle. Did the kindly old man actually believe he was Santa Claus? He didn't seem delusional. She glanced at the tickets again, noting the return date: December 26th.

"I don't understand," she murmured. "Why—"

"I won't be using these," he explained, "since I'll be traveling over the holidays. I've got a nice, cozy cabin in the woods outside Noel, a little town north of Fairbanks. It's a bit rustic, but it would be a good place for you and Holly to celebrate that old-fashioned Christmas you've been hankering for. Oh, and since you're wondering, Kringle is my given name. It's on my passport."

"It suits you." Joy stared at the eccentric stranger, touched by his generosity. "But I can't possibly accept these—"

"Not even for Holly's sake?" he asked, eyes twinkling merrily.

A change of scenery might help take Holly's mind off wishing for a father, Joy conceded. Compared to the prospect of standing in an unemployment line, spending the holiday in a cabin in the Alaskan woods held an irresistible appeal.

"Thank you," she whispered, her eyes misting

over as she closed her hands around the envelope. *Whoever you really are.*

"Merry Christmas." With a wink of his eye, he stepped into the waiting elevator. Odd that he was going up, Joy thought as she watched the elevator buttons light up, then stop at the roof level. Moments later, a jingling sound emanated from above. *Sleigh bells?*

Nonsense, Joy told herself, tucking the tickets into her pocket as the sound faded to a distant tinkling, than vanished into the night.

Chapter One

December 22, 1997 Noel, Alaska

Glancing at the map Kriss Kringle had given her, Joy steered the rented station wagon off the highway north of Fairbanks and turned onto an icy side road. Snow-covered pine trees lined the narrow road like ghostly sentinels in the darkness.

"How long till we get there, Mommy?" Holly asked, pressing her nose against the passenger window.

"Not too long," Joy assured her. "Why don't we sing 'Jingle Bells' again?" She glanced in the side mirror as the car bounced over a bump, glad to see the Christmas tree she'd purchased at a Fairbanks tree lot still seemed securely tied on top of the station wagon.

Holly giggled. "I like the song about Santa Claus better. 'Here comes Santa Claus, here comes Santa Claus,'" she sang. "Santa's gonna bring us something real special this Christmas, Mommy."

A knot tightened in Joy's throat. "Honey, sometimes Santa can't give everything that children ask for. He—"

"He can too!" Holly crossed her arms, her lower lip jutting out stubbornly. "He's Santa. He can do anything. Just wait till Christmas—you'll see, Mommy."

Joy tightened her grip on the wheel. Snowflakes drifted downward, casting lacy images in the headlights. Apparently distance hadn't distracted Holly's attention from her Christmas wish one bit.

The road narrowed. A solid coat of ice covered the pavement, broken only by patches of newly fallen snow. The snow tires no longer provided traction; Joy felt the wheels sliding on the ice. *Maybe we should've spent the night in Fairbanks*, she thought, growing nervous. She hadn't realized it would be dark so early, but near the Arctic Circle daylight lasted only a few hours this time of year.

She rounded a curve and struck a pothole, then skidded on a slick patch of ice. The back of the wagon fishtailed. Joy cranked the steering wheel in the direction of the spin, fighting to regain control. "Mommy!" Holly screamed as the station wagon careened toward a snowbank.

Choking back fear, Joy hit the brakes. Nothing. "No," she whispered, slamming down harder. Instinctively her right arm shot out to shield Holly as the vehicle plunged into the snow, then shuddered to a stop.

Joy stared through the windshield, which was half-obscured with snow. The entire front end of the station wagon was embedded in the snowbank. Beside her, Holly whimpered, clutching Joy's arm.

Mr. Wright's Christmas Angel

Joy gave her daughter a hug. "Are you all right?" Holly nodded, still trembling.

Joy shifted into reverse. The rear tires spun uselessly. She pulled on the parka she'd bought at a camping supply store and stepped out into the bitter cold. With mittened hands she scooped snow from behind the front tires, only to jump back as more snow cascaded down from the top of the snowbank, burying the hood. *If we stay here, we're liable to be buried alive by morning,* she thought, fear twisting in her stomach. *That is, if we don't freeze to death first.*

A mailbox half-buried in snow caught her attention. She pushed away snow and found the name KRINGLE in red lettering on the mailbox. "Looks like we're in the right neighborhood, anyhow," she observed.

She spotted a narrow lane leading into the snowy woods. In the distance, a light shone dimly. A house! "Come on," she urged Holly, bundling the child into the extra-warm jacket, knitted cap and galoshes she'd purchased for the trip. "We're going for a little walk."

Joy glanced at the tree strapped on top of the station wagon, then at the luggage in the back. She'd have to leave the suitcase, she realized, hoping no one would steal anything before she could come back to retrieve it. She picked up her carry-on flight bag and led the child into the woods, praying no wolves or polar bears were lurking nearby.

"It's scary out here," Holly moaned, squeezing Joy's hand.

"We'll find help soon," Joy promised as her boots sank into snow up to her knees. Snowflakes covered the hood and shoulders of her parka; moisture seeped through her white, fleece-lined running suit straight down to her skin, chilling her to the bone. Snow flurries fell harder, becoming a curtain of white. Joy squinted, focusing on the light ahead.

"Mommy, I'm cold," Holly moaned, falling onto one knee. "I can't walk anymore."

Praying Holly couldn't sense her fear, Joy looped the flight bag over her shoulder, scooped the child up into her arms and trudged onwards. Snowflakes clumped together as the storm worsened; Joy could scarcely see the light through the blizzard's blinding whiteness.

Wind howled in her ears, sending a shiver up her spine. Wind—or wolves? Her nose and cheeks stung from the bitter cold. Her hiking boots, caked with snow, felt too heavy to lift and her arm ached from the flight bag's weight. She paused to catch her breath, dizzy and disoriented.

Closing her eyes, she brushed away the ice crystals forming on her lashes. So terribly cold . . . "Merry Christmas," she intoned.

Suddenly the world seemed to collapse around her. She couldn't catch her breath; the very air surrounding her seemed to condense. She heard Holly's startled gasp, and clutched the child tightly. "Mommy, what's happening?"

Joy opened her eyes and blinked. The world spun around her in a blur of light, shadows and mind-numbing cold. She glanced at the sky and caught her breath; a vision of hazy colored lights danced and sparkled on the horizon. The Northern Lights? Confused, Joy tried to recall when the spectacle was visible. Then as quickly as it had appeared, the mysterious vision faded from view.

"I don't know what just happened," Joy admitted, fighting down the chill that crept up her spine.

Holly stared up, wide-eyed. "It's not snowing anymore."

Dazed, Joy looked around. Somehow, she'd stumbled into a clearing. She looked back over her shoulder but couldn't see the car—or the road. She whirled around, looking for the light she had followed into the woods.

It was gone.

Inside a barn nearby, a large white dog raised his regal head. He cocked an ear, detecting a faint sound carried on the winter wind. *C'est bien. Our visitors have come at last*.

He barked loudly, nudging open the barn door with his nose. Ignoring the shouts behind him, he ran outside and raced into the wind.

From somewhere in the night, Joy heard a bone-chilling howl. Something crashed toward them through the woods, closer and closer. Joy hugged Holly tightly against her chest, heart pounding as her gaze swept the newly fallen snow in search of a stick—anything—to use as a weapon.

Dimly she discerned a huge, white blur break into the clearing, barreling straight at them. A white wolf? *No*, she realized as the animal raised its enormous head and barked. *A dog!*

"Mommy, look!" Holly squirmed free and raced to the animal.

"Don't touch, he might—" Joy began, but Holly

had already thrown her arms around the massive furry beast. The dog licked Holly's face and snuggled against her, welcoming the attention.

Relief flooded through Joy. The dog appeared well-groomed, which meant its owner was probably somewhere in the vicinity. Tentatively she reached a hand out to pat the dog's broad head. The dog nuzzled against her, radiating warmth into her icy limbs. "Where's your master, handsome fellow?" she asked, staring into the creature's soulful, dark eyes, which stared back at her with an unnerving intensity.

The dog sniffed perfume-scented hands and gazed up at the vision before him. *Mon Dieu!* He tilted his head to one side, taking in every detail of Dr. Joy Winters and the child beside her. *C'est bien . . . My master has chosen well.*

A deep, male voice resonated through the night, startling Joy. "Frank? Frankincense! Where the devil did you run off to?"

The dog let out a loud bark.

Joy shouted, "Help! We're over here!"

Holly's eyes widened. "Mommy, it's the doggie in my book!"

"That's only a fairy tale," Joy said, jarred at the coincidence. "Though maybe this dog's owner read the book and named his dog after the character."

A moonbeam cast a golden spotlight on the man as he strode into the clearing, illuminating the startled gleam in his dark eyes. Why hadn't she noticed the full moon before? Joy wondered fleetingly, then turned her attention to their would-be rescuer.

Dressed in a sheepskin coat turned up at the collar, heavy gloves, fur-lined cap, jeans and sturdy boots strapped onto snowshoes, he looked like a cross between an old-time fur trapper and the Marlboro man. He was tall—well over six feet, with the muscular build of a man accustomed to hard work.

He moved toward her, then paused, gaping, leaning against a walking stick. Not a stick, Joy realized, heart catching in her throat. A rifle.

"Sweet Lord, Frank! What have you fetched this time?" the man addressed the dog. Moonlight illuminated the concern etched on his rough-hewn face. Joy's heart caught as the man moved forward with the strength and swiftness of a grizzly bear. Something stirred inside her as her gaze wandered over the hardened planes of his unshaven, tanned face. He must spend a great deal of time outdoors, she thought. Yet there was a ruggedness about him that somehow told her he hadn't picked up that suntan hanging around a ski resort.

"We seem to have lost our way," she said, finding her voice. Silently she prayed he carried the rifle for hunting or self-defense, realizing she had no choice but to seek his help.

Nicholas Wright stared, thunderstruck, at the golden-haired woman and small, dark child embracing the dog in the middle of the clearing. A halo of moonlight encircled the woman's hair, casting a warm glow on her heart-shaped face and angelic features. Spots of color stained her cheeks, which looked soft and smooth as rose petals. She wore a puffy, pink and white hooded coat of an unusual fabric over soft, white britches tucked into sturdy, short-topped boots. Nicholas recalled a stodgy, salty-tongued farm widow he'd known who'd taken to mucking out stalls in men's trousers. Yet the female before him now looked anything but stodgy—and those snug-fitting white britches she had on didn't look like anything any male in these parts would wear.

Definitely not from these parts, he thought, mesmerized.

"Who are you?" he asked. "And how the devil did you wind up in the middle of these woods?"

"I'm Joy Winters," the woman replied in a melodic voice. Nodding toward the cherubic child with tousled black curls, she added, "This is my daughter, Holly. We flew into Fairbanks, then rented a wagon and drove the rest of the way."

"Flew?" Nicholas echoed, dazed. He shook his head; he must have heard wrong. The dog trotted over and he scratched Frank's favorite spot, behind the ears, trying to make sense of the woman's babbling. Perhaps she was suffering from frostbite.

"I'm Nicholas Wright." He laid down his rifle and picked up her hand, then stripped off the mitten she wore, wondering where she'd procured yarn with shimmering threads. At his touch, a startled gasp slipped from her lips, which had a faint blue tinge. He pulled off his own glove, then rubbed his fingers over her smooth palm and perfectly formed fingertips.

The tips of her fingers were ice-cold, though she seemed to have feeling in them, he noted, when she responded to his pinch. "No frostbite," he informed her, ignoring the warm sensation building inside him as he slipped her mitten back on. "At least, not on your fingers. What possessed you to go walking through the woods in the darkness, anyhow? Do you have any idea how dangerous it is?"

She slid her hand free. "We rented a station wagon in Fairbanks, but it broke down when we hit a snowbank. We saw a light, and started walking. Only it started snowing so hard, we must've lost our way."

"Snowing?" He peered at her more closely. "It hasn't snowed since this morning, Miz Winters."

"Joy," she said numbly, staring at him as if he'd gone snow-blind. "Of course it was snowing. That's why our wagon skidded off the road and got stuck." She pointed behind her and continued, "We started walking, only we got caught in the blizzard. Holly couldn't go any farther, so I had to carry her."

He glanced in the direction she was pointing and froze. Tarnation! There were no footprints in the snow where she claimed to have been. In fact, he realized, as his gaze swept the perimeter of the clearing, there wasn't a single footprint leading into the clearing, other than his own.

"What about your husband?" he inquired, wondering how any man could let his wife and child roam about the woods alone at night. "Won't he come looking for you?"

She looked discomforted. "I don't have a husband."

Noting his puzzled glance at the child, she lowered her voice. "Holly's father died years ago. There's just the two of us. If it hadn't been for your dog finding us, I'd hate to think what might have happened."

Frankincense cocked an ear. *Merci, chérie. Nice to be appreciated.* He glanced sidelong at Nicholas, wagging his tail approvingly.

"I'd just finished checking on the livestock in the barn when Frank here started barking," Nicholas said, amazed that the animal had warmed so quickly to a pair of strangers. "Then he took off in the storm. He must have picked up your scent."

How could a woman carrying a child wind up in the middle of a snow-covered clearing without leaving footprints? Nicholas opened his mouth to ask, then noticed the child shivering. At least the girl had on thicker mittens than her mother, and since she'd been carried her feet should be spared from frostbite. Still, he knew the urgency of getting both mother and child warmed up.

He knelt beside Holly. "Care to go for a ride?"

Holly nodded, smiling shyly. Nicholas suppressed a groan of pain as the child scrambled onto his back. Blast that fool excuse for a doctor who couldn't set an injured shoulder straight to save his soul. He picked up the rifle and straightened to a standing position, using the gunstock as a crutch to support his aching left shoulder.

Joy hesitated, doubt wavering inside her. She had no choice but to trust the man, yet couldn't help feeling uncomfortable at the prospect of entrusting her daughter to a total stranger.

"We're supposed to be staying at a friend's cabin," she informed him. "If you could just help us find Mr. Kringle's place—"

"Kringle?" He frowned.

"Do you know him?"

"I know him, all right. He's got a fine cabin, real comfortable—though you might find it a mite on the cozy side."

"Cozy sounds wonderful. Is it very far?"

"Not far at all," he assured her, taking a step forward and motioning her to follow. "But you'd best not mind some company."

"Company?" Joy asked, confused. "I thought Mr. Kringle was out of town."

"He is."

"He never mentioned any other guests," she said, feeling nervous. "Who else is staying in his cabin?"

Nicholas glanced over his shoulder and cocked a craggy eyebrow. "Me," he informed her, flashing a grin that sent heat rushing from her scalp to her half-numb toes. "I'm Mr. Kringle's caretaker."

Chapter Two

"Caretaker?" Joy gasped.

"Kringle hired me to stay and keep an eye on things while he's away," he informed her.

"Things," she repeated dully. "Including house-guests?"

Nicholas shrugged. "Reckon so." He trudged through the snow ahead of her. Holly shouted "Gid-dyup!" and squealed with delight as Nicholas broke into a lopsided trot—or the closest he could muster on snowshoes. Frankincense raced ahead, tail wagging as he led the way home through the woods.

Soon they came to a log cabin nestled in a clearing. Icicles hung like frozen lace trim along the eaves; pale smoke curled upward from a rustic stone chimney silhouetted against the ink-black sky. With a start, Joy realized the scene looked just like an illustration in Holly's favorite picture book— a fairy tale about Kriss Kringle's home in the northern woods—right down to the pine wreath hung on the front door.

Joy blinked, remembering the kindly old man

from the hospital. *Impossible*, she thought. He was just a typecast actor from some rent-a-Santa agency. *The cold must be affecting my brain,* she decided, suppressing a shiver.

"If you need to use the outhouse, best do so now," Nicholas informed them, gesturing toward a skinny wooden structure with a half moon carved in the door.

Joy stifled a groan. Kriss Kringle had warned her the place was rustic, but she'd never dreamed it wouldn't have indoor plumbing. Gritting her teeth, she stepped into the outhouse and took care of nature's calling, then helped Holly do the same.

Finished, they walked to the cabin's porch. Nicholas opened the front door and ushered them inside. He lit a pair of candles in wall sconces by the door, illuminating the small living room's knotted pine floors and rough-hewn furniture. Joy glimpsed a kitchen off one end of the living room and a hallway at the rear. An assortment of carved wooden animals lined shelves near a stone fireplace; green and red plaid curtains, cheerful woven rugs, and the aroma of bayberry candles gave the cabin an old-fashioned yet welcoming atmosphere.

Frankincense bounded to the hearth and curled up on an over-size pillow. Holly raced to the dog's side and snuggled against the huge, furry beast, which looked even more massive in the humble cabin. Nicholas lifted a knitted afghan off the sofa and laid it over both child and dog.

"You make yourself right at home, young lady," he said, a smile warming his face. "Your mother can sleep in the guest room. You can bunk with her—unless you'd rather stay here and keep Frankincense out of trouble." A twinkle lit his eyes and Joy knew he'd anticipated the child's choice. "That is, assuming your mother approves."

"Here!" Holly chimed in, wrapping her arms protectively around the dog, who tolerated the attention with remarkable patience.

Three pairs of eyes—Holly's, Nicholas's and the dog's—turned to Joy expectantly. Joy felt her resistance melting. "Okay," she agreed, "for tonight."

Nicholas added logs to the fireplace and stirred the embers, then hung a pot of water on an iron rod above the flames. Soon a fire blazed brightly. "Soon as we get you two warmed up, I'll hike back to the road and bring your horses to the stables."

"Horses? We don't have any horses, just a wagon. A *station* wagon," Joy said. How odd that he would assume she'd have a horse-drawn wagon, she mused. Though in this remote location, the locals must still rely on old-fashioned horsepower, especially during the winter months.

The caretaker looked at her as if she'd lost her mind. He clamped his mouth shut, shaking his head.

"Best check the girl's feet to make sure there's no frostbite," he said, dipping a cloth into the pot of warm water. Joy pulled off Holly's shoes and socks, relieved to find healthy pink toes—albeit cold to the touch. She accepted the cloth from Nicholas and wrapped it around Holly's feet.

"Mr. Wright, how'd your doggie get his name?" Holly asked.

"He's not my dog. I'm just looking after him for Mr. Kringle," Nicholas explained.

A loud snoring sound emanated from the mass

of white fur beneath Holly's head. "Guess Frank's plumb worn out," Nicholas said, winking at the child.

Joy gazed at the animal, struck anew by the similarity between the dog curled up beneath Holly and the fictional character in the child's storybook. "He's a Great Pyrenees, isn't he?"

"Don't reckon I know Frank's breed. But Kringle did mention something about the Pyrenees Mountains, on the border between France and Spain," Nicholas said, casting her a strange look. "Said he picked up the dog there on a trip abroad. He travels a good bit in his line of work."

Joy gulped air. "Just what line of work is Mr. Kringle in, anyhow?" she asked, determined to dispel the crazy thought whirling in her cold-numbed brain.

"An export business of some sort," Nicholas explained. He removed the damp cloth and dried Holly's warmed feet with a towel.

"Export business," Joy echoed, fighting the dizzying sensation that she'd somehow stepped into the pages of a child's storybook. Yet the parallels were uncanny. . . .

Shaking her head, she unzipped the flight bag and pulled out Holly's pajamas and toothbrush, then turned toward the child—only to see that her exhausted daughter had fallen asleep, cushioned on a pillow of white fur.

Joy removed her parka and laid it over the sleeping child. She kissed Holly's cheek, then sat down on the hearth. She exchanged a smile with Nicholas, who had the most delightful crinkles at the corners of his eyes.

Nicholas tugged at his collar, feeling hot as blazes. His gaze took in the rapturous vision before him: the cloud-colored sweater and shapely curves previously hidden by Joy Winters' shapeless coat. As she bent over to kiss her daughter, displaying those curious white britches molded to her pleasingly round backside, Nicholas exhaled a steamy breath. When she sat down on the hearth and gave him a smile to melt a glacier, he felt a tightening in his southerly region.

"Your turn to warm up, Miz Winters."

"Please, call me Joy," she said, unlacing her boots.

"Joy. It suits you." Without even asking him to turn away, she tugged off her boots, then unrolled her stockings and removed them. Nicholas drew in a sharp breath as he beheld her bare, creamy ankles. Averting his gaze to protect her modesty, he knelt beside the hearth and dipped the cloth in the warm water, intending to hand it to her.

To his astonishment, she stretched out her legs and set her feet on his knees without the least sense of shame, looking at him expectantly. Nicholas wondered fleetingly if she'd come from a house of ill repute, but one look at the pure innocence in her eyes made him ashamed to have entertained such a notion.

Gingerly he bathed her feet, which were surprisingly soft and smooth. Her toes had a faint blue tinge, he noted with concern, wrapping his hands around them to warm them faster. "Got to get the circulation back," he observed, massaging the soles of her feet with his thumbs. "Can you feel this?"

A pale pink hue stained her cheeks. "Oh, yes." She

wiggled her toes, sending ten tantalizing tingles across his palms and straight into his heart. "I feel . . . fine."

"Good." He withdrew his hands and handed her the towel, cursing himself for embarassing her, after all, with his intimate contact. Any suspicion he might have harbored about her purity was dispelled by her show of modesty.

Not that he'd have expected a female who paraded around in trousers to be concerned overly much with propriety. Especially one as unpredictable as this one—babbling about a wagon with no horses. He'd heard tales of snow madness from old-timers and wondered if Joy Winters had been driven to delirium from the cold. Though she seemed mighty warm to his touch . . .

"You could use some hot eggnog," he said, rising.

In the kitchen, he lit a lantern and set it in the middle of a square pine table beside a cast-iron stove, where it cast a warm glow that filled the quaint room.

Joy followed her benefactor into the kitchen, surprised to find the cabin apparently had no electricity. Or maybe the storm had knocked the power out.

"I'm sorry if we've inconvenienced you," she said as he added ingredients to an iron pot simmering on a pot-bellied stove. For an instant she felt as if she'd stumbled into another time as well as a distant place, but of course that was impossible. Though sharing close quarters with a stranger was more than enough adventure, Joy thought. Under the circumstances, it might be best to check into a hotel in Fairbanks for the holidays. "If you'll just let me borrow your phone," she said, "I'll call Triple-A and see if they can send someone out tomorrow to help me with the wagon."

"A phone?" He look surprised. "Don't have one of those new-fangled contraptions."

"You're kidding."

"Nope, but I'd be glad to take a look at your wagon tomorrow," he offered. "Just don't count on leaving anytime soon."

A tremor of apprehension rattled Joy's already frayed nerves. "What do you mean?"

"Road to Fairbanks's closed," he informed her, cocking a craggy eyebrow.

"I can't believe it! Why, there was only a little ice on the road just a few hours ago." She sighed. "My return trip's scheduled for the twenty-sixth. How long until they get the road cleared?"

Nicholas shrugged. "Depends on the weather. Could be a couple of weeks. Could be months. You might just be stuck here till the spring thaw."

Joy gasped, remembering the bills stacked up on her desk at home. "I can't afford to stay up here for the next two or three months!"

He stared at her intently. The lamplight illuminated his eyes, and Joy's gaze fixed on his midnight-blue irises with flecks of charcoal hidden in smoky depths. "You haven't told me where you've come from," he said in a voice low and deep as distant thunder.

"We flew in from L.A., the so-called City of Angels."

"Flew!" His eyebrows rose. So he'd heard right, preposterous as it seemed. "City of Angels?"

"Some name, isn't it? What with all the smog,

traffic and gangs. No wonder I couldn't wait to get away."

"Smog? Gangs?" Nothing about Joy Winters made sense, from the moment he'd found the peculiar beauty wandering in the middle of a snowy clearing, leaving no tracks. First, she'd insisted she'd arrived on a wagon with no horses. Now she claimed to have flown in—from the City of Angels—whatever the devil that meant. Her explanations defied logic, unless . . .

A disturbing thought struck him with the force of a lightning bolt. *Unless she's an angel sent to reform you, Nicholas.* Damned if that sharp-tongued preacher hadn't warned him he was heading straight for perdition. Missing church services and laboring Sunday mornings to rebuild his place, not to mention cussing and drinking too much of the "devil's brew," as Preacher Haggarty called it.

"Is something the matter?" Concern shadowed Joy's lilac-colored eyes—eyes no ordinary human could possibly possess, Nicholas mused. He crossed to the stove and ladled up two ceramic mugs full of piping-hot eggnog. His shoulder ached as if it had been skewered with a hot poker. Carrying the child had hurt like the dickens, not that he'd had any other choice. He poured a shot of whiskey into his mug to ease his pain, noting the frown on Joy's face. He downed a swig, welcoming the nutmeg-laced warmth.

"A shot of this would warm you up faster," he advised, gesturing toward the whiskey bottle. She shook her head, pursing her lips. As he handed her a mug of plain eggnog, her hand brushed his, igniting a hot spark that made his skin sizzle. The woman might look like an angel, but she felt soft and tempting as any flesh-and-blood female, Nicholas thought, confused. Even if she was a darn sight prettier than any mortal he'd ever laid eyes on.

Joy took a sip of the eggnog. "Thanks," she said, running her tongue across her full, tantalizing lips. "This really hits the spot."

"You haven't told me what brings you here." Nicholas swigged down his whiskey-laced eggnog, refilled his mug, then sat down across the table from her.

She hesitated, then spoke. "I guess you could say fate brought me here. I—I've got some important matters to straighten out."

He spluttered, nearly dropping his eggnog. "Lord Almighty," he mumbled. Shouldn't a man be entitled to peace of mind without some heaven-sent do-gooder turning up to change his ways?

Joy stared at the caretaker, disturbed by the dark scowl that had appeared on his face. "What is it, Nicholas? What's wrong?"

"You tell me," he said in a frosty tone. "I don't believe in fate, Miz Winters. So you'd best stop talking in riddles and tell me the real reason you've come here, or I just might be tempted to toss you back out in the snow where Frank found you."

Chapter Three

Joy stared at the caretaker, stunned. What had triggered the change in him? He'd seemed so kind and considerate before, yet now his temper had flared for no apparent reason. Her gaze fell on the whiskey bottle. Was Nicholas Wright nothing more than a mean-tempered drunk?

"Not that it's any of your concern, but I've come here to give my daughter an old-fashioned Christmas—the kind I used to have with my family, a lifetime ago," she replied cautiously.

"A lifetime ago," he repeated, a glazed look in his eyes.

"Noel sounded like a good place to come, away from all the hustle and bustle back home," she elaborated, not wanting to divulge her job loss.

"Back home. In the City of Angels?"

"That's right." She nodded. Why was he staring at her so suspiciously, as if she'd just dropped in from another planet?

Uncomfortable beneath his probing gaze, she stood up. "It's been a long day. I really should get to bed."

He nodded. "Good night, then."

"Good night."

She walked out of the kitchen, feeling the heat of his gaze on her back. She picked up her flight bag and carried it into the dark bedroom. Shivering from more than the cold, she changed into her nightgown.

A sliver of moonlight through the shuttered window illuminated the sleigh bed in the middle of the small room. Joy slipped beneath the covers and sank into the soft mattress, which felt as if it were filled with down.

Everything about this place was old-fashioned, Joy thought, snuggling deeper. Especially Nicholas Wright, whose speech and actions seemed borrowed from some bygone era. One minute, he'd seemed compassionate and kind, the next, stubborn and demanding. How could one man be so contradictory?

Conflicting visions of her rescuer swirled in Joy's exhausted mind as she drifted off to sleep, wondering if she'd wound up with more than she bargained for when she accepted Kriss Kringle's offer.

Joy rubbed her eyes, then blinked. Pale light filtered through wooden shutters, forming amber lines across a wood-plank floor. *Where am I?* She glanced around the bedroom lined with rough-hewn cedar paneling and clutched a patchwork quilt against her chest. *Kriss Kringle's cabin ... holed up for heaven knows how long with a total stranger.*

A stranger too handsome for his own good—or hers, she recalled, as remembrance of the previous

314

night's events filtered into her half-asleep brain.

She'd felt agitated the night before, when Nicholas had demanded to know the reason for her visit. It certainly wasn't any of his business to know that she'd just been fired and needed a safe haven in which to sort out plans for the rest of her life.

Not that "safe" quite described how she felt about sharing an all-too-cozy cabin with the charismatic yet quick-tempered Nicholas Wright. His sullen attitude was no doubt due to the whiskey he'd imbibed, she told herself.

Memories flashed in her mind—the family car careening out of control, her mother's scream, then terrible silence; her father's pallor as sirens wailed futilely in the night . . .

She clamped her eyes shut, blocking the images that assailed her. No way was she going to tolerate staying cooped up with a man who drank too much. Though in fairness, she shouldn't judge the man a drunk after a single episode.

A knock on the door drew her attention. "Mommy, are you awake?"

"Come on in," Joy called out.

The door burst open and a cannonball of white fur hurtled onto the bed, closely followed by Holly. "Good morning to you, too," Joy laughed beneath a barrage of licks and hugs.

"Mr. Wright promised to get our Christmas tree off the wagon this morning," Holly informed her mother. "He's making pancakes—only he calls 'em flipjacks."

"You mean flapjacks," Joy said, suddenly aware of the aroma of freshly brewed coffee. "Why don't you take Frank into the kitchen? I'll be in for break-ast as soon as I get dressed."

Child and dog raced out as fast as they'd appeared. Joy pushed back the covers, climbed out of bed and closed the door. She poured cold water from a pitcher into a porcelain basin and splashed some on her face, shivering. Quickly she stripped off her nightgown and pulled on corduroy slacks and a cream-colored angora sweater she'd packed in the flight bag, making a mental note to retrieve her suitcase from the station wagon later on. She dabbed on makeup and pulled a brush through her tangled hair, then glanced at an antique clock on the bureau, startled to learn that it was already past eleven. But of course, daybreak came late in December this close to the Arctic Circle, she reminded herself.

She walked into the kitchen, flabbergasted at the sight of Nicholas flipping a large pancake off the woodburning stove with a metal spatula. It sailed across the room, landing precisely in the middle of Holly's plate.

"Flipjacks," Holly beamed. "Told ya so."

Nicholas flashed a boyish grin. "Morning, sleepy-head." Joy chuckled, unable to maintain her annoyance at him for his curtness the night before. The man had an amazing way with children. Holly, usually shy around strangers, had taken an obvious liking to both caretaker and dog.

"Your turn," Nicholas announced, eyes sparkling like an impish child.

Rising to the challenge, Joy picked up an empty plate and held it aloft. "Ready, aim, fire!"

He scooped up a pair of flapjacks and sent them

soaring toward her. Joy shifted the plate to catch the first one, missing the second by a fraction of an inch. It tumbled toward the floor but was intercepted in midair by Frankincense, who caught it Frisbee-style, then hastily wolfed down the remains.

"One for two. Not bad." Nicholas shrugged. The corners of his mouth tugged upward as he scooped a final pancake off the skillet and plopped it onto her plate.

Moments later he joined them at the table, where he'd already filled a plate for himself. Joy spread butter and maple syrup on the flapjacks, unable to keep her eyes off their unconventional host as she consumed the delicious fare.

"You'll help us find the station wagon?" Joy asked, fortified by a cup of the strongest coffee she could recall tasting.

"I told you I would, didn't I?" he answered, an inexplicable wariness in his tone.

After breakfast, Nicholas led the way to the road. Holly rode on Frankincense's back, shouting "Giddyap" and squealing with delight.

The transformation in the scenery amazed Joy almost as much as the transformation in her daughter. Sunshine shone through lacy branches sheathed in shimmering ice, creating a fairy-tale setting. Funny how the trees had seemed so much taller last night, Joy thought as they passed the clearing where Nicholas had found her and Holly.

A few minutes later, they emerged on a snow-packed road. Joy recognized Kriss Kringle's mailbox. She glanced up and down the empty road and felt her heart stop. "The wagon—it was right here," she gasped.

"Are you sure?" Nicholas asked. "After all, it was dark when you came and—"

"I'm positive," Joy insisted, pressing her hands against her forehead. "I can't believe this! Someone must've stolen it."

"Stolen?" Holly wailed. "But what about our Christmas tree? How can we have Christmas without a tree?" She dissolved into tears, burying her face in the dog's fur.

Frankincense whimpered sympathetically and carried Holly to her mother. *Don't cry, ma petite fille.* He fixed an exasperated stare on Nicholas. *For Heaven's sake, do something!*

Joy pulled Holly into her arms. "Don't worry," she said with more conviction than she felt. "We'll still have a special Christmas somehow. I promise." She fought down the knot of dread in her throat. She'd have to notify the rental agency, and the police—just as soon as she could find a phone.

Nicholas knelt in front of Holly, wiping her tears with his gloved fingertips. "How would you like to help me pick out an even better tree?" he asked. "I'll fetch my saw from the barn, then we can go tree hunting."

Holly's eyes brightened and a smile split her face. "You mean, we can cut our very own Christmas tree? For real?"

Nicholas nodded soberly. "For real."

"Yippee!" Holly jumped up and slapped his palm in a high five. Looking slightly startled, Nicholas returned the gesture. Frankincense barked, as if voicing his approval of the plan.

Mr. Wright's Christmas Angel

Joy gazed at the dog, who stared back intently, head cocked, dark eyes gleaming. If she didn't know better she'd swear the animal had understood every word spoken. *But of course that's ridiculous*, she thought, turning to follow Nicholas into the snowy woods.

One hour later, Joy's gaze rested on Nicholas's broad, muscular back and taut forearms as he wielded a saw through the base of the six-foot-tall pine tree Holly had chosen. "Stand back," he cautioned. With a powerful stroke, he severed the last portion of trunk. The tree plummeted to the snow-covered ground below, spewing white powder into the air.

Holly clapped her hands with delight as Nicholas hoisted the fallen tree trunk onto his shoulder. He grimaced, as if in pain, Joy noted. A moment later the expression faded as he began dragging the Christmas tree toward the cabin. *The man just sawed down a tree single-handedly*, she reminded herself. *Naturally he's bound to have a sore muscle or two.*

Nicholas's shoulder burned like hellfire. It was throbbing, sure to be stiff as a tree stump by morning. He clenched his teeth, determined not to show his weakness. The last thing he needed was sympathy from a do-gooder angel . . . if she really *was* an angel, he amended, wondering if he'd allowed his imagination to run wild. She surely was the most attractive incarnation ever to set foot in this neck of the woods, he thought, gazing appreciatively at her pink-tinged cheeks and the soft swirl of golden hair cascading over her shoulders as she fell into step beside him.

A spasm wrenched his shoulder, ricocheting down his arm. Nicholas winced, nearly dropping the tree. Blast that fool excuse for a doctor who couldn't set an out-of-kilter bone to save his miserable hide! He gritted his teeth, wishing he could reach his hip flask of whiskey to ease his pain.

"Here. Let me help." To his surprise, Joy fell into step behind him, gripping the narrow end of the tree trunk.

"I can manage."

"I'm sure you can. But since you've done so much for us, the least I can do is lend a hand."

Nicholas opened his mouth to protest, but a fresh spurt of pain silenced him. He shrugged, triggering a new spasm in his tormented shoulder, then turned away to hide his humiliation at being too weak to tote home fresh-cut timber without help—from a woman wearing trousers, no less!

Unscrewing his hip flask, he downed a swig of whiskey. He glanced over his shoulder and saw the tight-lipped expression of disapproval her face. Damn her for looking down her perfect little angelic nose at him, anyhow! What right did she have, coming here, turning his life upside down, telling him what not to do? He shoved his hip flask back in its sheath and trudged forward, glowering at the trail ahead.

Back at the cabin, he rekindled the fire in the stove and made a fresh batch of eggnog. Carrying the tureen to the table, he ladled out mugs for Joy and Holly, then poured a liberal dose of whiskey into the remainder. He downed two portions, irked to note the disapproving glint in Joy's eyes.

Frankincense prodded Nicholas with his nose. *Stop it! Mon vieux, this won't do. No, it won't do at all.*

Nicholas glared at the dog, who lowered his muzzle and rested it it on his paws. *I've got to do something about this. But what?*

"If you could see what alcohol does to your liver, you'd take it easy with that stuff," Joy said softly.

Annoyed at her rebuke, Nicholas poured a third helping and drank it. "I reckon that's my business, not yours." He could tell by the spark in her eye he'd rankled her, but before Joy could respond, Holly spied a cannister of popping corn and picked it up. "Mr. Wright, can we string popcorn to decorate the tree? Please?" the child asked excitedly.

A few minutes later, Nicholas found himself holding a long-handled iron pot over a roaring blaze in the fireplace, shaking it back and forth as the kernels popped against the underside of the lid.

His tortured muscles soothed by the alcohol, he set up the tree in the parlor while Joy helped Holly thread the popped corn onto a long piece of fishing twine.

A slurping sound drew his attention. "Oh no!" Joy exclaimed, racing to the kitchen doorway. "Frankincense drank up all the eggnog!"

Nicholas hastened to her side and groaned at the sight of the dog lifting his eggnog-coated muzzle out of the now-empty tureen. Frankincense licked his chops, then let out a large burp.

"Please excuse his manners, ladies," Nicholas said, irritated at the waste of good whiskey.

"Have you given him liquor before?" Joy asked, frowning.

"Of course not! Though given his size, I wouldn't worry. He may be a mite fuzzy-headed for a spell, but there shouldn't be any serious effects."

As if to prove the caretaker's point, Frankincense padded into the living room and sat down. Joy shrugged, picked up the popcorn garland and began winding it around the base of the tree. As she passed the strand to Nicholas on the other side, his hand grazed hers, supple and warm. Taking a step back, he strung the popcorn over the next section of branches, then passed it back to Joy.

As they neared the top branches, she stood on tiptoe. Her corded trousers accentuated every curve in her all-too-pleasing figure. Why the devil didn't she wear skirts like other women, anyhow? Perhaps she wasn't an angel after all, he mused, wondering what it would be like to explore every tantalizing inch of those curves. Surely heaven wouldn't tempt a man by sending down an angel even a saint would be hard-pressed to resist.

"I can't quite reach," she said, stretching her arms up higher. Her breasts strained against her sweater, sending an arc of fire straight through Nicholas. Instinctively he stepped forward, reaching around her to grasp the garland.

"Here, let me—" he began, but was interrupted by a furry ball that catapulted itself against his left side, sending him and Joy tumbling to the floor. Pink color rose in her face as he landed face down on top of her. Suppressing a gasp, he sensed the soft mounds of her sweater pressed against his chest, her lower torso squeezed firmly beneath his abdomen. Holy heaven, just how much temptation was a man supposed to stand?

He propped himself up on his elbows, staring down at her startled eyes and round, pink lips sucking in air. "Are you all right?" he heard himself ask.

"No . . . y-yes," she stammered. "I think I just had the wind knocked out of me. It's never happened to me before."

Suddenly aware that Joy's left palm rested on his right thigh, he felt his loins grow taut. Seeing the flush deepen on her face, he realized she'd sensed his predicament. Her tongue flicked over her lower lip, a nervous gesture, no doubt. Yet in her eyes he'd swear he saw a hunger to match his own. No angel could look and feel so sinfully tempting, he told himself. Giving way to temptation, he bent forward and brushed her lips, eager to savor her all-too-sweet charms.

"Frank, no!" Holly's cry snapped him to his senses. He glanced around in time to see the Christmas tree teetering precariously. Deftly he rolled off Joy and bolted to his feet, catching the tree in midfall. Pain shot through his shoulder; he cursed under his breath.

Frankincense slinked from beneath the tree, head down. He staggered across the room, then plopped down on his favorite pillow beside the hearth. *I tried, chérie. Guess I got carried away, though, with too much eggnog. Mon Dieu, but my head is aching!*

Holly curled up beside the dog, whispering reassurances to the intoxicated animal. Joy scrambled to her feet, brushing pine needles off her sweater self-consciously.

Nicholas stabilized the tree, then moved to stand

beside her, careful to maintain a discreet distance between them. "I apologize—both for that skunk-drunk dog and for myself. I shouldn't have taken such liberties. Forgive me."

"I—don't worry about it. Accidents happen."

She turned away and disappeared into the spare bedroom, returning a moment later with a spool of red ribbon. Nicholas chided himself for nearly believing she was an angel. There must be some other explanation for her appearance out of the blue, footprints or no. Perhaps City of Angels was a nickname for her hometown. "Flew" might just be her way of referring to a fast journey. She couldn't actually have flown here; after all, that sweater she wore could scarcely hide a pair of wings, he assured himself.

"Good thing I packed this ribbon in my flight bag," she announced.

Nicholas felt his jaw drop. "Flight bag? You mean, you really did fly here from—from the City of Angels?"

Frankincense perked up his ears, opening one eye groggily. *City of Angels . . . Oh, no. Nicholas can't think she flew here from Heaven, can he?*

"Yes, of course," Joy confirmed, giving Nicholas a puzzled look. "It was a rough flight, landing through all those storm clouds."

Mon Dieu! Frankincense shut his eyes. *Il fait—he does.*

Nicholas felt thunderstruck as Joy unrolled a length of red ribbon and added, "I brought this to wrap Holly's gift, but there's plenty extra. I thought we could cut it up and make bows to decorate the tree."

Mr. Wright's Christmas Angel

Regaining his wits, he clamped his mouth shut and stepped into the kitchen to find a knife. Joy must be an angel, he concluded. Why else would she insist that she can fly? The child didn't contradict her, he noted. Was the little girl an angel too? Frowning, he pulled a knife out of a drawer and slammed it shut. Blast Kringle's dog for fetching trouble, anyhow!

Back in the parlor, he took the ribbon and sliced it into small strips. Joy and Holly tied the ribbons onto the tree branches, forming them into tidy bows.

Nicholas fetched a piece of hammered tin and a tool from his workshop, then punched out a star shape.

"It's heavenly!" Holly beamed, admiring his handiwork.

Unable to restrain his curiousity, Nicholas asked, "How do you know?"

"Know what?" the child asked, tilting her head to one side.

"What Heaven's like."

"Oh. Why, it's glorious," Holly exclaimed. "Way up in the clouds, all puffy and soft. The houses are gold and white and sparkling, and the angels all wear pearls in their hair. They play harps and sing beautiful songs, and pick gumdrops and cotton candy right off the trees!"

"You sound as if you've seen it," Nicholas said cautiously.

"No, but I know it's true," the child insisted, " 'cause Mommy told me so."

Nicholas's heart stopped. So it's true, he thought, his chest aching at the realization that Joy really was an angel—and a loving mother taken prematurely from her child. Startled to feel a trace of moisture in his eyes, he found himself wanting to protect the innocent little girl from any more pain. He glanced at Joy, whose face had reddened, and felt ashamed of his earlier base desires. Lusting after an angel! *Lord forgive me,* he said to himself, the closest he'd come to praying in longer than he could recall.

Staring at him with luminous eyes and trusting innocence, Holly asked, "Mr. Wright, please can you hang the star now?"

Nicholas fastened the star to the top of the tree, not trusting himself to speak. What had happened to rob Joy Winters of life so young? And how would her innocent daughter cope when Joy returned to the City of Angels?

Chapter Four

Joy stirred a pot of stew on the stove, marveling at the mingled aromas of moose meat, onions, boiled potatoes and cloves. It had taken quite an effort to start a fire in the cast-iron stove and assemble the meal, yet she felt more relaxed than she had in a long time. There was something enchanting about Kriss Kringle's old-fashioned cabin and its caretaker, Nicholas Wright. Enchanting yet disturbing, she amended, recalling the way she'd tingled from head to toe when he'd started to kiss her beneath the falling Christmas tree.

Closing her eyes, she imagined what it would be like to be well and truly kissed by Nicholas Wright—wrapped in the comfort of those strong arms, engulfed by the scent of woodsmoke and the lingering taste of eggnog and nutmeg . . .

She blinked, startled at the strength of her feelings. Nicholas was a man unlike any she'd known before—down-to-earth, good with children; a man with old-fashioned values. She smiled, remembering the way he'd paid attention to Holly's vivid de-

scription of the hereafter—a description Joy had
made up to ease the orphaned girl's concerns over
the deceased parents she'd never known. Nicholas
had listened indulgently, almost as if he'd actually
believed the fanciful vision Holly had described.
He'd make a good father someday, she mused . . .
If only he didn't drink so much. But any man who
started imbibing before noon clearly had a problem
with alcohol, she knew.

What drove such an otherwise strong man to
drink? Isolation, perhaps. Cabin fever. Or something else . . . She frowned, recalling how he'd fa-
vored his right shoulder, propping his left with a
rifle while carrying Holly the evening before and
again today, dragging home the Christmas tree.
Could he have turned to drink to escape pain from
an injury? The nearest doctor might be miles away,
and she doubted many physical therapists, osteo-
paths or chiropractors hung out shingles in such a
remote location. She'd just have to ask him at the
first opportunity, she resolved. If she could help
him professionally, at least she could leave with a
clear conscience after Christmas, knowing she'd re-
paid his hospitality.

Part of her longed to stay past the holidays, to
delay the inevitable hard choices. Yet Joy knew that
was impractical. *You'd better start thinking about
the future—and how you're going to support yourself
and Holly,* her rational half chided.

Yet in truth, Joy felt relieved to be out of the in-
ner-city emergency room. She'd gone into medicine
to heal people—yet lately she'd found herself
spending most of her time patching up gangban-
gers, addicts and drug dealers who returned to the

streets, only to commit new crimes. Besides, she hated the idea of bringing up Holly in an urban area. Though she'd done her best to find a condo in a decent neighborhood, Holly's school had graffiti-scarred walls and had recently expelled a student caught carrying a knife. Somehow, she'd just have to find a way to pay for private school, or relocate. Take out a new loan, if need be.

The idea of practicing in a small town sounded more and more appealing—if only she could find just the right place.

She heard the front door open, followed by the sound of Nicholas stamping his boots on the boot scraper just inside the door.

Joy tucked her hands into the pockets of Mrs. Kringle's floor-length gingham apron, which Nicholas had insisted she borrow. With a ruffled smock top and embroidered reindeer, the garment made her feel like a holiday version of Betty Crocker, and she smiled at the thought as she stepped through the kitchen doorway.

Holly was napping by the hearth, curled up against Frankincense, who was still sleeping off the effects of too much spiked eggnog. She glanced from the hearth to Nicholas, who stood framed in the doorway, ice clinging to the unshaved stubble on his chin. "Mmmmm, sure smells good," he said, closing the door. He carried an armful of logs across the room and set them down in the woodbox by the hearth.

He caught her gaze and held it, staring at her as if he'd seen a vision. "Looks good too," he said softly.

Joy felt her face grow warm from more than the

heat in the kitchen. Nicholas hung his coat on a peg, then took a step closer. Joy's heart fluttered against her ribs. She'd be crazy to get involved with Nicholas Wright, a backwoods caretaker she'd never see again after Christmas, or whenever the road to Fairbanks reopened.

"Nicholas," she began. "I—"

"Snow's falling too hard to get to town," he informed her. "Drifts are too deep. First thing in the morning, I promise I'll take you to Noel—assuming the weather cooperates."

Joy swallowed her disappointment. Notifying the rental car company and the authorities of the theft would just have to wait another day. On the other hand, she consoled herself, chances are the car thieves didn't make it too far, with the highway to Fairbanks snowed in.

"It's all right," she assured him.

He rubbed his shoulder, a pained expression on his face. Joy moved forward and rested her palm on his shoulder instinctively. "You're in pain. Nicholas, what's wrong?"

He jerked back as if burned. "Nothing."

"Nicholas, I can tell you're hurting. If you'll just tell me about it, I could—"

"Could what? Nag at me some more about my vices?" His voice held a steely edge. "Seeing as you're Kringle's guest, it's not my place to send you packing. But I'd thank you to mind your own business as long as we're stuck sleeping under the same roof!"

Stunned, Joy opened her mouth to protest his rude response to her good intentions, but was halted by a mournful howl from Frankincense.

Mr. Wright's Christmas Angel

"Bad dreams?" Nicholas crossed the room to rub the dog's enormous head. "Must be that demon whiskey," he said in a sardonic tone. Frankincense opened one eye and yawned widely.

Holly rubbed her eyes and sat up. Spying Nicholas, she grinned. "You're back!"

"You bet, partner. And it smells like your Mama's rustled up some mighty fine grub. What do you say we go have some supper?"

"Yum!" Holly exclaimed, gripping Nicholas's hand. He pulled her to her feet and steered her toward the kitchen, leaving Joy to wonder how one man could be so exasperating and desirable all at the same time.

Chapter Five

After dinner, Nicholas boiled wash water in a large kettle. Amazed that the cabin didn't even have running water, Joy wondered how Kriss Kringle had managed to avoid all the trappings of the twentieth century as she dried the dishes and put them away in a hand-hewn pine hutch. She'd heard tales of modern-day mountain men living in rustic cabins in the wilderness, of course. Clearly the man was as eccentric as his name implied. A name he'd probably had legally changed from something far more mundane.

Joy doused the kitchen lantern and stepped into the living room. Her heart warmed at the sight of Nicholas telling a story to Holly, who was tucked comfortably beneath a quilt in front of the fireplace, Frankincense curled at her side. Holly deserved to have a father like Nicholas, Joy thought, anguish stirring inside her at the memory of Holly's Christmas wish. If only she could find a way to protect her little girl from being disillusioned on Christmas morning, she thought for the thousandth time.

Mr. Wright's Christmas Angel

Nicholas looked up and flashed a grin. "Come on over," he said, patting a cushion on the floor beside him. Joy sat down, heat from the fireplace radiating into her chilled bones. Seeing her shiver, Nicholas draped his right arm around her and pulled her closer. Warmth from his arm burned a molten trail straight to Joy's heart as Nicholas opened Holly's favorite storybook.

He read the title aloud. "Frankincense, Santa's Christmas Dog." Nicholas glanced at Holly, clearly startled.

"The coincidence threw me for a loop at first too," Joy said. "Then I realized Mr. Kringle must've read this story and named his dog after the character in the book."

Frankincense lifted his noble head and blinked. *Ah, chérie. You have much to learn. Nicholas, too, it seems.*

Nicholas stroked his chin, pondering Joy's words. "That's a logical explanation." He flipped past the title page and began to read the tale in a voice rich and warm as melted honey. "Santa Claus loves traveling around the world, bringing toys to children everywhere each Christmas Eve," he read. "But things weren't always so merry. Once, Santa's reindeer spent all day frolicking across the tundra, playing reindeer games. When the sun set, they refused to come back inside their nice, safe barn."

He went on to recite the antics of the disobedient reindeer, who scampered onto an icy pond, narrowly escaped a hungry bear and tracked slushy hoofprints all over Mrs. Claus's freshly mopped floor.

Joy smiled at the delight evident in Holly's eyes as Nicholas described Santa's journey to a faraway land in the Pyrenees mountains, embellishing the story with vivid details. He retold how Santa met a young shepherd boy with two large, white dogs named Gold and Myrrh—and a bounding puppy called Frankincense. While Santa watched the dogs herd sheep into a pen, the shepherd boy told of the dogs' origin—descended from an ancestor in Bethlehem.

"Wise men and kings came to see the Christ child, bringing marvelous gifts," Nicholas read, describing how a long-ago shepherd gave up his beloved dog—a scraggly brown animal that was the boy's most precious possession. "The kings were amazed to see a poor boy give up all that he owned to honor the newborn child," Nicholas read. "One of the kings decided to reward the shepherd boy for his generous spirit. So the king gave the boy his royal mascot, a glorious white dog."

Nicholas told how descendants of the Bethlehem shepherd emigrated to the Pyrenees mountains in Europe, bringing offspring of the regal white dog with them to tend their flocks. "Touched by the boy's story," he read, "Santa asked the young shepherd in the Pyrenees what he wanted for Christmas. 'A good home for the puppy, Frankincense,' the boy replied, explaining that his family already had two dogs and couldn't keep the pup. 'Would you like a puppy for Christmas, Santa?'" Nicholas read.

Joy's eyes misted as Holly begged Nicholas to finish the tale. He described how Santa brought Frankincense back to his home in the arctic, where the dog learned to herd reindeer and became Santa's faithful mascot.

As Nicholas turned the last page and saw the illustration of Santa's log home in the Northern woods, she saw the startled spark of recognition in his eyes. He held the book closer, studying the full-color illustration.

"The similarity is uncanny, isn't it?" Joy observed, peering over his shoulder.

"Yes, though there must be hundreds of log cabins very much like this one in this territory," Nicholas pointed out. "And as you've observed, Kringle probably read this book. Obviously he was inspired to add features from this illustration when he built his cabin."

"Of course, you're right," Joy agreed. Santa Claus is only a make-believe figure, she reminded herself. And Kriss Kringle is just an eccentric old man with a Santa Claus complex. *Get a grip, Joy, or next you'll be looking for elves in the woods and imagining reindeer can fly.*

She kissed Holly good night. Before she could ask Nicholas about his shoulder, however, he informed Joy that he had chores to take care of in the barn.

Soon Holly was sleeping peacefully. Joy tiptoed into the bedroom and changed into her nightgown, then unzipped the flight bag and pulled out the autoharp she'd found in a music store. It wasn't a daddy, but Joy hoped Holly would love it anyhow. She'd known the moment she laid eyes on the instrument that it was the perfect Christmas gift, since Holly loved to sing.

Joy pulled out the tuning wrench she'd purchased and began tightening the tuning pins, grateful for her years of voice lessons and the fact that she'd been gifted from birth with perfect pitch. After poking her head around the corner to make sure Holly was still asleep, she cradled the autoharp in her arms and strummed her fingers across the strings.

Soothed by the melodious sound, she donned fingerpicks, pressed the chord buttons with her left hand and plucked the strings with her right hand, creating graceful arpeggios. She smiled, envisioning Holly's delight in the instrument, and began leafing through the music book she'd purchased.

Nicholas slipped off his boots and turned the doorknob quietly, so as not to awaken Holly. He tiptoed into the kitchen, shoulder blazing like hellfire from lifting hay bales to feed Kringle's livestock. Finding the whiskey bottle, he chugged down a hefty swig. Tilting the bottle up, he finished off the last drops, grateful for the fiery warmth he knew would soon lessen his pain. Blast Joy for prying into his personal affairs, he thought, his annoyance flaring anew at her meddlesome questions earlier. If only—

A sweet, flowing sound broke his concentration, filling the tiny cabin with music. *Harp music*. Tarnation! Nicholas nearly dropped the empty whiskey bottle. Staggering into the parlor, he stumbled towards the source of the sound. He braced himself in the doorframe of the guest bedroom, struck dumb as if seared by a bolt of lightning.

Joy was seated on the bed, her back to him, cradling an instrument in her arms. Nicholas had never seen a harp before, but the sweet strains cascading from the strings Joy alternately plucked and strummed were the most beautiful sounds he'd ever heard. *She's an angel, you fool. It stands to reason she'd play the harp as if she'd been born to the practice.*

Then she started singing "Silent Night," and he knew beyond a doubt that Joy's voice was surely the most melodious sound in heaven or on earth. The pure, perfect voice of an angel . . .

Spying his reflection in the looking glass above the bureau, she stopped playing and turned toward him. "I hope I didn't disturb you, Nicholas."

Disturbed was an understatement, Nicholas thought, fighting down the all-too-unchaste thoughts racing through his brain at the vision of Joy, draped in a flowing white gown, her womanly shape silhouetted in a halo of light from a lantern beside the bed.

Joy put the autoharp back in its case, startled at the look on Nicholas's face—as if he'd seen a ghost, she thought disjointedly.

"I know why you've come." His low voice, slightly slurred, held an underlying sensuality that made Joy's cheeks burn.

"You do?" she asked, sensing the desire in his tone as he stepped closer, then sat down on the bed beside her. She smelled the whiskey on his breath and realized he was drunk, or close to it.

"No point denying it." He brushed a curl off her forehead, his fingertip grazing her burning cheek. "I'm curious about one thing, though. What happened to bring your former life, as I believe you termed it, to such an untimely demise?"

Joy blinked, swallowing hard. "The hospital—you know about that?" Had Holly somehow overheard her talking about losing her job and confided in Nicholas? He knew she was a doctor out of work.

It seemed the only logical explanation. Not that anything had seemed logical since her arrival in Noel, Alaska.

He lifted her chin with his index finger, forcing her to meet his penetrating gaze. "I know that something terrible happened, something that made you leave your old life behind."

She felt as if the air had been knocked from her lungs a second time. "I was terminated," she confessed.

"Terminated?" A flash of anger sparked in his eyes. "You mean, this wasn't an accident? A tragic whim of fate?"

"I didn't see eye-to-eye with the powers that be," she explained, intrigued at his quaint choice of words even as she fought down a tremor at the realization that she was alone in a bedroom in an isolated cabin with an angry, drunken man.

"That doesn't justify what happened to you—or Holly," he said, his pupils flaring with indignation. "With such unforgiving powers that be, I can see why you'd want to fly away from that City of Angels and come here for a spell."

Reassured by his apparent concern for her welfare, Joy nodded. "Yes. You can't imagine how wonderful it is to be free—just to hear birds singing and feel snow crunch beneath my feet and breathe fresh, mountain air again," she went on, recalling scenes from her childhood near the Cascade range in Washington. "If only—"

"If only what?" Startled at the depth of emotion reflected in his eyes, Joy clamped her lips shut. She'd been on the verge of saying "if only I didn't have to leave," but stopped herself in time.

Mr. Wright's Christmas Angel

"Nothing. I was just remembering happier times, that's all."

"Tell me about them."

Finding it hard to concentrate on anything other than the distracting way his blue eyes crinkled at the corners, she replied, "I was thinking about the time my father took me sledding, before he and my mother died. They were killed by a drunk driver when I was twelve years old."

"Good Lord." He sucked in air. "Guess that explains why you started like a spooked calf every time I downed a swig of whiskey." Grasping her shoulders protectively, he pledged, "Joy, I promise I'd never do anything to hurt you."

"You're hurting yourself, Nicholas," she said gently. "Though I suspect you're drinking to escape some hidden pain. I've seen how you favor your right shoulder. Did you injure it somehow?"

"That's not your concern." His jaw clamped shut.

"Tell me what happened, Nicholas," she persisted. "I might be able to help."

"You already know more than is decent about me," he said, his words growing more and more slurred. "Though I guess that comes with the territory, doesn't it, Miz do-gooder angel? Next I suppose you'll be telling me you're a faith healer too."

"You're not making any sense," she chided. She pressed her palm against his shoulder, eliciting a pained grunt. "You know what I am," she reminded him, "so you may as well know that I'm quite adept at treating injuries—provided the patient isn't too stubborn to let me examine him."

Nicholas's head throbbed nearly as badly as his shoulder. *Liquor must be dulling at least some of my senses*, he thought, sure that he'd heard wrong. Had his self-appointed guardian angel really claimed to have the power to heal his pain?

"You've done this before?" he asked, wary of letting anyone else—even a do-gooder angel—poke at his sore shoulder.

She nodded. "Oh, yes. Lots of times. We'd get accident victims in where I came from, poor souls with mangled limbs and—"

"Good Lord." A vision of wounded souls passing through the Pearly Gates waiting for Joy's healing touch flashed in Nicholas's befuddled brain. "Aw, hell. Go ahead and give it your best try. Lord knows you can't do any worse than the jackass who tried before."

"Take off your shirt," she ordered.

"What? But—" He started to protest the impropriety of stripping down half-naked in front of a female, then remembered Joy was no mere mortal woman. He could hardly tarnish the reputation of an angel! Nicholas recalled illustrations he'd seen of buck-naked cherubs and figured she'd seen her share cavorting around the City of Angels. "Oh, hell." He unbuttoned his shirt and tossed it aside.

"You shouldn't swear, especially with a child in the house. Now, stand up," she instructed.

Grudgingly, he obeyed. "Holly's asleep—ouch!" he yelped as she poked beneath his shoulderblade.

"Sorry about that. I've got to do a complete examination, find the trigger points and check your range of motion," she explained.

"Raise your arm," she directed. Following her instructions, he rotated his shoulder as far as he could, gritting his teeth to keep from flinching as he completed the series of movements she requested.

"Now, lie down on the bed," Joy instructed, pursing those ever-so-luscious lips of hers.

Nicholas's mouth went dry. The only times he'd been invited onto a mattress by a female, it had definitely not been for a physical exam. At least, not the clinical sort Joy Winters had in mind. Fighting down lustful thoughts and an impulse to pull her into his arms for a sinfully pleasurable tumble, he lay on the bed, face-down.

Her hands felt cool and soothing as they moved expertly over his upper back, neck and shoulders, alternately pressing, prodding and massaging his aching muscles. A man could do far worse than to have his own personal guardian angel, he decided as he closed his eyes and surrendered himself to her touch. Sweet Lord, but it felt good to have her caressing his tortured flesh.

Joy bent forward and prodded a sore point behind his shoulder, triggering a bolt of pain. "Da— er, drat," he gasped.

She traced her fingertips across the ravaged scar on his forearm. "You've been burned." Her voice filled with concern. "Is that how you knocked your shoulder out of joint—escaping from a fire?"

Surprised that the powers that be hadn't filled her in on the details of his case, Nicholas replied, "I was building a house when the wind blew over a lantern on the porch. Whole place went up in flames—all I could save were some tools from my workshop."

"It was your house that burned?"

He nodded. "Bad enough losing the house, without having a blasted beam fall and knock my shoulder out of kilter."

"I'm sorry," she murmured. "So that's why you're working as a caretaker for Mr. Kringle."

"Had to live someplace," he said hoarsely, "till I get the place rebuilt."

"So you're a builder?"

"A carpenter."

Returning her attention to his shoulder, she lifted his arm and tilted it forward, then back. "Someone's set this wrong. Who treated you?"

Stopping the string of curses that threatened to escape his lips, he glowered at the memory of the so-called doctor who'd ground his boot heel into Nicholas's armpit, yanking the arm until Nicholas hollered from the pain. "Blasted fool should have stuck to barbering," he muttered under his breath.

Joy looked at him as if she'd heard wrong. "Are you telling me you let a *barber* treat your injuries?"

"Who else was I supposed to get?"

"Isn't there a doctor in this town, or one nearby?"

"Not for a couple of hundred miles. Might as well be a million in winter, though. Cassidy, the barber, claimed to have some medical training, though frankly I doubt that butcher could heal a blister on his own ass—er, backside."

Shaking her head, Joy instructed him to hang his arm over the edge of the bed. "This might hurt a little," she cautioned.

Pressing one hand into the hollow behind his shoulder blade, she fastened a surprisingly strong grip around his upper arm and pulled outward. Nicholas held his breath. She tugged again, harder this time, and rotated the arm forward in its socket.

A loud pop and a moment of intense pain gave way to a sudden sensation of relief.

Nicholas sat up and rubbed the sore spot behind his shoulder, then turned his neck from side to side. The tight, painful place where his shoulder muscles joined his neck scarcely felt stiff at all.

"Merciful heavens, you are a miracle worker," he whispered.

She smiled, illuminating the night. "I'm glad the spasm's better, though it will take a little time for you to reach full recovery. You've probably been compensating for your injury by using your muscles differently than normal, so you'll need to start a program of exercises to rebuild your strength."

Nicholas's mouth went dry. "What kind of exercises?" he asked, thinking of one particular exercise he'd very much like to undertake.

"Slow, gradual movements," she said, bending over to demonstrate a stretching maneuver. She was so close Nicholas could scarcely stand not to reach out and pull her onto his lap. The top button of her nightgown had come undone, revealing creamy white flesh underneath. Lord, he thought, heat rushing to his lower regions, how much temptation do you expect a man to resist?

"I'll help you at first," she was saying, "then later you can build up stamina."

A groan slid from his lips. Knowing if he tarried a moment longer he'd be in danger of debauching an angel, Nicholas pulled himself to his feet and reeled toward the door. "Much obliged, Miz Winters," he managed, his tongue thick from whiskey and desire.

Turning away from temptation incarnate, he

staggered out of her room and shut the door behind him. He made his way to the kitchen, where he picked up his last bottle of whiskey.

He carried it out to the front porch and opened it. Raising the bottle, he stared longingly at the fiery liquid gleaming in the moonlight.

"Aw, hell," he cussed for the last time. Then he tilted the bottle upside down and poured the liquor onto the snow.

Chapter Six

Joy tossed beneath the covers, sinking deeper into the softness of the down-filled mattress. If only she could put the image of Nicholas's bare-chested, dusky-haired masculinity out of her mind. Yet try as she might, all Joy seemed able to think of was the raw power she'd felt as she'd stroked her palms and fingertips over the corded muscles in his back—lean and powerful, except for the injured area.

She'd have to have been blind not to have seen the desire in his eyes, or heard the husky tone in his voice fueled by more than whiskey. Why, then, hadn't he acted on his desires? For an instant she'd been certain he'd intended to kiss her—at the very least—and to her surprise, had found herself hoping that he would. For an instant she'd envisioned Nicholas pulling her into his strong arms and making wild, passionate love to her beneath this very quilt, filling her with the need she'd seen emblazoned in his eyes. . . .

Eyes that might not find her attractive when he's sober, Joy reminded herself. She sighed, telling herself she should be grateful Nicholas had exhibited restraint, even in his alcohol-soaked state of mind.

Then why did she feel so empty inside?

The next morning, Christmas Eve, Joy stood in front of the mirror, hardly recognizing herself. At Nicholas's insistence, she'd borrowed a forest green wool dress with black velvet trim and a full-length skirt from Mrs. Kringle's wardrobe chest—which was filled with long dresses. Mr. Kringle's wife must be as eccentric as her husband, Joy thought. Or maybe the older woman simply preferred long skirts for warmth in the arctic climate.

Apparently Mrs. Kringle was a bit on the plump side, she noted, grateful that she'd managed to pin up seams on the inside to adjust the fit. As a finishing touch, she swept up her hair in a bun to match the quaint costume and topped it off with a broad-brimmed green hat trimmed with black felt and a ribbon that tied beneath her chin.

"Mommy, Mommy! Come look!" Holly burst into the bedroom, eyes widening. "Wow, you look like one of those storybook people."

Joy smiled, feeling a bit like she'd stepped into a Victorian stage play. "What's all the excitement about?" she asked, pulling on a long cloak.

Holly grabbed her mother's hand and towed Joy out the front door. As she stepped off the porch, Joy saw an empty whiskey bottle on the ground. A cold feeling penetrated her heart; had Nicholas done more drinking after he left her room? Then she saw the broad, tell-tale stain on the snow and realized Nicholas had spilled his liquor. But was it by accident, or on purpose? Buoyed by the thought that there might be hope for him yet, she turned to Holly. "Now then, what did you want to show me?"

"Frankincense is playing with the reindeer," Holly announced gleefully.

Joy nearly stumbled in the snow. "R-reindeer?"

Holly's head bounced up and down. "Come see!"

The child mounted a snowy hill and pointed to a valley on the other side. Joy scrambled up to stand beside her daughter, certain that the frosty air must be affecting her brain cells.

Below, in an icy meadow, the Great Pyrenees was running in a zigzag pattern, nipping at the heels of a half-dozen reindeer. As she watched in disbelief, the dog rounded up stragglers and herded the entire group into a barnyard pen at the far side of the valley.

Nicholas, holding the gate open, spotted them. For an instant he stood stock-still, then waved. "Come on down," he shouted, cupping gloved hands around his mouth.

Climbing down the hillside, Joy found herself scanning the herd in search of a red-nosed reindeer. Finding none, she managed a nervous chuckle. She really was starting to lose her grip on reality, she chided herself.

"They're mighty high-spirited this morning, so I let them out for a romp before we head to town," Nicholas said, gesturing toward a wooden sleigh parked inside the open barn door. Flashing a smile that warmed Joy to her toes, he added, "You look mighty pretty in that getup, even for a healing angel."

Angel? Joy flushed at the compliment as he

closed the gate and walked into the barn, Frankincense and Holly at his heels.

The dog halted in mid-frolic, staring at Joy in Mrs. Kringle's dress. *Ooh-la-la! Chérie, you are magnificent in that ensemble. Nicholas, can't you see she's the perfect mate for you?*

"I can't believe Kriss Kringle actually owns a sleigh," Joy exclaimed, her breath frosty as she followed Nicholas inside.

He shrugged. "Nothing so strange about driving a sleigh around these parts."

"But the reindeer!" She stared suspiciously at the herd milling in the pen outside. "Don't tell me their names are Dasher, Dancer—"

Nicholas waved a hand dismissively. "Of course not."

Joy breathed a sigh of relief, chastening herself for letting her imagination run wilder than Kriss Kringle's reindeer.

"This is the spare team," Nicholas continued.

"What?" Joy blinked.

"Dasher and the rest of the number-one team are with Kringle on his travels."

Holly tugged at Nicholas's arm. "Do they really fly, Mr. Wright?"

Nicholas knelt beside the child. "I haven't actually seen them fly," he informed her, winking at Joy over Holly's shoulder. "Though with Kriss Kringle's reindeer, I imagine anything's possible. Just like in that storybook of yours."

Joy shook her head, unable to dispel the disturbing thoughts taking root in her mind. Reindeer couldn't really fly, she told herself. Nicholas was merely trying not to ruin the Christmas myth for

Holly. And Kriss Kringle's eccentricity apparently extended to naming reindeer after Santa's fabled herd.

"How's your shoulder?" she asked, anxious to change the subject.

"A tad stiff, but better than its been in months." A shadow darkened his tanned face. "I've got you to thank for that." He cleared his throat, then added, "Reckon I owe you an apology. I was wrong for being so all-fired stubborn, and losing my temper when you only meant to help me."

"Apology accepted. I'm just glad my medical training came in handy. I've written out some exercises that should help," she added, handing him a folded piece of paper.

"Why did you become a healer, anyhow?" He pocketed the paper. "If you don't mind my asking."

"After my parents died in that accident, I kept wondering if there wasn't something, anything, that could have been done to save them. The doctors at the hospital tried their best, but . . ." she sighed. "So I decided to study medicine, hoping to spare other families the pain I went through. I helped a lot of people in my prior life," she said, adding softly, "before my termination."

He scratched his head, surprised to hear she'd been a healer before she ever got to Heaven. Before he could ask how a female managed to get medical training, Joy said softly, "I'm still trying to sort out where to go from here."

Nicholas felt something twist inside him at Joy's mention of leaving. Of course, she'd be moving on soon now that her work here was finished. She'd sweet-talked him into giving up drinking and swearing, and managed to heal his bad shoulder to boot. She'd fallen out of the sky and into his life only two days ago, yet already it seemed he'd known her all his life. And wanted to know her better still. For the first time, Nicholas found himself unable to look forward to Christmas, knowing that after the holiday, Joy would be going back to the City of Angels. Her return trip was scheduled for December 26th, he remembered glumly.

There's nothing you can do about it, Nicholas. You can't fight the powers that be. Choking down anguish, he headed into the barn, striding past the empty reindeer stalls. At least he could make sure Joy and Holly's last days here were happy ones. "I've got to load up a few things from my workshop, then we'll head for town."

To his consternation, Joy trailed after him. Now that she'd accomplished what she'd set out to do, couldn't she leave him be?

As he reached his makeshift workshop at the far end of the barn, he heard her startled cry of surprise. Turning, he saw her gaze sweep the room, taking in the shelves filled with hand-carved wooden toys and dolls. "Oh, Nicholas, they're marvelous! Did you make them all?"

He nodded, pleased at the sparkle of approval in her eyes. "Most of my work is on contract for Kringle's export business," he explained. "But not these. I always make a few extras for the children of Noel."

"What a wonderful thing to do," Joy whispered in an awestruck tone.

He shrugged. "Most everyone in Noel works for Kringle. Lumberjacks, sawyers, weavers, a painter or two . . ."

Mr. Wright's Christmas Angel

Seeing Holly gaze longingly at a curly-haired doll with a red gingham dress, he picked up the doll and handed it to her. "For you, young lady," he said, his heart warming at the bittersweet sight of Holly's blissful expression. "Now then, how would you and your mother like to help me deliver all these toys to the rest of the children in this town?"

With a delighted cry, she raced toward the sleigh, clutching the treasured doll. Nicholas lifted the child into the backseat and tucked a blanket across her lap.

Frankincense woofed loudly, then bounded into the sleigh beside Holly. *Keep smiling, ma petite. Things will work out—if only we can find a way to get through Nicholas's thick skull by tomorrow morning.*

Nicholas harnessed the reindeer and hitched them to the sleigh, shaking his head as he noted the odd way that dog of Kringle's was staring at him. He helped Joy into the front seat, then climbed in beside her. Taking the reins, he urged the reindeer to a brisk trot.

Soon Joy and Holly began singing Christmas carols, their angelic voices mingling with the jingle of sleigh bells and the whistling of the wind. Nicholas joined in the merriment, unable to remember when he'd felt so alive.

Yet when Joy struck up a chorus of "Hark, the Herald Angels Sing," Nicholas's heart froze. How could he bear to lose the angel he'd come to cherish—and the one woman who would never be free to love him in return?

* * *

Seated beside Nicholas, gliding over the snowy terrain, skin tingling from the cold, Joy felt an exhilaration she'd never known before. After so many years of working in a sterile, urban environment, she'd forgotten how enjoyable simple pleasures could be. And some not so simple . . . Gazing at Nicholas, she found herself mesmerized by his every word, movement, and facial expression: the way the wind ruffled his hair, the beauty of the sunshine gleaming through the ice crystals on his thick, dark eyelashes, the way his face seemed to light up when he smiled, without pain. She'd been amazed when he'd shown her the toys he must have spent months making for the town's children, touched by the generous spirit inside the heart of this rugged, reclusive man. Nicholas Wright was an enigma; an old-fashioned man who had somehow managed to escape all the trappings of a modern day world. She snuggled against him, longing for him to wrap his arm around her and draw her closer, disappointed when he did not.

Nicholas guided the sleigh into town. A towering pine tree stood in the middle of the town square, festooned with ribbons and bows.

"Welcome to Noel," he announced, tethering the reins at a hitching post.

"Mommy, it looks just like Frontierland!" Holly exclaimed, recalling a recent visit to Disneyland.

Joy looked around, her amazement growing with each new sight. Indeed, the rough-hewn log buildings and wooden boardwalks festooned with green and red bunting did bear a striking resemblance to something out of the nineteenth century, no doubt a throwback to the region's frontier past. Even the stores bore names chosen, she supposed, to attract tourists—a mercantile shop, haberdashery, general store, even a blacksmith! Presumably some of the townspeople still relied on horses—not cars, and certainly not reindeer—for transportation in areas too remote for any snowplow to reach. Odd that there weren't any cars or even snowmobiles in sight, though . . . For a moment she wondered if she really had slipped magically into the past, but dismissed the idea as quickly as it had come.

"I need to notify the rental company about the stolen station wagon," she reminded Nicholas. "Where's the nearest telephone?"

"A small town like Noel way up in these Northern woods won't likely get telephone service for years, if ever." He stared at her oddly. "But there's a telegraph office across the street."

Her mouth opened in surprise. Was it really possible at the dawn of the twenty-first century for there to be a town so remote that it didn't have phone service?

"Fine, then. I'll send a telegram." Keeping her concerns to herself, she walked with Nicholas and Holly into the Western Union office.

Frankincense waited outside, wet nose pressed against a frosted windowpane. *This could be a problem . . . Mon Dieu! She's as strong-willed as Nicholas.*

Inside the telegraph office, Joy spied a clerk behind a barred window, dressed like an extra from a *Gunsmoke* rerun. She gave him the name of the rental car company. He creased his brow, rubbing his chin thoughtfully. "Can't say as I've heard of any such business, ma'am."

A warning bell sounded in Joy's head. "But I rented a car from them in Fairbanks, just a couple of days ago!"

"A cart, you say?"

"Car! A station wagon, brown with green trim. Only somebody stole it."

The clerk frowned. "Never had no highway robbers in these parts, not in recent memory, anyhow."

"There must be something you can do," Joy insisted, exasperated.

"Tell you what, ma'am. I'll wire the sheriff's office down in Fairbanks," the clerk offered. "Tell him to keep a lookout for your stolen wagon."

Nicholas paid the clerk, wondering why Joy had raised such a ruckus over a missing wagon when she could simply fly back to the City of Angels. More importantly, why had her face turned pale as snow the moment she'd laid eyes on the town?

"Much obliged, Cyrus," he said to the clerk. "Any news comes in, you let me know."

Outside, Joy noticed the old-fashioned clothing worn by seemingly everyone in the town. It reminded her of Williamsburg or Mystic Seaport—one of those places where everything had been historically recreated and everyone dressed in costumes to please the tourists. *Except that I'm the only tourist here in the middle of winter*. The thought jarred her; what logical explanation could there be?

"In celebration of Christmas Eve, all the shops close at noon. There's a festival in the town square, with dancing and food and good old-fashioned fun," Nicholas informed her.

Joy expelled a nervous laugh. "That sounds great," she said, relieved to discover there was a logical explanation for the old-time attire after all.

They stopped at a candy shop, where Nicholas bought a bagful of peppermint sticks for Holly. Joy slipped next door to the leather goods store and tried to buy a hand-tooled belt with silver buckle as a Christmas gift for Nicholas, but was dismayed when the proprietor not only refused to accept her traveler's check, but acted as though he'd never seen one before. She'd packed most of her cash in her luggage, since at the time it had seemed wise to keep cash and traveler's checks separate. But how could she possibly find a gift suitable for Nicholas without money?

Emerging from the store, she met up with Holly and Nicholas on the boardwalk. Around the square, merchants were closing up shop. "Mommy, look!" Holly squealed with delight, pointing at a large bonfire blazing on one side of the square. Nearby, tables had been set up, topped with delightful looking baked goods; someone was ladling out cups of hot cider from a large keg. Frankincense perched atop the sleigh, guarding Nicholas's stash of toys. Spying the trio, the dog wagged his bushy white tail, jumped down from the sleigh and trotted over to greet them.

"So there you are!" A tawny-haired man bearing a striking resemblance to Nicholas took the steps two at a time, halting on the boardwalk two paces in front of them. He glanced at Joy, who had linked arms with Nicholas. "Looks like you've been holding out on me, little brother," he said, his face splitting into a broad grin. "Are you going to introduce me to your lady friend here, or do I have to do the honors myself?"

"Matt, this is Joy Winters and her daughter, Holly," Nicholas obliged. "They're visitors here—friends of Kriss Kringle's."

Matt's eyebrows shot up. "Visitors, at this time of year?"

"Nice to meet you." Joy smiled, surprised to learn Nicholas had family in town. She extended her right hand; Matt kissed the back of it, staring at her intently.

"You've got yourself a real angel, here, Nicholas," Matt observed, still staring at Joy as he rose to his feet.

A strangled sound came from Nicholas's throat. "Please excuse my brother," he informed Joy after a moment. "Subtlety has never been one of his many charms."

Frankincense barked, nuzzling against Nicholas's brother.

Doffing his hat, Matt looked suitably chagrined. "Nicholas, Felicity sent me to find you and invite you for Christmas Eve dinner, right after the festival. She and our sisters are home cooking up a feast, so I brought the young 'uns to town," he said, gesturing across the square to a crowd of frolicking children. "Reckon Felicity'd have my hide if I didn't invite your charming companion and her daughter too."

Seeing the uncomfortable expression on Nicholas's face, Joy wondered if he was merely trying to avoid second-guessing how she might want to spend Christmas Eve. "I haven't been to a family Christmas dinner in many years," she said softly. "It sounds lovely."

Matt winked at Holly. "I'll bet this young lady

would enjoy playing with our girls." To Joy, he added, "Our sisters, Hope and Faith, will be there with their families—five boys and four girls between them, plus our three makes a dozen youngsters. Should be enough to launch quite a snowball fight."

Holly clapped her hands, looking at Nicholas with eyes gleaming excitedly. "Please, Mr. Wright?"

"All right, you've convinced me." Nicholas surrendered, warming Joy's heart. "Matt, tell Felicity we're looking forward to her good cooking."

Watching his brother stride away moments later, Nicholas wondered if he'd taken leave of his senses. He'd had little choice but to accept Felicity's invitation, but he didn't have the foggiest notion how to explain where Holly and Joy had come from, or what they were doing in Noel. Sharing a family dinner was one thing, he thought as he took Joy's arm and escorted her across the street. But how in blazes was he supposed to explain Joy Winters and the City of Angels to his all-too-curious siblings?

Chapter Seven

Beside the Christmas tree in the town square, Nicholas tapped his heel in rhythm with a fiddler's lively rendition of "God Rest Ye Merry Gentlemen."

He glanced at Joy, who was singing blissfully, along with Holly and the townspeople: "To save us all from Satan's fire when we were gone astray, o tidings of comfort and joy . . ."

Joy was a comfort—and an enticement to any man, he mused, mesmerized by the rapturous look on her face and the pure, bell-like quality of her voice nearly as much as by the sensuousness of her touch and the loving nature of her spirit—a spirit that no doubt had saved his own misguided soul, he thought, frowning at the thought of the impending family gathering.

How on earth was he supposed to explain Joy to his relatives? If he told them she was an angel, his brother would think he'd gone stark raving mad— a surefire case of cabin fever. But if he kept mum, his sisters would undoubtedly try their best at matchmaking—again.

Mr. Wright's Christmas Angel

Nicholas half-wished the icy street would crack open and swallow him up before supper. He shook his head, stifling a groan.

Mercifully, the music stopped. "Mr. Wright, what's inside your bag?" A child's voice called out. Looking around, Nicholas saw his nieces and nephews, along with the rest of the town's children, gathering around him, Joy and Holly.

"Something special, just for you, Tommy," Nicholas answered, pulling out a wooden toy cart. The boy's eyes widened as he accepted the gift. Next, Nicholas produced a wooden top and set it spinning on the table, winning squeals of delight from the four-year-old girl next in line. He passed out a bear puppet on strings to a boy behind her, relishing the happiness on the child's face when he made the bear dance on command.

Raising his eyes, he saw the light of approval in Joy's gaze as she watched him pass out more gifts, until the last of the town's children gratefully accepted a miniature locomotive. As the child hobbled away, Joy whispered, "He's limping. Why?"

Nicholas lowered his voice. "Accident. Poor waif got kicked by a horse."

"Hasn't he seen a doctor?" Joy asked, clearly upset.

"Noel doesn't have one," Nicholas reminded her. "Until recently, most folks relied on Cassidy, the barber, to doctor festering wounds or stich up bad cuts. But he left town last month."

"But that's terrible!" she exclaimed. "I can't believe children are going without medical care, in this day and age—"

The fiddler struck up a lively reel, drowning out

the rest of her words. Frankincense thumped the ground with his tail, keeping time with the beat. *What are you waiting for, Nicholas? Ask mademoiselle to dance!*

Struck by an irresistible impulse, Nicholas grabbed Joy's hand and towed her out to the middle of the street, where the townspeople had cleared away snow to form a makeshift dance floor. He placed one hand at her waist and clasped her fingers with his remaining hand, her warmth seeping into his hand straight through his gloves. Whirling her around and around, he heard a startled gasp slip from her lips and saw the bright flush of color in her cheeks. For an angel, she sure seemed to be enjoying this earthly pleasure, Nicholas noted with satisfaction.

He drew her closer, his heart pumping in his chest until he felt sure he would explode. Around them, people had begun clapping; the sound pulsed in his temples as the music's tempo increased. The wind loosened her hair, blowing stray wisps freely around her face. Her lips glistened like dewy rosebuds in the waning light; Nicholas wondered what it would be like to taste them, tenderly at first, then crushing his mouth against hers, savoring every inch of Joy Winters—

Lord Almighty! What had gotten into him? Nicholas closed his mind against the devilish notions lurking there, wondering how in blazes he could feel hot all over in the middle of a freezing arctic winter.

Frankincense watched Nicholas leave Joy standing, dumbfounded, in the middle of the street. *Mon vieux, but you are denser than a flock of bleating sheep!* Tilting his head back, he howled at the celestial sky above.

Joy drew in a breath, charmed at the sight of Nicholas's brother and sister-in-law's home on the outskirts of town. The cheery red-and-white house reminded her of a Victorian cottage, with a steeply-pitched roof, wide porch and an abundance of gingerbread trim.

The front door burst open and a crowd of children raced outside, eagerly drawing Holly and the dog into their midst. "Come with us—we're building a snow fort," shouted one of the boys Joy had met at the festival. Two of Nicholas's nieces about Holly's age with braided, beribboned hair tugged at Holly's mittens. "Mama says you could use some hot cocoa and molasses cookies to warm up," Sarah, the taller girl, informed Holly, smiling to reveal two missing front teeth. "Then we can have a snowball fight."

Matt ushered them inside, where Nicholas introduced Joy to the rest of his extended family—brothers, sisters, spouses, and more children than Joy could keep track of.

Felicity Wright smiled warmly, dark eyes shining in her olive-toned face. "Perhaps you'd like to join Hope, Faith and me in the kitchen so we can get to know you better," she said to Joy, brushing floured hands on her pinafored apron.

"I'd love to," Joy replied, eager to learn more about Nicholas from his relatives. She glanced at Nicholas, startled at the discomforted expression on his face. What on earth was bothering him, anyhow? At the festival she'd sensed his desire as she'd swirled in his arms, dancing in the protective circle of his embrace, his heart pounding in rhythm with her own. Then abruptly, he'd tensed, the glimmer in his eyes turning distant as the stars now powdering the evening sky.

Felicity's kitchen looked every bit as old-fashioned as Kriss Kringle's, though filled with a delightful assortment of clutter: cookie cutters in an array of Christmas shapes, quilted potholders, jars of candied fruits and spices, and a basket filled with steaming-hot muffins all rested on a checked gingham tablecloth atop a pine table in the middle of the room. A mixture of aromas reached Joy, reminding her of childhood holidays long, long ago.

Felicity opened an antique oven and pulled out a pan containing a large, stuffed bird with brown, glazed skin. "Our goose, it is almost done," she said with a trace of a Spanish accent, basting the bird a final time.

Glancing around, Joy noticed a ham studded with cloves on the countertop. "Hope brought the ham, along with candied yams," Felicity explained, gesturing at a petite fair-haired woman arranging cookies on a platter.

"And I made the corn chowder and mincemeat pie," said Faith, smiling, apple-red cheeks aglow.

"So," Felicity inquired curiously, "tell us where you're from, Joy, and what brought you to Noel."

"I'm here on vacation, more or less. From Los Angeles."

"Los Angeles," Felicity repeated. "Spanish for 'angels.' I've always thought that was a lovely name for a town. I'm from Monterey," she explained. "My grandfather, he was a Spanish missionary."

362

Before Joy could respond to Felicity's odd statement, Faith chimed in eagerly, "Are you enjoying your stay here in Noel?"

"It's been wonderful," Joy said honestly, warming at the memory of the past two days. "Like something out of a fairy tale. Kriss Kringle's cabin is the perfect place to spend the holidays, and Nicholas has been terrific. More than terrific," she rambled on, struggling to put her feelings into words.

Three pairs of feminine eyebrows shot up. "You're staying at the Kringle cabin—with Nicholas?" Hope's mouth formed a startled *O*.

"Yes—no, not exactly," Joy said, flustered. She'd assumed Nicholas had told his relatives about her circumstances. "That is, Nicholas has been a perfect gentleman." Too perfect, she thought, recalling how he'd apologized after their lips met under the fallen Christmas tree, even as she'd longed for him to wrap his arms around her and . . .

"He has?" The sparkle in Hope's eyes lessened. "Oh, dear. And we had such high hopes this time."

"This time?" Joy asked, confused.

Nicholas cleared his throat, startling everyone.

"Nicholas, we didn't hear you come in," Faith said, red cheeks turning rosier as she turned toward her brother.

"Obviously," he observed, crossing his arms.

"Now, Nicholas, you needn't look so cross. We're only looking after your own good," Hope chided.

"The way you 'looked after' my well-being when you tried to fix me up with the preacher's daughter?" he reminded his sister, looking cross enough to melt nails.

"Agatha Haggerty has a good heart," Hope said defensively.

"And a face homelier than a horse," Nicholas retorted.

"Luella Parsons, she was pretty," Felicity piped up.

"The grocer's widow," he recalled. "True, but Kringle's dog has more brains than Luella Parsons. Poor woman can't even figure the price on a can of beans without getting the vapors."

"That French woman we introduced you to—Georgette, the one who came into town visiting from one of the lumber camps last summer," Faith recalled in a wistful tone. "She was beautiful, and she certainly spoke intelligently. You never did tell us what you found wrong with her."

"Apparently she was a hard worker up at that camp," Nicholas said wryly, "judging by the number of lumberjacks who claimed to know her, ah, very well."

"Oh dear." Faith clasped a hand over her mouth. "We had no idea. We meant well, Nicholas. After all, you did say you wanted to find a bride—"

"When and if I take a wife," Nicholas interrupted tersely, "she'll be a woman of my own choosing."

Suppressing her amusement at the misguided matchmaking efforts, Joy felt a spark of excitement. *Nicholas is looking for a wife.* For a fleeting moment she imagined life as Mrs. Nicholas Wright, and to her surprise found the prospect undeniably attractive. *I'm falling in love with Nicholas . . .* The thought struck her harder than the beam that had injured Nicholas's shoulder.

It could work, she realized, her heart fluttering

against her ribcage. I've been looking for a small town to set up practice, and Noel needs a doctor. Holly is happier than she's ever been. . . .

She swallowed hard, mentally slamming against the one major stumbling block in her plan: Nicholas. Recalling his standoffish manner, she realized that her feelings must not be mutual. Nicholas had passed up every opportunity of pursuing intimate involvement; the man seemed positively gun-shy of so much as a kiss. *He just doesn't see me as wife material,* she concluded glumly.

"Joy?" Nicholas's voice penetrated the fog in her brain. "Did you hear me? I asked if you'd like to come see the snow fort Holly's helped build."

She nodded, not trusting herself to speak, and followed him out the back door. A lantern hung on the back porch, illuminating a wall of snow on an embankment. Popping up from behind the fortress wall, Holly and the other girls were gleefully hurling snowballs at the boys. Joy felt a bittersweet tug at her heart; Holly deserved a family like this one.

"My sisters mean well, but sometimes they can be meddlesome," Nicholas apologized, his breath frosty in the cold air. He stood close, close enough for Joy to mentally trace the shadows flickering across his features in the lantern light.

"They s-seem to have your best interests at heart," Joy replied.

He laid his palms on her shoulders, staring at her intently, his charcoal-gray eyes deepening to inky black in the shadows. For a heart-stopping second, he seemed on the verge of kissing her; Joy's pulse quickened at the thought that perhaps she'd been mistaken about him, after all.

"Joy," he said, his voice hoarse. "I've come to care for you a great deal."

"I care for you too, Nicholas," she whispered, her hopes rising.

"We're from different worlds, you and I." He shook his head. "But I want you to know, if things had been different—"

The loud clanging of a bell silenced his words. "Dinner's ready!" Felicity called out, poking her head out the kitchen door.

Joy bit her lip to hold back the disappointment welling up inside her. Nicholas didn't want her. Didn't believe she could fit into his world. Turning her back on him, she blinked to clear away the tears threatening to burst forth.

The she stiffened her spine and headed for the door.

The eight adults sat around a long dining table, while the children ate in the kitchen. Not wanting to offend Nicholas's sisters, Joy forced herself to eat, her appetite gone. Even the fact that Nicholas declined a glass of wine failed to cheer her, although she was relieved to know he genuinely intended to stay sober.

Unable to meet Nicholas's gaze, she focused on her surroundings. Quaint yet rustic, without a trace of the usual entertainments one would expect to find in a family household, she mused. No TV or VCR. No electricity; only candles, lanterns and wall sconces. Not even a current novel or magazine. There was something vaguely disturbing about an entire town that seemed to be living in the past, Joy thought, frowning. Of course there must be an explanation. Perhaps the townspeople belonged to some religious order, like the Amish or Mennonites, choosing to shun modern amenities. . . .

"I heard a rumor the gold bug's bit you, Zeke." Nicholas's voice caught Joy's attention as he addressed Hope's husband. "Is it true you're headed to the Klondike?"

"Klondike?" Joy nearly dropped her fork, recalling what she'd read of the Klondike gold rush—in history books. "In Canada?"

Zeke grinned. "Yep. Ever since I heard they struck gold at Bonanza Creek, I've got the itch. Guess it runs in the family."

"Our Pa was a forty-niner, in his younger days," Nicholas explained.

"Forty-niner?" Joy repeated, her tongue thick in her mouth. "In California?"

"Of course," he said.

"I, uh, seem to have lost track of time since I left on vacation," Joy mumbled. "Just what is today's date, anyhow?"

Nicholas and his relatives stared at her as if she'd lost her mind. "December twenty-fourth, eighteen ninety-seven," he said. "Christmas Eve, remember?"

"Christmas Eve. Of course. How silly of me." *1897? A century ago!* Like an avalanche, the truth cascaded over Joy. Somehow, some way, she really *had* been transported into the past. Sent by Kriss Kringle, straight into the pages of a Christmas fairy tale . . .

"Joy, are you feeling well?" Concern filled Nicholas's voice. You look peaked."

She swallowed hard. "I'm a little tired," she said, wondering suddenly just how this fairy tale would end. Would she wake up after Christmas, only to find herself back in 1997—a hundred years and more than a lifetime away from Nicholas Wright? Her stomach knotted. If she had a choice, would she stay or go? Could she adapt to life in the Victorian Era, without modern medicine? Suddenly she recalled her wish for an old-fashioned Christmas, and her flippant comment to Kriss Kringle about wanting to practice medicine before insurance companies began dictating treatments. Ironically, she might just get exactly what she'd wished for . . . all except for Nicholas, who'd made it all too clear he saw no future with her.

"We'll head back to the cabin right after dinner," Nicholas promised. "Besides," he added with a wink, "you'll want to get Holly tucked in early so that Santa Claus can come calling."

Joy nodded, her mind numb. She laid down her fork, incapable of tasting anything but bitter disappointment.

Chapter Eight

As soon as Holly fell asleep, Joy tiptoed to the mantel and filled the child's stocking with treats she'd purchased before leaving Los Angeles. She tied a red ribbon around the autoharp and laid it under the tree, her heart breaking as she envisioned Holly's inevitable disillusionment. How could she explain to Holly why Santa Claus didn't bring her a daddy? Or why she might never go home again?

"What's wrong?" Nicholas whispered, sitting down beside her in the darkness.

Joy shivered. The cabin was cold, since Holly had insisted no fire could be lit, or Santa wouldn't be able to come down the chimney. "I'm just not looking forward to leaving, that's all." *Are Holly and I free to leave on the 26th and return to our own time,* she wondered? *Or will we stay here, as permanent residents in the past?*

Nicholas turned her to face him, his touch igniting a fire within her heart. "I wish you didn't have to go."

"Do you?" She trembled, aching for him to ask her to stay.

Nicholas heard the pain in Joy's voice and longed to find some way to ease it. Yet he knew she had no choice but to obey the powers that be and go back to the City of Angels, now that her mission here was completed. She'd reformed him completely—he felt like a changed man, healed in both body and soul.

"I've never wished for anything harder in my whole life," he admitted, his voice breaking.

Joy's lips trembled; in the flickering candlelight Nicholas detected a gleam of moisture in her eye. Unable to stand her pain a moment longer, he bent forward and slanted his lips over hers, determined to let her know just how much she meant to him. If it cost him his soul for tainting an angel, so be it, he resolved.

She melted into his arms as if made for his embrace. A soft moan escaped her; she arched against him, sifting her fingers through the hair at the nape of his neck. Her all-too-feminine curves brushed seductively against his chest, stretching Nicholas's self-control to the limit.

Deepening the kiss, he drank in the touch and taste and scent of her, knowing the memory must last him a lifetime—and Joy, an eternity. How heavenly it would be to spend this night with Joy, making love to the angel in his arms . . .

Lord Almighty, she's an angel, Nicholas! Not some fancy woman to warm your bed. He tore free, breath ragged, fighting down an urge to curse the powers that be for making him fall in love with an angel.

"Nicholas?" Her voice, faint as the distant whistle of the wind, stung his tortured soul.

He shook his head. "It wasn't meant to be," he

whispered. Unable to stand a moment more, he pulled himself to his feet and propelled himself out the door.

Outside, he propped his elbows on the porch rail. He stared at the darkened heavens above, wondering how in Creation he would ever get Joy Winters out of his mind—or his heart.

Unable to sleep, Nicholas awoke hours before the arctic dawn. He made a pot of strong coffee and poured himself a cup to brace himself for the ordeal ahead. Finishing it, he tiptoed into the parlor, mindful of Holly and Frankincense still sleeping soundly beside the hearth. He knelt down and laid his gifts for Joy and Holly beneath the Christmas tree.

"Mr. Wright?" Holly's voice held a tone of awe. "It's you, isn't it?"

Kneeling beneath the tree, he turned around to see Joy's daughter standing barefoot, staring at him wide-eyed, Frankincense at her heels.

"It's me, all right. Who were you expecting, Santa Claus?" Nicholas winked, nodding at the filled stocking hung on the mantle. "Appears to me he's already paid a visit."

Holly stepped closer, a smile exploding across her face. "I knew it! I knew Santa would bring me a Daddy for Christmas!"

Nicholas felt as if he'd been gut-punched. "A what?"

"A daddy! Just like I asked for."

"Listen, Holly, I think there's been a little misunderstanding. I'm not—"

Frankincense pressed his nose against the child's

back, urging her forward. *Go on, ma petite.*

"Mommy said Santa might not be able to give me what I wanted," Holly pronounced, her curly head bouncing up and down in a decisive nod, "but I knew he would. He promised!"

"He did, did he?" Nicholas felt short of air. It had been bad enough loving and losing an angel; now he had to break the news to her daughter that he wasn't the daddy she'd been hoping for. Lord Almighty, what next? A plague of locusts would have been easier to cope with.

Holly launched herself at him, throwing her arms around him and smothering his face with kisses. "I'm glad you're going to be my daddy, Mr. Wright," she informed him, snuggling onto his lap.

"Holly," he said, his discomfort growing. "Sometimes no matter how much we want something, it just can't come to be. I'd like nothing better than to be your daddy, if only—" A flicker of movement caught his attention. Turning his head, he saw Joy standing across the room, her face white as the snow in which he'd found her.

She stepped forward; Holly leaped out of Nicholas's lap and ran to greet her mother with a big hug. "Merry Christmas, Mommy! Come, look what Santa brought!"

"Nicholas, I'm sorry." Joy shook her head. "I should've warned you—"

A sudden thought took hold in Nicholas's mind. He'd worried about what would would happen to Holly when Joy returned to the City of Angels. He couldn't have Joy, but perhaps there was something he could do to help her daughter. "Don't worry," Nicholas said softly. Leaning closer, he brushed a kiss across her cheek and whispered, "Let's talk about this later. No need to spoil Christmas morning for Holly."

"But—"

"No arguments," he insisted, then turned to Holly. "Now then, young lady, let's see what else Santa brought."

Holly dumped out her stocking, exclaiming over each item inside—from the festive hair bows to the multi-hued peppermint candy canes. Next she opened her mother's gift, her delight evident as Joy demonstrated how to play the autoharp.

Nicholas hauled out a large package from beneath the tree. Holly gasped with pleasure as she pulled out the wooden sled he'd carved.

"Thank you, Mr. Wri—I mean, Daddy," she said.

Joy and Nicholas exchanged an uneasy look. "I'll take you sledding later today," he told Holly. "That is, if your mother approves."

Joy consented. Nicholas handed her a small, wrapped package. "This one's for you."

She blinked in surprise. Carefully she untied the ribbon and removed the paper, then opened the box. She lifted out the miniature angel he'd carved and painted, cradling it in her palm. "It's beautiful, Nicholas," she said, her eyes misty. "No one's ever made anything special, just for me, before."

Nicholas's throat felt swollen. "Something to remember me by."

"I'll never forget you, Nicholas," she said softly. Picking up an odd-shaped package, she handed it to him. "For you."

He opened it. Inside lay a long, cylindrical stuffed object stitched together at the ends and covered in a soft, ribbed fabric—the corded material from the pants she'd worn the day before, he realized.

"It's a cervical pillow," she explained. "If you tuck it under your neck when you sleep, it should help keep those muscles in your back and shoulder from flaring up again."

Touched by her concern, he turned the pillow over in his hands. Underneath, in embroidered stitches, were the words "With love, Joy." A lump formed in his throat; he lifted his gaze and saw his own emotions mirrored in Joy's eyes.

Holly presented him and Joy with a gift she'd made herself: a picture of Holly, Nicholas and Joy all holding hands and smiling. "Thank you," he managed, his voice breaking. "I'll make a frame for it and treasure it always."

Peering beneath the lowest branches, Joy discovered a gold box. "It's from Kriss Kringle," she said, her eyes widening.

"I found it in my workshop, after I cleared out the toys yesterday," Nicholas said, wondering how he'd missed it before.

Joy opened the box. Inside were four individual packages.

The first contained a red leather collar for Frankincense. The dog woofed with approval as Nicholas fastened it around his neck. *Merci beaucoup. Quite dashing, don't you think?*

The second package held a plaid wool scarf for Nicholas. Holly's contained a charm bracelet with a miniature silver dog bearing a striking resemblance to Frankincense.

Joy held her breath as she opened the small box with her name on it. She lifted out a pendant-style watch engraved with her name. Old-fashioned—except for the calendar function, she noted, peering closer to check the date.

December 25, 1897. Heart hammering, she read the small slip of paper tucked beneath the watch:

> *Dear Joy,*
> *I hope you've found Noel to be everything you'd hoped for.*
> *If you reset the date on this watch, your return tickets will be good for tomorrow only. The choice is yours. I trust you and Holly are enjoying the old-fashioned holiday you always wanted.*
>
> *Merry Christmas to all,*
> *Kriss Kringle*

"What does it say?" Nicholas asked.

Joy folded the note and slipped it into her pocket. "Just instructions for setting the watch." She could hardly expect him to believe she'd come from the future, she told herself.

She slipped the chain over her head and felt the pendant watch nestle against her heart, which pounded as Kringle's meaning sunk in. *I don't have to go back. I could stay here, with Holly, and Nicholas . . . If only he wanted me to stay.*

She had nothing to go back for—no job, no family, no wholesome community in which to raise Holly. No future . . .

Could she build a future in the past? Did she dare take the chance of leaving everything she'd known behind, to risk building a life with a man who could kiss her until her toes curled one minute, then declare their relationship "wasn't meant to be" in his next breath?

Kringle's words echoed in her mind, awareness dawning with the beauty of an arctic sunrise: *The choice is yours.*

Heads turned as Nicholas escorted Joy and Holly into the whitewashed chapel for Christmas morning services. Spying Nicholas and the newcomers in the foyer, Preacher Haggerty nearly lost the spectacles perched precariously on the bridge of his nose. "It's been a long time," he said, clasping Nicholas's hand. "Welcome back."

After the services, Nicholas helped Joy and Holly into the sleigh. Frankincense, guarding the reindeer, barked a greeting, then jumped in beside Joy. Nicholas urged the team forward on a road leading into the woods. A few minutes later, beside a frozen lake, he turned into a narrow, rutted lane that ended at the top of a hill overlooking the lake below.

Joy stared at the house in front of her, certain it was the most charming home she'd ever seen. The two-story, Victorian-style cottage was painted white with fishscale-shingle siding, forest-green trim, shutters and window boxes. A large porch with gingerbread trim wrapped around the front and side of the home; snow drifts atop the steeply pitched roof added to the fairy-tale effect.

"It's beautiful!" she said. "Who lives here?"

Nicholas tethered the reindeer to a porch rail and helped her dismount. "I do. Or will, soon as Kringle returns and I'm free to move in. I've been working on rebuilding the place for the past three months, and it's finally finished."

"I'm amazed—you built this all yourself? And with a bad shoulder." She walked through room after room, marveling at his skill.

"I wanted you to see it before you leave. I—I'm not sure why." He turned away. "This time tomorrow, I reckon you'll be long gone."

Frankincense laid his paws over his ears. *I can't take much more of this. Nicholas, mon vieux, can't you see you're running out of time?*

Holly raced into the room. "Mommy, it's wonderful here!" Plopping down on a window seat, the child peered out the second-story window. "Look, you can see the lake and everything." She turned toward her mother, eyes shining. "Please, Mommy, say we can stay. I don't want to go home—not ever!"

Joy exchanged glances with Nicholas. Holly had convinced herself Nicholas was her new daddy—a conclusion no amount of discussion had managed to dispel when Joy had broached the subject earlier, before church services. Leaving here would break Holly's heart. Yet Nicholas seemed convinced she must leave tomorrow. "Holly," Joy began, kneeling beside her daughter. "You know we have to—"

"Come on outside, young lady, and I'll show you how to use that sled you got for Christmas," Nicholas interrupted, boosting Holly onto his back. With little choice but to follow them outside, Joy swallowed her irritation and watched as Nicholas dragged the sled up a small slope, then sent Holly sliding downhill, squealing gleefully.

Frankincense grabbed the sled rope and hauled it uphill, child in tow. As Holly slid down a second time, the dog loped alongside her, cushioning her fall as she tumbled sidelong into the snow.

"Incredible, how good that dog is with her," Joy said, watching as dog and child repeated the effort two more times, without a spill. Glancing at Nicholas, she took a deep breath. "Nicholas, we have to talk."

He nodded. "Holly, do you think you and Frank can play by yourselves for a few minutes?"

"Sure, Mr. Wright—I mean, Daddy."

Nicholas swallowed hard. "Just be careful, and stay clear of the lake, all right? It takes it a long time to freeze all the way."

"Okay." Holly nodded, rubbing Frankincense between his ears.

Nicholas led Joy down to the water's edge, out of Holly's earshot. "I've been thinking," he began, feeling awkward.

"What about?"

"Holly," he said. "What happens to her, when you have to go?"

She gave him a puzzled stare. "She'll go with me, of course." She seemed on the verge of saying something more, but stopped.

"To the City of Angels?" Horrified, Nicholas dropped his jaw open.

She nodded.

His heart lurched to a halt. *Joy's little girl is going to Heaven.* The thought of Holly missing out on a normal, happy childhood grieved him as deeply as the thought of losing Joy. How could the powers that be allow something so cruel to happen to an innocent child?

"We can't let that happen." He grasped her shoulders, desperate to shake some sense into her. "Joy, I love you—more than I ever thought possible."

"I love you too. And I'd give anything to stay here, in Noel, with you." Her eyes glistened; Nicholas felt his heart wrench at her words.

"Lord, if you weren't an angel I'd—"

"Angel!"

"But you are, so we can't. But I won't stand by and let you take Holly to the City of Angels too! She's so young. Let me adopt her, Joy. I promise, I'll make a good father. I'll—"

Joy stared at him, mouth open, lilac eyes wide as coins. "You really think I'm an angel, don't you?"

"Of course you're an angel! Flying in through a snowstorm, no footprints, even bringing that harp with you. At first I got riled that the powers that be sent you here to reform me. But after you healed me—and sweet-talked me into giving up drinking and cussing—I figured they were right, after all. But taking Holly's life is just plain wrong!"

"Oh, Nicholas." Tears streamed down Joy's cheeks. She flung her arms around his neck and buried her face against his chest. "I'm not an angel."

"Not an angel?" Confusion fogged his brain. "But your own daughter described Heaven to a T. Said you'd told her all about it."

"I did, but it's just a story I made up to make her feel better when she'd ask me about her parents. Holly's an orphan—I adopted her after her real mother and father died."

He stared at her, dazed. "You said you flew here. If you're not an angel, just how in tarnation did you wind up in Noel—and where in Heaven's name did you come from?"

"This sounds crazy," she said, "but the truth is I'm—"

Barking, loud and incessant, drowned out her last words.

Nicholas looked around in time to see Holly's sled racing toward an embankment jutting out above the frozen lake, some fifty feet up the shoreline from where he and Joy stood. "No!" He shouted, breaking into a run. "The ice is too thin—"

Joy bolted past him, instinctively hurling herself into the path of the sled. She slipped, stumbling backwards over the edge of the embankment, onto the frozen lake below. Nicholas heard the terrifying sound of ice cracking; a split second later Joy disappeared into the icy waters.

Chapter Nine

"Mommy!" Holly screamed as Nicholas snatched the sled rope and stopped the child from careening over the edge.

He stared at the hole in the ice and felt his heart rip in two. *If Joy isn't an angel, she'll drown.* Every fiber in his being urged him to dive beneath the ice and try to rescue Joy, even if he killed himself in the process. Which he undoubtedly would, since he couldn't swim. Yet how could he risk leaving Joy's daughter alone, with no one to look after her?

A white blur knocked him to the ground. Staggering to his knees, Nicholas saw Kringle's dog dive into the frigid water, then vanish beneath the ice.

Frankincense forced his way downward, his thick fur no shield against the cold that penetrated to his marrow. *Mon Dieu! Joy, where are you? It wasn't supposed to end this way . . . not this way at all.* Heart pumping, lungs bursting, he dove deeper into the icy, dark water.

"Dear Lord, save them," Nicholas prayed, scrambling down the embankment. He wrapped the sled rope around his ankle and tethered it to a large tree root, then crawled on his belly to the edge of the hole in the ice. "Come on, Frank." He dipped his hands in the frigid water, reaching as far as he could and then some. How much longer could Joy survive without air?

Suddenly the dog's head appeared above the water. There was something in his mouth . . . Joy's clothing! Frankincense gripped the back of Joy's collar, struggling, unable to haul himself out of the water with Joy in tow. Swiftly Nicholas grabbed hold of Joy's arms and pulled her onto the ice. He felt the ice cracking beneath their combined weight . . . Lord, she looked so blue!

With a powerful heave, he dragged her off the ice and hoisted her onto the embankment. One foot on dry land, he gripped the rope and felt the ice give way beneath his other foot. Hearing paws thudding on the ice behind him, he realized Frankincense had swum ashore. The dog leaped past him, showering him with an icy spray.

Nicholas pulled himself onto the embankment and rolled Joy onto her stomach. He pressed his hands against her upper back, forcing water from her lungs. She felt so cold. . . . Forcing down the fear darkening his thoughts, he turned her onto her back. He wrapped his fingers around her wrist, thankful to find a pulse. Then he touched her lips and his heart stopped. "Lord, no." He gasped. "She isn't breathing!"

Holly, eyes bright with fear, knelt beside him. "You're gonna have to do that mouth-to-mouth thing Mommy taught me."

He stared at Joy's trembling daughter, wondering

just how much the child knew of her mother's healing powers. "How?" he heard himself ask.

"Put your mouth over her face, like this." Holly cupped her hand over her nose and mouth, her voice rising in panic. "Hurry up!"

Nicholas turned Joy faceup and commenced blowing breaths into her lungs. He paused when Holly instructed, then repeating the procedure. "Breathe," he whispered, his own pulse racing. *I can't lose you. Not now. Not ever.*

Joy made a sputtering sound, her lips trembling. "She's breathing!" Nicholas hugged Holly, relief spreading through him at the sight of the pendant watch on Joy's chest rising, then falling.

"Joy, it's Nicholas." Her eyes fluttered, but didn't open. A shiver shook her from head to toe; he knew the danger was far from over.

"We've got to get her warmed up, fast," he informed Holly. He lifted Joy's limp, wet body into his arms and ran to the sleigh. Holly and a shivering Frankincense leaped aboard; Nicholas urged the reindeer forward and raced to Kriss Kringle's cabin a half-mile away. Cradling Joy in his arms, he ran inside and carried her into the bedroom.

"Dry off Frankincense and fetch all the blankets you can find," he told Holly. As soon as the child left the room, he stripped off Joy's wet clothes and wrapped a robe around her very-female form. How could he have mistaken her for an angel? Nicholas asked himself, wondering just where Joy Winters really had come from.

Together, Nicholas and Holly spread quilts and blankets over Joy. Still, Nicholas feared it wasn't enough. He climbed under the covers and pulled

Joy into his arms, infusing heat from his own body into her chilled flesh.

Holly curled up at her mother's feet. The mattress sagged as Frankincense hopped onto the covers, adding a mountain of warmth. *That's the way, Nicholas.* He shivered, his fur still damp despite Holly's towel-drying. *C'est temps; it's time.*

An eternity later, Nicholas felt warmth return to the woman in his arms. Her breathing was regular and color had returned to her cheeks. Yet she still hadn't regained consciousness.

Had she been in the icy water too long? Nicholas met Holly's concerned gaze, his limbs turning to stone. What if Joy never recovered?

He got out of bed and tucked the covers tighter around Joy. "She'll come around," he told Holly with more confidence than he felt. "She just needs to rest awhile."

Nicholas's gaze fell on Joy's flight bag. She'd told him once she'd studied medicine. Perhaps there were medical supplies inside. Or an address for next of kin, he thought grimly.

He opened it and sifted through Joy's belongings. Sure enough he found a black medical bag, though he recognized none of the medications inside. He found a wallet with strange currency inside. He pulled out a small card with a photograph of Joy on it. A color photograph, he noted, surprised to know such a thing existed. He studied the card, which had the words "California Driver's License" at the top. It listed an address in Los Angeles. Angels . . . "City of Angels," he realized aloud.

The card listed a birthdate and an expiration date. Nicholas gasped, estimating Joy's age. *Joy*

Mr. Wright's Christmas Angel

Winters had a license to drive in California—until 1999!

He tore through the remaining cards in her wallet, all dated in the 1990s. His hands closed around Holly's storybook; opening it. He read the copyright date: 1997. Stunned, he recalled all the strange things Joy had spoken of—telephones, horseless wagons. No wonder she'd acted baffled by Noel's lack of such devices, Nicholas thought. Joy Winters didn't come here from Heaven, but from the future! One hundred years from now. But how, and why?

Joy moaned softly, her eyes fluttering open. Suddenly, Nicholas recalled his last conversation with Kriss Kringle, when the whimsical old man had asked what Nicholas wanted for Christmas. "A good-hearted woman to share my life and warm my bed," Nicholas had replied flippantly, his thoughts blurred by whiskey-steeped eggnog. "Smart, compassionate, and prettier than sin. How's that for a tall order?"

Staring down at Joy, Nicholas realized his Christmas wish had come true. *It's a miracle. An honest-to-God, bonafide miracle.*

"Nicholas?" she whispered, staring at him with those heaven-sent, lilac-colored eyes.

"It's all right, Joy," he answered, squeezing her hand. Bending low, he brushed her lips with his own. "I promise, my love, from now on everything's going to be all right."

Holly hugged her mother, a cherubic smile lighting up the room. "I knew it!"

Concern shadowed Joy's face. She lifted her head, her fingers closing around the pendant Kringle had given her. "The watch—"

Miriam Raftery

Nicholas examined the water-logged time piece. "Astounding that it's still running."

Joy stared at the watch, hand poised above the mechanism to reset the date. "Time itself is an amazing thing," she whispered, raising her eyes to meet his.

"I know where you've come from, Joy."

Her eyes widened, revealing violet sparks in the lilac pools. "You do?"

He nodded, lifting her fingertips to kiss each one. "I want to hear all about this time of yours, my love—provided I can convince you to stay here with me in mine. I want to share more than a winter holiday with you, Joy Winters. I want to show you the beauty of a summer day in the land of the midnight sun. I want to see your face when you look at our golden aspen in the fall, and walk with you through meadows filled with forget-me-nots in bloom come spring."

"Nicholas," she whispered, sitting up straight. "Are you saying—"

"I'm asking you to marry me," he said, brushing his lips across her forehead, "and Lord knows, this town could use a doctor. Care to apply for both jobs?"

"I've never wanted anything more," Joy said, a misty haze enveloping those enchanting lilac pools.

Holly jumped up, clapping her hands with delight. "Daddy!" she exclaimed, hurling herself into his arms.

"Looks like I've got myself a family," Nicholas said, embracing them both warmly.

Finally, you've got it right, Nicholas. C'est bien, mon vieux. Frankincense laid his head on his paws and yawned, exhausted from his exertion.

Epilogue

Noel, Alaska December 27, 1897

The entire town seemed to have turned out for the wedding, Joy noted, arranging the lacy train on the dress Felicity had loaned her for the occasion.

Glancing ahead, she smiled at the sight of Holly walking down the chapel aisle, clutching a bouquet of flowers Faith had found Heaven knows where in the midst of an Alaskan winter. Beside Holly walked the ring bearer: Frankincense, regally displaying a pair of gold rings fastened around his new red collar.

Over the pump organ music, Joy heard the distinctive jingle of sleigh bells. Moments later, Kriss Kringle strode through the doors in the back of the chapel, dressed in a plain, dark suit with red suspenders. Except for the full white beard, he looked positively ordinary, thought Joy. But she knew better.

Frankincense barked, welcoming his master home.

"Good to see you again, Dr. Winters," Kringle said merrily.

"So you've come back," she said softly. "A hundred years back in time. I'd never have believed time travel was possible before, but—"

"How else do you think all those toys manage to get delivered in a single night?" Kringle replied, raising his snow-white eyebrows knowingly.

Just then, Joy noticed a plump, kindly-faced woman standing behind Kriss Kringle. "The Missus here points out you could use a matron of honor," Kringle announced as his wife stepped forward.

"I'd be pleased to help out," Mrs. Kringle offered, cheeks glowing like ripe apples.

Joy divided her bouquet in two and handed half to Mrs. Kringle. "Thank you," she said, her voice trembling with emotion.

Giving her a wink, Kriss Kringle asked, "Mind if I give the bride away?"

"I'd be honored." Joy smiled, then whispered, "Thank you for making my Christmas dream come true—and Holly's."

It's true, she thought as she accepted his arm and walked down the aisle toward Nicholas, whose love shone brighter than a Christmas star. I thought I'd never find Mr. Right, yet here I am marrying Nicholas Wright, the man of my dreams—and the loving father Holly always wanted.

Nicholas fixed his gaze on his bride-to-be, certain no angel had ever been more beautiful. As he repeated the solemn vows, he gave silent thanks to the Lord for bringing Joy into his life—and for His four-footed matchmaker, he added, removing the wedding rings from the dog's collar.

Mr. Wright's Christmas Angel

That's the way, Nicholas. Frankincense wagged his tail, nearly knocking the flowers from Holly's hands. *Ah, vive l'amour!*

Nicholas slipped the golden band onto Joy's finger and felt a rush of warmth as she slid the other ring onto his hand. He took her hands in his, gazing into her loving eyes as Preacher Haggerty pronounced them husband and wife.

"You may kiss the bri—" Preacher Haggerty began, but Nicholas had already swept Joy into his arms. Lifting her veil, he pressed his lips against hers and kissed her the way he'd longed to ever since he'd found her in the snowy woods. Mindless of the murmuring crowd, he deepened the embrace, savoring the passionate woman in his arms.

Frankincense barked. Nicholas released Joy, glancing sidelong at the dog. If he hadn't given up cussing, he'd swear the old boy was smiling.

"Thanks to you, Frank," he said softly, ruffling the snow-white fur on the dog's majestic head, "for fetching me an angel, after all."

IT'S A DOG'S LIFE ROMANCE

Stray Hearts by Annie Kimberlin. A busy veterinarian, Melissa is comfortable around her patients—but when it comes to men, too often her instincts have her barking up the wrong tree. So she's understandably wary when Peter Winthrop, who accidentally hits a Shetland sheepdog with his car, shows more than just a friendly interest in her. But as their relationship grows more intimate she finds herself hoping that he has room for one more lost soul in his home.
__52221-7 $5.50 US/$6.50 CAN

Rosamunda's Revenge by Emma Craig. At first, Tacita Grantham thinks that Jedediah Hardcastle is a big brute of a man with no manners whatsoever. But when she sees he'll do anything to protect her—even rescue her beloved Rosamunda—she knows his bark is worse than his bite. And when she first feels his kiss—she knows he is the only man who'll ever touch her heart.

__52213-6 $5.50 US/$6.50 CAN

Dorchester Publishing Co., Inc.
P.O. Box 6640
Wayne, PA 19087-8640

Please add $1.75 for shipping and handling for the first book and $.50 for each book thereafter. NY, NYC, and PA residents, please add appropriate sales tax. No cash, stamps, or C.O.D.s. All orders shipped within 6 weeks via postal service book rate. Canadian orders require $2.00 extra postage and must be paid in U.S. dollars through a U.S. banking facility.

Name_____
Address_____
City_____ State_____ Zip_____
I have enclosed $_____ in payment for the checked book(s).
Payment <u>must</u> accompany all orders. ❏ Please send a free catalog.

APOLLO'S FAULT

TIMESWEPT

MIRIAM RAFTERY

Taylor James's wrinkled Shar-Pei, Apollo, is always getting into trouble. But the young beauty never expects her mischievous puppy to lead her on the romantic adventure of a lifetime—from a dusty old Victorian attic to the strong arms of Nathaniel Stuart and his turn-of-the-century charm. One minute Taylor and Apollo are in modern-day San Francisco, and the next thing Taylor knows, a shift in the earth's crust, a wrinkle in time, and the lovely historian finds herself facing the terror of California's most infamous earthquake—and a love so monumental it threatens to shake the foundations of her world.

_52084-2 $4.99 US/$6.99 CAN

Dorchester Publishing Co., Inc.
P.O. Box 6640
Wayne, PA 19087-8640

Please add $1.75 for shipping and handling for the first book and $.50 for each book thereafter. NY, NYC, and PA residents, please add appropriate sales tax. No cash, stamps, or C.O.D.s. All orders shipped within 6 weeks via postal service book rate. Canadian orders require $2.00 extra postage and must be paid in U.S. dollars through a U.S. banking facility.

Name_____

Address_____

City_____ State_____ Zip_____

I have enclosed $_____ in payment for the checked book(s).

Payment <u>must</u> accompany all orders. ❏ Please send a free catalog.

A FAERIE TALE ROMANCE

VICTORIA ALEXANDER

Ophelia Kendrake has barely finished conning the coat off a cardsharp's back when she stumbles into Dead End, Wyoming. Mistaken for the Countess of Bridgewater, Ophelia sees no reason to reveal herself until she has stripped the hamlet of its fortunes and escaped into the sunset. But the free-spirited beauty almost swallows her script when she meets Tyler, the town's virile young mayor. When Tyler Matthews returns from an Ivy League college, he simply wants to settle down and enjoy the simplicity of ranching. But his aunt and uncle are set on making a silk purse out of Dead End, and Tyler is going to be the new mayor. It's a job he takes with little relish—until he catches a glimpse of the village's newest visitor.

_52159-8 $5.50 US/$6.50 CAN

Heart's Magic

Flora Speer

Bestselling author of *ROSE RED*

In the year 1122, Mirielle senses change is coming to Wroxley Castle. Then, from out of the fog, two strangers ride into Lincolnshire. Mirielle believes the first man to be honest. But the second, Giles, is hiding something–even as he stirs her heart and awakens her deepest desires. And as Mirielle seeks the truth about her mysterious guest, she uncovers the castle's secrets and learns she must stop a treachery which threatens all she holds dear. Only then can she be in the arms of her only love, the man who has awakened her own heart's magic.

___52204-7 $5.99 US/$6.99 CAN

A Faerie Tale Romance

Let Me Come In

LINDA JONES

It's been fourteen years, but Benjamin Wolfe remembers it like yesterday—the day his father was run out of town by Hamilton Pigg. Now Ben is back to give the three remaining Piggs—lovely Cecilia and her sisters—a taste of their own medicine. But Ben doesn't count on Hamilton's daughter being such a beautiful woman, or so stubborn. And suddenly he finds himself questioning—despite all his huffing and puffing—whether it's revenge he really wants, or just for the lovely Cecilia to let him come in.

___52217-9 $5.50 US/$6.50 CAN

Dorchester Publishing Co., Inc.
P.O. Box 6640
Wayne, PA 19087-8640

Please add $1.75 for shipping and handling for the first book and $.50 for each book thereafter. NY, NYC, and PA residents, please add appropriate sales tax. No cash, stamps, or C.O.D.s. All orders shipped within 6 weeks via postal service book rate. Canadian orders require $2.00 extra postage and must be paid in U.S. dollars through a U.S. banking facility.

Name_____
Address_____
City_____State_____Zip_____
I have enclosed $_____ in payment for the checked book(s).
Payment <u>must</u> accompany all orders. ☐ Please send a free catalog.

A Faerie Tale Romance

Prince of Kisses — Colleen Shannon

Daughter of wealth and privilege, lovely Charlaine Kimball is known to Victorian society as the Ice Princess. But when a brash intruder dares to take a king's ransom in jewels from her private safe, indignation burns away her usual cool reserve. And when the handsome rogue presumes to steal a kiss from her untouched lips, forbidden longing sets her soul ablaze.

Illegitimate son of a penniless Frenchwoman, Devlin Rhodes is nothing but a lowly bounder to the British aristocrats who snub him. But his leapfrogging ambition engages him in a dangerous game. Now he will have to win Charlaine's hand in marriage–and have her begging for the kiss that will awaken his heart and transform him into the man he was always meant to be.

——52200-4 $5.99 US/$6.99 CAN

Dorchester Publishing Co., Inc.
P.O. Box 6640
Wayne, PA 19087-8640

Please add $1.75 for shipping and handling for the first book and $.50 for each book thereafter. NY, NYC, and PA residents, please add appropriate sales tax. No cash, stamps, or C.O.D.s. All orders shipped within 6 weeks via postal service book rate.
Canadian orders require $2.00 extra postage and must be paid in U.S. dollars through a U.S. banking facility.

Name_____

Address_____

City_____ State_____ Zip_____

I have enclosed $_____ in payment for the checked book(s).

Payment <u>must</u> accompany all orders. ❏ Please send a free catalog.